CUP OF BLOOD

Cup of Blood

A Crispin Guest Medieval Noir Prequel

JERI WESTERSON

Old London Press

The Crispin Guest Novels by Jeri Westerson
available from Minotaur Books

Veil of Lies

Serpent in the Thorns

The Demon's Parchment

Troubled Bones

Blood Lance

Shadow of the Alchemist

www.JeriWesterson.com

Cover design by Jeri Westerson. Photography by Craig Westerson.

ISBN-10: 1497476127
ISBN-13: 978-1497476127

First Edition: July 2014

To Craig, who has always stood by me, even when it seemed like a silly idea

INTRODUCTION

If you have been reading the Crispin Guest Mysteries, then perhaps you were wondering how Jack came into Crispin's life. In this prequel, your questions have been answered.

But let's back up a bit. Sometime in 2003, I developed the first Crispin Guest book, having never penned a mystery before. Despite capturing the interest of my agent, it failed to capture the hearts of editors. But because this was my first venture into mysteries and because mysteries like to travel in packs, that is, in a series format, and since I had also never written a series before, I jumped right into writing the second book, and then the third.

I couldn't have known when I wrote *Cup of Blood* and sent it in to my agent that this would also be the year that Dan Brown's explosively popular book, *The DaVinci Code*, would hit the bookshelves. When that happened, believe me, editors were sick to death of Templars and grails.

And so, when an agent sends out a manuscript to all his editors that he thinks will be the best fit for the book and it doesn't pan out, agent and author decide to retire that book. That was this book. Some fourteen months later, an editor at St. Martin's Press, who had read *Cup of Blood* but had sadly declined to publish it, contacted my agent. For some reason, he couldn't get the characters out of his head, and did the author have another book in that series he could look at?

Why yes. Yes, she did. That one was *Veil of Lies* and it was the one St. Martin's published, along with five more—six in total—before they said good-bye to the series. However, I was by no means done with the series myself, and so I decided to dust off that first book, give it a hefty rewrite, and present it myself as a prequel. And here we are.

I hope you enjoy this peek into Crispin's life as Jack pushes his way in from outcast to servant…along with some lovely murders and swashbuckling escapades.

ACKNOWLEDGMENTS

A whopping big thank you to Steve Mancino. He was the first to see that there was something to this hardboiled medieval detective and he was the one who got him into print. An additional big thank you to him for giving this book the once over once again.

Another thank you goes out to the Vicious Circle of Ana Brazil and Bobbie Gosnell, offering critique and suggestions just where they are needed.

Thank you to Chris Kasianczuk, for offering his time and his features as the new face of Crispin.

ICG in Norco, CA has been more than generous, supplying the printing for bookmarks, postcards, and invitations. It is much appreciated.

Thank you to Rebekah Hendershot of Semper Editing and Kris Jacen for helping out with the formatting. Thank you librarians for offering me the opportunity to swing my sword around when I visit. Thank you bookstore owners for giving me shelf space. Thank you reviewers for the nice things you say.

An especial thank you to the fans and readers. You have stuck with me through thick and thin. I shall endeavor to be worthy of you.

And finally, a grateful thank you to the love of my life, the Long Suffering Husband, Craig. He has stood by me throughout all my wacky ventures, always with a smile...and a drink in his hand.

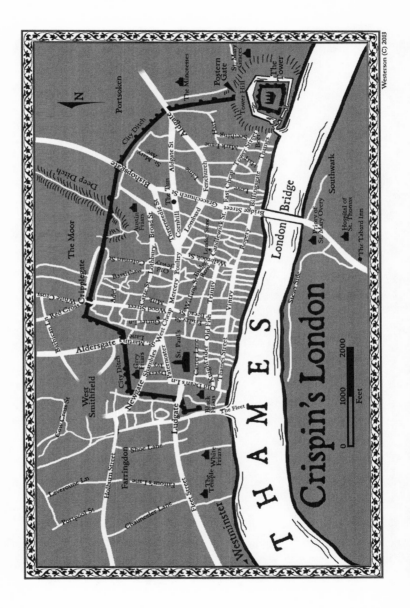

Crispin's London

CHAPTER ONE

London, 1384

Cold. His fingers were cold. Digging them into his tunic sleeves did little good, as ragged and as full of holes as they were.

Jack Tucker lifted his face to the wet sky. Droplets pelted his numbed cheeks, but he barely felt them. Yanking his hood lower over his face, he scanned the street. So few were abroad now, what with the rain and the dim moonlight peeking beyond the tall buildings and shops. The bells in the nearby churches were tolling compline and soon the Watch would be roaming the streets, looking for stragglers like him.

"Jack." It was almost a growl but it was only because it came out a gravelly whisper. He turned, looking for the maker of the sound and found him in the doorway of an abandoned shop. Jack's eyes widened as he slowly approached.

The face of the young man looked far older than his fourteen or fifteen years, and Jack swallowed, looking him over. "What you doing there, Will?"

Will made a movement that might have been a shrug. "Spare a coin for your old friend?"

Jack approached and then saw the leg. It was twisted and the scant stocking covering it was torn and damp from sores and running pus. He gasped and then looked again into Will's face. Will

1

was the smartest lad he knew, taught him some of his trade in purse-cutting. Now his bright eyes were dull and shadowed. Jack's gaze fell again to the sour leg, the leg that was slowly killing him.

"What happened, man?"

Will's mouth curved up in a slight smile. "Rat bit me. I think. So here I now sit."

Running a hand over the back of his neck, Jack crouched low. He couldn't stop staring at the leg and the horror of it. "By the saints, Will. How could a small bite do that to you? You were as hearty and hale as me."

But now that he was closer, Jack noted the sallow and sweat-damp cheeks and how sunken-in they were.

He'd been saving the hard crust of bread in his pouch for later. The last time he'd had a bite to eat was that morning and he well knew the dreadful hollow feeling. But without another thought, he threw open the flap of the scrip at his belt and withdrew the crust, handing it to Will. "Here, Will. Take it. And this, too." His fingers lighted on a coin—the only one he had—and gave it over.

"Ah, look at you, Jack," he said, closing his fingers on the bounty. "That's right charitable of you, my lad."

Still crouching, Jack rocked back. He said nothing as Will nibbled on the crust, tumbling crumbs onto his breast. He'd seen it before, many times. The pallid complexion, the slow movements, the deadened eyes. Will hadn't long. And with a jolt to his heart, he knew it could easily have been him, dying alone in an abandoned doorway.

He snapped to his feet.

"I…I have to go."

Will nodded. Yes, he knew. Knew that boys like the two of them saw death regularly on the streets of London. Saw it, skirted it, said their prayers, and moved on. Jack's charity was a small kindness that would not last. But Jack vowed that if he could get a purse or two this night, he'd come back and share it with Will, bring him something warm to drink maybe.

"I have to go," he said again.

Will merely closed his eyes and laid his head back against the doorpost. The hand holding the bread drooped over his chest.

Swallowing hard, Jack rose and trotted away. He becrossed himself and looked back, but saw only shadows. He *would* return, he vowed, though his guts churned from the thought of that leg, of Death hovering so closely. The fear of it kept him moving.

A boy on the streets courted Death, at least that's what Will used to say. Courted her, bowed to her, but you were to always keep your distance. A clever young lad could avoid her grasping hands. But not always, they had both noted silently when they'd seen boys floating face down in the Thames, or broken in an alley from a man who hadn't liked getting his purse cut.

He turned a corner, just another corner like any other in London. He looked back once, and then only ahead.

Shopkeepers urged their young sons and apprentices with a gentle nudge to their shoulders, heading indoors. Some of the boys were little older than Jack.

An ale stake rose out of the gloom and then the sound of a pipe filtered onto the muddy lane from the shuttered window. A tavern. That meant warmth and perhaps a purse or two to cut. The painted sign was of a spiraled horn. Tusk, maybe?

"God be praised," he muttered, blowing on his fingers. Had to bring life back into them if he was to do a proper job of it.

Gingerly, he pushed open the heavy oaken door and glanced about the dim room. So few men. There was one slumped over the table. His arms were crossed before him and he was surrounded by many bowls of wine. He sat next to a slumping man, a servant likely, from the badge on his arm.

Looking across the room through the haze of smoke, he saw another asleep by the fire. And yet another man at another table, barely able to sit up as he swayed, staring morosely into his horn beaker. A piper played in a corner, and it appeared that the tavern keeper was himself asleep, leaning back against the wall on his three-legged stool.

Jack raised his face to the heavens and smiled. *Ah, blessed saints.*

You are *looking out for a poor thief like me.*

If he could cut the drunken men's purses and make off, he'd eat tonight. If he was able to find a baker with his shop still open and buy a day-old pie, something with some meat in it, that would fill his belly. That would be worth it. And he could share it with Will, who could use a few hours with a friendly face.

Yes. He'd get in and get out. No need to linger. Though the warmth on his cheeks was particularly inviting.

He slipped past the door and made his way carefully toward the hearth. He couldn't help himself and stood before it, warming his face and hands. He almost groaned from the wonderful heat. But he knew he had a job to do.

Turning to the first man asleep near him, he crept closer. The man's rust-colored cotehardie looked as threadbare as Jack's own tunic, with a few missing buttons on his sleeve and shiny at the elbows where the material—good wool, he noticed—was nearly worn through. His black hair hung long over his face, hiding his features, and the man's fingers, curled on the table, were dirty and calloused. He wondered what manner of work the man did, but only briefly. He didn't truly care. Only that the man's purse had at least some silver in it, though by the looks of him, he likely didn't have much.

Jack glanced once more back toward the snoring tavern keeper, and drew his small knife. The piper played on and never seemed to notice what Jack was about.

Jack listened intently to his victim, to his slow and even breathing in and out, followed by an occasional snore. Sidling closer, he looked over the man's shoulder. His dark cloak hid his purse, but if Jack was careful, he could move it out of the way, cut the purse strings, and move on to the next man.

Kneeling behind him, still listening, Jack gently pushed the heavy, damp cloak aside. It smelled strongly of smoke and wet wool. He moved it only enough to reveal the dangling black, leather purse. Jack knew his knife was sharp. He kept it that way by necessity. What thief would keep a dull blade? He needed it as much for his work as for protection. Holding his breath, he eased the knife forward.

The deep breathing changed, shortened. Jack froze. Had he awakened the drunkard? After a long tense moment, the man's breathing resumed in a lengthy, slow exhale and Jack didn't hesitate to snip the leather ties. The pouch landed neatly into his other palm and he immediately slipped it down into his tunic neck until it rested warm and snug next to his body.

He smiled and gently withdrew, becrossing himself with quiet thanks to the Almighty. The man slept on and he quickly turned his attention to the other, the one surrounded by wine bowls. Jack licked his lips. The wine was tempting. He was thirsty, truth be told, and now seemed a good time to snatch a bit of spirits.

He moved away from the man by the warm hearth and crossed to that far table with its two occupants, one a hooded servant in dark blue livery with a broach pinned to his breast, and the other asleep, his face lying in the nest of his arms. At that moment, the first of the two, the servant, snapped from the bench as if his seat were afire. It was an easy thing for Jack to stumble into him and he fell into Jack's accommodating arms. The pouch wasn't within reach but the broach was, and he snatched it from the servant's breast and secreted it like the others.

The man stumbled away, none the wiser. Jack knew his fingers were nimble and his touch light. But a drunken man was ten times easier than a sober one, and by the time the man realized what happened, Jack would be long gone.

He knew his luck would soon run out and this last one needed to be dispatched as quickly as possible. Sliding onto the bench next to the sleeping man, he toyed with the wine bowls. There were plenty there with still the dregs of wine within, and he took up one and slurped it down. It warmed, and the tangy berry flavors filled his mouth like a gift.

He measured the man beside him with a sly look and noted a necklace in the shadows and folds of his gown. *'Slud!* he thought. Jewelry was always hard to come by and here it was, like it was being handed to him. But first and foremost, the purse. He scooted along the bench until he was right up against the man. He was dead to the world, was this one, and Jack easily snipped off his purse without his ever moving. It was just as easy to reach up and unhook the necklace and he slipped both jewelry and pouch into his tunic. And now the wine! He slid a bowl toward him, took a long drink and sighed. He would eat tonight. And now he even had his wine. Not bad for a scrap of a thief.

"Oi!"

Jack looked up at the first man by the fire, who seemed to have awakened. The man swayed, his cruel gray eyes narrowing. "Thief!" he cried, lurching to his feet.

Uh oh. Jack didn't hesitate. He dove across the table, tipping a candle and spattering hot wax. Like a startled rabbit, he wove in and out of the tables and slipped out the door, leaving a wake of turned heads and puzzled faces.

Down the lane he ran, but God's teeth! That man in the rust-colored cotehardie followed right after him! The sound of feet pounding behind forced him from Gutter Lane to the swell of West Cheap. The smooth road gave way to rutted mud and gray puddles.

He rounded a corner and turned, panting. A gray silhouette against the dim light of a sputtering cresset appeared in the middle of the street. The man hadn't seen him. Jack crept forward, stealth foremost on his mind. His foot slid on the wet paving and he nearly lost his balance. He spit a loud curse and instantly realized his mistake.

The man turned. His moonlit face was a shield of stark white and dark eyes. His gaze locked on Jack bent over and wind-milling to keep his footing. The man pursued at a run, and Jack put heel to mud, zigzagging away down a crooked alley.

Jack scrambled over a low fence at the end of a long lane and dashed across a dark courtyard into the gloom and came up against a wall. It was so deeply shadowed he reckoned he could hide in the darkness until the man passed by and then he could double back.

He waited, slowing his breathing, touching the pouches that jumbled against his skin under his tunic.

A low growl rumbled next to Jack's ear. Eyes wide he turned slowly and stared into the face of a dark, shaggy mongrel. Teeth bared, it growled a bark.

Jack was on his feet in an instant, ran back through the yard, and leapt for the fence.

Out of the blackness, the man lunged and caught Jack in midair by his hood. Yanked back, he struggled and swung a fist, but the man dodged, and darted his own fist forward, landing a solid blow to Jack's jaw. Stars exploded behind his eyes and he sagged like a rag doll. He was shoved to the ground with shoulders pinned, and his last thoughts were, *Here I am in no better stead than Will.*

Taut at the end of its tether, the dog barked until someone hurled a bone from a window and hit the mutt in the head. After a prolonged howl and a yip, the dog took the bone and padded away.

The man shook Jack till his senses returned.

"Harken! I have you." Immediately, Jack began to struggle, but those hands were strong on his shoulders. "Stop it!"

As if a string were cut, Jack surrendered, flopping back. There was no way out of this. But he sent up a prayer anyway, hoping for something swift and painless. Jack shook his curly ginger hair out of his eyes and raised his chin, deciding that he wouldn't beg. Face Death like a man, that was the idea. "Aye, m'lord," he said, his voice a bit more strident than he liked it to be. "You got me. And for what, I'd like to know?"

The man smiled. His gray eyes fixed on Jack's. His accent was that of a lord's, though a shabby one. His dark hair, hanging nearly to his shoulders, was a match to those heavy brows. He had a sharp nose and a self-satisfied twist to his lips that seemed to suggest amusement, though the situation was far from amusing.

Jack's heart hammered, but he tried to appear calm and innocent, even as the man reached into his tunic and pulled out both stolen pouches.

"For these, perhaps."

Christ! The man had known all along. Jack *knew* he had awakened! "Them's just purses I come by," he said quietly.

"Came by them, did you? Well one of them came by way of *my* belt."

"O-o-o-h! So *you're* the lord what lost it."

With knees pinning Jack's shoulders, the man picked out his pouch from the two. Since the straps were cut, he maneuvered the flap over his belt and managed to secure it there one-handed. "As for you, what's to be done? Turn you over to the law?"

"For what, m'lord? I done naught. I told you. I come by them purses."

"Not afraid of the law, eh? Do you know what they do to thieves in London?"

"I'm not afraid of gaol," he said, though his voice quivered.

"Gaol? You'd be lucky to be thrown in gaol. No, for your type of thief, the sheriff prefers to cut off that sinful hand of yours."

Jack gasped. Hadn't meant to. Fear closed his throat. If the man turned him in he'd be hanged for sure!

With a flourish, the man suddenly brandished his knife. "Perhaps I should do it myself."

The brave façade fell. Terror welled up in him and he squirmed, eyes pouring forth tears. "M'lord! Have mercy. I'm just a poor lad all alone in the world! I got naught. Please, m'lord, have mercy!"

The man considered. He looked once at his blade before he shrugged and replaced it. "Then what shall we do? Go to the sheriff?"

"There's no need to trouble him, is there, m'lord?" He sniffed and longed to wipe his dripping nose on his sleeve, but his arm was still trapped at his side by the man's knee. "You have your property back. I would say that is all fair and done with. Wouldn't you, m'lord?"

"Not all. There is this other pouch. And I have a mind that you should be the one to personally restore it to its owner."

Jack grimaced. "Aw now, m'lord. He might not be as fair-minded as you are. Can't *you* take it to him and be done with it?"

CUP OF BLOOD

"Not possible. 'First be reconciled with thy brother.' You have sinned against your fellow man. You will take it to him yourself, or we will go to the sheriff now." The man released him and rose.

Slowly, Jack got to his feet and shook the cold mud from his cloak. He frowned up at the man. "If it's to be done, let's do it quickly."

Any thoughts of escape quickly faded as the man grabbed Jack by his cloak in a tight grip. He smiled. "Perhaps he will be merciful. A genuine show of repentance will do much for a man's disposition. I suggest you add remorse to your apology."

"Aye, m'lord," he grumbled. Jack fell silent and did not struggle even when the man hoisted him up and his toes barely danced along the ground. It could have gone worse, he decided. The man could have been cruel, could have beaten or cut him. It wouldn't have been the first time.

They made the long walk back to the tavern in silence. Yellow light pierced the broken shutters, though many of the candles had burned low. The place was quiet when they opened the door. The tavern keeper no longer dozed at his place by the kitchens, but was instead picking up the mess Jack had left when he ran.

The piper had left his pipe aside and quaffed his cup of ale from a clay cup. A male servant lay asleep and snoring near the door, his feet hanging off the end of a cot. Most of the patrons had gone, but Jack's latest victim never moved, sleeping where he had left him.

When the man shut the door, the tavern keeper looked up. "Oi? Is that you Crispin?"

"Yes, Gilbert."

"Come, man. I thought you left for the night. In truth, it is time I send these last two away so that I can go to my own bed."

The musician looked up from over the rim of his cup and pointed to it.

Gilbert waved him off with a huff. "He'd nurse that 'til dawn if I let him. But what is this?" He gestured toward Jack, who shrank away from the brawny man as much as he could while still in the clutches of the man called Crispin. "What have you brought me?"

"I return him to the place of his crime for the betterment of his soul."

Gilbert rubbed his face with a fat hand, wiping away the sweat from his bearded chin. A big-boned man, he stood nearly as tall as Crispin. "Crime? What mean you by that?"

"I mean that this knave is a cutpurse…"

"Oh! It's that way, is it?" Gilbert lunged for the knife at his belt and pulled it free, advancing on Jack. "I'll have none of that in my house!"

Jack recoiled and tried to wriggle free.

"Peace, Gilbert. I have already pardoned the knave on condition that he returns his spoils to the rightful owner."

Gilbert glared and pointed with his knife. "You do not know how fortunate you are, young lad. Crispin Guest is a right honorable gentleman. That's the Tracker you're fooling with. I'll wager you've heard of him. Any other man would have first sliced you open for your thievery—" and he made cutting motions— "and only then asked questions. He's coddling you, and in all probability you don't deserve it."

Jack glanced once at Crispin before licking his dry lips. Tracker? He *had* heard of the man, though he thought it was more of a legend than a real person. He slipped further into the neck of his tunic held firm in the Tracker's fist. Were he thinner, he might have slipped entirely free of the tattered garment.

"I think first you owe Master Langton an apology for using such tricks in his establishment." Crispin shook him. "Well?"

Hanging from his own hood, Jack smiled weakly up at Gilbert's taut face. "I…I am heartily sorry for plying me trade in your ale house, good Master."

"Hmpf," snorted Gilbert. "The words are spoken but the sincerity is lacking. Let me never see your face in here again, lad."

"Aye, Master." He glanced up at Crispin's stern expression. "I doubt I'll be back."

"Well then," said Crispin, casting his glance toward the sleeping man. "Let us awaken your victim." Crispin maneuvered the boy forward and kicked the table. "Awake, Master. Come, now."

The man remained stubbornly motionless.

Crispin chuckled and looked up at Gilbert. "The character of your wine must be particularly potent today." With Jack's hood still firm in his grip, he reached down with his other hand and shook the man's shoulder before frowning.

"He sleeps like the dead, this one," said Gilbert.

"You are partly correct," said Crispin. His fist slackened on Jack's hood, and Jack took advantage by stepping back and adjusting his loosened collar. Crispin's fingers touched the sleeping man's neck and turned his face, revealing wide bulging eyes.

Jack gasped.

"This man isn't asleep at all," said Crispin. "He *is* dead."

CHAPTER TWO

Crispin examined the dead man's face and grimaced, not at the pale and waxy skin, for he was used to corpses both on the battlefield and off, but at the manner and incongruity of such a body in such a place. The man looked as if he had suffered. His eyes bulged and spittle whitened his lips. Crispin cautiously bent to sniff the corpse's opened mouth but didn't detect any unusual odors or obvious poisons. One arm extended across the table ending in curled fingers as if he were reaching for something. Crispin tested the arm by raising it. Stiff.

He shook his head. "It's a wretched thing, Gilbert. Poor man. Dying and not a soul aware of it."

Gilbert stood behind Crispin's shoulder and nodded. "You don't think it was the food? Or the wine?"

"Not the food, though you would think so."

"Crispin! This is no time for jesting."

"Who's jesting?" He saw the look on Gilbert's face and laid his hand on his shoulder with a hasty smile. "Rest assured it was nothing in your food or drink. However, it was most certainly something he consumed, though I fear not by choice."

"Poison?" Gilbert whispered.

"I don't see any other way about it." His temples throbbed again and he groaned. He was too tired to entertain this now. Let others content themselves with it. He hated to leave Gilbert with such a thing, but he had spent too much time today at the Boar's Tusk already. He glanced at the boy, still cringing in the corner. "Gilbert, I would be off to my own bed. There's little I can do here, at any rate. You'd best wait for Ned to get back with the sheriff and the coroner."

"Oh, Crispin, don't go! You know how the sheriff is."

All too well. Crispin rubbed his face. It felt like damp leather. "Gilbert. For God's sake."

"Please, Crispin."

He sighed and opened his eyes to glare at his friend. "Very well. But you owe me for this."

"I'll take it from your overdue bill," Gilbert muttered and stared at the dead man. He wrung his hands on his apron, shuffled backward to a table opposite, and sunk to the bench.

The ginger-haired boy stealthily made for the door but Crispin leaned over and grabbed his hood again. "I am afraid you cannot leave either, little thief. For the sheriff may wish to question you as well."

"But I don't know naught!"

"That remains to be seen." He shoved him down onto a stool while he sat on a chair, rocking it back, and plopped his feet on the table. He stared over his muddy boot tips at the dead man and waited.

The nearby monastery bells rang for Lauds by the time Sheriff Simon Wynchecombe entered and looked across the smoky room, legs wide with gloved fists dug into his hips. There was nothing particularly ostentatious about his dress, for another man might have made more use of bright colors in more combination. The sheriff's pretension sprang from his person, some of it by choice and some of it by nature. A tall, ruddy man with dark bushy brows and an equally dark mustache and beard, he seemed to relish this darkness and clothed himself equally so.

Two of his men entered after him and stood at the ready in his shadow.

The sheriff clucked his tongue, but when he spied Crispin his expectant expression melted into a scowl. "I should have known you were somehow involved."

"Me? I have no involvement. I am merely a bystander."

Wynchecombe grunted. "Why do I find that so difficult to believe?" He cast about again and bellowed, "Who is master here?"

"I-I am, Lord Sheriff," said Gilbert. He sprang from his bench and shuffled forward.

"Then what mischief is here?"

"We only found him an hour ago," said Gilbert. "Such a terrible thing." He glanced at Crispin. "To have him dead like that and no one the wiser."

"So he's been dead an hour."

"Longer," said Crispin.

Wynchecombe leveled a glare at him. "I did not ask you, *Master* Guest."

"Nevertheless." Crispin didn't look at the sheriff. "He has been dead longer. Possibly all evening."

"And how do you know that?"

"Try to move his arms. They are stiffening with rigor."

Wynchecombe snorted. He eyed the stark faces looking expectantly back at him. "Well. Does anyone know who the man is?"

"I know not," said Gilbert. "I do not remember his coming in, and I have never seen him before. Perhaps he's a merchant. His cloak is plain enough, but his boots are well made."

"He's a knight," said Crispin.

Wynchecombe strode toward Crispin and measured him with a pinched expression. His mustache twitched. "And how the hell do you know that?"

"He's wearing a hauberk under his gown. I felt it when I touched his arm. Further, those clothes are not of local origin. That gown is a Damascus weave. I remember it well…from a long time ago."

Wynchecombe glared a long moment before he slapped

Crispin's feet from the table. "Have you no respect for the dead?"

Crispin clenched his fist at his side but turned an indifferent expression to the sheriff. "I have very little respect for anything. Isn't that what you've heard?"

"Yes." Wynchecombe chuckled and nodded. "That is exactly what I've heard."

The sheriff studied the dead man, peering at him at close range. "I don't suppose," he said over his shoulder, "*you* know who he is?"

Crispin shrugged. His lids hung heavily. "I do not. He wears no signet. But he did wear a necklace. A thin chain. His neck."

"What?" The sheriff bent to look closely at the man's neck.

Crispin yawned and waved in the dead man's general direction. "See the red stripe? As if it were pulled off. I wonder by whom?"

He did not need to turn his head to know that the cutpurse cringed. The sheriff caught the movement and swiveled, directing his attention to the boy on a stool.

"Well? And who are you?"

"N-no one, m'lord. Jack Tucker. Just an innocent witness."

"Innocent?" The sheriff swept the anxious faces of Gilbert and Jack with a scowl. "No one here looks innocent to me." He crossed the room with heavy steps and leaned on the table. The wood creaked under his weight. "What time did *you* get here, my Lord Guest?"

Crispin slowly withdrew his knife and began cleaning under his fingernails with the tip. "I am no one's lord," he reminded tolerantly. "Are you suggesting *I* killed the man?"

"It was not established he was killed. There is no blood, after all."

"Natural causes? In one so young? Surely even you are not that dim, Wynchecombe."

Wynchecombe grabbed Crispin's hood. He leaned in so close that Crispin could smell the stale wine on his breath. "I am 'my *Lord* Wynchecombe' to you, Guest." Wynchecombe's eyes flicked to the dagger in Crispin's fist, but Crispin never flinched nor took his gaze from the sheriff. "Give me an excuse," the sheriff whispered, twisting Crispin's hood tighter. "*Any* excuse."

The sheriff's two men at the door took several steps closer. Their hands clutched their sword pommels.

Crispin blinked. He took his time curling his lips into a slow smile. It made the sheriff's scowl deepen. "I am your servant as always... Lord Sheriff."

Wynchecombe released him and straightened. "Then I repeat. What time did you get here?"

Crispin smoothed out his coat and shoulder cape and resumed cleaning his nails. "Sometime after sundown. I am not certain of the hour."

"How many were here?"

"The usual number. It was nearly a full house, wouldn't you say Gilbert?"

"Aye, Crispin. A goodly number."

The sheriff smiled an unpleasant grin. "Been drinking here all evening, eh, Crispin?"

Crispin snapped his blade back in its scabbard without looking up. "I am no longer concerned with the running of estates, Lord Sheriff. What I do with my time is surely my own business."

"Yet death seems to stalk you."

"Death stalks us all. And in this case, I believe the man was poisoned. I'd stake my—" He paused, wondering what exactly was left to stake. Certainly he possessed no reputation to wager, no property, and no money. And his life? Likewise discounted. He smiled grimly and looked the sheriff in the eye. "I am certain," he continued. "See how he struggled? And the foam at his mouth? Yet no one noticed his dying."

"Poison, is it?" Wynchecombe glanced at the bowls scattered on the table. Wine still glistened in the bottom of both clay cups. The one of wood stood empty. He pushed one bowl with his fingers. It wobbled and sloshed red wine onto the table. "Poison is the choice of cowards and conspirators," he snorted. "Which bowl was his?"

Crispin grinned crookedly. "I do not recall. Why don't you try them and find out?"

The sheriff gritted his teeth in a steely smile. "Not today, Guest." With his gloved hand he tipped over both bowls. The wine ran red like blood. "Tavern keeper!" he said, stepping away from the dribbles spattering the floor. "Clean this mess."

Gilbert moved quickly and plucked up the bowls with apron-covered fingers.

The sheriff edged toward Crispin. "What sort of poison?"

"The sort that kills quickly. There are a few that would do the trick."

"You know a bit too much about this."

"I have a habit of knowing a bit too much about everything. Jack of all trades—"

"Master of none," the sheriff chuckled. "Then of course you—a man who knows everything—would know where to obtain such poisons."

"Any apothecary knows of them, but only the more unsavory would sell them. Do not waste your time. It will be difficult finding the purveyor."

"The king has appointed me to waste my time, as you say."

Crispin shrugged. "Then be my guest."

"And what about this fellow, Jack Tucker. Tucker?" Wynchecombe turned, but Jack had vanished. The sheriff glanced a warning at his men. Their faces flattened with guilty apology.

Crispin chuckled. "Your fish slipped the hook."

"Damn the boy! You two! Go get him!"

"Surely you do not suspect Tucker?" said Crispin over the noise of the sheriff's men clamoring out. "What cutpurse would waste money on poison? That boy's a thief not a murderer."

"I care nothing for what you think you know of it."

Crispin glanced at the window and groaned at the sight of gray light tinting the open shutters. "As you will," he sighed. "It is nearly dawn. Are you done with me?"

Wynchecombe's bushy brows lowered. Crispin well knew that if the sheriff wished, if taunted enough, he could arrest Crispin and put *him* on trial for the crime. Evidence could be easily cobbled to make him look guilty enough. Especially since the dead man's money pouch still lay tucked in its hiding place inside Crispin's coat.

Wynchecombe snorted and turned his back. "Go home. If I need you further, I know where to find you."

Crispin gathered his sluggish body and rose, made a cursory bow that Wynchecombe did not notice, and dragged himself from the tavern.

He groaned again, squinting at the eastern sky visible now as a bluish-gray wash behind the dark silhouette of rooftops and spires. The morning hung in the air as cold and as damp as last night's laundry. He put up his hood and wrapped his worn cloak over his chest to protect his chapped fingers. His empty belly complained, but he did not feel well enough to eat, even if there was bread or cheese in his larder. There might be the dregs of wine still left in his jug at home, and that thought sustained him while he leapt the puddles and trudged down gray-edged alleys.

At last he turned the corner and surveyed the familiar haunts of the Shambles. The structures in the narrow lane tilted inward toward one another, their protruding second stories sometimes only separated by three arm lengths, making the lane dim during the day and dismal at night.

The street lay in quiet. Soon the market bells would ring when the shadows reached the first gatepost at the far end of the lane making it after Prime. Then stalls would be unfolded from their shuttered windows. Hearths, dreaming with only the gentle puff of white from covered embers, would be stoked and billow oppressive smoke from their dormant chimneys. Yet even in the stillness of the morning, the odor of butchered meat still hung in the air.

Poor as it was, it was better than digs in Southwark, the parish situated across the Thames, which housed the brothels, thieves, and the poorest of the poor. Crispin could not bring himself to live there, though the rent was far cheaper. If it were not possible to live at court as he used to, then he would at least live close enough to sneeze at it. London was his city, after all, and no one—no matter how high their rank—was going to chase him from its walls.

Crispin opened the money pouch for his key and the pouch fell to the ground. He cursed and picked it up. He must remember to repair that, and gave a grudging chuckle at the brashness of the clever young cutpurse. He climbed the rickety wooden stairs, trying to keep quiet. The still sleeping tinker who owned the shop below, made his living repairing large cooking pots for beef tallow, and sharpening and mending butchering knives and meat hooks. The forge in the back courtyard sent black smoke into Crispin's window during the day, but even this could not smother the stench of the meat markets below.

He took out the rusty key and unlocked the door to his lodgings. He knew well the small room's full compliment of furniture and sundries. Nothing adorned the walls, not even a crucifix. The only items he owned were the clothes on his back, a wax slate, a quill, a small ink pot, and a journal—all of which resided in the rented coffer.

"Home and hearth," he sighed. He wrinkled his nose. The cramped room smelled of old smoke and the smothering closeness of sweat. He reached for the wine jug and found it empty. Too weary to divest himself of the cloak, he leaned toward the pallet and tumbled onto the straw-stuffed mattress. It crunched under his weight and released the smell of musty grass. Throwing his arm across his face, he lay on his back, closed his eyes, and settled into the lumpy cot, hoping to lie there the rest of the day.

He hadn't slept for more than a few moments when the sound of doors slamming and pots rattling below stairs woke him. He jolted upright and stared uncomprehendingly at his surroundings. His mind reluctantly fell in step as a door slammed a second time. The Kemps, the tinker family, had awakened and begun their day. "God's blood." He threw his legs over the side of the bed and dropped his head into his hands. He wasn't drunk enough anymore to simply sleep through the morning. That time had been taken up with the sheriff and the dead man.

A dead *knight*. The idea fascinated. A poisoned knight. But what was this dead man to him? He only solved such puzzles when he was hired to do it. There was no profit in wasting time with such without pay. He needed to find a puzzle for which someone *would* hire him. Let the sheriff fool with this. He'd muck up the job like he always did. Arrest the wrong man and hang him. It was far too much work for the sheriff to muster the real culprit. And no truer a scoundrel there was than this killer. Poison. In the middle of a crowded tavern. That took gall. He almost admired the knave but stopped short. Poison was a horrible way to die. Knowing you had ingested the venom and incapable of stopping it from rushing through your system. A horrific loss of control. At least with a knife blade you had a chance to fight! He shook his head. He'd even rather die by the noose than by poison.

Who was that poor bastard anyway, murdered in plain view? Crispin thought he was a knight not just because of the ring mail he wore but of his groomed hair and nails, his clean-shaven face. He was no mere soldier. He had jewelry and weapons. But why was his armor hidden? Was he killed because of that secret?

Crispin unbuttoned the top buttons of his coat and reached inside to bring out the dead man's purse. He dropped it on the table and it pooled on the nicked wood like a bad pudding. He supposed he should take it to the sheriff but not before he satisfied his own curiosity.

He looked inside. Coins, mostly silver with one or two gold. Reaching in, he pulled out a thin gold chain that held a cross potent set with small green stones. Etched on its reverse was the word *pocillator*. He turned the object in his hand again, feeling its heft before laying it aside. He then withdrew a pinky ring, also with a green stone, though not like the cross' jewels. After examining it for any markings, he shrugged and laid it, too, on the table.

He glanced toward the window and sighed. The cracked shutters hung ajar and bleary sunshine cast irregular stripes across the floor. Dawn had given way to morning. However long he slept at the Boar's Tusk was not long enough. He passed a calloused hand over his face and felt the beard stubble for the first time. He rose to go to the basin and jug and poured the icy water into the bowl. He washed his face quickly, but a sound on the landing stopped him. He listened. Water dripped from his chin. He stepped clear of the basin and pricked his ears.

The landing creaked.

Crispin edged his dagger free from its sheath and crept with slow steps toward the door. He gently pressed his ear to the wood and held his breath.

The landing creaked again. But before Crispin could respond, hard footfalls thumped on the wooden steps and hurled down the stairs.

Crispin threw the bolt and cast open the door. The tail end of a robed figure disappeared at the bottom step.

Crispin leapt down the stairs, two, three at a time and landed with an unsteady thump at the bottom. He took to the middle of the street and looked up the road.

No robed man.

He ran up the lane, splashing his boots in the gutter, pushing stray passersby out of his way.

No one in a robe. No mysterious stranger.

He ran his hand over his hair, damp from washing his face. Was he seeing things now?

A tug at his coat. He spun, brandishing his knife. A lad of ten years stood behind him. He wore the sheriff's livery but the tabard was too large for him. The boy shrunk from Crispin's scowl and from the menacing blade, and held up his hands to fend off the expected blow. "Master Guest!" he squeaked.

Crispin breathed. He looked at the knife in his hand and quickly sheathed it. "What is it, boy?"

The boy gathered himself and gave the message in a rush. "M-my Lord Sheriff sent me to tell you they have captured the murderer and he commands you to come to Newgate at once."

The murderer? That was quick. Especially for Wynchecombe. Crispin looked back up the lane. Shopkeepers and passersby paid him no heed. "Commands, does he?" He ran his hand over his chin again and finally shrugged. "Then I suppose a shave will have to wait."

CHAPTER THREE

Panting, with tears blurring his eyes, Jack Tucker ran for all he was worth. "Jesus mercy," he muttered desperately, over and over, frantic gaze searching the streets and the frosty signs swaying from a morning breeze. No one yet stirred on the deserted lanes but he didn't care. That man, that Tracker had said that those wine bowls were poisoned and he had drunk them! Drunk every last one of them and knew he was doomed.

Finally, his eyes caught the sight he was looking for, a sign of an apothecary, and he dove for the front door. Finding it locked, he pounded on it. "Master! Master, for God's mercy, please open your door, I beg of you!"

The thud of steps approached and the bar scraped back across the door. It opened slowly and only a crack revealed an eye staring beadily at Jack. "What's all this?"

"Please, good Master. I need your help!"

The eye darted back and forth. "My help? It can wait an hour, can't it? It is not yet time to open my doors."

"Please, good sir. I've been poisoned! I haven't long."

The door flew open and a man in an open robe revealing his long linen gown beneath, stood on the threshold. "By the Virgin, young man! Did you say poisoned?"

"Aye, Master. A cruel thing it is. Please. Can you help me? Oh! I feel faint." A wave of dizziness overcame him and Jack sank to the stone threshold. The man caught him but just barely and hoisted him upward.

"Now lad. By the saints! Can you walk? Come inside." Half dragging him, the apothecary pulled Jack inside where the immediate warmth of the small shop revived him. The man sat Jack on a stool before the hearth and jammed a poker into the small fire, urging the flames to rise.

Blearily, Jack watched the fire, a play of light and shadows that he could barely discern. His belly roiled and he clutched the stool to keep upright.

The man bent toward him. "Tell me, boy. Do you know what manner of poison you ingested?"

He shook his head. "I don't know, Master. I drank it in the wine. But another died of it. All foamy at the mouth, struggling to breathe."

"Hmm." The man nodded, placing a finger to his lips in thought. He suddenly took Jack by the shoulders and studied his face. He pulled opened Jack's jaw and sniffed his breath and then he laid his head against Jack's chest.

"Here! What you doing?" Jack demanded.

Withdrawing, the apothecary narrowed his eyes. "Are you certain you were poisoned?"

"I swear by my Lady, Master. I saw the dead man, and I drank the same wine."

"Then it is likely it was merely a small dose and already purged from your system. Did you sick up, boy?"

"Aye. I did. Right before I found you."

"You see. You are fine."

Jack grabbed the man's robes in his clammy fists. "No! I must have a cure. Please, sir!"

The apothecary threw his hands up and sighed. "Very well, but I am certain you do not need it."

Jack shot from the stool to follow the man into his shop, behind a ragged curtain. He crumpled his tunic hem in nervous fingers, all the while watching as the man pulled down canisters and bottles, and mixed the strange ingredients into a mortar. He then mixed them about and poured some ale into a beaker, carefully measuring in the now powdered ingredients. He stirred it with a metal wand and finally handed it to Jack. "There. Drink it."

Jack stared into the beaker and to the greasy rings floating on the top of the ale. "This will cure me?"

The man shook his head. "As I said, you do not need a cure, but this will help you amend your belly."

Jack nodded and put the beaker to his lips. Holding his nose, he downed it and nearly lost the rest of what was in his belly from the sour taste. The beaker dropped from his hands and he covered his mouth.

The apothecary stood over him. "Better?"

Jack grimaced and licked his lips. It took a moment, but the taste and the sick feeling subsided. "Aye," he said unsteadily. "I do feel better."

"Of course you do," the man muttered. "That will be a ha'penny."

Sheepishly, Jack stared at his feet. "I have a confession to make to you, good Master."

The apothecary rocked on his heels. At any other time, it would have been an amusing sight to Jack: the man in his sleeping gown and fussy robe, and hair in disarray. But Jack's emotions had been wrung dry in the span of a few hours. He had nothing left inside of him. He felt as hollow as a bell.

"I confess, good Master, that I haven't a coin to my name." He raised his chin and met the man's gaze. "But I swear to you on me mother's grave, that I will repay you. I…I can work for you. Sweep your floors and fetch wood. I can do that."

The apothecary rolled his eyes and laid his hand on Jack's shoulder. "I thought as much. Fear not. You have no need to repay me. I have done you a Christian deed and there is only reward in Heaven for that."

Jack fell to the ground on his knees and grabbed the man's

hands. "Oh sir! I am grateful for your kindness and charity. I'll say a prayer for you, sir. Many!"

"Thieves and beggars' prayers!" chortled the man. "I must be mad. Off with you, then. And keep away from poisons!"

"Good Master, I will indeed. And thank you again. The Lord's blessings upon you and yours." He pushed through the doors and looked back. The man waved and turned away, back to his curtained alcove and maybe to bed.

Jack stood on the lane. The air was fresher, brighter. The sun's light stretched down the muddy road making the shop fronts golden with its rays. The damp signs and trees glistened with droplets like gems. Jack inhaled deeply and sighed. Life! It was a precious thing to behold.

He turned his face toward the sunshine and its feeble warmth and sighed again. Empty, he was. Of silver and of belly. He had wanted to bring Will a meal but now that was out of the question. He sniffed, catching the scent of baked bread. Or was it?

He trotted down the lane, letting his nose lead him. It wasn't a baker but just an ordinary shop. He stopped before it and put his eye to the shutter. A plump woman, her head covered in a kerchief, was just setting browned loaves on the table. Jack pushed his wayward fringe away from his face, stepped back, and knocked gently on the wooden shutter.

Hesitantly, the shutter opened. The woman, rosy nose and cheeks, stuck her head out. "Eh?" she said upon spying Jack. "Are you knocking on my window?"

Jack lowered his face and curled his tunic hem in his fingers. "Good damosel, I smelt your bread from the street and God's angels and saints urged me to ask. For to ask ye shall receive. So I knocked and you answered. I come asking if you could spare only a small portion of them loaves you just baked."

Eyes downcast, he knew he looked humble and yet sympathetic. It was still an advantage his being so young with a voice high and light. God help him when his bollocks dropped.

Silence greeted him and he slowly looked up through his ginger fringe. She stared at him with her hands at her hips. But she hadn't slammed the window shut, so that was a good sign. He becrossed himself, for piety was highly prized by those to whom charity was given, and he even formed his hands in an attitude of prayer. It never hurt to go that extra mile.

He could see in her features that she was relenting and she left the window momentarily and returned with half a loaf. "You're a scoundrel," she said, handing it to Jack's eager hands. "But you are a charming one. Off with you, lad."

"Thank you, kind damosel!" He saluted with the warm loaf and ran.

As he ran he put the loaf to his face, feeling its warmth and inhaling its sweet aroma. He couldn't resist taking a bite and it was just that much Heaven.

He stopped under an eave and leaned against the wall and slowly ate a small portion. The fact that it was fresh was a novelty. He certainly was used to rougher, older fare. This was a treat to be prized. And yet. His thoughts fell again to Will and he pulled the crusty bread away from his lips. He tucked it into his tunic, where the bread kept him warm, and he trotted on, back toward Gutter Lane and to find Will.

The early warmth from the sun had faded behind a sheath of clouds and he yanked his muddied cloak across his chest, warding off the cold wind. He hadn't thought beyond giving Will the small remnant. He didn't dare think what he could do for the lad, for he had no home to go to himself. But God's grace would surely show him the way as He had done many times before—he had no doubt of that—and so he hurried, turning the corner and heading directly for the small alcove where he had left his friend the night before.

Will was there, hunched over in the damp shadows, his head lying on his chest.

Jack dropped to his knees in front of him and touched the good leg. "Will, look who it is, but Jack Tucker. And lo! I've brought a feast." He withdrew the bread and brandished it, a smile curling his lips.

But Will didn't move. "Oi, Will," he said again, shaking the boy's shoulder. The head lolled back and Jack yelled and fell back on his bum. Will's eyes were open but they were dry and clouded.

"Oh, no." Jack sat and stared. It wasn't as if he hadn't seen corpses before. He had, many times. But they hadn't been anyone he had known.

Slowly, he reached forward and touched the cold cheek. Nothing moved. Not an eyelash. Not a flicker of breath. Eyes and mouth dry, Will didn't know pain or hunger or even loneliness any longer.

It was Will who had helped him on the streets when Jack had run away from a master who hadn't wanted him. Though the man had, at least, spent the coin to bury Jack's mother, who had also been his servant. But it was Will who taught him to cut a purse, taught him which man to target and which to stay away from. Will was the master of it. And though they had often gone their separate ways, they always managed to find one another again, either at the alms door of a church, or at crowded gatherings outside ale houses, or watching processions. Without ever exchanging a word, they'd catch each other's eye in the crowd and begin to coordinate their thievery, and meet up later, sharing a bowl of wine or ale, and laugh and laugh.

Will was unstoppable, bright, wary, invincible, immortal! But maybe…not as much as Jack had thought.

He sat in the mud, staring. His throat was thick and hot, but he had no more tears. Will wouldn't have wanted them in any case. Jack becrossed himself and sent up a silent prayer.

After a long moment, he picked himself up and stood, staring down at his friend, but aware that people would soon be on the streets. "I know you will forgive me," he whispered, "but I cannot be seen with you. Besides, what do you care? You're with God now." And despite what he thought before, tears did streak their way down his dirty cheeks.

After another long moment, he finally turned and walked away, stuffing the bread back into his tunic and dragging his feet. He choked on a prayer. Fear, caught up with other innumerable emotions, left him confused and mute.

He looked back only once and shivered. Death stalked so close. Too close. He had been only too lucky himself. If that Tracker hadn't said and that apothecary hadn't cured him, he was loath to consider what would have happened to him.

His steps were lighter as he thought about it. Gratitude surged within again. "And a prayer for Crispin Guest, too, I reckon," he muttered. "If he hadn't have caught me, I'd be a dead man now."

Turning the corner, he smacked right into the sheriff's men. Disoriented for only a moment, he jerked back when one of the men pointed at him and said, "It's him. Grab him!"

Jack took no time at all to pivot on his heel and took off running.

He was young and full of verve, but the sheriff's men had a task set to them and they stayed close behind.

Jack knew the city like no one else. No nobleman, no shopkeeper, knew it like he did. He scrambled down a narrow close and skidded low through an open arched window. He slid down and hit the straw-laden floor of the storeroom and kept running. Up the stairs and behind him, he heard them struggling to squeeze through the tiny window.

He threw open the door and looked around. The abandoned storeroom often served as a dry place for him and others, and was strewn about with broken barrels, shattered pottery, and blackened floors where vagrants like him had dared to make small fires for warmth. He dashed for the front door, pulled it open, and fell into the arms of more of the sheriff's men. Fingers closed over his arms, yanking him one way while another man yanked him the other.

"Mercy! You'll pull me apart!"

"Don't think it hasn't crossed my mind to do just that," growled one of the men in a mail hood. He gave Jack's arm a particularly hard pull, one that nearly dislocated Jack's shoulder. "Be still or I'll wrench every limb from your body."

Jack stilled and sagged. It wasn't his day. "What's this about, Master? I haven't the strength to fight you, so I'd like to know at least what you think I'd done."

The men who had finally gotten through the window of the storehouse met them at the door.

"What you've done?" said the mail-coifed man. "Listen to him." He gestured toward the men and they surrounded Jack with shadowed faces and dark intent. "What you've done? I'm arresting you in the name of the king and the Lord Sheriff. For murder."

CHAPTER FOUR

Newgate prison stood high above London's streets, flaunting its gray stone walls to the encroaching sun like an armored knight challenging all-comers.

Crispin sauntered behind the nervous page all through the district's streets. From time to time the boy looked back at him, pleading with desperate eyes for him to hurry.

Crispin couldn't help but look back over his own shoulder, wondering if the man in the robe was following somewhere behind.

They arrived at the gates and the high walls. It was late morning and Crispin had yet to properly sleep, eat, or shave and now it seemed the day wore the possibility of being a long one.

The messenger took Crispin up the familiar wooden stairway and through an arched door. The aroma of roasted meat clung to the room and when Crispin turned he saw the capon and a haunch of pork steaming on a platter. Nestled beside it sat a round loaf of white bread on a board and a wooden bowl heaped with glistening yellow butter. The sheriff poured himself a cup of wine from a jug.

"My lord," said Crispin with an abbreviated bow.

"Crispin. Since you were a witness to this business, I thought you might be interested in its conclusion." He quaffed the entire contents of the silver cup before he reached across the table for the bread. He tore a hunk, swathed it with butter, and shoved into his mouth. A shower of crumbs speckled his chest.

Crispin shut his eyes. He wasn't certain if his belly rumbled more from hunger or intemperance.

"Are you hungry?" Wynchecombe asked, mouth full. "Have some. Here. Have some wine." He poured Crispin a goblet and slid it across the table. Without a word Crispin took it, but before he touched the rim to his lips, Wynchecombe raised his cup and said, "To the king."

Crispin paused. He considered casting the cup away in a defiant gesture; laughing outright and returning the cup to the table untouched, leveling a steely gaze at Wynchecombe; cursing the king and taking a long quaff.

In the end, he did none of it. He lifted the goblet politely in salute and murmured, "To the king," before downing the wine. He felt it worth a little swallowed pride to get the taste of all of last night from his mouth.

Wynchecombe chuckled, refilled Crispin's cup, and slid the tray of meats toward him.

"I shall continue to reserve my doubts about you," said Wynchecombe after another quaff. He ran his finger under his wet mustache. "But I shall never doubt your cunning."

"I do not believe my cunning was ever in doubt," said Crispin, tearing a leg from the capon and taking a bite. He muffled his groan of pleasure.

Wynchecombe shook his head. "There you stand. Are you a mockery to the court or a defiant martyr? I have never been able to distinguish which, and the longer I know you the less I can reckon it."

"Do you truly know me?" he said quietly between mouthfuls.

Wynchecombe laughed. He narrowed his eyes at Crispin over the rim of his cup. "No. I suppose I don't."

Crispin continued to chew.

Wynchecombe leaned forward. His large hand surrounded the cup of wine. "I'd like to get to know you, if for no better reason than to cut your legs out from under you from time to time."

Crispin raised his brows but said nothing while he ate.

"Still," said Wynchecombe, sitting back while Crispin stood. "You must admit, your circumstances forced you to learn new skills."

"Starving?" he said, mouth full. "Yes, it is a new skill. One I would rather not have learned." He swallowed the meat in his mouth, set the stripped bone aside, and wiped his hand on the tablecloth. "Though in France one was often required to go without the comforts of roasted flesh or wine. Ah…but, of course, since *you* never did battle in the king's army, you would not understand such sacrifice. My lord."

Wynchecombe's face flushed and darkened. He threw down the slice of pork. It slipped off the plate and hit the floor with a slap. He grabbed the tablecloth and jabbed at his beard and mustache. "I did not summon you here to eat," said Wynchecombe, "but to show you our prisoner."

"I am curious, my lord, who you apprehended. There were so few clues."

"Don't be coy, Crispin. It doesn't suit."

Taking one more hasty bite of food and one last gulp of wine, Crispin followed the sheriff out.

They descended the stairs into a dim passageway that smelled of a blend of musty damp, old smoke, and urine. The stench caused a chill of remembrance to ripple down Crispin's spine.

The passageway opened into a slightly wider chamber with a smoky fire blazing from a center hearth ring. Four guards hovered near the fire, ghostly gray shapes that snapped to attention when they noticed the sheriff. "Bring out that prisoner," he told them, and one man with a large ring of keys on his belt ran to comply.

In a few moments the sound of dragging chains caught Crispin's attention. When the prisoner reached the yellow nimbus of hearth light, Crispin snorted in disgust.

Paler, even sickly-looking, the boy's shackled feet lost all their youthful spring, but there was no mistaking the cutpurse Jack

Tucker.

"What have you gone and done, Wynchecombe?" The words left Crispin's mouth before he could stop himself, but the sheriff, in his triumph, took no notice.

"No one escapes from me, Guest. Especially murdering cutpurses."

Recognizing Crispin, Jack's face lighted. "My lord!" He threw himself at Crispin's feet. "Tell the Lord Sheriff it is all a mistake. I didn't murder nobody! I swear on the Holy Mother's veil. I never killed nobody!"

Wynchecombe leaned toward Crispin. "He told us he'd been to an apothecary. He said he was looking for a cure. For poison."

Crispin nearly laughed, but he turned his sharp nose toward Wynchecombe instead. "My Lord Sheriff, I can easily explain this otherwise guilty behavior of our young friend besides the actions of a murderer."

Amused, Wynchecombe cocked his head. "Can you? By Christ, Guest, you astound me. Protecting the likes of cutpurses now? How low will you stoop?"

"Never have I said he is innocent. Of thievery, he is abundantly guilty."

"Aye, sir," said Jack, bobbing his head. "I am that. Christ help me for the sinner I am."

"But of murder?" continued Crispin. "No."

"Then explain to me why such an innocent boy should seek an antidote to a poison to which he had no knowledge and no familiarity."

Crispin smiled. "He drank some. Or at least he thought he did."

The sheriff's smug expression fell. "What? What is this nonsense? Why should he drink it himself? He knew how lethal it was."

"Precisely. Had he known our knight was dead from poison he never would have touched that wine. But I saw with my own eyes what he did: He cut the man's purse, took a few baubles, and took a sip of wine before he left. Like me, he thought the man asleep, never suspecting the truth. He did not drink from the dead man's wine, but another of the many on the table. Else he would certainly be dead himself."

Wynchecombe could deny it all. Crispin braced for it, studied his changing expression, and wondered just what he would do: Save face and hang Jack Tucker anyway, or be a good Christian and admit his faults?

"Damn you!" Wynchecombe spewed at Jack. "Why didn't you say?"

"I did, m'lord! I tried to tell you, but I'm only a thief, not a great lord like this gentleman."

"And damn you, Guest. You could have saved me the trouble."

"You believe me, then?" Crispin denied himself the pleasure of reminding Wynchecombe that Crispin specifically told him to forget about Tucker.

"Yes, I suppose I do." The sheriff made a reluctant wave of his hand, and the guard took this as a command to release Jack from his shackles.

Jack rubbed his bloody wrists and fell to his knees before the sheriff. "Thank you, m'lord! God's blessing on you, m'lord."

"There is still this crime of thievery," said Wynchecombe.

"My Lord Sheriff," said Crispin wearily, "he has made good. And he promised me not to thieve again. Didn't you, Jack?"

"On me mother's heart, Lord Sheriff. I have learnt the error of me ways. I'm a new man."

Wynchecombe breathed through clenched teeth. "Just get him out of my sight."

Two guards shoved Jack in the direction of the arch.

Wynchecombe tapped his foot and opened and closed his sword hand. "Look what you have done to me," he growled. "You have made me magnanimous!"

"Lord Sheriff…"

"Oh, hold your tongue, Guest." The sheriff turned and stomped back through the passageway to his warm hall.

Crispin followed slowly and lingered in the doorway, studying the floorboards at his feet.

Back in his tower chamber, Wynchecombe sat in his chair and brooded. He stared at the food getting cold.

"Did you discover who the dead man was?" asked Crispin.

"No. We found no clue to his identity."

Crispin pushed away from the wall and reached into his coat. "Perhaps this may help." He held the pouch forward and pulled out the gold chain with the bejeweled cross.

Wynchecombe sat up and snatched the cross. He turned it over in his hand and ran a thick finger over the inscription. "Where did you get this?"

"Tucker may be no murderer, but he is an accomplished cutpurse. He took my money pouch before stealing the dead man's. I gave chase and captured the boy along with his spoils."

Wynchecombe gave him only a cursory glance while examining the cross. "How enterprising of you." He touched the engraved letters and muttered, *"Pocillator."*

"It means 'cup bearer'."

"I know my Latin, damn you." He examined it another moment more before asking, "But what exactly does 'cup bearer' mean? Is he a priest?"

Crispin shook his head. "I know not. There was also this." He showed Wynchecombe the pinky ring.

"No signet. No inscription. This does not help." Wynchecombe discarded both and grabbed the cloth pouch.

Crispin noticed its embroidery for the first time and without a word of apology, seized the pouch out of Wynchecombe's hand. "Let me see that." He turned the pouch and ran his finger over the needlework. "I did not note this carefully before," he said, pointing to the stitching of a red cross. "This is a *Templar's* badge."

"What? Are you mad? There are no more Templars. Not since King Edward of Caernarvon's day."

"Nevertheless, it is the Templar's sign." Crispin tapped his lip with a finger. "Why would a man carry such a thing?"

"A family bequest?"

36

"It is practically new."

"Part of his arms?"

"What fool would add this to his arms? Surely ill-luck would follow him."

Wynchecombe turned the pouch again and shook his head. "Strange, indeed. I know of no knight who would own such a thing."

"Where is the body now?"

"God's teeth, Guest. What is on your mind?"

"Nothing, perhaps. May I see it?"

Wynchecombe relented and led Crispin outside and across a courtyard to the stone chapel. The body lay on a platform inside the dim interior. Two friars in dark robes knelt beside it. The clerics were startled to their feet when both men marched down the aisle and stopped before the corpse.

"Our apologies, brothers," muttered Crispin to the cowled men. The friars nodded and stepped aside for them, finding a new place at two prie-dieux beside a fat, white candle.

Crispin cast aside the gauzy shroud covering the body and stared at the plain surcote. No arms or badge to indicate the man's background, title, or name, but Crispin whispered a curse when he saw that the surcote was white. A Templar color.

"That means nothing," said Wynchecombe, seeming to read his thoughts.

Crispin ignored him and examined the hauberk of finely linked rings. The clerics had dressed the man in his mail hood and hauberk and covered it all with his white surcote. They laid his hands over the hilt of his sword that now rested on his legs, point downward. He wore no shin armor. This would have been observed peeking out from under his merchant's gown, Crispin supposed. His leather belt was cinched tightly about his waist, and on it hung a dagger and an empty pouch like a scrip.

Just as he had completed his examination, the candles flickered, casting light across the dead man's chest. Crispin bent lower. The shadows of some irregular stitching marred the otherwise smooth line of his surcote, as if something had been embroidered there. No, not on the surface but beneath, on the other side.

Crispin reached for the corpse's surcote but Wynchecombe stayed his hand.

"Crispin, even you would not desecrate a body..."

"I mean no disrespect," he said more to the corpse than to the sheriff. "But there is something I must see."

Crispin pulled down the surcote, and looked on its inner face. There. The Templar's cross stitched lightly over his heart in white. It matched the cross on the pouch.

Crispin stepped aside so the sheriff could see it.

"Mother of God," Wynchecombe gasped.

Crispin returned the surcote in place over mail, padded gambeson, and lambskin shirt.

"I would not believe it—"

"—if I had not seen it," Crispin finished. "It seems the Templars are not extinct after all," he whispered, mindful of the friars.

"But what does this mean? Now what's to be done? Do we notify Rome? The Knights Templars were disbanded and abolished seventy years ago." He bit his lower lip. "Perhaps we should send a message to the Archbishop of Canterbury..."

"No. Do nothing yet." With half an eye fixed toward the friars, Crispin's voice drew low. "This business of an abolished order and a poisoned man. It smells of treachery."

Wynchecombe licked his lips and changed his weight from one foot to the other. "I do not like this."

"Nor do I. There is much to discover. Do I have your leave to go, Lord Sheriff?"

The sheriff eyed him darkly. "Crispin. Leave it alone."

"I am the Tracker. It is now my vocation."

"Tracker of what? There is nothing lost here."

"A life is lost. A murderer is worth discovering."

Wynchecombe stuck his thumbs in his belt and stared down his nose. "You are mad to pursue this, especially since no one will pay you. Do you have leisure now to waste time on such? Leave it alone, I say."

"'There is no great genius without some touch of madness.'"

"Scripture?"

"Seneca. Do you need me further, my lord?"

Wynchecombe scowled. "Perhaps you would do better with Scripture and not with pagans, no matter how sage."

"Are you suddenly concerned with my soul, Lord Sheriff?"

"What? What nonsense. Off with you. Let me see nothing of you and corpses from now on."

Crispin grunted his reply, but becrossed himself cursorily before leaving the chapel. Once free of Newgate, he breathed the smoky air of London with relief.

His mind worked on Templars and poisons, of crosses and Latin phrases. The sheriff would not help him. Nothing unusual there. But this was no ordinary murder if it involved a long abolished order. Templars? He could scarce believe it.

Poison might be administered by anyone. It could have been stealthily done with the victim none the wiser. It was best to discover just who was at the Boar's Tusk last night…

He chuffed an airless sound. Hadn't he scolded himself earlier for taking up diversions that did not pay? Ah well. He supposed it wasn't good for a tavern keeper's business having a dead man in one's tavern, and it was the least he could do for Gilbert and his wife Eleanor.

He left the prison and walked down Newgate Market where it became the Shambles. Gilbert might even be willing to erase Crispin's debt if he discovered who so ill-used the Boar's Tusk. He let fantasies of free wine for the rest of his days fill his mind. He even licked his lips at the thought…before a dark sack thrust down over his head.

Before he could react, a heavy club contacted with his skull and drove his racing mind into black oblivion.

CHAPTER FIVE

Crispin stared at it a long time, but his hazy mind refused to understand. When finally he could focus, he recognized a single candle flame sputtering on its wick, hovering over a pool of liquid tallow.

And then pain shot down his neck. The pain radiated down from his scalp, and when he tried to raise a hand to it, he found he could not. He tugged harder but his arms were bound behind him.

"God's blood!"

"Oaths? A very poor use of language."

Crispin jerked up his head. He searched vainly for the face that belonged to the male voice, but all he saw was dark and the bright spot of the candle flame.

"Would not a prayer be more appropriate to such a setting?"

"What setting? Am I in Hell?" Crispin asked half-heartedly, though once the question left his lips he worried over the answer.

The voice laughed. "No. Though you may think Hell preferable."

"What is the use of such mummery? Unbind me." Coming to his senses, Crispin took inventory of his numb body; hands tied behind him, each leg likewise fastened to the legs of the chair. His coat had been unbuttoned and pushed back over his shoulders, and his chemise had likewise been opened, his chest bared to the cold.

What in heaven—? "Who are you? What do you want of me?"

"We are men who seek answers."

"'We'?"

"We will ask the questions. Understand?"

Before Crispin could reply, a whip lashed across his chest. The stinging pain rolled up and down his body. The back of his knees tingled and weakened.

"It is a simple question," said the voice. "We want to know where it is." Through his pain, Crispin detected the faint pinching of words, of a man cultivating very carefully how he spoke with the under layer of a French accent.

"Where 'what' is?"

The whip lashed out again and Crispin stiffened against the taut ropes. He blinked away the pain.

"Wrong answer."

"How can I tell you if I don't know what you seek?"

The whip slashed again, raising a wash of hot pain across the warming skin.

"You know very well what it is. We want it back, and if it means removing your flesh one strip at a time, then so be it."

Crispin's belly tightened. His head throbbed, and now his chest flamed with deep red welts. Soon he would lose the tenuous consciousness he fought to keep.

"It's not too far," he gasped. "I'll get it for you."

The voice came closer, speaking into his ear. "Where?"

"You'd never find it. I will have to show you."

"Liar." The whip slashed twice, catching him once across the throat. He choked on a gurgling breath before the candle's brightness dimmed to a bronze haze.

"You must understand," said the voice. "We have no desire to cause you harm." He gave a low chuckle. "It is only a bonus."

"What would you have me say?" Crispin gasped.

"Say anything at all," said the cultivated voice. "But finally speak the truth, for it is the only thing that will keep you alive."

"This thing you want. I am certain once I produce it, my life will be terminated. So what is the point?"

"You may be correct. Well then. It will not *prolong* your life. Surely that will be a mercy."

Crispin huffed. "A small one. You will have to untie me in order for me to show you."

"As I said. I do not think I trust you."

"That trust goes both ways. First, tell me who you are."

"That is not for you to know. And trust need not necessarily go both ways. Only our way." To prove the point, he slashed the whip across Crispin's chest again.

Tears of pain squeezed from his eyes and he held his breath while the sting subsided. "As I said," said Crispin between breaths, "there seems little point in this. It will not help you if I die. Or faint."

"I cannot help the dying, but of fainting…We can revive you."

Crispin's vision blurred. The shadowy figure before him wavered. He knew he was blacking out and he welcomed the respite, though he knew it would be brief. But before the room darkened completely, he heard something behind him crash. A chair? Men grunted in a wordless struggle. More crashing and scuffling. Empty barrels toppled and rolled across the wood floor. Someone shouted, calling for help. Light flooded the chamber and more voices added to the melee. Footsteps shuffled and finally lit out.

Men's voices conversed above him and something sawed the bindings at Crispin's hands. He tensed his jaw, wondering what new torture awaited.

"I've almost got you free." A new voice. "It's me, Master. Jack Tucker. Them bastards may come back, so you must help me once you're free."

"Help you?" There were far too many questions for the state of his mind. His hands were suddenly freed and he stared at them, opening and closing the fingers. Then his feet were free, but he had no urge to rise.

"Come now, Master. You must get up."

"No, no," he said, lowering to the ground. His head hurt, his chest flamed, and when he reached up to his face, he felt the sticky wetness of blood.

"Master Guest, arise!"

Crispin lay on his side, wondering what all the chatter was about. In his clouded mind, he imagined a host of white-garbed Templars encircling him. They urged him to do something, trying to show him an object that he couldn't quite see. One reached down and shook his shoulder. "Master Guest!" the voice urged, his face masked by silver mail under a bascinet helm. The voice changed from that of a cultured knight to a young boy's of a lower class. Surely not a squire. Crispin opened his eyes and focused them on the lad. "Who are you?"

"Jack Tucker, Master. Remember? From the Boar's Tusk? Arise. You there! Help me."

Crispin's mind arrived back to the present and he grunted in pain. Gingerly, he rose. "Jack. Yes."

Jack slung Crispin's arm over his shoulder while another man helped Crispin to his feet. Jack told Crispin to lean on him while he quickly ushered him to the door and thanked the men who helped with the rescue. A few men offered to assist Jack, but the boy kindly refused them.

Silhouettes of men crowded the open doorway and eyed Crispin curiously. In a haze, Crispin felt himself dragged past them and through London's streets, his shirt and coat flapping. He flinched when they reached the sunlight.

After many turns and twists Crispin mustered his voice. "Where are you taking me?"

"Home, Master. To your lodgings."

"And how, by the Virgin, do you know where I live?"

"Everyone knows that, Master."

They reached the shop below his lodgings and Martin Kemp, the tinker, met them at the door. "By the Mass, Crispin! What's happened to you?"

"Help me get him to his room, good Master," Jack pleaded.

Kemp quickly complied. With Jack above and Kemp behind, they managed to wrestle him up the narrow stairway. The tinker unlocked the door and they laid him on the bed.

Kemp hovered and stared at the blood on Crispin's chest while Jack stoked the meager fire. Thin and wiry, Kemp was almost as tall as Crispin. His brown hair, cut carelessly, was kept tucked under a plain, leather cap. A leather apron covered him from his jaundiced chest to his knobby knees.

"Have you wood or peat, good Master?" Jack said over his shoulder. "This room's as cold as a brothel's back door."

"Wood? Aye, I do. I'll fetch some, shall I?" He turned but stopped in the doorway. "You are a most blessed Good Samaritan, my boy. Praise God for your timely arrival."

"There wasn't no timely arrivals. I'm his servant, is all. Jack Tucker."

"Oh? Indeed?"

"The *wood*, Master."

"Oh aye. The wood." He hurried away with heavy steps down the stairwell.

Jack raised Crispin and settled his pillow more comfortably behind him. Gingerly he made certain Crispin's coat and shirt were open and pushed away from his wounds. He ticked his head. "Bastards," he muttered and brought over the basin and water jug. He found a rag and dipped it into the water. "This will smart a bit, Master. Have you wine?"

Crispin gritted his teeth and shook his head.

"Then water will have to do until that fellow comes back." He pressed the soggy rag to the bleeding wounds and Crispin jerked back, pain renewed.

"Sorry, sir. Can't be helped. Don't want them to fester. We'll have to put warm water to that, too."

Kemp returned and placed the sticks on the fire. "Whatever has happened to you, Crispin?"

Crispin smiled weakly. "I do not rightly know, Martin. It seems I met some men who mistakenly believe I am in possession of something they own. Or something they want."

Kemp put tin-grayed fingers to his lips. "Should you not call the sheriff…"

"Master Kemp," said Jack quickly from his place beside Crispin. "Have you wine for these wounds? They're right foul."

"Wine? Oh yes."

Jack watched the tinker leave again. "I think it best to keep the sheriff out of it, don't you, good Master?"

He turned his gaze toward the boy. "I thought I rid myself of you."

"Well now. About that." Jack wrung the bloody water from the rag into the basin. He laid the cool rag again over Crispin's wounds. "After I left Newgate, I followed you for a bit." He lowered his eyes and a blush reddened his pale cheeks. "I wanted to thank you proper, sir, but there isn't much a lad like me can offer. Before I could speak, you turned down an alley and out of me sight for the blink of an eye and when I got there, I saw these monk's carrying you off, and you with a sack over your head like you were turnips going to market."

"Monks?"

"Aye. They looked like monks, all robed in dark cassocks."

"Hmm. Go on."

Well, sir, they didn't see me. I can keep to the shadows like I am one. So I followed them. When you didn't come out, I gave the hue and cry and some shopkeepers come running. I suppose the noise scared them villains off. Do you know who they were?"

"No." Crispin reached for his head and then thought better of it. He looked down at the wet rag covering his chest. Red stripes welled up through it. "You probably saved my life back there."

"Well now. It's only proper, isn't it? My being your servant and all."

"You are not my servant. You must stop saying that."

"I might have been a fine servant, if my mother and sire weren't taken when they were. Both died of the plague, you see. And my worthless sister abandoned us. I had to make me own way, didn't

I? What's a lad of eight to do?"

"What *is* a lad to do? You were orphaned at eight?"

Jack nodded. "But I managed, sir. By the grace of God."

Crispin studied the boy's dirty face and crusted hair. He well knew the sting of losing family at an early age. "How old are you now, boy?"

"Eleven, m'lord. Maybe twelve."

"Stop calling me 'lord'. I am no one's lord. Not anymore."

"Oh. What shall I call you, then?"

Crispin shifted his position with a grunt. "Call me Crispin. Everyone else does. Now suppose you tell me about this antidote you took."

Jack offered a shy smile. "You *are* as smart as they say, eh? Well, when I heard you and the sheriff talk of poison, I said to m'self, 'Jack, you had best get your arse out of there or all is lost.' And almost right away I started feeling all queer in me gut. I heaved soon thereafter and kept on heaving till there was naught left. Saints' toes, I thought I'd vomit m'self inside out! Well, I never been so scared, and I found an apothecary and begged him for a cure. I got in one swallow, went on me way, and then the sheriff's men nabbed me, and I reckon you know the rest."

"You are fortunate. I know of no antidote to such a poison."

"That's what the apothecary said. He said it wouldn't do no good for me, but here I am."

"Yes. Here you are."

"Right then. What victuals shall I fix you?"

"You will not cook for me." He closed his eyes half from pain and half from embarrassment. "At any rate...I...I have no food."

"That's simple, my lord. I'll return anon."

"I am *not* a lord...Tucker!"

Jack flew over the threshold with a wave. Kemp passed him at the door.

"A fine servant, that," said the tinker. "Looks like you acquired him just in time."

"He's *not* my—oh hell." Crispin fell back surrendering to the pillow, and stared at the cobwebs among the rafters.

"I brought some wine." He lifted the full jug to show him. "It will serve to cleanse your wounds and warm the belly. Now then, if there is more you need, send Jack down to fetch me. Oh. Where was he off to?"

"To get some food."

"I see. Then circumstances for you must have improved. What with a servant and such. Perhaps, well, perhaps this isn't quite the proper time, but my wife would hide me if I did not remind you…"

"The rent. I know it well, Martin. I will send Jack anon to pay you."

"Well then!" Kemp nodded and rubbed his long hands together.

Crispin watched him leave with a pang of guilt. The rent was days overdue, but he had lied about paying him. He had already borrowed from Gilbert and could not even repay that. Vaguely he wondered how Jack was acquiring food and decided he didn't want to know.

He cast a glance at his money pouch, but it lay undisturbed.

Crispin slowly awoke to savory aromas. He opened his eyes and spied Jack stirring a pot on a trivet over his fire, humming to himself.

"You again? Why are you here?" Crispin asked groggily. "And what's that?"

"Rabbit stew. Will you have some?"

"How did you afford this rabbit and the rest of it?"

Jack didn't answer and Crispin rose from the pillow. "Tucker?"

"I'm here to help, Master. As to the rabbit…well now. It isn't polite to ask after a gift, is it?"

Crispin sighed and laid back.

The mattress sank under Jack's weight. Crispin sat up, squinting at the boy. Jack offered a steaming bowl.

"It smells good," Crispin grunted and grudgingly took the

spoon.

Jack poured wine into the other wooden bowl and then sat again on the mattress. "Them men," Jack began while Crispin tasted the stew with a tentative tongue. "What did they want?"

"I wish I knew," he answered between spoonful's.

"Must have mistaken you for someone else, eh?"

"Possibly." Crispin felt Jack's eyes on him before he looked up at the boy's anxious features.

"Is it good?"

Crispin offered a crooked grin. "Yes, Jack. Much thanks. For everything. Now, suppose you prepare to be on your way."

Jack frowned. "After all I done, you'd still be rid of me?"

"Jack, I told you the truth. I haven't any money to pay you. I haven't even enough for my rent."

"Oh, that! That's taken care of."

Crispin lowered the spoon. "I'm afraid to ask."

"I've taken care of it, is all."

Crispin set the bowl aside and lay back. "Jack. What have you done? You did not cut a purse, did you?"

"Aw no, Master. It's just that I went downstairs to thank Master Kemp for his kindness, and it seems some of his loose coins were sitting there on his accounting books. Well, they were just sitting there and all, and I just naturally come by 'em. So then I ask him, 'Master Kemp, how much is it that Master Crispin owes you?' So he looks in his book and he says the number and I hand him the coins."

Crispin bit his lip. The pain helped but didn't entirely dull the smile from curving the edge of his mouth. "You paid him with his own money?"

"Now Master. Don't you think it's time you lay back and rest?"

Crispin allowed Jack to push him gently into the pillow. He watched the boy stoke the fire and listened to his humming. He must have slept again, because he awoke some time later and Jack was standing over him. Crispin raised his hand to his forehead. A roaring headache was in full bloom. "What is it, Jack?"

"There is a message for you."

Crispin noticed the paper in Jack's hand. "Who brought it?"

"I know not, Master. It was left tucked into the door."

Crispin unfolded the small bit of parchment and inhaled a sharp breath. There was no writing on the parchment. Only the careful rendition of a red cross. The cross of the Knights Templar.

CHAPTER SIX

Crispin wracked his brain, trying to remember as much about the Templars as he could recall with a sore head and an equally sore chest. Templar history hadn't been part of his studies as a young man and it certainly wasn't part of the conversation at court. But he did recall some snippets at various tournaments and battles. How the Templars fought at Mansurah. The Battle of Arsuf under Richard Lionheart. And the last decisive battle in the Holy Land, Hattin. But as with talk of any battle, it was strategy and failure that was studied and discussed, not the wisdom of an order of warrior clerics.

He moved to the chair and stared at the wall. The parchment hung limply from his hand.

Jack cleared his throat and Crispin looked up.

"Pardon, sir," said Jack, crumpling the hem of his tunic in dirty fingers. "But what *is* that?" He pointed to the paper in Crispin's hand.

"This is a cross of the Knights Templar."

"I see. And what, sir, is a Knight Templar?"

"What's the matter with you, boy? Born under a rock? Has not all the world heard of the Knights Templar?"

"Maybe all the world, Master Crispin...but not me."

Crispin looked at him before chuckling. "Well, Master Tucker.

Perhaps you are too young. Come here. Sit down." He offered him the stool. Jack moved closer and gingerly took the stool, drawing it into the light. He slid atop it smoothly. His legs dangled. Crispin leaned on the table toward Jack and Jack leaned forward to match him. "They were an order of warrior monks who guarded travelers in the Holy Land. But then they took to warfare. They chiefly fought in the Holy Land during the Crusades. You *have* heard of the Crusades, have you not?"

"Oh aye," he said with a casual sweep of his hand. "So them monks went off fighting, did they?" He took a swing at the air. "I like a good melee m'self."

"Yes. Well. These Templars were more knight than monk, so it is said. And they were supposed to have a cache of treasure hidden somewhere in France. But that is long past. The order was suppressed by the pope seventy years ago."

Jack pointed to the paper on the table. "Then what's that for?"

"The dead man in the tavern was a Knight Templar."

"God blind me! I thought you just said they was no more."

"So they were. Or so it was thought. And now this."

"Oh!" Jack shot to his feet. "Them men what grabbed you! They're them Templars!"

"I was just thinking that. And yet how can that be? And why torture me? Why this missive?"

Jack slowly sat again. "It seems plain enough to me, sir," said Jack. He dropped his voice to a soft whisper. "They don't want you poking around no murders. If I was you, I'd take that counsel."

"Then it is a very good thing I am not you." Crispin rose, tied the laces of his chemise, and gingerly buttoned up his cotehardie. Retrieving his belt from a peg, he buckled it around his waist and pressed his hand to the dagger hilt. He headed for the door when Jack scrambled from his seat and yanked on Crispin's sleeve. He looked down at Jack's hand clenched about his wrist.

"Master! Are you well enough to go out? Them men. They're still out there. And besides, you didn't know the dead man. What's this man's murder to you?"

"If you think I'm going to allow these scoundrels to put me to torture without penalty, you are mistaken." He eyed Jack's hand on him and Jack quickly released his grip.

"If it's all the same to you, sir, I will stay here."

Crispin opened his mouth to tell the boy to be off when he thought better of it. Those men *were* still out there. They probably were none too happy with Jack either. Might it be safer for the boy if he stayed locked inside?

"If stay you will—and only temporarily, mind—then it is best you lock yourself within." He grabbed the door handle but Jack leaned against the door.

He dropped his gaze and fidgeted with his tunic hem. "So you're this Tracker they talk about, eh? Isn't it the sheriff's job to catch thieves and murderers?"

"And you've seen for yourself the fine job the sheriff's done of it."

Jack flicked a grin. "The king appointed him. He's just an armorer, after all. But you. It isn't worth getting y'self killed now, is it?"

"What do you care? What is your investment? I told you I cannot pay you. I do not need a servant."

Jack's eyes took in the room, the hearth, the table. "It's shelter, isn't it? And food."

"And it's dangerous. You saw what those men did to me. You could be next."

Jack crossed his arms tightly over his chest and tucked his chin down. "I've seen danger before. Never you fear."

Jack's face might have been comical in its sincerity if it had not pressed a nerve somewhere in Crispin's heart. At thirty, he still had no sons...well, none that he was aware of. He fostered no children, mentored no squires or pages. Looking at Jack, then looking at the empty room caused a hard knot to tighten in the center of his belly. "There's truly no place for you here, you know. For anyone." He raised his arms in a gesture of futility and dropped them to his sides. "No matter what tales you have heard, you do not know my situation. You do not know *me*!" He rubbed his head but it only roused an ache on the bruised lump.

"You were kind…and fair to me, sir. That is all I know. That is all I care about. Isn't that enough?"

His gaze tracked over the boy's hopeful expression. He grabbed his cloak. "I do *not* need a servant." He pushed Jack away from the door, and left through it.

CHAPTER SEVEN

Crispin retraced his steps of that morning and stole back to the alley where they had abducted him. Like a hunting dog, he followed the trail along the edges of the buildings, searching for anything that might yield him clues. But there was nothing.

He stood at the mouth of the dank alley and listened to dripping water and creaking eaves. His gaze glided over the dew-slick rooftops, and he pulled his cloak over his sore chest before striding toward the storeroom where he was imprisoned. Its mews emptied onto a dark and colorless alley. The shutters that first blocked the daylight from the windows now hung wide from the efforts of his rescuers.

When he crossed the threshold and stood in the center of the room, coldness numbed the pit of his belly. With a scowl he surveyed the broken chair, discarded ropes, and spattered droplets of blood. *His* blood. A candle stub sat on an upright firkin, but there was nothing else.

Crispin looked at the remains of the ropes and shivered. Though the room was empty, he could not help but feel the evil that once inhabited it, charring its plaster and stone walls with unseen malevolence.

He left the room with relief and sought out the owner of the building, a man who owned a number of similar mews along the same lane. He told Crispin that these particular stores were unoccupied for the last six months and that he was unaware of anyone using them. He promised with all solemnity to board them up.

Crispin made his way to the Boar's Tusk and sat in his usual place close to the fire with his back to the wall, the best place to observe anyone entering or leaving.

At that early hour few patrons occupied the benches and stools under a familiar haze of candle and hearth smoke. He glanced at the table where he had found the dead man. The place was conspicuously unoccupied. Word traveled fast on Gutter Lane.

Crispin settled on the bench and drank. His elbow sat in something wet but he didn't care to move it. A shadow paused over the table and when he looked up he saw Gilbert's wife, Eleanor, above him. She brushed off the table with a rag before glancing at the jug of wine. "Crispin," she said softly. Her friendly but careworn face, lined at her brown eyes, seldom wore a sour expression, though her clientele often gave her cause. Her hair was a dull blonde or possibly gray, but Crispin rarely saw it, for she kept it tucked under a white linen headdress.

"What is it, Nell?" He waited for her usual rebuke; ordering the more expensive wine instead of ale. Wine reminded him of better days and he felt it was the one luxury he could not afford to do without.

"There's a sadness about you today, Crispin," she said instead. She sat opposite him and slid the wine jug aside. "Usually you're just cross. But today, it's sadness."

Sadness? Nothing particularly saddened him today. There was the usual poverty, but that made him more angry than sad. So, too, his treatment at the hands of those mysterious men. He rubbed his chest, thinking of it. Yet, in a small way, Jack Tucker made him sad, he supposed. Here was a boy who had nothing. Far less than Crispin, no prospects, no shelter, no hope. Yet he was as cheerful a soul as he had ever met. What made him so damned happy?

Crispin shrugged. "Maybe so."

"Care to say?"

"No."

"Sometimes," she said, pouring more wine into his clay bowl, "when a body feels sad and he tells his troubles, he feels better. It's like confession. It's cleansing."

"And sometimes a body likes to be left alone."

She smiled, wrinkling the bridge of her nose. "Well now. If I thought that for a moment, I'd leave you be." She set aside the wine jug and laid both arms on the table, leaning toward him. "Have some wine. It seems to be from a better cask today. Those who drink it are in a merry mood."

After a moment he sighed and reached for the bowl.

"It must be a woman," she said, ticking her head.

Crispin swallowed the harsh wine and grimaced. If this was the good wine he didn't want to sample the bad. "How do you reason that?"

"Well! Just look at you."

He studied her face and took another swallow. "It's not always about a woman, you know."

"Well now!" She settled her rump and leaned closer. "Tell me about it. It'll help."

"No. It won't."

"Crispin." Her hand covered his. "A woman is sometimes fickle. She does it to inspire her man to artful courting."

"It's not a woman! It's…" He searched for the words. "What purpose do I serve, Eleanor?" The words came out of his mouth, but they weren't quite what he had wanted to say. But Jack Tucker's insistence on serving him had crept into his mind and opened his thoughts from a place that should have been long buried. "I do not serve a lord. I do not serve the Church. I am…nothing."

She sighed and wrapped her fingers around her rag, winding the material into a twisted rope. "I've known you a long time, Crispin. Even before I knew your name or you knew mine, you and your friends would come here. And I remember thinking what a jolly lot they were. But looking at you now, you're not the same man."

He scowled. "I'm *not* the same man."

"It's despair you're feeling. I tell you, Crispin. It's as if you stopped living from that day. It seems to me that you cannot live on disappointments and hopes of revenge all your life."

He gulped his wine and stared at the table. "No? I seem to get on well enough."

"No," she said in a firm voice and reached for him again. Her hand closed on his wrist. The fingers felt warm on his cool skin. "You *don't* get on. And the more you dwell on it the more it shall devour you from the inside out."

He shook his head. "Nell—"

"Tell me. How many friends have you, eh? True friends. Friends to tell your troubles to."

"There is you and Gilbert."

"Aye. And who else?"

Crispin paused to think. His questing brow soon lowered into a scowl. Slowly he extricated his hand from hers.

Eleanor sat back and folded her arms over her ample chest. "That's what I thought. You make no friends, you meet no women—"

Crispin hunched forward and surrounded his cup with both hands. "I am a solitary man."

"That is not how I remember it when you were a knight. You had many associates then. And many women before your betrothal. Now you live like a monk."

The corners of his eyes crinkled as he offered a slight smile. "Not quite as a monk."

"But even so. You have no cause to be so glum. It's been seven years. You're one of us now."

Crispin stiffened his shoulders and dug a fist into his temple, leaning into it.

Eleanor scowled, no doubt reading his gesture for what it was. "I'm no fool, Crispin. I know you would rather hang than consider yourself one of us, poor lowly class that we are. The class that welcomes you, by the way. The class that hasn't rejected you. The class that won't. Maybe someday you'll lose that stubborn pride of yours and realize that. What's it gotten you anyway? Heartsore and humiliated, that's what."

"I'm glad we had this talk, Eleanor" he sneered, raising the wine to his lips.

"All I'm saying is that it wouldn't hurt you to be merry; to find some friends. And for heaven's sake to find a lovely girl. She'll take that frown from your face."

"I can think of no woman save Rosamunde." He stopped. He hadn't spoken her name in years. Was it years? The sound of it jabbed his heart, brought back all the memories.

"Rosamunde? Your betrothed?" He nodded. "Crispin Guest! That was seven years ago! She is wed. You told me so."

"Yes. Her dog of a brother betrayed his honor and broke his oath to me." He lifted his bowl. "Here's to Sir Stephen St Albans. I hope to God he is dead."

"Sir Stephen? Oh, he's not dead. At least he wasn't yesterday."

"Indeed. Too bad."

"Aye. He was arguing with that dead man…before he was dead, of course."

Crispin's eyes snapped up. "What?"

"He was here. And I haven't seen him in years. Not since…well." She took up her rag again and twisted it into a lumpy rope. "Oh, such a sad thing. Who would go and poison such a fine man as that?" She shook her head and pressed the rag to the corner of a glossy eye. "I tell you, Crispin. I do not know what this town is coming to."

Crispin edged forward and sat up. "Stephen was here, you say? What did they argue about?"

She sniffed and drew the rag into her lap, pulling on its errant strings. "I know not. They did it in whispers, if you know my meaning. But the other, the dead one, he would have none of it."

"And when was all this?"

"Right before you came in. Sir Stephen saw you, put up his hood, and left."

"Did he?"

"Sir Stephen tried to get something from the man. I did not see what it was. I thought it best to stay out of sight."

"I wish you had not done so."

"Aye. I see that now. I told as much to the Lord Sheriff."

Damn. "You spoke to the sheriff?"

"He came back this morning and demanded I tell him what I knew."

"But Gilbert never said—"

"He was not here at the time. He was below in the mews. I was here alone."

"Then what more did you say?"

"Only that John the piper was here. A few other men who looked to be servants. And the monks."

"Monks?"

"Aye. Two friars."

"What did they look like?"

"I could not say. They wore their cowls the whole time. They each called for a cup of ale but never drank any of it."

"Were they here before or after Stephen?"

"Before, I think. But I cannot be certain."

"Anyone else?"

"Only the woman."

Crispin squinted hard at her. "By all that is holy, Eleanor. Why did I not hear this before?"

She straightened and lifted her chin. "No one asked me before."

With a puff of air he leaned in. "Yes. Well, then. What woman?"

"I could not see her face."

"Naturally."

"She spoke to that dead man, too, for a brief time after Stephen left."

A busy fellow, this dead Templar. "How long did she stay?"

"Not long at all. She was gone after I turned round again. She could not have exchanged more than a few words with him."

"A servant woman or higher?"

"Oh, much higher. Fur-trimmed cloak and all."

He nodded. "You were correct on one account, Eleanor. It *was* good to talk." He climbed from the bench and before Eleanor could speak again, he slipped out the door.

A soft rain gentled the street, hazing its somber features. He pulled the leather hood over his head and clenched it over his chin. The chill still permeated the scuffed leather, and it suddenly reminded him of warmer capes and cloaks he once owned, fur-lined with fox or miniver. Some were sturdy weaves of wool while others were of velvet and brushed serge. His boots, too, had been sturdier and also lined with fur, except for the courtly slippers with their impossibly long, pointed toes.

His fist tightened on the hood and he felt the raw skin stretch. He used to have gloves, too. Masculine things for the hunt or on the lists. He remembered the feel of his gloved hands curled around a sword hilt, or pulling back the strings of a hunting bow with the gloved fingers veed around a nocked arrow.

One man took all these things away. Stephen.

Crispin felt giddy. If Rosamunde's brother was the last man to see the Templar alive—a man he had argued with—then there was a good possibility *he* could be the murderer. It was almost too good to be true.

Crispin exhaled a laugh more like a bark. "Then you'll hang," he whispered into the hood. "I will make certain that you'll stand in disgrace on the scaffold and hang for your crime. And *I* will be the one to bring you to justice. Thank you *Jesu* for this mercy!"

It fit nicely into his plots of revenge. Stephen guilty of murder. Stephen hanging.

Until his thoughts suddenly drew up short. What about the woman?

He rubbed his face. Who was she and what did she discuss with the dead Templar? Did she have anything to do with the murder?

"Perhaps not," he reasoned. "Perhaps it is mere coincidence."

A crowd blocked the avenue and stopped his momentum and his musings. People seldom gathered in the rain. Most Londoners did their best to escape the muddy streets and raw wind. Why then should this mob gather here?

Crispin peered through the throng and saw an ordinary man who smiled and waggled his arm. The crowd seemed to be excited by this.

"What the devil is going on?" Crispin demanded to no one in particular.

One of the men standing beside him pointed at the man in the center of all the attention. "Said his arm's been healed."

"Healed? How?"

"Miracle, I suppose. I don't know the man. Don't know what all this foolery is."

Crispin watched the man in the center of the crowd. The people guffawed or congratulated him on his good luck, but did not seem interested in dispersing. Crispin observed them for a moment more before he gave up with a shrug and pushed his way through.

The lowly were always making more of such events than were called for, he decided. A physician's remedy somehow becomes a miracle. The simple truth of it, Crispin knew, was that the body healed on its own. He himself sustained many a battle wound, some horrendous. Nasty gashes from swords; blows from maces that dented his helm. But he recovered each time, some under a physician's art and some simply because of his own obstinacy.

He walked on, thinking of Man's folly, of his own, and even of revenge. "Living on revenge," he muttered, considering Eleanor's words. He had not liked those words when she spoke them, but now he could not erase them from his mind. They rang in his ear, punctuated by each of his plodding steps. They prevented him from immediately noticing Jack Tucker standing in his path until he nearly ran him down.

Crispin stopped and looked up. "My shadow," he said with a

frown.

"Aye, sir. A good servant knows what his master is about."

Crispin felt in no mood for the "not my servant" roundelay, so he said nothing and side-stepped him.

"The sheriffs are awaiting you at your lodgings, Master," Jack said to Crispin's retreating back.

Crispin took one more step then stopped. He raised his head and stared up into the raining sky. It misted his cold cheeks with the patter of drops. "Of course they are," he muttered defeated. "Then I must see them at once, no?"

"They are not patient men."

Crispin yanked his cloak across his chest and cursed under his breath. "Neither am I."

Crispin found Sheriff Wynchecombe and Sheriff John More staring at his meager hearth flames when he entered. Jack took up a post in a corner of the small room. Crispin nearly told him to be off but at the last moment decided against it. He turned to Wynchecombe and More and bowed. "Welcome, my lords," he said without a shred of welcome in his voice. He strode past the sheriffs to stoke the fire.

"So these are your lodgings." Wynchecombe looked about with distaste. His gaze swept over Jack but there did not appear to be any recognition in his eyes.

"What would you expect?" said More. He was a shorter, rounder man than Wynchecombe, appearing his opposite in every way. Where Wynchecombe was dark, More was light with sandy blond hair. And where Wynchecombe sported beard and mustache, More was clean-shaven like Crispin. His houppelande was scarlet with small pearls sewn onto the chest. He chuckled and placed his thumbs in his wide belt. "For my part," he went on, "it appears *better* than I anticipated."

Wynchecombe scowled. London well knew that he did not approve of his partner being elected to the post of sheriff and in fact, More was more absent in most proceedings than not. He sniffed, ignoring More. "Why London, Crispin? One would think you would hide yourself far from here."

"A man can lose himself in London. Or at least..." He set the poker aside and faced them both. "He can try." He felt a wave of uneasiness with the sheriffs standing in his place of safe and private surroundings. "My lords, to what do I owe—?"

Wynchecombe looked at More before answering. "The body is gone."

Crispin raised a brow. "Indeed."

More shook himself. "Is that all you can say?"

"What would you have me say, Lord Sheriff?"

"Damn you, Guest," said Wynchecombe. "You couldn't let it go, could you? Couldn't let me hang that useless cutpurse who now seems to be your lap dog. Now it's missing Templars and dark mysteries. I want none of it, I tell you."

"You have a sworn duty—"

Without warning, Wynchecombe slammed his forearm into Crispin's chest and pinned him against the wall. Jack made a half-hearted lurch forward, but truly, what could he do?

More stood beside the fire uncomfortably, shuffling from foot to foot.

Inhaling a sharp breath through his teeth, Crispin swore softly. The freshening pain of his wounds smarted. "Don't tell me my duty," Wynchecombe spat at Crispin's cheek. "I know it right well." The sheriff waited, but Crispin said nothing. Wynchecombe snorted. He held Crispin one moment more before releasing him. He paced, as if nothing had happened between them. "But this," he said. "This is beyond me. Templars. Bah! I tell you I know not what to do." He snarled in Jack's direction and the boy cringed. There was a pause and Crispin waited for whatever pronouncement Wynchecombe would surely hurl at him. Instead, he was surprised by Jack scurrying around them offering bowls of wine. Wynchecombe took one, looked into his bowl, but did not drink. More refused the offer, lifting his face in disdain.

"Perhaps...we might work together on this," offered More.

The wine proved interesting again to Wynchecombe, but only to look at. "Eh? What is it, John?"

"Well, might I suggest, just this once, mind you, that Master Guest...I mean him with his history as a knight and us with... with..."

"With the might of the king's majesty?" said Crispin.

Wynchecombe nodded abruptly. "Yes. Yes, to be sure. Am I right in assuming you mean to hire this churl, John?"

"It is just that he has inconvenienced us, has he not? With his distractions of cutpurses and Templars. We must be about the king's business, not this nonsense."

Wynchecombe smiled, though not a pleasant one. "So? What say you, Guest?"

Their mummery was good, he mused. Not as practiced as it could have been, but good enough. "'Evil draws men together'," he muttered.

"What's that?"

"Nothing. Pardon my asking, but what do *I* gain from this extraordinary partnership?"

More stuttered.

"What?" cried Wynchecombe. "You mean *pay* you? Ha!" He finally drank and then grimaced, looking quizzically into the bowl. He handed it off to Jack who took it and sniffed its contents, shaking his head.

"My wages are sixpence a day," said Crispin.

Wynchecombe laughed. "Sixpence? I pay my archers as much and they work harder."

"Sixpence is my fee, archer or no. And more often than not, *I* hit the mark."

Jack snorted a laugh but quickly suppressed it when both sheriffs eyed him with twin scowls.

"Yes," said Wynchecombe. "I do recall something a year ago about your finding Westminster Abbey's missing altar goods. They were returned forthwith."

"Not so forth*with*," said Crispin, shying from the warmth of flattery. "A fort*night*, perhaps."

Wynchecombe pushed More aside to glare hard at Crispin. "You think yourself very clever."

"As long as I am clever, my lord, I eat."

Wynchecombe smirked. His dark mustache framed his white teeth. "You were fortunate they did not execute you for treason." The low growl of his words reassured them both of their status with one another.

Jack froze while setting the empty bowl back on the shelf.

"Was I?"

"Come, Crispin," Wynchecombe said, magnanimous again. "You live." He glanced about the dingy room. "Such as it is."

"My title, my lands all taken with my knighthood," he managed to say without gritting his teeth. "Yes. I live. Such as it is."

More snorted and clutched his gloved hand on his sword hilt. "By God! The gall. You were a traitor, sir! Conspiring with other traitors to put Lancaster on the throne over King Richard, the rightful heir."

Wynchecombe leaned against the wall, his arms folded in front of him. "You do not think you deserved to lose your knighthood over that? Better your knighthood than your head, eh?"

Crispin eyed their swords still in their sheaths before flicking his gaze away. "I know not. In similar circumstances, I, too, might have cast my vote to degrade such a knight. But when it is oneself, the circumstances seem...unjustified." The flames caught his attention and he shook his head. "Richard is king now. There is nothing to be done. But 'they should rule who are able to rule best'. I stand by that now as then."

Wynchecombe laughed. "Still quoting that pagan Aristotle? No wonder you are without your sword."

"And without food. Do you pay my wage or not?"

Wynchecombe frowned. "Yes. I agree to your fee."

"Now wait a moment..." said More.

"Be still, John," Wynchecombe said wearily. "These matters are best left to me, are they not?" More scowled deeply. It was true that Crispin rarely saw More in these duties except to take his place of pride in processions and other high profile events. Still, for Wynchecombe to rub his face in it…

"Though I may not need to pay it," the sheriff went on. "I know now who killed our missing knight, and it may cheer your heart to hear it."

Crispin nodded. "Stephen St Albans."

"How the hell——? Oh! That wench at the Boar's Tusk."

"You forget. She is my friend." Crispin took two steps to the fire and warmed his knuckles near the blaze. Behind him, rain drizzled against the half-closed shutters and misted the floorboards. "Will you arrest him?" The idea tingled Crispin's neck, coursing an energized sensation throughout his gut.

He did not even look at More. "Yes. Unless you have a better idea."

"My better idea isn't exactly legal." He twisted back to look at both sheriffs. "You do not seem as concerned as one would expect that your corpse has vanished."

More waved his hand in dismissal. "We no longer need the corpse to know he is dead. It is the same as if he were buried."

Crispin turned. "But he is *not* buried! He is stolen. Do you make nothing of that?"

More moved as if to speak but Wynchecombe cut him off. "I do not care."

"*We* do not need the body," assured More, face glowering comically.

Crispin chuckled. "The Templars are now out of your hair, eh? One problem solved."

"That is not your concern. Your concern is only to help me find Stephen St Albans."

"You forget, Wynchecombe. The body must be produced for a trial."

"I can get round that, never you fear." He huffed at More and turned back to the fire to warm his hands. "What troubles you? I would have thought nothing would please you more than to put

66

that particular man on the gallows."

Wynchecombe was right. Nothing could possibly please Crispin more except to drop the rope over Stephen's neck himself. But something about Stephen's guilt gnawed at him. He worried at it, like a widow at her rosary.

"Yes," was all he said. Stephen a poisoner. Crispin hated him with all his being, but was Stephen dishonorable enough to use poison? It was mostly that thought that kept him silent when he and Jack followed the sheriffs out to the street and watched them and their entourage of horses and men finally depart up the avenue back toward Newgate.

CHAPTER EIGHT

Stephen St Albans. Was there a day gone by where Crispin had not thought of him? It was he who revealed the conspiracy that felled many a knight and threw Crispin into the poverty he now suffered. Stephen. Rosamunde's guardian.

Standing in the street, his mind flitted unbidden to the image of Rosamunde. She had been the most beautiful creature he had ever set eyes on. Did love still haunt him, or was she only one of many objects wrapped in his past like hurts and dashed dreams?

He remembered her pale face on that day when they cut his scabbard and unsheathed the sword. Though all of court watched, only she had mattered. They smashed the blade against the stone floor, but it was well made and expensive, and refused to break. It took three such blows to finally knick the tip. Then they cut his family arms from his surcote, tore off the whole garment, and broke his spurs. Left with nothing but the clothes on his back, the whole court turned away from him. Humiliated, he dared not look at Rosamunde. Did she turn her back, too? Even now he couldn't decide what was worse: his complete degradation and dispossession, or his loss of her.

She never even fought it. She never stood up to Stephen and came to me. I thought she might. But what woman would have done? Willingly become a pauper and the laughing stock of court, all for him? How could he blame her? Yet he did. A year earlier they had both signed the betrothal contracts and the families thought it a fine match. But something happened between the contracts and the courtship: Crispin fell in love.

How could I not? She was so beautiful. There were many days they would steal away, leaving her maidservants behind. They would kiss and touch and whisper those silly phrases only spoken in romances and love songs. And though he loved and desired her, often raining kisses along her throat, he would go no further. A proper courtier was he.

A proper fool!

Only a mere fortnight after his disgrace, another man conquered that virginity which should have been his. It was *that* pain that pierced him the most, that could not be undone.

He looked at Jack standing in the tinker's doorway, waiting for orders. What was he to do with the boy? Jack was like a stray dog that would not leave, even when kicked. "Tucker, I appreciate your loyalty, but this has to end. Now. When I get back, I do not expect to find you here."

"But Master…"

"I am not your master. You must leave." He turned on his heel, uncertain where he was going. Did it matter? He needed to think, but it was difficult with a headache pounding between his temples.

He turned up the street to Gutter Lane—walking toward the Boar's Tusk—when he saw it. A man in a long, dark robe, hood up over his head, standing under the eave of a shop across the way. He merely looked in Crispin's direction, or at least his covered head and shadowed face was turned toward him.

A fleeting sense of recognition propelled Crispin toward the man, but the man abruptly turned and dashed up the lane.

Crispin paused before he leaped forward, sprinting after the man.

The robed man flew ahead, dodging stalls and townsfolk.

Crispin ran hard. His feet sucked and slapped the mud, pounding the lane, swerving to avoid people and wandering dogs.

The man looked back once but kept going. Crispin cursed. He still could not see his face. But his legs were visible as they pumped. He was wearing mail chausses and boots with spurs. He wore no weapon, but scabbard frogs flapped from the belt as if he had only just divested himself of a sword.

Flying down the lane, Crispin caught only a glimpse of the man. Pushing himself harder, Crispin panted, rushing forward. If only he could cut him off. Was it possible? The man was heading up Monkwell toward Cripplegate. If he got past the gate, he could disappear into the marshland.

The man neared a cart full of bundled firewood. He leapt up and ran over the laden cart and jumped off the end. He whirled, grabbed the cart, and upended it, filling the street with scattered sticks and cordwood. Then he lit off.

The merchant howled his protest. Crispin's momentum hurled him forward. He spun and tumbled backwards, rolling over the bundles. It smarted, but he bolted upright and leapt free of the debris. But it only propelled him awkwardly, stumbling over the cart's handles. He flew into the air, flopped on his belly, and skidded forward several feet before he came to a stop. His sore chest flamed with pain and he was covered face to chest in mud.

There was no need to look. He knew the man was gone.

Slowly he picked himself up amid raucous guffaws and curses. He stood and looked down. Mud everywhere. He ran his hands down his coat and scraped some of it off, did the same to his face. He took the end of his cloak and wiped his eyes and lips. Saying nothing to the cart owner or the crowd, he limped back toward the Shambles, thinking of little but to wash his face and clothes. The robed man was now long gone, whoever he was. It galled that these men continued to shadow Crispin, leaving him cryptic parchments and no other clues. If he and his ilk wanted this object so badly why not just come out with it and say what it was? Was he not the

70

Tracker? Did he not find lost articles for a living? Surely they knew that by now.

He got to the tinker shop and trudged up the stairs, flicking the mud from his hand to retrieve the key from his pouch. He put the key to the lock but the door swung open freely. He dropped the key, grabbed his dagger, and shouldered the door wider.

The room lay in disarray. The table, the chair and stool were all cast aside. His bedding had been tossed about with some of the hay from the ripped mattress making a long trail across the floor. His bowls and spoons were scattered as well as his basin and water jug which sat in a pool of rippling water under the far window.

His first thoughts were of Jack Tucker, and a very descriptive curse left his lips. But when he made a circuit of the room he found his family rings scattered on the floor, thrown from their hiding place. If Tucker had ransacked his room, these prizes would not have been left behind.

The chase. It had been a ruse. But what were they looking for?

He stood with shoulders sagged for a few moments, simply surveying the carnage. Then he knelt by the overturned chest and picked up his spare pair of underbraies that had been cast from the coffer.

The floor behind him creaked and he whirled, drawn dagger in one hand, underbraies in the other.

The woman stared at him, her perfect brows arched in surprise.

"Are you Crispin Guest?" she asked. "I've been looking for you."

CHAPTER NINE

"I am Crispin Guest." He felt warmth spreading throughout his muddied cheeks. Trying not to look at the garment in his hand, he sheathed the knife and struggled to his feet. He stood in the center of his shambles of a room, mud on his clothes, and a jagged smile slashed across his face. "I fear you have not caught me at my best."

She returned his smile with a rueful wince. "I should hope not."

He tossed the underbraies under the bed and lifted a chair upright. Stooping to raise the table he found the wayward candle stub and set it in the center of the nicked wood. "I...er...seem to have had unwanted visitors. Please." He gestured to the chair but she did not sit.

Her dark eyes studied him suspiciously, eyes as dark as her hair braided into two plaits and framing her head in tightly wound buns. A ring of pearls ran across her forehead matching a pearl necklace at her throat that led Crispin's eye to a neckline cut in the French fashion and to breasts mounding the brushed wool of her gown. "I have heard how you helped others find lost things...lost people," she said and strolled into the room, glancing at his few possessions sprinkled about the floor.

Crispin pulled at his muddy coat to straighten it, mustering as much dignity as he could. "I am honored."

"Can I trust you, sir?"

"I am trusted in all my endeavors. I may not be a wealthy lord—" and he opened his arms unnecessarily to display himself and the room— "but none can speak ill of Crispin Guest. Not these days, at any rate."

Her taut shoulders relaxed. "Yes, I have heard much about you. I wonder if you have recently recovered an article of any import. Such I sometimes hear of at court and I find it…fascinating."

He measured her. "Nothing lately that would interest the court. And surely you did not come all this way to the Shambles merely to ask to be regaled of my feats of investigation."

"Indeed not." She turned at just the correct angle to catch the best light from the window. She thrust out her chin, artfully elongating her neck. "You do get to the point."

Crispin watched the display with admiration. "The point, damosel? The point is for you to make. What would you have me seek? Thing or person?"

"Person."

He retrieved the water jug—glad it still had water in it—and repositioned the tin basin on a shelf. He pushed up his sleeves and poured the water in the basin and then paused. He looked back at her for permission and she gave a slight nod for him to continue. He offered her the chair again and she took it this time, though she made a show of it, arranging her skirts about her legs, but not quite to hide them.

Crispin took a moment to consider her. He knew she came from court by her jewels and the expensive cut of her gown but seldom did his clients include the highborn. Only shopkeepers and a few landowners used his services. Those from court were another matter. Memories ran long at court, and certainly his name still conjured the same amount of head wagging and varying degrees of revulsion and sympathy as they had these last seven years.

"Your name, damosel, eludes me," he said. "I do not traffic in court these days."

She smiled politely and showed by her silence that she knew his history. "My husband is Henry FitzThomas," she said simply.

73

"Lord Stancliff."

"Then you are Lady Vivienne." His mind shuffled the names and painted them with vague likenesses. It settled on Henry FitzThomas, the corpulent fool whose wife of twenty years spent him nearly to poverty. When she died, he married this one, some twenty years his junior and all the court jeered. Apparently the man had wealth enough to woo the young Vivienne into an old man's bed.

He dipped his hands into the cold water and splashed his face. The cake of soap had not been disturbed in the aftermath of the ransacking. He took it up and wetted it in the basin. "Is there a reason you come to my lodgings without an escort? A woman of your position would surely send for me, not come to my doorstep."

She sighed. "These are personal matters, Master Guest. I have my reasons."

"Indeed. I am the friend of last resort. This is how I make my living."

He continued washing and in that time his words finally sunk in. She raised her head, forming her lips into a charming red "o". "Payment? Of course. I have coin, sir. I can pay."

He raised his hand magnanimously and even smiled, though it was the kind he reserved for such occasions. "Perhaps you should first tell me who this person is and why you search for him."

Her features darkened, whether from anger or shame he could not tell. "That is a long tale. And I shall not burden you with particulars." Vivienne gazed steadily at Crispin. "I merely need you to follow him."

He scrubbed the back of his neck and up his arms until the basin was as brown and murky as the Thames. "Follow, Lady? I am not in the habit of shadowing men without good cause."

"But this is a matter of much import!" She controlled the panic in her voice by laying her delicate hands on her thighs, thighs that were easily defined by the cascading gown's drape. "He has something of mine. An object of great price. I naturally want it back."

"Naturally."

"It is something I desperately need. I want him followed so that I may retrieve it."

"And what is this object?"

"That is not your concern. You have only to follow him. My coin buys that and only that."

He took up a relatively clean cloth and wiped his face and hands. If she was trying to intrigue him she succeeded. "I take it he is an important man. May I know his name?"

She hesitated. "Is a name important?"

"It makes it easier to inquire."

"Then you shall have to work that much harder, Master Guest."

Crispin made a half smile and clutched the damp cloth. But she offered nothing more. "My lady, do you jest with me?"

"No indeed. It is a puzzle for you."

He waved his hand. "Very well. Continue. The rest should be just as disarming."

"He was staying at the Spur," she offered suddenly. "Perhaps he is still there."

"If you know that, then why don't you inquire at the Spur yourself?"

She raised her chin. "Don't be absurd."

"And once I have found this man what am I to do?"

"Stay clear of him. Inform me only." Her eyes never wavered from Crispin's. "I need to know his movements. If he leaves London, for instance. Who he meets. And if he exchanges any...packages."

"Packages? Of what size?"

"Of any size."

"I see," said Crispin, amused. He vigorously rubbed out his coat with the damp cloth. "And so, a man with no name with an object of no particulars is staying God-knows-where. Is that correct?"

"Be flippant if you wish, sir, but I am willing to pay."

Crispin sighed as he worked on the coat. "My empty larder is convinced of your desperation. When was the last time you saw him?"

Lady Vivienne blinked her thick lashes and slowly rose. When she sauntered toward him, he dropped the cloth. Her hips rolled and the sinewy body followed, the whole suggesting the gait of a slender cat. She stood close to him, measuring him up and down. He smelled the scent of lavender but it did little to mask the muskiness of woman. "It might have been a sennight. It might have been less."

"'Might have been'? My lady, you are imprecise in the extreme. If I am to help you at all, I need more from you."

"You need *more* from me?" She stepped closer. "I have told you what I know."

"But only as you want me to know it."

She laughed, giving her the excuse to touch him lightly on the chest. He winced from the renewed pain of the raw flesh beneath the coat. Her face betrayed her displeasure and he felt the need to explain.

"A wound newly received, Lady. I wear bandages beneath." He gestured to the rust-colored coat.

"Oh. For a moment I thought my touch revolted you."

"Now how could that be?"

She touched his shoulder. "Better?"

"Yes."

Her features softened with sympathy. She took in the room before settling again on Crispin's face. "Have you no one to see to your needs? It is a terrible thing to be alone. And in pain."

Crispin drew a deep breath. "I have seen to my own needs for quite some time now."

"But a wound so close to the heart...." Her fingers brushed his neck. She suddenly noticed where her hand lay and she blushed and drew it back.

Her face in its crumpled sympathy was far too close to his and he felt the warmth of her, and even smelled a faint breath of anise sweetening her lips. The effect intoxicated and he stepped closer.

"You are too familiar with me, my lady. And here you are in a man's room unescorted. What could you be thinking?"

She did not step back as expected. "It only seems to me that I recognize a kindred spirit. A man who is perhaps as lonely and as vulnerable as I."

Was it his imagination, or was she leaning closer? He was a little too light-headed to debate it, and he found himself slanting toward her and met her mouth with his. His arms drew her into his sore chest causing only a hissing inhale through his nose. A dream. It must have been. He wasn't in the habit of kissing strange women on their first meeting, but Vivienne's palpable distress beckoned him. And her lips did nothing to repel his own. In fact, they seemed particularly inviting. He wanted to kiss her, but the circumstances restrained his full passion, and good sense finally made him push her back.

"My lady," he whispered, and then cleared his throat. He offered an awkward bow. "You are quite correct. We are both most vulnerable."

She offered a sad smile and sauntered the long way around the table to the door and touched the post. "Forgive *me*, Master Guest. I have a habit of giving in too easily to my…whims."

A creeping sense of embarrassment reddened his ears. He pulled his coat partly to straighten it, partly to give him time to think. "Yes, well. It…it will help if I know what he looks like," he said hastily. "I have been known to find a man by his description alone."

She measured him coolly under her lashes. She seemed unmoved by their encounter. "He is slightly taller than you, clean-shaven, dark hair, with cruel, blue eyes. Ask for the Frenchman with the foreign gown. He is fond of wearing it."

"A clean-shaven Frenchmen at the Spur. This shouldn't be too difficult."

"It is *very* important you find him and follow him. Not merely for me, but…" She cut herself off and shook her head slightly. Clearly she felt she had revealed too much.

"When I discover something, how shall I contact you? Shall I…send to court?" Court wasn't a place Crispin was welcomed. He hadn't passed through its doors in many a year now and he did not relish even passing by it.

"I will contact you." She pulled a silver coin from the purse at her belt. "Your payment."

He shook his head. "It is too much."

"I am certain you will earn it."

A smile lifted one side of his mouth, remembering their kiss. "I am certain I will." He took the coin and watched her leave.

CHAPTER TEN

No sign of Jack Tucker. The boy had obviously taken Crispin's words to heart. As usual, the timing was excellent. He wanted to ask the boy if he'd seen anything and help him clean his cotehardie and his room. Alas.

He tidied his lodgings as best he could. Nothing was broken or missing but it did not please him that strangers had been through his private things. What was it they were looking for? He rubbed his sore chest distractedly.

His pouch was heavier for a change. Usually it was feast or famine. And today it was raining clients. First the sheriffs and now Lady Vivienne. He sighed thinking of her. What a fool he was. How a flicking eyelash could bestir him!

Vivienne sought an "object of great price" and since she was not forthcoming he could only speculate as to what that might be. Some rare jewel, perhaps. Or something else. How could he begin to know?

He dismissed thoughts of Vivienne for the moment and thought of the other job. Yes, he wanted to solve this murder, and yes, he wanted more than anything to see Stephen hang for it, but now there were these damned men hunting him and ransacking his place. It was all getting to be a bit more trouble than sixpence a day might be worth.

Well, one thing at a time. He had no idea how to find Stephen, but he could first go to the Spur and find Lady Vivienne's unnamed mystery man.

Crispin locked his lodgings and traveled down the Shambles, making the long walk west. He turned a corner and went down Friday Street before he stopped, measuring the two-story tavern, the Spur. Its front steps were washed, its sign newly painted.

He stood across from the tavern for a while before he ambled across the lane and pushed open the door. Making a slow circuit around the great room's perimeter, he measured faces and characters of its noble inhabitants.

No one fit the description given by Lady Vivienne. At length, he decided to ask.

The innkeeper, a solitary man, stood very tall and very thin. He eyed Crispin's clothes as Crispin inquired. "Nay. I do not remember a man of that description."

"Perhaps it was a sennight ago. A man in a foreign gown or cloak. A Frenchman."

"A Frenchman you say? Aye. There was such a gentleman. He's been a lodger here for a sennight."

"Is he still here?"

"His room is here, but as to the gentleman, I have not seen him for two days, maybe three, yet he paid for a full fortnight."

"His room. Where is it?"

The innkeeper suddenly brought himself up short. "And just who might you be, my lord?"

Crispin straightened his shoulders. The cloak resting on them felt almost like it used to. "I am Lord Guest, and this man has something of mine. I would consider it a courtesy if you would take me to his room."

The man jerked his head in a hasty bow. "If it's as you say…then follow me, my lord."

The man led Crispin up the stairs along the gallery where he glanced down below at the long tables and raucous drinkers. The hearth flung its light across their drunken faces.

The innkeeper unlocked a door and pushed it open. The room smelled musty and stank of old smoke. Crispin toed a gray log that rolled out of the cold hearth. On a corner side table he saw what looked like a shrine; a crucifix, a candle stub, bumpy with hardened drips, and a red velvet cloth. He trailed his fingers over the velvet and spied a chest by the bed. He glanced at the inn's host still standing awkwardly in the doorway. Crispin approached the chest, knelt, and opened it.

Empty.

He strode to the bed and yanked up the pillow, crushing it with both hands. He turned over the mattress and flung the cheap bedding across the floor. He went to the wall and felt with his fingers along the timber frames, but he found nothing hidden, no clues to the man's identity.

"Does a chambermaid come in here at all?"

"No. We do not disturb the travelers who come here unless they request it." He eyed the crumpled mattress with distress. "A man likes his privacy." He rubbed his neck and looked behind, perhaps expecting the owner to return at any moment.

"Then no one would enter here unless asked?"

"Aye, my lord."

Crispin dug his fists in his hips and swept his gaze across the room one last time before leaving. He stood on the gallery while the innkeeper ticked his head and locked the door.

"Will there be anything else, my lord?"

Crispin enjoyed for that fleeting moment the feeling of being a lord again. "That will be all," he said, and leaned on the railing to look down on the room below, dismissing the hovering innkeeper. He would have offered the man a coin, but since he had only a few, he could not spare it.

The innkeeper thumped down the stairs. When his head disappeared beneath the landing, Crispin glanced at the closed door. He drew his dagger and snipped some threads from the inside collar of his coat. He used the blade's tip to insert the red threads between the door and the jamb. Satisfied, he sheathed the dagger and hurried down the stairs and into the main room. The clink of cups and hearty laughter stoked his thirst, but he had no wish to find a place at a long table amongst the knights and squires. Instead, he left the Spur to seek his comfort in the familiarity of the Boar's Tusk.

Crispin turned the wooden bowl with his two thumbs and index fingers and watched the red wine gleam and swirl against its smooth sides. He did not drink as much tonight as he expected to. In fact, he was still on his first cup, but what few sips he took seemed to settle his heart into a calm numbness. It even warmed his chest with a radiance resembling vague contentment. He wasn't exactly happy, but not too morose either. Gilbert's good cask seemed to have done the trick. Even his chest no longer felt sore. He sipped the wine again and felt its warmth glide down his throat and infuse him. He raised his head. The hearth flames seemed brighter, more alive. Faces glowed with merry expressions. Even the room's normally stale air filled with pleasant toasty aromas of burning logs, rich wine, and savory roasted meats, their juices dripping and sizzling over the flames.

Crispin drank and sighed. It would be so pleasant to simply sit in the Boar's Tusk the rest of the day and absorb his surroundings, but with another sigh that had no contentment in it, he knew he did not have the luxury to do such a thing.

He glanced over his shoulder at the place the mysterious knight died. How was Stephen involved in this? Skillful with a sword like any knight and certainly ruthless, would he ever resort to poison when face-to-face violence would do? Unless he showed himself and offered some answers, the sheriff would use Eleanor's testimony to prove his guilt. With a short chuckle, Crispin realized Wynchecombe didn't care who was hanged, as long as his writ was complete.

Crispin considered the murder scene: Stephen arguing in hushed whispers to the knight, perhaps threatening him for something that the dead man possessed. Did he give him the poison then, during this bitter argument? Afterwards, he must have spied Crispin and hastily departed. Then, in came the woman. What of her? He could not help but wonder at the message she conveyed to the dead knight. A warning given too late? How did she fit into the tapestry?

It bothered him not to know, but in the end, it would not matter. If Stephen hanged, the inquiry would be over.

But it would not solve all Crispin's problems no matter how satisfying it might be. It would not return his knighthood. It would not entirely erase the past.

"You are a thorn in my side, Stephen St Albans," he muttered, "living or dead."

Crispin felt the sharp prick in his flank, thinking of thorns and sides. He chided himself for never noticing the man beside him on the bench and allowing him the opportunity to press the knife blade to his ribs.

A voice, course like the crackle of ancient parchment, hissed in his ear. "You will be silent."

He took in the blurred impression of a monk's robe and cowl, and a frieze of white hair that ran the rim of his forehead.

"You will come with me and we will talk. Only talk."

Not the voice in the torture room, Crispin was certain of it. He heard instead a slight purring accent. Welsh?

More curious than afraid, Crispin slowly rose, allowing the man to withdraw his blade from Crispin's side. "I warn you against fleeing," the little man said when they reached the door. "I have compeers all around."

They walked several feet into a rain that fell hard and harsh, slanting across their path and spattering mud against the stone foundations. They entered an alley and traveled down its long, narrowing path before taking a left turn to what looked like a dead end. The old monk instructed Crispin to push a barrel aside revealing a jagged hole cut in the wattle and daub. Crispin peered into the dark hole but could not see what lay beyond it.

"I will go no further until you tell me who you are and what you want."

Another monk popped his head out of the mysterious hole. He, too, brandished a blade and gestured for Crispin to enter.

Crispin turned to look over his shoulder. Two silhouettes in robes stood at the alley's mouth, their unsheathed blades gleaming in the rainy twilight.

He weighed the circumstances and shrugged. "Very well. We will do it your way."

He bent nearly double to fit into the tight opening and found himself creeping forward in a crouched position through a long wooden passage, much like a flour chute. He followed the man toward a light and felt relief to step out into a room where he could finally stand erect.

Candles in sconces flickered but did little to light the space. Dusty barrels, sacks, and kegs lined the walls. Not the same site of his imprisonment but it might as well have been.

The two monks greeted him, both their daggers drawn.

Crispin spread out his empty hands. "What? No sacks over the head? No bindings? No whip?"

The two exchanged inquiring glances.

"Play no more games with me. Isn't this enough?" He tore open his coat and bandages, revealing the welts on his chest.

Their faces seemed to light with recognition and as one, they both sheathed their weapons.

"Forgive us, Sir Crispin," said the older man. "You mistake us for others. That is the work of the henchmen of the false pope of Avignon."

Crispin dropped his hands. His coat fell closed over his bare chest. "*What?* Then who the hell are you?"

Both men tossed back their hoods and opened their robes revealing hauberk and white surcote. When they opened their collars, Crispin felt no surprise to see the embroidered Templar cross on the underside of their surcotes.

CHAPTER ELEVEN

"I am having a nightmare."

"No, Sir Crispin. Indeed not. Please. Sit."

"Do not call me 'Sir Crispin'! I am a knight no more!"

"Your pardon," said the younger one, his black hair and white tonsure in sharp contrast in the flickering light. "You still bear the unmistakable nobility of knighthood."

"Sitting drunk in a tavern? You have an odd perception of knighthood. But then again, you two would."

"You do not believe our identity?" asked the older.

"There are no more Templars. You must be mad!"

"Please, Sir Cr—*Master* Guest," pleaded the older one. "Sit. Listen to what we have to say. If it is to your liking, you may stay. If not, then you are free to go. Is that not fair?"

"Brought here by the point of a dagger? Is *that* fair?"

"Not fair," said the older one, "but necessary. Indulge us?"

Crispin frowned and looked back toward the dark passageway. His curiosity encroached on his good judgment. With a petulant thud, he sat on a keg and rested both balled fists on his knees. "Well then?"

The monks exchanged looks and the younger deferred to the older. The white-haired man began. "As you seem to have guessed, we are Knights Templar, Master Guest. Though it was true that His Holiness Pope Clement V seemingly abolished the order over seventy years ago—allowing the savage execution of many of our French ancestors—some *did* survive...under the secrecy and protection of Rome."

Crispin rolled his eyes and rose, but the younger one pleaded, urging him back down. With a dramatic sigh, Crispin complied, cocking his head impatiently.

"Yes. Pope Clement V's own emissaries were sent to Chinon castle to interview the Grand Master Jacques de Molay." He frowned when he added, "He and his Templar brothers were accused of sodomy and blasphemy. We do not take well these accusations."

Crispin twisted his lips. "Very well. You do not like being called sodomites. I concede it. Go on."

"The pope's emissaries heard as much from the knights themselves," the older one went on. "They did not believe the lies against the Templars. After the emissaries sent word to Rome, the pope was convinced of their innocence and immediately absolved and pardoned them."

"That is not how history tells the story."

"No, Master Guest. These erroneous and sensational rumors about the Templars aroused such passions that the pope did not make this absolution public, fearing a schism." He shrugged. "A schism happened anyway. At any rate, King Philip had his own agenda. Although it was in his power to do so, the French king did not pardon the knights. He coveted their wealth and put them to the torch instead, some 2,000 of them, before the pope could make his decree public. By then, of course, it was too late."

"This is all only by your word."

"I assure you, Master Guest, that it is the truth. Succeeding popes knew of the decree and of the small band of remaining Templars. You see, they understood the necessity of our order."

"And what is that necessity? It was said the Templars only wanted to seize power, and possessed an enormous cache of hidden wealth to back it up."

The older man gazed at his boots and took a deep breath.

"They never sought the kind of power attributed to them, Master Guest, though it is true that some of our ranks…" He darted a glance at the younger man, who nodded his agreement. "Well, some failed to live up to our high ideals. And as for wealth." The old knight raised his arms and dropped them to his sides. "If any there was, there is little left now."

He walked slowly around Crispin, weighing his words. "Master Guest, we are now a humble order, our former status a thing of the past. As knights and as monks, we follow the proscribed path given to us from ancient days. We have our duties."

"To protect the way for travelers in the Holy Land."

"Yes. Once. But that is a thing of the past."

"Then what? What are you dancing around? I'm losing my patience."

The old monk stepped uncomfortably close to Crispin. "We have been given a singular honor in all the world, Master Crispin. We alone have been entrusted to safeguard an object of immeasurable value."

"Gold? Then there *is* a cache."

"Not gold. A relic."

"Relic?" Crispin's collar suddenly felt too tight. He licked his lips. "What relic?"

"Surely you have heard the tales."

A weak sensation tingled in his bones. He didn't like the look in the old man's eyes. "I've heard the tales. Everyone has. But…it can't be true."

"No?" The old man shrugged and turned away. "Then you are free to go."

Crispin eased his fists along his thighs. He laughed nervously. "You aren't going to say…you aren't going to tell me that…"

"That we are the keepers of the most Holy Grail? The cup of Christ?"

Crispin snapped to his feet. "I am at my wits end! There are no Templars, there is no Holy Grail, and you are fools or madmen…or both! I listened to your tale and I have been wholly amused. Now I wish to go."

"You must believe us," said the younger man, his hands pressed together prayerfully. "The good of the world depends on it."

"The good of the world?" Crispin grumbled. He marched toward the chute and rested his foot on its edge. "You are mad," he said over his shoulder. "The murdered man, then? One of your madmen?"

The old monk smiled gravely. "Yes."

"He's dead. Nothing more can be done for him." He measured the old man. "Maybe he's the lucky one."

"Yes. Perhaps. But Master Guest. There is a reason we brought you here."

"And had me followed?"

The old monk looked at the younger monk. "We have not followed you, Master Guest."

"Robed like the ones you are wearing. And you claim you have not shadowed me?"

The old monk bowed. "You have my solemn oath."

"And this?" Crispin took the folded parchment from his pouch and shook it open revealing the red cross.

The old monk smiled. "Yes, Master, that was us. We left it thinking you might know what it meant. That we would soon speak with you."

Crispin snorted and crumpled the parchment, tossing it to the floor. "You didn't have to be so melodramatic."

The monk stepped toward him but stopped when Crispin laid his hand on his dagger. "The reason we brought you here, Master Guest," he said, "is the grail. The cup Christ drank from at the Last Supper—was stolen from our dead companion."

Crispin blinked. An uncomfortable feeling started in his gut and traveled up his body to his chest. "He was the 'Cup Bearer'?"

"Yes."

Crispin turned and faced them. He listened to his own breathing and watched it cloud in the frigid storeroom, felt his heart pound. "Suppose...what you say is true—I am not saying I believe it. But if so, why? How did such an object get to England?"

"If you will sit, I will explain," said the older man.

Crispin blew out another long cloud of air before he finally returned to the wooden keg and sat.

"My name is Edwin," said the older knight.

"And mine Parsifal," said the younger.

Crispin guffawed. "You jest."

"No. It *is* my christened name. A very interesting coincidence, wouldn't you say?"

Crispin ran his hand over his beard-stubbled face but said nothing.

"And so," Edwin began. "It happened that our Lord drank from this cup at the Passover and was betrayed that very night. Joseph of Aramathea obtained the cup, and while our Lord suffered on the cross for our transgressions, he lifted the cup and saved some of our Lord's precious blood within it. He kept the cup safe for many years and was eventually called by the Apostle Philip to evangelize the Britons, our ancestors.

"Joseph sailed along England's rocky shores and finally came to the place known as Glastonbury Tor. He thrust his staff into the stony hillside and it miraculously stuck and took root. He took this as a sign that his journey had ended. The Angel Gabriel directed him to build a church on the spot and Christ Himself appeared in a vision declaring that the humble church of wattle and daub be dedicated to His mother.

"Joseph, feeling his life nearing its end, buried the grail at the base of the church."

Crispin put up his hand to interrupt. "And why have we heard nothing of this miraculous church?"

"Alas. It burned to the ground in 1184."

Crispin leaned back and folded his arms. "Alas."

Edwin smiled. "Even so, legend followed myth, and myth flowed into history, blending with the old tale of King Arthur and his Camelot knights—including one Sir Parsifal charged with the quest to find the grail." He smiled at Parsifal who grinned and blushed in reply. "But knights *were* chosen to guard the cup," he continued, "yet they did not hale from misty Camelot. They were called from the Holy Land by the hand of God, and were chosen by that same angel who directed Joseph of Aramathea to guard the grail and keep it free of the plunderous hands of man.

"We, the few Templars left, are warrior monks. We live by vows of poverty and chastity. Our single purpose on this earth is to guard the grail. One man is chosen each year to be the single bearer of the holy relic. And as you know, he was foully murdered."

"Then the cup is gone?"

"Yes. We have failed in our mission." Edwin's bravado cracked, and he slumped, shaking his head in disbelief. "We failed. We believe it may be in the hands of the anti-pope's men. Should it fall to the false pope—the one who is not the true successor of Peter—we fear for the fate of Christendom."

Crispin's heart drummed in his ears. Surely he could not believe such a wild tale, but their earnest faces and patrician manner tinted their narrative with credence. After all, how could so many of these noble men be under the same strange delusion?

"So who killed your knight?"

"We do not know. Perhaps the anti-pope's men."

"Possibly. But they did not obtain the grail, for the men who captured and tortured me still do not know where it is."

Parsifal glanced at Edwin. "Then there is no time to waste. We must search for it. Crispin, will you help us? You are the celebrated Tracker. Yes. We know who you are. Will you help us find the greatest of lost articles?"

"I work for a fee," he said.

"Of course. Name your price."

"Sixpence a day, plus expenses."

"Done," they said.

Crispin immediately regretted agreeing. He'd agreed to too many dances with the Devil this week. "There must be some great power in this relic. What is it?"

"Its power," said Edwin, "is...indescribable."

Crispin sneered a smile. "Try."

Edwin turned to Parsifal. "It has the power to change men," he said. Parsifal nodded. "To redirect their course. To transform."

"Transform? What do you mean? This is all very vague, gentlemen…"

"The power of God, sir," said Edwin. "The power of God."

CHAPTER TWELVE

Crispin walked the muddy streets of London, little minding the driving rain that raised the foul odors of the gutter. Enclosed by his hood, Crispin mulled his fractured thoughts. "The power of God," he muttered. In his head he called it absurd. But it had sent a chill down his spine he could not explain. Even now, the pit of his belly tightened like a hard core. They explained how possession of the cup could change the tide of events, win battles, confuse one's enemies. It still seemed very vague to Crispin but he felt a sense of impending disaster when the Templars described the possibilities.

He also knew the Templars had stolen back the body of their comrade. Crispin hadn't asked but hadn't needed to. Why had they? Probably to keep their secret. No body, no evidence. No more talk of a secret society.

He tightened the hood about his face and inhaled the tang of wet leather. Who killed the man, then? The anti-pope's men were first on his list. It was obvious that they believed in these wild tales. Enough to torture innocent men for it. Could murder be far behind?

But how did Stephen fit in? Crispin shook his head, trying to picture Stephen with the Templar. Did he steal the grail for himself hoping to sell it? That did not seem like the character of the man he knew all those years ago. He had to admit that Stephen was an honorable man, even if that honor was sometimes misplaced.

But Crispin also knew that time could change anyone, and circumstances could force good men to perform ill deeds.

Still. These henchmen of the anti-pope. These men seemed capable of killing the Templar. But if so, why then do they not possess the grail? Who had it? The woman?

"The grail," he whispered. Could such a thing truly exist? During his travels throughout the Christian world, Crispin saw many such relics boldly displayed, often for a fee. He did not believe easily. He knew the tricks of the craft. The blood of martyrs that miraculously changed from dried powder to liquid. Made of red ochre powder, the "blood" was encased in a monstrance with paraffin and oil. Once handled and warmed, the paraffin and oil would loosen and melt, mix with the dry powder, and look to all the world like liquid blood. Hen's bones served for saint's remains; ordinary oak splinters for a piece of the cross; dried pig's skin for a saint's flesh.

How could something as precious and as holy as the cup of the blood of Christ be hidden for so long?

Crispin stopped and looked upward. He found himself staring at the oaken doors of a humble church. The moment seemed to call to him and he pushed at the yielding door and slowly trudged inside.

The nave was only a few yards long. A crucifix hung above the altar rails behind a rood screen in the candlelit darkness. Seeing no one about, Crispin walked up to the altar rail, becrossed himself, and knelt.

He looked up at the shadowed crucifix. "You know I do not come to You as often as I should. But today...today, well. You heard them. Do I believe it? How do I approach such a task? Dare I even try?"

He heard a shuffled step. Instinctively he grabbed his dagger and spun.

The white-faced young priest raised his palms in defense.

Crispin sheathed the blade and shrugged. "I beg your pardon,

Father. It is an old habit."

The priest's weak smile reassured. He lowered his hands. "Such habits! Should they not be curtailed in the house of God?"

"A reflex. But…" He scanned the small chapel and detected no one else amongst the shadowy arches and apse. "If you have the time, I should like to talk to you."

"Do you wish to be shriven?"

"Me? No, Father. No. Not today. It is information I seek."

The priest shrugged and gestured toward the rectory door. "There is a warm fire there," he said walking toward it. "Come. We will be more comfortable."

Crispin followed the young cleric through a low doorway into a small, warm room. Vestments with gold embroidery lay folded in an open coffer.

"Father—"

"Father Timothy," the priest interjected and settled opposite him beside the hearth.

"Father Timothy, then. Tell me. What do you know of religious relics?"

"Well, let me see," he said, poking the fire with an iron rod. His face both gilded and darkened with the jumping flames. "I have seen many."

"But how many of them do you believe in?"

"Oh, I see." Timothy nodded and smiled when he set the poker aside. "Yes, there are some for which I have my doubts. Which ones trouble you?"

"Only one. The Holy Grail."

"*The Holy Grail?* Who has filled your head with such privy waste?"

Crispin perched on the edge of his stool. "I take it by your reaction that you do not believe in its existence."

Father Timothy pressed his lips together and stared into the fire. "I did not say that. I merely have my doubts of anyone who claims to possess such a rare object."

"But if someone did? What would be its worth?"

"You jest. It would be priceless. Kingdoms could be traded for it."

"Then it seems the safer course is to have such a thing under lock and key, guarded day and night."

Timothy touched his lips with ink-stained fingers. "Not necessarily. I would choose to keep it a moving target, if you will. Keep it guarded, to be sure, but never in the same place."

"And create a band of men for the sole purpose of its protection?"

The priest nodded with a smile. "Yes. Legend has it that the Knights of the Temple had that duty."

"So I've been told."

"But if such a thing were true, then it would already be lost, would it not? The Templars were a ruthless order of shrewd warriors who were not above treachery to further their agenda. They were rightly destroyed."

"'Rightly destroyed', Father? Strong words from a cleric…about fellow beadsmen."

"Beadsmen," he sneered. "Greed and the gluttony of power overtook them. I shed no tears for the passing of the Templars."

Crispin drew his lip between forefinger and thumb. His words muffled under his hand. "In France they were betrayed by their king and put to the torch."

"Yes, but in England they were spared and became cloistered monks, not warrior monks. So it is said."

He eyed the young priest's face, smooth and unlined, his dark hair likewise unmarred by white or gray. Still, his manner and words seemed far beyond his age. "You do not believe it."

"No," said the priest. "There are many secrets about the Templars I fear we will never know. Secrets harbor evil. In God there are no secrets, only light."

"'The secret things belong unto the Lord our God,'" Crispin quoted.

The priest smiled. "Just so."

Crispin edged forward and bathed himself in the warmth of the rectory hearth. "Then you do not believe the Templars' place in the tale of the Holy Grail?"

"No, I do not. They are said to be the cupbearers, but I fear their treachery. I fear they would use it to ill ends."

"Why?"

"Because domination was their goal and nothing has changed that. If they were to use the power of the grail to that end, what could stop them?"

Crispin's frown grew deeper. "Then what of the pope of Avignon? He, too, must be a danger to all that is good and Christian in the world."

The priest cocked his head. A smile raised one corner of his mouth. "Your mind worries over many things. It spins from one thing to the other like a whirlwind." He rubbed his hands close to the fire. "Very well. To answer your question, the anti-pope *does* pose a danger to the Church. Anything that may force good men to split their conscience is not good for the soul."

"Does he not pose a greater danger than the Templars? If they exist."

The priest's expression changed while he concentrated. The hearth light made his face appear as young as Jack Tucker's. "Difficult to say. The anti-pope has many followers on the continent, but the Templars had compatriots in all lands known to civilized man. And they worked in secret. Who can say who the bigger threat would be?"

Crispin muttered under his breath.

"But you must tell me, my son. What is it that you know of the Holy Grail?"

He stared at the priest. "What is the grail's power? Do you know?"

"Other than it touched the lips of Christ and held His precious blood both in the guise of wine and in the blood on the cross? Is that not power enough?"

"The power of God," Crispin muttered. "But how can one wield this power to do ill in the world?"

Timothy twirled the ring on his finger in a thoughtful gesture. He stopped when he noticed Crispin stare at it. "It is said to be a cup of healing. Whoever drinks from it shall not die."

"Is that all? Healing?"

"No, not all. The power is said to be much more than that. More terrible than can be imagined. Man is not prepared to wield such power."

Crispin shivered though he sat close to the fire. He glanced once more at the ring before looking away. "Then, are you saying that the Templars may be no better to guard the grail than, perhaps, the anti-pope?"

"Perhaps not."

"Then its safety may be better served by someone like you."

"Me?" Timothy laughed and shook his head. "I should be a poor guardian. I would neglect my parish for the sole purpose of keeping watch of the precious relic." The humor momentarily washed from his face and a wistful flicker curved his lips. "Who would not wish to…to touch such an object? To even adore it."

Crispin stared at the light playing against his boots for a long time. At last he rose. "I thank you, Father Timothy for our conversation."

"I fear I have told you nothing useful."

"On the contrary. Every bit of it was useful. It is just that I am no more enlightened now than I was before."

The young cleric smiled sadly. "If someone has told you a tale I beg you, do not pursue it. Leave it to others."

"What others would that be, Father?"

"Yes. You may be right. Go in peace, then." He blessed him with the sign of the cross.

Once out in the rain of London's streets again, Crispin turned to measure the little church up the daubed walls to its tower of wood. A brass cross perched at the very top.

Who could resist the urge to be closer to God in some tangible sense? To own the cup, to touch it.

If the cup were real then it could be coveted by anyone. But who should have it? The Templars? Their discourse seemed honest enough, yet this priest had a different tale to tell. *Who am I to believe?* If he should find it and return it to the Templars would he be doing the right thing or exactly the wrong thing?

How to make this decision? He would have to confide in someone, someone who often made solemn decisions.

He looked over his shoulder one last time at the little church disappearing behind the sinewy frames of houses and shops. He snorted. "The one time I could actually use the help of Jack Tucker and he is gone for good."

"Who is gone for good?"

Crispin turned.

Tucker stood behind him, ringing the hem of his threadbare tunic in dirty fingers. His eyes darted uncertainly until he finally rested his gaze on Crispin's face.

Crispin couldn't repress his laugh. "*You*, my shadow. I thought I rid myself of you."

"No, Master," said Jack firmly. "I followed you since you went into the chapel."

"I told you I did not need a servant."

The boy sniffed, ran a hand under his nose. "Thought you might change your mind."

Crispin glared. "Oh, did you, now? Just where is it you go when you disappear? You are more mysterious than a sprite."

"Oh, here and there."

"You aren't cutting purses are you?"

Jack frowned. "And what if I were? What it's to you? You insist I am not in your employ."

"But I do follow the law. You do not want to return to Newgate and lose an ear, do you?"

Tucker stepped back, alarm on his face. "But you wouldn't do that, sir. Would you?"

Crispin sighed and surveyed the street. "You have the better of me now, Master Tucker. I would feel distinctly uncomfortable doing so to you." The boy visibly relaxed. "But it doesn't mean I will allow you further to engage in such activity."

"No, sir." He smiled.

Crispin felt as if he had been baited, the line tossed in, the hook set. "You were most conveniently absent when unknown persons ransacked my lodgings."

Jack's face blossomed into shock. "You don't think I—"

"I must admit. Only fleetingly. Where did you go?"

"You seemed dead set against my being there so I lit out until you'd calmed down. Did I do wrong, sir?"

"No, of course not. It was, after all, my one order you followed." He ticked his head looking at Jack. "Why do you vex me, I wonder?"

"You're a great lord!" said Jack, not quite correctly interpreting Crispin's lament. "I never been this close to a great lord like you, sir. And here you are, struck as low as a man can be. But you're the same as ever you were. And you're always thinking, thinking. It… contents me, sir."

"Thinking is hard work sometimes." The boy rocked on his heels. His tunic was a disgrace. His face was dirty. He looked like any number of strays on London's streets, begging, stealing. Of course that was exactly what he was. It made Crispin wonder why he should care about the boy at all. But then his mind drew in all his most recent memories, of Templars and murdered men…and poisons.

"Tell me, Jack, which apothecary did you go to for your cure?"

CHAPTER THIRTEEN

Crispin and Jack slipped into the apothecary's doorway. Sour aromas issued from a pot hanging over a brazier. A board spanned two trestles and stood guard before a wall of shelves filled with glass jars and clay pots, all with wooden or ceramic lids. Crispin eyed some of them warily, thinking of sorcerers with their fanciful ingredients like frog's toes and lizard tails. Nothing looked remotely like those things, though some dried leaves in a glass jar could easily be mistaken for something more alarming.

"Now Jack," he said quietly, "keep silent while I talk, eh? Pay no mind to what I say."

A curious Jack prodded a bag full of God-knows-what and then looked up at Crispin. Pale-faced, he nodded silently.

"Good Master," said the man, startling Crispin with his abrupt arrival. The tapestry covering the doorway to the back of the shop swayed and settled. "What is your pleasure?"

The large man's fleshy cheeks rested on a furred collar and his bright eyes studied Jack and Crispin under thin, black brows.

Crispin removed a coin from his pouch and laid it on the board. With index and middle fingers, he slid it toward the apothecary. "I seek something unusual."

The man stared at the coin. "Something unusual for you, good Master? Of course. Tell me, then."

"I have a kinsman with whom I have a special arrangement. Of necessity I must break this arrangement. Can you think of a convenient way in which this can be done?"

The man lifted his head with rounded eyes. "I do not understand your meaning, sir," he whispered.

Crispin leaned forward, hands resting on the board. "I think you understand my meaning well. I need something quick, something easy. What say you, Master Apothecary?" He hefted his coin pouch. The few coins within sounded like many. "I can pay your price."

"There is no price you can pay me, sir," he answered breathlessly, "for surrendering my soul. I beg you. Leave my shop at once."

"You are opposed to this, then?"

"Most assuredly. Now pray you, sir. Leave at once. I...I will say nothing of this to anyone..."

Crispin laughed and scooped the coin off the counter. "I am heartily glad to hear it, Master Apothecary."

The man froze.

"Come, come, good fellow. I only jest with you. Two nights ago you helped this boy here who accidentally poisoned himself. Do you recall it?" He took Jack's shoulders and pulled him forward. Jack stumbled and looked up at the apothecary from under an unruly fringe.

Warily, the man nodded toward Jack. "Of course. How fare you, lad?"

"God please you, I am well and happy your art saved me."

"I did nothing. Had you swallowed such a dose there would be nothing I could do, save call in a priest. I suspect it was *digitalis purpurea*," he said to Crispin, "based on the lad's description. Even if the boy had taken only a few grains of such a dose he might have felt strange and ill, perhaps even swooned. But a lad in good health would quickly recover. The sheriff was most rude when he came to inquire about it."

"Naturally. Did he ask if you sold such a poison?"

"Yes. It is not a poison when properly applied. It is for the heart, you see." He tapped his chest. "It stimulates the heart's humors. In an old man, it can revive those near death. But in high doses to a healthy individual, it makes the heart race to the point of bursting. I only sell it to physicians I know well. And I told the sheriff as much. I value my soul very highly indeed."

"And you keep it well."

Jack shook his head. "'Slud! That's right nasty, isn't it?" He looked from Crispin to the apothecary and back again. "You'd have to be a devil to use it on a man. I don't like it at all."

Crispin rested his hand on Jack's shoulder. "Thank you, Jack. I surmised your opinion."

"What man would have cause to use—"

"Tucker! You're interrupting me." He tightened his grip and maneuvered Jack aside. "But surely, Master Apothecary, there are others in your guild that are not so mindful of the afterlife."

The man nodded. "Perhaps. But I know of no one."

Crispin leaned closer and in a harsh undertone said, "I need to know who sold this poison and to whom he sold it. A man has already died. I do not know how many more are at risk."

The apothecary considered, forehead wrinkled. "The sheriff also asked me, but I assured him I could not say."

"Did he offer coin for your memory?" asked Crispin, thumbing the silver piece.

The man pressed his lips tightly. "No, Master. It is just that...the sheriff. It is best to deal with him as little as possible."

"I couldn't agree more."

"If I may be so bold as to ask: who are *you*, good sir, if not the sheriff's man?"

Jack edged forward, almost pushing Crispin aside. "This here is Crispin Guest. He's the Tracker."

"*You* are Crispin Guest?" The apothecary chortled and wiped his big hands down his stained apron. "A very great pleasure to meet you."

Crispin bowed.

"I've heard up and down this ward how you've helped men find stolen goods and saved an innocent man or two from the gallows. And here you are in my shop." The apothecary chuckled before his expression sobered. He lowered his voice. "Are you on the trail of this murderer?"

Crispin leaned in and with the same tone said, "Yes. It is my hope to find this villain before the sheriff does. As a matter of honor."

"Oh! To be sure. Well then. There *is* a shop owned by a man named Rupert of Kent on Fenchurch Street. Be careful of him, good Master. He is an evil man. I am certain this is where the poison came from."

"I shall be careful. And I thank you." Crispin left the coin on the board and bowed before he departed.

It wasn't long until they reached Fenchurch Street. Rupert's shop was not as clean as the other. Crispin told Jack to wait outside, but Jack protested. "I want to come in and watch you talk to this knave! That story will be worth a farthing's worth of ale in any tavern, I'll warrant."

"I did not bring you along to entertain you nor to fill you with drink. I am here for a purpose. Now wait outside."

Jack kicked at the dirt and threw himself against the wall, digging his heel into the hard daub. His petulance almost made Crispin laugh but he didn't want to encourage the boy. Instead, he schooled his features and laid his hand on his dagger when he entered, measuring the frail man at a writing desk. The apothecary looked up with tiny rodent eyes.

"You are Rupert of Kent?"

The man kept his seat. "Who wants to know?"

"Who I am does not matter. What matters are your wares. I think you are a seller of death."

Crispin expected at least some look of astonishment but the man only smiled. He slid off his stool and postured against the heavy drapery that separated the shop from his private rooms.

"Seller of death, am I? And who are *you*? An avenging angel? Bah! Off with you. I have work to do."

"You sold a most lethal poison. No man of conscience would do so."

"There is no blood on my hands. I only supply what is asked for. Whatever the use it is put to is strictly up to the buyer."

"'Things that cause sin will inevitably occur, but woe to the person through whom they occur.'"

The man's smile faded. He made a dismissing gesture and turned away, but Crispin lunged and dragged him in, almost nose to nose. He flailed against the curtain until Crispin's dagger pressed to his throat. "Who did you sell it to? I have a strong need to know. Almost as strong as the need to push this blade to the back of your throat."

The dagger tip dimpled the flesh so deeply it produced a pearl of blood. Rupert's lips worked but no sound issued forth.

Crispin pressed harder. "After all, it is not *I* that killed you, but this blade. There will be no blood on *my* hands. Is that not correct?"

"I sell such all the time!"

"*Digitalis purpurea?*"

The man's eyes widened. "I sold only a dram!" he squealed.

"To whom?"

"I do not know the name—"

The apothecary screwed up his face, arching away from the pressure of the knife. But when Rupert stretched to reach behind, Crispin spied the dagger imbedded in his back. The apothecary gurgled and lurched forward, falling with his full weight into Crispin's arms. Crispin pushed the man away and the apothecary crumpled to the floor.

Tossing the tapestry aside, Crispin scanned the dark storeroom. Something caught the candlelight. Crispin took a step but instinct made him pause.

A shelf tilted forward. Crispin barely had time to lurch out of the way before jars and canisters exploded on the floor. They blocked Crispin's path but he caught sight of a dark, hooded figure opening the rear door before escaping into the alley.

He pushed back through the curtain, tripped over the apothecary's body, ran into Jack running in, and staggered over broken pottery littering the threshold. He looked out to the deserted street and swore.

The sheriff paced across the apothecary shop, stepping over the body on the floor. "He gave no name, no description?"

"No," said Crispin. "He was killed before he could say." He looked up the street for Tucker who hid in the shadows as far away from the sheriff as he could get.

Wynchecombe frowned at the bloodstain oozing under the corpse. Its irregular shape took on the appearance of a skull. "How do we know this is the only seller of such a poison? There could be others."

"Why else was *he* killed?" They both stared at the body. "But if you doubt it, send your bailiff to question the others."

"I shall."

Crispin sighed. The sun had only just set, and weariness etched the marrow in his bones. He wanted to sleep for a long time but knew he had too much to do.

Wynchecombe's shadow fell across Crispin's chest. "And you say you saw the murderer?"

Crispin shook his head. "Not exactly, my lord. Only a shadowy glimpse."

"Anyone you recognized?"

He frowned. "No."

"So you say."

"My lord, I would tell you if I knew anything."

Wynchecombe scowled. "If you are lying to me…"

"No, my lord. What cause would I have to lie?"

"The more I know you the less I believe I can trust you."

"The curse of being an enigma. May I go now, Lord Sheriff? I must continue pursuing Sir Stephen."

Wynchecombe knelt and grabbed the corpse's hair and raised his head. "What of this? You said he was stabbed in the back. What about this on his throat?"

"That?" Crispin brushed a bit of straw from his coat. "He fell against my dagger."

"An accident, eh?"

"Yes. I am certain you have similar accidents when you question a man."

Wynchecombe smiled. "Yes. Accidents do occur." The sheriff waved him off. "Go on, then."

Crispin looked back. The shop with its swarm of sheriff's men receded behind him. It was just as well. Let the sheriff deal with the body and let Crispin deal with the murderer. Someone plainly did not want there to be witnesses. A dagger was something Stephen would be more familiar with, not this business of poisons. And speaking of poisons...

He checked the street for Jack Tucker, but the boy was nowhere to be found.

Crispin trudged wearily up the stairs to his lodgings. When he looked up, he saw the young cutpurse crouched by the door on the landing. Jack raised his head.

"I suppose I should not be surprised to find you here. Why did you run?"

"I was afraid the sheriff would question me again."

"I see. And why sit in the dark?"

"I can better see who approaches without their seeing me, Master."

Crispin nodded. "You know this business well."

Jack frowned. "Not as well as you." He stayed in his huddled position and hugged himself tighter. "Is this what you do with your time? Get yourself involved in murders?"

Crispin chuckled gravely and pulled the key from his pouch. "It does seem to consume my days and nights. Why? Does it trouble you?"

"God's teeth," said Jack, shaking his head. "That's no work for a gentleman."

"In case you have not noticed, Jack, I am no longer a gentleman. A fact I weary of repeating. But what is it to you? This is my business not yours."

Jack sighed through his blunted nose but said no more. He shivered and pulled his meager cloak tight over his chest.

Crispin held the key near the lock. "Is this where you intend to sleep?"

The boy shrugged. "It isn't bad. It's dry."

"Where do you usually sleep?"

"Anywhere I can. But, being your servant now, I'd thought I'd be hard by."

Crispin tapped his finger on the key. He called himself three kinds of fools before he spoke quietly into the wood of the door. "It is warmer inside."

"Oh no, Master," he said shaking his head, all the while rising and drawing near the door. "What, me? Sleep by a fire?" Jack's face brightened with hope.

Crispin smiled. He turned the key and pushed open the door. "Go on in, you fool. And you are *not* my servant!"

Jack moved forward but stopped abruptly halfway over the threshold.

Beyond him, a feminine shape sauntered forward. The glow from the hearth embers painted only a golden line down the curves of one side of her silhouette. Until she reached the doorway and stepped out of the shadows.

Crispin staggered back as if struck by an arrow. His chest contracted with an old and unpleasant twinge. His voice was rough when he could speak at last. "My God. Rosamunde."

CHAPTER FOURTEEN

She was the very image of the Holy Virgin: genteel, enigmatic, and distant. Her light green gown, modest at the neck, draped in generous folds to the floor, revealing only the long tips of her shoes. A fur-trimmed cloak covered her shoulders clasped by an agrafe with the ivory image of a crane. Full lips opened, prepared to speak or breathe, to admonish as much as to bless. Her face, shaped like a heart with its wide, pale forehead and small chin, emphasized round eyes, green as England's pastures. Green as Crispin remembered them. Nothing about her seemed to have changed—except for the gold band on her left ring finger.

Gone were all thoughts of dead Templars, apothecaries, and poison. He cleared his throat but did not step inside. Jack's body blocked the threshold.

"Rosamunde...I mean...Lady Rothwell." His mouth twisted on the last.

She breathed and formed one word: "Crispin."

Crispin looked away yet the gesture failed to stop the stabbing pains in his chest. "Madam. I am more than surprised to see you here. And after all these years. In fact..." He glanced into the landing. Jack tried to make himself as small as possible. Crispin leaned further. Her manservant Jenkyn was sure to be somewhere nearby. "You should not be here at all."

"Crispin." She said it sadly. With regret? Perhaps it was with the more unromantic sound of pity.

Her gaze hovered on his face but slipped to his stained coat and threadbare cloak. "It has been a long time."

"Seven years," he said tight-lipped.

Neither spoke for several heartbeats. Crispin vaguely wondered if he were dreaming, especially with the familiar fragrant cloud of roses about her.

"Shall I tell her to leave, Master Crispin?"

Crispin stared at Jack with growing unease. Jack swallowed. "Or…maybe *I* should leave." The boy backed out of the door and looked once at Rosamunde and once at Crispin before he made himself scarce in the shadows of the stairwell.

"What are you doing here, Rosamunde?" asked Crispin.

"I will explain."

"This is entirely improper."

She flashed a brutal smile. "When did that ever trouble you?"

"How did you get in?"

"Your landlord was most gracious. But it has been an hour at least." She found the courtesy not to wince at the surroundings. Her soft skirts followed demurely like servants, and she sat in the only chair.

He stood awkwardly in the doorway, trying to recall courtly manners he hadn't used in seven years. He didn't think he had any wine. There was no food to offer, save for some of Jack's day old stew.

A draft churned up from the stairwell and he shivered, glanced once at Jack, and closed the door. He advanced on the hearth to stoke the embers, taking his time with the poker, and he carefully laid the last square of peat on the awakening flames. Another long moment passed before he tore his gaze from the fire, took a breath, and turned.

It was a mistake. The fire threw gold onto her smooth features, emblazoning her round cheeks with a blush of rose.

"Crispin," she said again, her voice tender.

"My lady." He bowed. "How did you find me?"

"I am not so sheltered that I do not follow such tidings. It is known where you live."

He grunted. "I do not know if I am consoled by this information." He stepped away from the fire to the low coffer by the door and gingerly sat. "Still. It does nothing to explain your presence."

She smiled playfully. "No words of greeting? No 'how have you fared, Rosamunde?'"

He glanced away. "I should think that when my sword was broken before your eyes and my blazon torn from my surcote that there were no words left."

She squared her shoulders and drew her lips into a brooding frown. "And you blame me."

Crispin leaned back and crossed his arms over his chest. "Why are you here?"

"You blame me for your dishonor? I say again, as I said seven years ago, I had nothing to do with it."

"No. Your brother saw to everything. My dishonor, the seizing of my titles and lands, and the end of our betrothal."

"How could I go against my brother, my only kinsman?"

He snapped to his feet. "I was to be your husband! I would have defended you to the death had *your* honor been questioned!"

"It wasn't a question of honor!" She bit off the rest of her words and shook her head. "You know very well," she said quietly, "it was a question of treason."

Crispin stiffened. "Why are you here? I have nothing to offer now. But riches were important to you then, weren't they? Is that why you married only a fortnight after our betrothal ended?"

Rosamunde tilted her head but otherwise did not move. He fully expected her to stalk away, silent and enraged as she had done so many times before. He well knew her moods and the performances that accompanied them. He waited for her to cast her skirts aside, flash her teeth in a grimace of disgust, and stomp away, whereupon he was to follow behind and plead an apology. ·

No more. Those refined games were long over.

At last she rose, head bowed, hands fumbling at the pin of her cloak. "I *need* your help."

He laughed, an unfamiliar sound. "That is doubtful."

"No. It is the truth."

He strode to the door and pulled it open. The draft gusted the hearth smoke and it rolled out of the fireplace, across the room, and over the threshold.

"Please. There is no one who can help me."

"What of your husband, Madam?"

She sighed and lowered her eyes. "He is dead, Crispin. More than a year now."

Widowed? It took a monumental effort to keep his face impassive. "Indeed."

"Yes. I am alone."

He almost spat the words but checked himself. "Your *brother*, then."

"But Stephen is missing. I need you to find him."

Stephen missing. Of course. Committing a murder. He better damn well be missing. He longed to say it aloud, but held his tongue.

Her gown rustled when she came up behind him. "A woman needs the protection of her kinsman. The lands…" She drew back and he watched the shadow of her gown move across the floor. "There were no children from this marriage to Lord Rothwell. Had there been an heir, I might be in a better position now. But as it is…"

He listened to his own breathing a long time before his hand of its own accord closed and latched the door. The same hand rested against the door's worn surface before he turned again. She stood only an arm's length away. With one bold step, she crossed the space between them, forcing Crispin's back against the door.

He took a breath and then another. Rasping, he said, "Of all people, why me? You know what he did to me. To us."

"There is no soul I trust more."

He lifted his hands and reached for her shoulders. He felt her warmth, her nearness. It had been a long time. Too long.

After only a moment, he dropped his hands limply to his sides. Leaning forward slightly he stood almost close enough to kiss. "If I find him for you…"

"No, Crispin. *When* you find him."

"When I find him, then. What is there for me?"

She drew back. "I will be grateful."

His flesh warmed. He remembered such gratitude. "Is that all?"

She took another step back. "What do you want?"

"Can't you guess?"

"Your knighthood?"

He leaned back and rested his head against the doorframe. "King Richard will not restore my shield. And there is little you could do on that account, at any rate."

"Then what *do* you want?"

His tongue slid over a tangle of desires, but he could not speak any of them. The next thing that came to mind crossed his lips, but he never meant to say those words either. "I am paid to find things. It is now my sole means of living."

Her face hardened. For a moment, Crispin expected her to slap his cheek. It would be better than that coldness with which she regarded him.

She moved her hands, but not to slap. Instead, she reached up behind her neck and released the clasp to the gold chain at her throat and thrust the bauble toward him.

"Your payment, Master Guest. If this is what is required for you to do a lady a courtesy, then so be it."

The chain, a thumb-width of gold filigree in clever knots, boasted a pendant with a ruby the size of a sheep's eye surrounded by white fresh-water pearls.

Far too much. He wanted to refuse it, but her tone urged his hand upward and the metal pooled in his cupped palm. It was still warm.

"I see these years have caused your memory to lapse on courtly manners."

His fist closed over the gem and he lowered it to his side. "Honor does not fill the larder." She said nothing. He felt the necklace in his hand grow cold. Breathing deeply, he wondered what more to say when he suddenly blurted, "Stephen is accused of murder. A man at the Boar's Tusk. Perhaps that is why he is missing."

"Murder? How can the sheriff accuse Stephen?"

Slightly ashamed of himself for the relish with which he told Rosamunde, Crispin stood stiff as a reed. He wanted to go to her and enfold her in his arms. But to tell her what? *'Sweeting, once your brother is hanged, we are free to marry. Does that not cheer your heart?'* If Stephen died, Crispin's vengeance would be paid in full, and one part of him wanted to caper about the small room.

The sober part of him, the part whose pride kept him within the nimbus of Westminster Palace and its court, kept harrying the facts like a child poking a badger's warren.

"Circumstances point in his direction," he answered, "but we must discover the entire truth."

Her eyes shined with a veil of unshed tears but her lips pressed tightly with a surge of pride. "You do not believe it?"

"I did not say that. But I still must find him."

Rosamunde strode across the room and before he could react, she took his face in her hands, brought it down to hers, and kissed him.

She meant the gesture to be a short kiss of gratitude, and Crispin knew it for what it was once his initial shock wore off. But her nearness and her touch destroyed any scrap of sense. Still clutching the necklace, he grasped her shoulders and crushed her small frame to his chest. He deepened the kiss, savoring her lips, her taste, her tongue.

It lasted only a moment more until, reluctantly, he withdrew from her.

"Rosamunde," he whispered, still clutching her arms, caressing her forehead with his own. "After all this time, do you still love me?" He drew back and searched her face. "For God sake, at least lie to me!"

"Which lie do you desire?" she asked, her breath steaming on his lips. "The lie that says I feel nothing, or the lie that says I do?"

"Seven years have passed and I burn for you still!"

"You should have wed by now."

"How could I, with thoughts of you smoldering in my heart?"

"And still you would defend Stephen's innocence?"

Stephen. The name cooled his flesh and he released her. "You put words in my mouth. If he is guilty, then I know my duty."

She inhaled a trembling breath. Tears quivered on the tips of her lashes but never fell. "But I came here to tell you he has been abducted. I want to hire you to find him."

"The sheriff has already hired me to find him."

"But Crispin, you can't—"

He took her hand and slapped the necklace into it. "Take it back. When I search for Stephen it shall be under the auspices of the sheriff."

She stared at him, eyes wide and dark. She did not put the necklace back around her slender neck. Instead, she clutched it in a trembling hand she kept close to her thigh. "I tell you he's been abducted."

"How long since you last saw him?"

"A sennight. Surely a ransom would have been demanded by now?"

He narrowed his eyes. "A sennight? Are you certain?"

She looked at him with hollow eyes, shook her head, and sank to the chair. "I'm not certain of anything anymore."

Walking to the window he took a deep breath. The cold air seeped in through the cracks in the shutters and he inhaled it, though it was filled with the stench of the meat markets below.

"Whom do I trust, Rosamunde? You—whom I have heard no word from in seven years—or my good and honest friends?"

She raised her eyes. "Why did he go to such a place as the Boar's Tusk? It was far outside his usual havens." She blushed when she said it. She must have realized it was now Crispin's favorite refuge. "Was he meeting someone?"

"Yes. He did meet someone. The man he killed."

She raised her chin defiantly and he backed down.

"Rosamunde, could this man be someone you knew?"

"He could be any number of Stephen's acquaintances."

Crispin hesitated. He needed to ask, but knew it might also put her in danger. He measured her, remembering her strength of character, her fearlessness. "Rosamunde, do you know whether Stephen knew any unusual knights? Any…Templars, for instance?"

"Templars? There are no Templars."

"It was said Stephen argued with this man about something he possessed that Stephen wanted. Is any of this familiar?"

She shook her head. "Nothing, I am sorry to say."

"This man also met briefly with a woman. If we could ascertain her identity it might throw light on the matter."

"None of these tidings mean anything to me. I wish they did." Rosamunde rose and laid her hand on his sleeve. "I know Stephen has caused you much grief. But many years have past. And he is my brother." Her head lowered. "I am staying at the White Hart. If you discover anything, you may send a message to me there. Please help me, Crispin."

She pulled the latch and passed halfway over the threshold before he asked, "And if I cannot? If he is dead? Then…what of us?"

He cringed immediately upon saying it. He expected her expression to change, wanted dearly to see something in her face to indicate her feelings. But he saw nothing. Only an expression of duty seen often on the faces of chatelaines and obedient, submissive wives.

"Fare well, Crispin," was all she said. Her long fingers touched the empty spot where her necklace had been, and then she turned, her train fluttering after.

Crispin stood in the doorway and listened to the last of her footfalls disappear before he closed the door. He glanced at the table and saw the necklace there. He scooped it up, weighed it in his hand, and tossed it on the bed.

He sat heavily on the chair and scooted it to the table. He ran his hand up over his head and mashed down the thick tangle of black hair in an attempt to quell his many thoughts.

The door whined open and Crispin expected Jack Tucker to be standing in the doorway twisting his tunic hem into a knot. But when he looked up it was not Tucker.

Vivienne stood with a hand still on the door. She glanced back down the stairs at the receding Rosamunde and then lifted her chin to look down on him through her long lashes. "Is this a bad time?"

CHAPTER FIFTEEN

"A bad time?" He sighed. "No, of course not."

She walked into the room. When last she stood there the room was in chaos. At least now his lodgings were in a better state.

At the threshold Jack poked his head in for only a moment before he sighed and pulled the door closed.

"I tried to shadow your knight," Crispin said, remembering his manners and rising. He wiped his face, trying to excise the emotions. "But he was not there."

"I am not surprised."

"And why is that?"

"Things have changed."

"You have news then? Is there something you wish to share with me?"

"I only wish I could. But there is much I cannot say."

"Because of this...object?"

"That and more." She stepped to the window and peered through a broken slat to the street below. When she turned to Crispin again, her face seemed paler.

"Lady Vivienne?"

"We must speak quickly. I fear..." She looked back at the window and then moved hastily away as if afraid of it. Her face was tight when she intoned, "The man I sent you to follow may in fact be dead."

"Then the situation is lost."

"No. There is still another man. I am certain he is now in possession of the object. You might find him at the Rose."

"And *his* name?"

"That I still cannot say. But I can describe him. This man is tall and auburn-haired. And he has something of mine I need. It is a desperate need." She lowered her face and whispered, "He is a dangerous man." Her gaze darted once more toward the window. "I fear he will find me."

"What is it you fear?" he asked quietly.

"He is a violent man. I know he means me harm. But this thing he has stolen from me. It could mean my own death if I do not retrieve it. You do not know, you cannot know, how helpless a woman is."

His gaze roved over the sensuous curves of her body and he almost smiled. *Not so defenseless.*

"I suppose I must tell you who this man is. Whatever he says of me, you must not believe him."

"And I should believe you because you are my client?" What was left of Vivienne's coin still rattled in his purse. "I do not enjoy being made a fool of even for coin. Your manner has been strange, my lady. You have offered nothing but obfuscation…and you have behaved most wantonly."

Instead of the contrition he expected, she gave a wry smile. "Other women find their comfort in prayers and solitude. But mine has always been in the company of men. Their attention, whatever form it takes, gives me solace. Have you ever felt alone and frightened?" She laughed carelessly. "Of course not. How foolish of me. You're a man."

"There are times," he said, voice husky, "that I feel alone."

"How brave of you to say. It makes me think…" The tip of her pink tongue pressed against small teeth. "No. That, too, is foolish." She toyed with the brooch. "Have I spoiled your trust in me because of our kiss?"

Crispin clasped his hands together. "Not exactly. I was surprised, to be sure. But I know what manner of woman you are."

"Oh. I see." She threw back her head, but instead of laughing she heaved a sigh.

Crispin's attention drew to her shoulders and neck, and then down to her neckline moving in rhythm to her breaths.

"A young woman marries the wealthy old man," she said. "The butt of many jests. Certainly ambition plays its role at court. But you must remember it was not by my choice I married, but by my uncle's. A woman is always at the mercy of her kin, unless she be an orphan. And if she were, she had better be a rich one."

He gazed into her brown eyes but thought instead of green. "Yes. I know well how a woman is not her own master."

"Just so."

"Then who is the man you fear?"

"Stephen St Albans."

Crispin heard the timbers crack in the walls, until he realized it was not the walls but his teeth clenched in his jaw. "Stephen?" he asked calmly.

"Yes," said Vivienne. "I think you know him."

His jaw would not loosen. "Yes."

"Then you know he is dangerous as well as heartless. The object he has belongs to me. Well, if not to me, at least it will keep me safe."

He fisted his hands, not knowing whether he should curse or punch the wall. Shuddering to control himself, he stared at her, unsure of himself in the veil of her vulnerability. "Whatever this object," he said cagily, "I will see it returned to its rightful owner."

"Good. But I wonder," she said, eyes downcast artfully, "what his sister was doing here."

"You know Lady Rosamunde?"

"Only by sight."

A heartsore sensation lingered in Crispin's chest when he mentioned Rosamunde's name. "You have nothing to fear from her. It is...other business."

She smiled. "I trust you. You are all that they say about you. No matter what the king did, you remain a knight in my eyes." She

119

breathed a sigh. "How clever you are. Such an interesting life you lead. It makes a woman jealous of her own drear life in the quiet of solars. You must discover some thrilling mysteries. Interesting objects. Any of late you would tell me of? It is only that my own life is so sheltered. Your antics are like those of a minstrel's song."

He doubted very much that *her* life could be all that sheltered, but he shook his head. This was the second time she asked this. "Nothing, I fear, that would interest you and your...*sheltered* life." He stepped closer to her, painfully aware of the scent of her and that red mouth. He remembered kissing her before. "What am I looking for?" he whispered. It seemed to be many questions at once. He wanted a kind of certainty from Vivienne, some clue that he pursued something tangible and real. The grail was a dream, part of the ethereal mist of Camelot. Rosamunde, too, was unreal, like a dream. He needed something to grasp, something substantial to believe in.

She slanted forward and touched her lips to his, and whispered, "You will know when you find it."

He had more questions but he couldn't seem to grasp them from his foggy mind. His mouth joined to hers and he kissed her deeply, like he had wanted to before.

She did not caress or pull him into an embrace. Instead, she clutched wildly at his clothing and yanked open the collar.

He hauled up the folds of her skirts and shoved her hard against the door.

Jack Tucker spent the night on the cold landing after all.

Vivienne left before Crispin arose. Amazingly, the boy was still on the landing. Crispin let him in to warm himself by the fire and offered him some cheese and a heel of bread. While he shaved, he endured Jack's quiet scrutiny, and then shook his head at himself as he left the boy alone in his lodgings in order to search for Stephen St Albans at last.

Crispin stood outside the Rose a long time before going in. The innkeeper spied him first and raised his arms in greeting. "Sir

Crispin! My lord, it has been many a day since you have graced my humble establishment."

Crispin cringed. *Jesu.* He hurried to meet the innkeeper, stifling the next declaration by laying a hand on his shoulder. "A long time indeed. But as you well know, Brian," he said, lowering the volume of his voice, "I am no longer 'Sir' Crispin. Nor am I 'Lord' Crispin."

Brian's merry demeanor melted, replaced by a humiliated mask. "Forgive me, my lord...I mean, Master Crispin. I would not wish to harm you with my words any more than..."

"Peace, Brian," he said reflexively, patting the man's arm and maneuvering him to a bench. How many times over the years had he played out this scenario with others? No wonder King Richard thought it a fine Hell for him. A never-ending ritual of mortification and dishonor.

"I have only come this morning to ask you some questions."

"Anything for you, Master Crispin."

"Thank you, old friend. I seek Stephen St Albans. Has he been here?"

"That whoreson." Brian spat and folded his arms over his chest. His pale freckled face pouted, wrinkling forehead up to his receding hairline.

"Now Brian. I would not have you disparage one of your loyal patrons."

"Now, Master. It was he—"

"I know well what he did. It is important I find him."

"If it is so, then I will help you. But alas, we have seen nothing of him for days."

"Has anyone seen him in, say, a sennight?"

"Here!" Brian called to a servant. "Rolf, bring Master Crispin some wine. And then tell us if you have seen hide or hair of Sir Stephen St Albans?"

Rolf's face broke into a smile. "Master Crispin!"

Crispin raised his hand in an attempt to stave off another scene. "Rolf. It is good to see you, too. But I must not delay. Can you tell me about Sir Stephen?"

Rolf scratched his head and pushed a cup in front of Crispin. He poured wine from a leather jug. "Aye," he answered. "He hasn't come in for at least two days. And him coming regular all these years. Mayhap he's off to France."

Crispin leaned in. "Why would you say that?"

"Oh, often he'd talk to his fellows about France and his business there."

"Did you happen to hear the nature of that business?"

"I know not. As soon as I come with the jug they'd all commence to talk that French talk."

"Who were these fellows of his?"

"Lords, I suppose. Men from court. Serious men. They came to talk and did very little drinking."

"Did they arrive together?"

"No. They'd meet here and depart separately."

Crispin tapped his fingers on his wine bowl and scowled into the ruby liquid. "Is there anything more you can tell me, Rolf?"

"No. That is all. Except for Lady Rothwell."

"Lady Rothwell came here?"

"Aye."

"How often?"

"In the last week, almost all the days he came."

"How about two days ago?"

"Aye. She was here."

He made a sound much like a growl deep in his throat. "Did they lapse into French when you approached?"

"Aye. That they did."

He thanked Rolf and Brian and took his leave, promising to return, though when he scanned the room and the darkly shadowed faces of squires who looked down their noses at him, and at knights who scowled and jabbed each other in the ribs when he passed, he knew he would not come again.

Like a spirit, Crispin traversed London, stopping only occasionally to partake of food from a purveyor of meat pies, or of roasted meat on sticks. He did what he should have done days ago, and slipped into the alleys to question those who knew the man, who had dealt with him, but his meticulous inquiries yielded nothing.

He rubbed the back of his neck as night fell, realizing with some dejection that he had been at it all day with little to show for it.

Clouds covered the oncoming stars but a cresset burned nearby and cast irregular shadows along the empty road. The wood in the cresset's iron cage crackled and snapped, flinging a bright ember into the air. For a moment, it illuminated a dark doorway. He saw a tall, slim shape of a man with a cloak and a sword.

Crispin studied the figure before the ember died and slipped the doorway back into thick shadow. He strained to see into the portico, but only velvety darkness engulfed the avenue and swallowed all but the faintest of details.

"It is well after compline, man."

Crispin spun.

The Watch, a man in hauberk and conical helm behind him, gestured with the torch. "The curfew is in force," he said.

"Yes," said Crispin. "I forgot the time."

The Watch studied him, stood stiffly, clutching the staff with its burning cage of coals dropping embers into the mud, and watched steadily as Crispin trudged away.

Crispin turned as he passed the doorway but the man had vanished. He blew a disappointed cloud of breath into the damp air and rested his hand on the butt of his dagger.

The anti-pope's man? The thought made him consider France and Stephen. "Now what, pray, were you doing in France, Sir Stephen?" he muttered. "Was your business in Avignon, perhaps?"

Hurrying back to his lodgings, Crispin became aware of another figure ahead of him in the misty night. A woman. He hung back, not wishing to alarm her, since by her cloak she appeared to be a highborn lady. He thought of waiting for her to pass completely since she happened to be going in the same direction, but the air was damp and he longed for his own hearth. He followed her for some time until she stopped at a tavern door. Crispin fell back into the shadows and watched as the door opened, throwing light onto her face.

Vivienne! Why was she abroad at this hour?

He moved forward to ask just as the door closed behind her. He reached for the door but thought better of it. Instead, he crept to the shuttered window and peered through the slats. He saw her sit at a table opposite a tall, hooded man with his back to Crispin. He could not hear their words but she was speaking to him in a forceful manner. The man merely shook his head. She insisted, slamming her hand to the table but the man leaned back, his shoulders moving as if he were laughing. She sneered, grabbed his beaker of ale, and tossed it into his face. The man shot to his feet and grasped her wrist. The few men in the tavern turned to them, but they were rougher men and knew they could not interfere with those of higher rank.

Crispin had almost decided to go in when the man released her. She rubbed her wrist but instead of the indignant anger he expected of any woman in such a situation, Vivienne's face softened. Her lips drew into a pout and an expression of coquetry washed over her features.

"God's blood," he whispered. "An accomplished wanton indeed." He left the tavern's window and trudged his way back to his lodgings.

He was strangely relieved to find Jack there, especially since the boy had gotten a warm fire glowing in the hearth.

"Are you still here?" he asked, removing his cloak and hood and hanging them on a peg by the door.

Jack jabbed the poker at the peat and then stood uneasily before it. He looked to Crispin as if he wanted to speak. At last, he took a breath and said, "I am no varlet, sir, as well you know. Maybe I'm not good for much. Maybe I'm only good for thieving. But I can fetch things for you and open doors and do your bidding. I'm a smart lad, I am." He twisted his tunic in his fingers before realizing he was doing it and dropped the ragged cloth.

Crispin sat in the chair before the fire and studied the lad. Young, half-starved, dirty. Pale cheeks overrun with freckles and wild ginger hair atop his head. He looked more like a creature from the forest than a boy. Crispin leaned back. "Where do you come from, boy? Who is your master?"

"I have no master," he said, chin raised defiantly. "Leastways, not no more. And I come from London."

"What do you mean you no longer have a master?"

"He was me mother's master. She served him down on Old Fish Street. And when she died he took me on...for a bit. But he didn't want me. And I didn't want him. So I left."

There was a smudge on that obstinate nose, which only made him look more rebellious. Crispin's gaze traversed his face and his earnest expression. His voice softened when he asked, "And when was that?"

"When me mother died?" He becrossed himself. "Four winters it is now."

"And how old are you, boy?"

Jack licked his lips and stared up into the rafters. "I reckon...'bout eleven or so."

Crispin let out a breath. The boy was orphaned and on his own at eight years old? How had he managed? How was it possible? He had learned the fine art of thieving, that was certain. Enough to keep himself alive, at any rate. Crispin well knew that men, under dire circumstances, could make themselves survive on will alone. *He* had done it. And Jack had, too, apparently.

He smiled, hoping it might ease the boy's tight fists. "Well...you have been very helpful, Jack." He rose. "Are you thirsty? I have wine."

Jack jumped up. "Master, it is for me to serve you!"

Crispin waved him away and poured two bowls, offering one to the boy. Jack stared but did not reach for it.

"Take it, lad. Today, we are not master and servant. Lady Vivienne's visit of last night put me in a congenial mood." But his humor darkened upon thinking about the inn. "Although that mood is...fleeting."

Jack muttered and took the bowl. He slurped the wine. "Isn't she a married lady?"

Crispin raised the bowl and turned it, eyeing the color at rim height. He scowled at the sudden reminder of that which he conveniently put aside. "Yes. What of it?"

"It seems that a man ought not to worry over his property when it goes about town."

"You have a strange morality for a thief."

"It isn't my morality I'm worried over."

Crispin's scowl deepened. "We will not discuss my personal business, Tucker. Nor my morality."

Jack shrugged. "Very well. Beg pardon."

Crispin sat in the chair and drank. "Lady Vivienne asked me to follow a man. It seems he possesses an object of great value that she says belongs to her. Yet she would not divulge the man's name nor the object. I do not know why. But at any rate, I have been chasing wild geese, for she now says it was not this man that so interested her, but another who now has this mysterious object."

Jack took a slurping gulp of wine and wiped his mouth with his sleeve. "And what is the object?"

"She would not tell me."

"By the saints!"

Crispin nodded and drew the dead man's pouch from his coat. "I don't know what to make of it all—these dissimilar cases—but Stephen St Albans is in the thick of all of them. This dead Templar had an object Stephen wanted as well as this Stancliff woman." He showed Jack the embroidery and pulled out the pinky ring and the necklace with the cross, and showed him the words inscribed on the reverse.

"What does that mean, 'Cup Bearer'?"

"It means he was the keeper of the Holy Grail."

Jack's jaw hung and he becrossed himself. "Christ Jesus! Can it be true?"

Crispin snaked the long chain back into the pouch and again tucked it inside his coat. "I see you *have* heard of the grail, at least. But whether it is the true grail, I am not certain. These Templars certainly believe it and they want it back."

"It's gone then? Stolen?"

"Yes."

"Aren't they the men what abducted you?" He gestured toward Crispin's wounded chest.

Crispin gulped his wine and shook his head. He stared detachedly into the flames coming to life with more peat (and where had *that* come from?). He glanced at Jack. The fire warmed and foiled the shadows. But Crispin realized it wasn't just the fire that gave the room its amiable quality.

Jack was just a boy. A boy! Small, insignificant. He would barely have aroused Crispin's notice back at his lost estates in Sheen. And yet here he was confiding in the churl. He would have laughed if he had thought it the least bit funny.

Setting his mouth into a somber line, he turned the wine bowl in his hand. "No. It was not the Templars who did this to me. I have since met these Templars. No, the men who abducted me were the French anti-pope's men. It seems they, too, want the grail for their own purposes."

"God's holy eyes!"

"Just so." Crispin saluted with his cup and drank. He listened to the congenial quiet, to the fire crackling, and inhaled the satisfying aroma of wine before the unpleasant memory of his encounter with the sheriff and the grail intruded.

Absently, Crispin rubbed his sore chest. "It all started as just a simple murder."

"Simple murder?" huffed Jack. "Is that what murder is? If so simple then why are so many now involved? Who *is* the murderer? Is it that man you hate? Stephen St Albans?"

Crispin chuffed a laugh. "Yes, Jack. But that is not the half of it. The first man Lady Vivienne would have me find was the dead grail knight. I am almost certain of it."

127

"What has Lady Vivienne to do with these two gentlemen?"

He thought of her encounter with the strange man in the tavern. Now he wished he had intruded. "That, my boy, is the puzzle."

Jack picked up his wine bowl. "That's a fine bit of pastie, isn't it? All these bits of dough pressed together." He slurped the wine and licked his lips. "So this is what you do, eh? Tracker. Well, I suppose it's a fair sight better than making a shoe or weaving cloth."

"It is also considerably more dangerous."

"Aye. It is that. But it is an occupation that makes a man think. Is there much money in 'tracking'?"

Crispin shrugged. "Look around you."

Jack did, but Crispin did not see disgust or pity in his eyes. To the boy, it was shelter and a damned sight better than the streets. "There *is* something satisfying in putting one's mind to it instead of one's back," said Jack.

Crispin watched the wheels turn in Jack's mind. He smiled.

The boy took a hasty sip and belched. "If you truly think the murderer is this man who betrayed you," said Jack suddenly, "then he must have the grail, eh?"

Crispin's smile faded. The thought made him uneasy and he leaned back in the chair. "He must. It appears he intends to sell it or give it to the anti-pope." He raised the bowl but didn't drink. "Such treachery. It is one thing to conspire against another man. But to conspire against the seat of Peter..."

"But if it isn't the true grail..."

"Who can know? Not I. I have yet to see it."

Jack drank thoughtfully, clutching the bowl with one hand. He wrapped his other arm around his upraised leg and scooted close to the fire. "It'd be funny, wouldn't it?"

"What?" Despite the warmth of the fire and the wine Crispin was wide awake.

"It'd be funny if your Lady Vivienne were looking for the grail, too."

Crispin leaned back and closed his eyes. He raised the wine bowl to his face and drank the sharp taste of the pungent liquor. "Yes. Funny indeed."

CHAPTER SIXTEEN

Crispin groaned and rolled his head along the stiff, linen pillow. Jack lay curled up like a dog before the hearth. He and Jack had ended up drinking all the wine and talking half the night before Crispin dropped off from exhaustion somewhere in the middle of one of Jack's recitations.

He glanced at the shutters. Early morning. His lids hung heavy and his body felt lethargic, but he could not find enough sleep, and little wonder with so much on his mind. So many tangles and snags. This whole business made him uneasy. He wanted his revenge on Stephen. Of that much he was certain, but the circumstances did not sit well with him. He did not like the idea of Rosamunde being anywhere related to conspiracies and heresies. But she was there with Stephen at the Rose not too long ago, much more recent than the week she admitted to. Why did she say nothing of this? And then there was Vivienne with her secretive schemes.

He threw his legs over the side of the bed and clutched his aching head. Rising, he stumbled to the washbasin and threw cold water on his face and stared at his reflection in the polished brass mirror hanging on the wall. His thoughts were as distorted as his image. He splashed more water on his face, shaved hastily and sloppily—nicking his chin—and toed Jack awake from his place before the fire.

"I need you to do something for me," he said to the drowsy boy.

Crispin paced before the White Hart. He looked up through a cloud of breath at the window he reckoned was hers. The foggy morning revealed nothing beyond the inn's slate roof but whiteness. The fog obscured the lanes, and London looked like it consisted of only a few alehouses and shops. Spires, smoke, even sounds were absorbed by the shrouding white.

Crispin could stall no more. He slapped his scabbard for comfort, strode through the door, and climbed the stairs to the rooms. Her manservant Jenkyn stood beside the door and stepped in front of it to block Crispin.

"My lord. What business have you with my lady?"

"My own. Announce me."

"My lord, it is early. I dare not."

"Then I'll announce myself." Crispin maneuvered around him and pounded his fist on the door.

"My lord! Please!"

"Who is there?" asked Rosamunde's maid and she opened the door a crack. Crispin saw her eye stare at him and widen. The door swung to close but he thrust his foot and leg between the door and the jamb before it could close.

"Leave us," said Crispin and pushed the door open.

"Master, I cannot—"

He grabbed the maid by the shoulders and shoved her across the threshold into Jenkyn's arms. Crispin slammed the door and bolted it. When he turned he inhaled sharply.

Rosamunde stood in the center of the room. Her startling beauty always gave him pause and today was no different.

She looked more annoyed than shocked. She wore her green gown again and a gold fillet encircled her head. She was softness and elegance; everything in its place.

"You lied to me," he said.

"I?"

"Do not compound them." Her gaze fastened on him, following his step as he made a slow orbit of her. "Why did Stephen argue with the dead man? What do you keep from me?"

She looked down. Her proud shoulders fell slightly, but her demeanor did not change. "Nothing."

The facts coursed through his head. Rolf at the Rose saw Stephen and Rosamunde together. Eleanor at the Boar's Tusk saw Stephen arguing with the dead man and also saw a woman talking with the dead knight after Stephen left, but Crispin assumed this must have been Vivienne. Now he did not feel so certain.

"Was it you?" he breathed. "Was it you who spoke to the man in the Boar's Tusk? I found a witness."

She did not raise her face when she said at last, "Yes. It was me. I did talk to him."

Crispin closed his eyes and could not speak for several heartbeats. When he opened them again her expression remained unchanged. "Why?"

She strode to the window and looked out through the open shutter. White, gauzy sunlight cast her skin in an ashen pallor. "Does it matter so much?"

"Yes. It does. It could make you a murderer."

She whirled.

"Rosamunde, you must tell me why you were there and what was said. I must know it all."

She shook her head.

"Rosamunde." He strode to her side and lifted his hands to touch her, but then thought better of it. Gently he said, "It is me, Rosamunde. Have you forgotten how it was with us? We could keep nothing from the other. What has changed that you cannot confide in me?"

"I did not kill that man."

"I know that. But if you tell me—"

Her eyes filled with tears. "I cannot tell you. Too much has changed between us. It is not as it was. It can never again be as it was."

"So much has happened. To the both of us." Her words, her face, all etched an unpleasant picture in his mind. "Lord Rothwell. Was he cruel to you?"

She shook her head and one tear traveled down the length of her pale cheek. It sat there like a diamond, didn't move even when she shook her head. "I do not know what cruel is anymore. Anyway, it is past. He is dead."

"You should have sought me earlier."

"To what end? Were you to save me, Crispin?" She brushed his arm lightly before letting her hand fall away. "I was a married woman. To commit adultery—"

"No, no. Never. Ah, Rosamunde, Rosamunde." With the word "adultery" all he could think of was Lady Vivienne. So accessible, whereas Rosamunde was as unreachable as always.

He inhaled a breath and held it. "What has Lady Stancliff to do with you?"

"Lady Stancliff?" Rosamunde's brow rose. "I only know her from court...and from your lodgings. I could ask the same of you."

He shook his head. "Never mind. Tell me about the Rose, then."

"I do not understand."

"You know me and yet you think me a fool? You were seen at the Rose only a few days ago speaking with your brother. What were you doing there?"

"I needed to discuss a private matter with Stephen."

He turned and looked at her. The tear on her cheek finally fell, leaving a crooked, wet track down her face. Her damp lashes made her eyes appear bigger, deeper. He walked the few paces to stand before her. Cupping her soft face in his hands, he bent and kissed her full lips. A tender kiss, meant to last for only a moment. But she prolonged it, fingers reaching up to his chest and closing around his neck. She opened her lips in a bittersweet embrace. He wanted more, clutched her to take more, but he felt her fingers release him and he knew that he, too, must step away.

She hugged herself and moved to the fire. "I cannot tell you what we spoke of. It is too private. It is likewise so what I said to Gaston D'Arcy, the dead man. You must believe me when I tell you our conversation had nothing to do with murder and everything to do with my private business, which I will not share with you and certainly not with that oaf of a sheriff."

The brief kiss did nothing to alleviate his craving. "I see. But that does not excuse your brother."

She scowled. "You only think him guilty because you hate him."

"It makes it easier to believe, but the evidence suggests it was him."

"Crispin! It is my flesh and blood you speak of!"

"It is justice I speak of. Do you not wish to bring to judgment the slayer of an innocent man?"

"Of an innocent man, yes."

He measured her words and slowly approached. "Do you mean to say that Gaston D'Arcy was *not* an innocent man? In what way?"

"Just go, Crispin! What do you think to gain by coming here like this, manhandling my poor maid? What are you thinking?" She wiped hastily at her face. "Did you think that we would grow close again once you hanged my brother?" Her brow wrinkled unpleasantly. "We are different people now, you and I. I loved you then. And yes, there is still something alluring about you; something earthy that always compelled me. But I do not love you, Crispin. Not anymore. You are too angry to love. Too lost. And I am too weary to try."

The pain in his heart rose to his throat and it thickened momentarily before he could speak. "I have been charged with finding Stephen," he said, voice coarse, "and find him I will. And if he be hanged..." He stalked to the door and grasped the latch. "If he be hanged, I will tie the noose myself. You and your brother can both go to Hell."

He pulled the door open and the maid fell into the room, followed by Jenkyn. They chattered like angry squirrels but he pushed them both roughly aside and departed.

Outside, Crispin mashed the muddy lane with his boots. The

case started as an interesting diversion, but now all of it disgusted him with its compounding twists and deceptions. He could trust no one, not a soul this side of Purgatory.

"This investigation is cursed," he spat, following the winding alleys and lanes.

Though now it was afternoon, few traveled the streets amid the dense white fog. Crispin trudged with head down and hood up. He listened to his own feet tramping. So long in fact that it took some time to notice the unmistakable echo to his steps.

Subtly he hurried. The echo fell slightly behind at first but sped to match his pace. Crispin remembered the man with the sword lit by a cresset's flame, and he cursed under his breath that he lacked a sword himself.

He rounded a corner and flattened against a wall, waiting for the moment his shadow appeared. He felt like pummeling someone and he did not care who.

He listened. Steps approached and stopped.

Tensing, Crispin expected a figure to pass by. The moment stretched. He leaned toward the edge of the wall and peered into the thick mist.

No one.

Unsettled, Crispin reached the Rose and sat by the fire with his back to the hearth and tipped a cup of wine to his lips. He watched patrons come and go but did not see Stephen. After two hours he stretched his back and left, kicking the tavern door shut behind him.

The fog never lifted since Crispin first entered the Rose and it tumbled down the narrow lanes almost as if following him to the Spur. He did not bother to scan the room for Gaston D'Arcy, the Frenchman in the foreign gown. He knew he would never return. Crispin instead climbed the stairs and walked across the gallery to stop in front of the room he visited before. He glanced at the floor surprised. Crouching on one knee, he ran his rough fingers across the floorboards and found the red threads. He tried the latch.

Locked. With his knife's blade he slipped it between door and jamb and managed to lift the bolt.

Quickly he assessed the room, but nothing had changed except for the shrine. The crucifix, the candle, and the velvet cloth were gone.

He frowned and left the room, thinking deeply. He slowly descended the stairs and left the Spur. He trudged to a privy at the edge of the riverbank, hitched up his coat, pushed his braies aside, and relieved himself into the filthy pit, sighing at the futility of the past several hours that were as black and as awful as the hole before him.

He tied his braies and turned to leave when he heard shouts outside his door.

Men scuffled and struggled just beyond the privy and he opened the door a crack in time to watch a man roll by. Two others picked him up. Loose ropes were bound to the escaping man's wrists, their free ends dangling like tassels. The two tried to drag the fugitive away, but the man swung at them. His fist mashed one in the nose and down he went. Then the other pursuer threw a wild punch and missed.

Crispin smiled grimly. He pushed up his right sleeve and opened the door. With relish, he smacked his fist in the face of one of the aggressors. A spray of blood fanned from the man's mouth and he tumbled backwards into the mud and lay still.

The first man struggled to his feet and, with a surprised look toward his companion on the ground, swung at Crispin.

Crispin dodged but not soon enough to escape hard knuckles glancing off his cheek. He felt his teeth crack and tasted salty blood. He shook his head to clear it.

Crispin swung his foot out and kicked the man's knee cap. The man went down in a howl of pain and the fugitive swiveled and then fell on his assailant and pummeled his face with his fists, cut ropes flailing.

The first attacker came to and pounced on Crispin. Crispin dug his fingers into the man's face until he growled in pain. Pushing him back, Crispin kneed him in the groin. While the man bent over, Crispin swung an uppercut and flattened him in the mud. The man lay stiff and still. Only low moans escaped his lips.

The other man wriggled away from the fugitive's beating and scrambled to his feet. With one glance at his companion on the ground, he limped away down an alley. Crispin pursued for a few half-hearted steps, but let him go.

The fugitive lay on his face huffing and panting until Crispin reached down for the man to take his arm. With lowered face, the man took it and rose.

"I must thank you," grunted the man before he looked up and froze.

Crispin stared into the man's face and spit the blood from his mouth. "God's blood," he said before a spiteful smile curved his lips. "Sir Stephen."

CHAPTER SEVENTEEN

"I do not care who you are, Wynchecombe," rasped Stephen through cracked lips. "Why the hell am I here?"

"I do not believe you understand the seriousness of your situation, Sir Stephen," said the sheriff. The stuffy chambers at Newgate closed in on them. Its hearth light flickered off their faces. The other sheriff, John More, was, as usual, nowhere to be found.

Stephen sat while the sheriff circled him like a raven looking for an opportunity to swoop down on a carcass.

Crispin leaned against a far wall in the shadows. Lips rigid, he studied the proceedings.

Stephen snorted at the sheriff's last remark. He wiped at his bruised face and again straightened his torn coat. Though he sat with legs wide in a seemingly relaxed manner, his features winced when he moved and the red blood on his left temple shone bright against his pale skin. He rubbed his wrists. They were ringed red with raw abrasions. "As I see it, my situation is no longer serious. I have been rescued." He smiled an unsavory grin at Crispin. "And I have you to thank."

Crispin said nothing. He moved only to breathe long, slow breaths.

Stephen dismissed him and glared again at Wynchecombe. "So why does it appear I am under arrest?"

"For the simple reason," said the sheriff, pouring himself some wine, "that you are."

Stephen launched from his chair. The sheriff shoved him back down with one hand. "Be advised, my lord, that my men are within hearing." Wynchecombe sat on the edge of the table and resumed pouring his wine. He lifted the cup to his lips and drank, wiped his mustache with his fingers, and set the cup aside. "You are here because of murder."

"Murder?" Stephen rolled his shoulders and slid to the edge of his stool. "What murder?"

"The man at the Boar's Tusk two nights ago."

"Gaston D'Arcy," said Crispin from his corner.

Stephen's lips parted. A retort appeared ready on his tongue. But he glanced swiftly at Crispin and then at the sheriff. Stephen slowly sat back and set his mouth into a thin line. "I know not what you speak of."

Wynchecombe rose, walked the few paces to Stephen's chair, and loured over him. The sheriff stood a head taller than most men. His dark features made him even more imposing, though Crispin suspected he could not intimidate the dour knight.

"Come, come, Sir Stephen," said Wynchecombe. "You were seen arguing with the man and not long thereafter he was dead."

Stephen scowled and stared at his feet. "I will say nothing."

"That does not bode well for you," said Wynchecombe. He stood with his feet apart and his hand on his sword pommel. "Did you know that this dead man—this Gaston D'Arcy—bore the mark of a Knight Templar?"

Stephen stiffened but remained mute.

"This surprises you?" asked the sheriff. "Or are you just surprised we know?"

"Say what you want, Wynchecombe. It changes nothing. You have no evidence. Release me."

"On the contrary. We have nothing but evidence against you. If you will not speak now, perhaps some meditation in a cell will do you good. Arise, my lord."

Scowling, Stephen rose and stood toe to toe with the sheriff. Wynchecombe opened his hand. "Your sword, Sir Stephen."

Crispin's chest filled with a warm flush. "Yes," he said just over Wynchecombe's shoulder. "Surrender your blade. See how it feels."

"You are behind this," Stephen said to Crispin. "Have you not learned enough? Do you require more lessons in humbling?"

"I am learning more each day." Crispin's mouth cracked into grin. Between clenched teeth he echoed the sheriff, "Surrender your sword."

"Very well, Lord Sheriff. I will pay whatever surety you require and we may end this."

"I have not yet prepared your writ for the jury, Sir Stephen. We will talk of sureties later. For now, I demand your sword."

"You mean to go through with this? To imprison me?"

"Indeed I do. Your sword."

Stephen's nostrils flared. With stiff fingers he unbuckled his baldric and handed strap, sheath, and sword to Wynchecombe, never taking his icy gaze from Crispin's face.

Crispin beamed.

The sheriff held out his hand. "Your knife."

Stephen yanked the frog from his belt and slapped the sheath into the sheriff's palm.

"And now a cell," said Crispin.

Stephen lurched forward with fists clenched, but Wynchecombe stopped him. His hands flattened against the knight's chest. "Peace," Wynchecombe said and glanced once at Crispin before motioning for Stephen to precede him to the door.

"You are making a mistake, Lord Sheriff," growled the knight. "I will have your head for this."

"Careful, Sir Stephen. If you wish to eat, you'd best be civil to the man who commands your gaolers."

"I will not be here long. When the king hears of this—"

"I will send my writ to him forthwith with all its evidence. King Richard loves the law but loves not lawbreakers. You *will* be my guest. For how long? Well, that is what your trial will decide. A gibbet is a simple thing to build."

Stephen's lips pressed tightly and paled. "The noose is already about my neck before I am even indicted, is it? Your folly, Wynchecombe, is to listen to Crispin Guest. He will get you both killed. No jury will convict me."

"You forget," said the sheriff, "*I* pick the jury." He thrust Stephen into the corridor. The knight stumbled against two gaolers. "This way, Sir Stephen," he said politely.

The gaolers took up their positions on either side of Stephen and escorted him toward an open cell, followed by the sheriff and finally Crispin. The gaolers pushed open the door and gestured him forward and Stephen walked onto the straw-covered floor before the gaolers closed and locked the door after him.

Wynchecombe looked through the small barred window. "Crispin played little part in putting you here," he said. "Perhaps you must look to your own actions. It is a man's actions, after all, that truly condemn him."

The sheriff turned away from the cell and glared once at Crispin to follow him before striding down the passage.

Crispin stared at the cell. He longed to gloat over Stephen in his disgrace. Hadn't he waited seven years for this? But he trailed the sheriff instead. They walked all the way back to his gatehouse chamber.

He should have been pleased that Stephen finally sat in a cell with the shadow of the hangman stretched over him. Yet there were many loose ends, too many questions yet to be answered.

The sheriff's voice startled.

"Well? You're free to go. Is not your business here complete?" Wynchecombe threw back his head with a huff of recollection. "Oh, I see. There is a matter of sixpence. Here." He dug into his pouch and pulled out the coins, more than six pence. "I feel generous today. Take these with my thanks."

Crispin took no notice of Wynchecombe but stared into the hearth. He sagged against the doorjamb and crossed his arms over his chest.

"Guest! Did you hear me?"

"My lord," he answered distantly. "When I first brought Stephen here, he had bindings on his wrists. And he thanked me, however grudgingly, for his 'rescue.' Yet neither of us have been able to determine why Stephen was in such a disreputable state with bindings."

"You heard him. He refused to say."

"And that is good enough for you? Why did he need rescuing? And where is the grail?"

Wynchecombe leapt from his chair. "God's teeth, Crispin! Are you still bringing that damn grail business into it?"

"Yes, my lord."

The sheriff gestured into the air. "I'll have none of it. Does the thing even exist? Rumor is not enough. I will believe only when I see it."

"So said Doubting Thomas."

"Nevertheless." Wynchecombe reached for his wine and paused. "I have never seen this side of you, Crispin. Why are you so willing to believe?"

"You saw the grail knight." He shouldered into the room and hovered near a chair long enough for Wynchecombe to relent and offer it to him.

Crispin sat heavily. "And I talked to other Templars, his companions. It's not that I believe in the grail itself, but that there is a cup that has been stolen. Surely it is valuable to these men for they wish for me to find it."

"You would make of this a conspiracy. I say lay it to rest. The murder is solved."

"Is it?"

Wynchecombe's wine poised at his lips when he slammed the goblet on the table. Red splattered onto his papers. "Now see here! Enough is enough. The murderer is in that cell."

"It remains to be seen."

"You heard him. He would not speak of it."

"A man is not necessarily guilty just because he is silent."

"And that's where you're wrong. According to the law, silence *is* affirmation. If he has nothing to hide, why not speak?"

"Perhaps he has something else to hide."

"Crispin..." Wynchecombe shook his head and rubbed his eyes with the heel of his palms. "Why must you always make more of it than there is? Is it the six pence? I already said I'd pay you extra for your trouble. Just take the coins and vex some other worthy." He tossed them to the table and Crispin watched them clatter and land, gleaming in the fire light.

"It is not for that, my lord, and you know it!"

Wynchecombe gulped from his goblet and gazed at Crispin steadily. "What is it that truly vexes you?" he said quietly. "I know your history. All of court knows it. By the mass, all of *London* knows it. So why are you suddenly so reluctant when before you were hot for his blood? Come now. You might as well tell me." He reached for his pouch and laid another two coins carefully on the pile already on the table.

Crispin licked his lips, eyes darting toward the bounty. "Stephen—despite my feelings and my personal history—has always been an honorable man. If he were guilty...I think he would admit it."

The sheriff glared at him, grinding his teeth. He jolted to his feet. "Very well. We will get it out of him. Now."

Crispin moved swiftly to block him. "Allow me to do it."

The sheriff guffawed. "I should let *you* interrogate him?"

"Commission me then."

"And what will that cost me?"

"My lord..." Crispin closed his fists and bowed his head. "I give my word as a tool of your office to interrogate him and behave in a fitting manner. For no fee."

They both fell silent. Even the crackling flames muted in the still air. Wynchecombe considered. His brows fumbled and his mustache buried his lips. He took his time deciding.

"Very well. See to it, Guest. But I tell you now, if you are wrong and he complains to the king, it's your head in the noose, not mine."

CHAPTER EIGHTEEN

Jack hurried through the streets, a tight happy feeling filling his chest. Four years ago, he hadn't wanted a master. The slovenly man his mother had served wasn't interested in cultivating an apprentice and certainly had no need of Jack, nor of feeding, housing, or paying him. The man was as relieved as Jack was when Jack left him for good, though it hadn't been long after that he would have gladly doffed his pride and begged to be back for the scraps to eat and a warm fire to sleep by.

But here was a master worth having! Master Crispin seemed like no ordinary man. And his vocation was strange and unusual. Jack knew he could learn the habits of a varlet but he liked better doing such tasks as Crispin had set him to today. Finding Lady Vivienne and following her would be simple, for he knew the streets of London better than the rats. Yes, it was good to find a home at last. He found he wanted to make the man proud of him, for he had the feeling that Master Crispin didn't suffer fools, and neither did Jack.

Crispin had said that Lady Vivienne would go to the Spur, an inn on Friday Street. Jack made his way there with no hesitation.

He held his chin up. For once, he was not skulking in the shadows, creeping upon his prey. He was walking in the clear light of day, taking in the passersby, watching curiously as boys—some his age, some younger—worked furiously for their masters by fetching water, carrying heavy loads, or sat crouching over tables and working their nimble fingers on some intricate trade.

The smells of the mid-morning wafted around him. Smells of cooking fires, dead fish, horse dung, sweet hay, wet wool, and roasted meats, all swirling together in an odor that said "London." Church bells began to chime, each claxon making its own unique sound, but all telling him it was terce, well before noon. He squinted up toward the gray sky but it was overcast and offered very little in the way of warm sunshine.

From West Cheap he turned down Friday Street and slowed as he neared the inn. A painted wooden spur hung from an iron hanger right before the inn door and Jack scanned the street around him. It was a strange thing, this task. For always before, he felt he was a little bit invisible. By necessity he had worked hard not to be noticed. But for some reason, now he felt gilded with a motely of colors, as if all eyes were upon him and knew what he was about. He tucked his hood down almost over his eyes and shuffled in place, kicking at a stone and stuffing his hands into his sleeves for warmth.

Don't be daft, Jack. No one's looking at you any more than they ever did.

He warily stole a look out from under his hood and saw that it was true. No one paid him any heed. He was just a boy, after all. What mischief could he be up to? Drawing his hands from his sleeves he adjusted his tunic and stalked forward across the dung-littered inn yard as if he belonged there. He crossed the threshold and pushed open the door.

The inn's hall was a riot of noise but the warmth and savory smells of food drew him in further until he was standing beside a table with a group of laughing men. They were enjoying their beakers of ale and spooning pottage from wooden bowls. Jack watched them for a moment, licking his lips, his belly growling, before he lifted his gaze to the rest of the hall. Tables and stools, all occupied with mostly men in traveling clothes. Some nuns sat off to the side and kept to themselves, their veils hiding most of their faces in shadow. Some other women in cloaks and sturdy gowns laughed alongside their male companions with bright eyes and smiles on their faces. Gowns in blues and cheerful crimson, yellow stockings, green cotehardies, gaily embroidered houppelandes. It reminded Jack of colorful chickens clucking in a barnyard.

He moved slowly through them, itching to cut a purse that was so carelessly hanging outside a cloak, or nab those laid on a table without a protective hand covering them. He pulled himself up short. He was here for a purpose, one Master Crispin had set him to and he was going to perform it as best he could. He rubbed his palms instead, keeping them occupied.

He listened as he moved, wondering if he'd catch some word or phrase that could help him. But it seemed a futile move, for nothing told him of Lady Vivienne. What made Master Crispin think she would come here?

He went to the stairwell and stood at the bottom. A gallery above the hall wound about three sides. Doors were tucked up there in the smoky gloom but they told him nothing.

He scanned the room again and caught sight of a familiar cloak on feminine shoulders. Just as Master Crispin had said. How had he known?

Jack moved back into the shadows of a pillar. He watched Lady Vivienne move away from the fire and go to the stairs. With her skirts raised, she walked up the treads and made her way to the second door on the gallery. She tried the handle but it was locked. Putting a finger to her lips, she turned suddenly, her cloak and skirts whirling out around her, and she descended the stairs and caught the sleeve of a man that Jack soon reckoned was the innkeeper. She talked quietly to him for a long time. He seemed disinclined to something she asked until she reached into the money pouch at her side and handed him a coin. He bowed and led the way up the stairs to the locked room, took a set of keys from a ring hanging from his belt, and unlocked the door. In she went. The innkeeper did not follow, but looked about shiftily before retreating down the stairs.

Jack hesitated. Should he follow? But wouldn't she notice him if he did?

A moment later she emerged and Jack thanked the saints for staying him. She walked all the way down the stairs and through the hall to the front door whereupon she passed through it to the outside.

Jack rose swiftly and followed, pushing the door slowly and peering through the slim opening before he stepped out himself. She was making fierce strides down the lane and Jack scrambled to keep an eye on her from a good distance behind. He side-stepped a gaggle of geese. One stretched out its long neck to snap its bill at him and he got out of its way just in time. "Sarding gander," he murmured, looking back.

A misty rain was falling and Jack tugged his hood up over his head, blinking the droplets from his lashes. Her pace was furious, as if she might be late for an appointment, and Jack followed some steps behind.

Once she looked back, and Jack whirled on his heel. He bent to pick up a bundle of sticks and hoisted it to his shoulder, pretending to walk into the nearest shop with it.

"Oi!"

He looked up at the man with the cart full of sticks, gesturing to him.

"What do you think *you're* doing?"

Jack gently placed the sticks where he found them. "Naught, good Master. I, er...farewell."

"Knave!" the man yelled, but Jack sprinted away around a corner. He stopped and slammed against the wall of a shop before peering back. No one was after him. Glancing forward, Vivienne was getting farther ahead so he pushed himself away and trailed after.

I wonder what is it I'm supposed to see, Jack mused. This tracking was more complicated than he thought.

They were traveling down Old Fish Street toward Trinity. The city was fully awake, and Jack blended in as he always had, walking just behind a man pushing a cart full of onions and turnips. He provided good cover as the avenue widened at Walbrook Street.

Vivienne turned down it and Jack lost the man with the cart but picked up the shadow of three monks traveling together.

Vivienne continued to march down the street until she turned again at Ropery. She seemed to be heading toward another inn, the Bell, by the wooden sign hanging before it. When she slipped inside Jack hurried. He got through the door and looked around hurriedly just in time to spy her up on the gallery with a key in hand and opening a door. Her room, he assumed.

Well then. What was he to do now? Master Crispin had told him to keep an eye on her and so he decided to wait. He looked about the place and found a stool near the fire and settled in, leaning the stool back until he rested his shoulders against the wall. Travelers and tradesmen sat in groups at the long tables, drinking, talking, or just eating by themselves. One appeared to be a rich cleric of some sort, all bedecked in the colorful robes of his office. He was hand-feeding a sleek greyhound sitting elegantly on the floor beside him.

Jack licked his lips and felt the emptiness in his belly again. Maybe just one purse. One purse from some unsuspecting drunkard would do, so he could get a meal.

Eyes keen, he began to examine the crowd for a likely victim. A drunken man to his right staggered to his feet and pulled out some coins. One fell to the floor and his shuffling feet kicked it beneath the table. Jack watched and waited. The man didn't notice, paid his bill, and shambled away.

The moment he was gone, Jack dove for it and pinched the silver between his fingers. A penny. He could buy pottage and ale for that, and he looked anxiously for the innkeeper before signaling to him.

Jack settled in. He'd eaten his bowl of soup, scraping the last bit with the wooden spoon, and wiped his mouth with his sleeve, nursing the ale in its wooden beaker. He kept half an eye on Lady Vivienne's room and the other on the rest of the hall. Men came and went. Others went to their rooms briefly and stomped out of them again. But Lady Vivienne's door remained shut.

Leaning against the wall, Jack waited. He took out his small knife and picked his teeth with the blade's tip. The innkeeper eyed him, but otherwise he went unmolested.

But after some hours passed, Jack squirmed. He'd never had to stay in one spot for so long. What did Master Crispin want, anyway?

He stood and stretched…and spied a man whose money pouch was there for the taking. He looked like a student or perhaps a law clerk, the type of young man with patches on his sleeves but with eloquent words on his tongue. His pouch was small and likely mostly empty, but it hung nearly on his back and he was in deep conversation with another of his ilk at the table.

Jack slid his gaze about the room and straightened his stool. No one was watching. The few customers in the hall were busy in their own conversations and Jack had been there for so long, no one even took heed of him any longer.

Certainly he had the time for it, he thought, snatching one last look up the stairs to Lady Vivienne's solidly closed door.

Slipping gently off his stool he moved closer to the student, pretending to dust off his tunic. He leaned over to tug up his sagging stocking, and while he was low, he raised his knife and swiped at the pouch's ties. The pouch fell neatly into his waiting hand. Standing up again, he pivoted to return to his seat when he smacked into the chest of a solid individual behind him. A tall, lean man in dark colors looked down at him. A scar pulled up an edge of his mouth and traveled up his face nearly to his eye.

Jack staggered back but the man shot out a hand and closed it over his shoulder. "How kind of you to retrieve that poor man's money pouch," he said in accented English.

Jack stiffened, especially when the hand squeezed hard on the bone.

The man kicked the student, who flashed angry eyes at him and rose, looking at the man askance. "Why do you kick, sir?"

His friends rose, too, and squared off with the Frenchman, for that was what Jack perceived him to be. After all, he had seen him before, and his gut chilled from the remembering.

The man smiled. "This boy retrieved your money pouch. You dropped it."

The student instantly put a hand to his belt and, feeling nothing there, glared down at Jack. Jack proffered the pouch, not knowing what else to do.

The student grabbed it from Jack's fingers and gripped it tightly. "Thanks, boy." He stared at Jack and Jack, frightened to do anything else, stared back.

"Should you not reward the boy for his honesty?" asked the tall Frenchman.

Sneering and clearly not wishing to do so, the student reached into his tightly cinched pouch and rummaged for a long time until he finally removed a farthing. He stuck his hand out toward Jack. "Here," he said. "God keep you."

Jack didn't hesitate to close his fingers on it. He bowed and nodded his head. "Thank you, sir. Bless you, sir."

The Frenchman let him go at last and stepped back. The others seated themselves again and resumed their conversation, albeit a bit cautiously.

Jack shrank away from the dark man. But the Frenchman winked at him, his scar whitening as he offered a half smile, before he stalked to the stairs and trotted upward. He knocked on Vivienne's door and when she opened it, she startled back upon seeing him. Jack watched as she exchanged a few quiet words before allowing him to enter.

The student was still glaring, and so Jack retreated to the back of the inn into the gloom. He could still watch the room from there, while keeping out of sight of the suspicious student.

After a brief time, the Frenchman emerged from the room and trotted back down the stairs and out the inn's door. Jack stayed in his corner a long time, until his bladder told him he needed to find a privy.

Out the door he went and toward the back of the stables when someone nabbed him by his hood and spun him around.

The Frenchman with the scar leaned close. "Don't I know you, boy?" He looked Jack over as he quivered in the man's grip. "Ah yes, I remember. Such a brave boy you are. So valiant. A proper squire, are you not? A fitting squire for such a knight." He chuckled at his own joke, before he peered closely, too close. "But, of course, your master is no longer a knight, is he? You must tell your master this: that I have not forgotten him. Oh no. Not at all. Eh, boy?"

Suddenly, he released Jack and he fell backward into the muddy hay of the courtyard. The Frenchman smirked and strode away, not looking back.

Trembling, Jack remembered well that man. He was the man who had held Master Crispin captive before Jack had led the rescue.

Jack looked down at his braies with shame. He no longer needed the privy.

CHAPTER NINETEEN

With the cell door closed and bolted behind him, Crispin experienced a raw chill of recollection.

Stephen sat on the wooden pallet, knees up and arms wrapped around his legs. He stared blankly into the cold hearth. The chiseled window allowed for a little gray light but made the room cold. "What do you want now?" Stephen snarled. "I thought I was free of you."

"It is none too comfortable, is it?"

Stephen glared at Crispin but said nothing.

"You will grow accustomed to it. I did. I, too, awaited judgment. You, of course, *will* die for this murder and justice will be served at last."

Stephen's face lay in shadow and his voice arose equally dark. "You will never succeed in this."

"I already have."

"You are spineless, Guest. They should have drawn and quartered you. They should have pulled out your worthless guts and set them ablaze before your eyes."

Crispin's mouth slanted in a crooked smile. "But they didn't. Perhaps God spared me for this day."

"How were you ever made a knight? Whose wife did you lay with to smooth the way of your pardon?"

Crispin grabbed Stephen's shirt and hauled him up. Nose to nose, he took a ragged breath and then another before he finally released him. Stephen fell back on the pallet and laughed, shaking his head. "You poor bastard. Even in revenge you fail. For if I am convicted, it will be for murder, while you will always be known as a traitor."

Crispin's fingers whitened on his dagger. He stepped back and took a cleansing breath. "And yet, your sister will be my wife. And all of your lands will be mine. When you are dead, it will be as if you never were. Consider that."

Stephen looked up only to sneer at him.

"The sheriff sent me to ask you questions."

"The both of you can go to Hell."

"I've already been there." Crispin kept his distance. "If you will not answer my questions, Sir Stephen, how can I help you? The sheriff will then ask, and his methods are far more unrefined."

"You? Help me? You must think me a fool. Anything I tell you will be twisted and used to destroy me."

"I see you still have no inkling about my character."

"I know a traitor when I see one."

The words stung, but Crispin only smiled in reply, the kind of smile reserved for menials. "Let us not dwell on history. Such is past and done. Today we talk of you. Of murders and of... other adventures. When I discovered you, you were being pursued. Your hands had been bound. Shall we begin there?"

Stephen rubbed his wrists. "Yes, why not?" Crispin watched him carefully. Stephen appeared to be weighing his words. "I was abducted. Held hostage for two days."

"Indeed. By whom?"

Stephen opened his mouth then closed it. He paused before starting again. "By disreputable men."

"What did they want?"

The knight laughed, a sound like crumpled parchment. "To torture me."

"Is that all they wanted?"

153

"No. They wanted something they thought I possessed. For a while I convinced them I didn't have it."

"And how did you accomplish that?"

"By telling them *you* had it."

Crispin pushed away from the wall and drew his knife. "You bastard. *You* set them on me!"

Stephen smiled broadly and leaned back against the wall. "I suppose I did. I take it you were also not in possession of this object. Did they torture you, too? I would have liked to have seen that."

Crispin felt his hand clench tighter around the dagger hilt. He took a breath. Took another. He tapped the flat of the blade against his other hand and quickly sheathed it. "What did they seek?"

"I am uncertain."

"No you're not. They seek the Holy Grail."

Stephen's smile dimmed and he scrambled to his feet. Crispin touched his dagger and stepped back, but Stephen did not draw near him. His face changed. The skin paled to a sickly gray. "God's toes, Crispin!" He trembled. "They hinted at such but I never believed...I couldn't! Does it...is it real?"

Taken aback, Crispin lowered his hand from his weapon. He angled slightly away from the knight but kept him within his field of vision. "I know not. I have yet to see it."

"Christ!" Stephen raked his hair with his fingers. His haughty bitterness lay forgotten. "I thought them insane, asking over and over. I could tell them nothing. How could I say? It's the stuff of legends, is it not?"

"Do you know who they were?"

"No."

Crispin eyed him, looking for any sign of deception, annoyed he couldn't find any. "It is rumored they are Clement VII's men."

Stephen's eyes widened.

"The anti-pope. Apparently they want the grail. The knight you killed, Gaston D'Arcy, was the cup bearer, the keeper of the grail.

Everyone assumed you took it after you killed him."

"Cup bearer? What riddle is here? You say Gaston D'Arcy was a *Knight Templar*?" Crispin nodded. Stephen sat and dropped his head in his hands. He said nothing for a long time. Crispin waited.

"A *Templar*!" Stephen spat. "A *Templar* indeed!"

"Tell me what you argued about."

With his head still resting on his palms, Stephen shook his head. "There is nothing further to say."

"You are a whoreson, but you are no idiot. Tell me!"

Stephen raised his head. "I repeat: Go to Hell."

Crispin nodded. "Then you are a fool. And you *will* hang."

"Then so be it."

Crispin turned and knocked on the door. "Gaoler! I am done here." When the door swung open he glanced once more at Stephen. "And so are you."

The door slammed on the knight and Crispin smiled with grim satisfaction, but the smile remained only briefly. The sense of triumph he expected fell short.

Crispin returned to the sheriff in his chamber. Wynchecombe did not gloat, or at least his expression did not show it. "Well?"

Crispin sighed. "He told me nothing."

The sheriff sat back and pressed his fingertips together. "Are you satisfied?"

Crispin shook his head. "My lord, I must leave now."

"Don't let me stop you."

Crispin would never understand the sheriff. Here was a puzzle of great import and he had no interest whatsoever in any of its intricacies. Did he not wish to know who captured and detained Stephen, the same who did so to Crispin? Had he no curiosity at all about the grail? Be myth or reality, dangerous men sought it, were willing to kill for it. Wynchecombe didn't care. If it didn't fall within his usual sphere of rogue, cutpurse, or murderer, he had no use for it.

Quickly, before he changed his mind, Crispin scraped the coins from the table into his hand. No use letting them go to waste. With a curt bow to hide his embarrassment, Crispin took his leave. He dropped the coins into his money pouch on his way down the stairs, and soon finally stood outside the prison. He looked up, scanned the walls. His eyes lit momentarily on each slotted window in the gate tower. Stephen's cell would be the one on the far left overlooking Newgate's sewage run-off that slipped in green tendrils toward the Fleet.

Why was Stephen so stubborn? What did he hide? He had concentrated so tightly on events surrounding Gaston D'Arcy and the grail that he'd quite forgotten to ask about Vivienne. No matter. Stephen was going nowhere and there would be time enough to discover what Lady Stancliff and Stephen had in common, as well as the subject of Stephen's earnest conversation with Rosamunde.

Rosamunde. He wondered if there would ever come a day when he thought of her name without a pang of longing in his heart.

He tried, with little success, to think of her in the abstract all the way back to his lodgings. When his boot touched the bottom step, he paused. Visions of Rosamunde fled.

A man. He felt more than saw him in the shadows at the top of the landing. It wasn't Jack, but that was all he knew. The landing above creaked and confirmed what his gut told him.

He braced himself against the railing, held his breath and shot up the stairs like a quarrel from a crossbow. The man had no time to escape—where was he to go?—and Crispin pinned him against the wall so hard the plaster gave way and flecked on the man's shoulders. The man groaned and hung his head.

"You have to the count of three to tell me who you are," Crispin rasped, cocking his fist at the man's eye level. "One...two...thr—"

"Hold! Hold! I am the sheriff's man!"

Crispin's gnarled fist remained near the man's face. "Say again."

"I am the Lord Sheriff's man!"

"Why have you been following me?"

"I was under orders." His gaze darted from Crispin's fist, to his face, and back again.

"Orders?"

"To follow you. My Lord Sheriff did not trust you to find Sir Stephen and report it immediately."

Crispin clenched his fist, wanting now more than ever to mash it into the man's face, but it was really Simon Wynchecombe he wanted before him.

He lowered his hand, released the man's shirt and stepped back. "Then your charge is done," he said coldly. "Get back to your master and never let me see you again."

"Aye," he grumbled. He straightened his cotehardie and skirted warily past Crispin down the stairs.

Crispin heaved a sigh and ran his hand through his hair. "Damn the man," he hissed, thinking of Wynchecombe and his suspicions. He took another breath to relax and lifted the key from his pouch. He pushed the door open, but stopped on the threshold, neck tingling.

Too late he sensed the men in the room. They dragged him forward, and slammed the door shut behind him.

CHAPTER TWENTY

The hearth had burned down to an undulating sea of red embers. Crispin could not see the men clearly. They moved like phantoms in the ragged light. He counted five men, possibly six. They wrestled him into his chair but did not bind him.

No use in angry protestations. Crispin simply sat where they put him and waited.

"I think you know who we are," said a chillingly familiar voice.

Crispin surprised himself by his composure. "You are the one who flogged me."

The man chuckled and ordered another man to stoke the fire. The room remained quiet except for the sounds of wood being moved. Sticks cracked over a knee and landed on the red coals. A man knelt and blew on the embers. It lit his profile and reflected on his cheeks and nose, giving him an uncanny resemblance to a demon. The coals awakened and ignited the sticks. White smoke curled around the man's still indistinguishable features and drifted in dispersing billows into the room. Someone stacked another square of peat onto the shimmering flames and illuminated the rest of the shadows, revealing the five men who stood along the perimeter.

One man leaned toward Crispin. An old scar ran from his left eyelid down to his lip, raising it slightly and revealing his white teeth. A face to the voice. "Now you see us," he said.

"I see you." He scanned the rough faces of the others. Many wore day-old beards and some sported bruises on their chins and around their eyes. Those were probably the men he encountered when rescuing Stephen. "What now?"

"It has occurred to me that you were unaware of the nature of the object which we seek."

"Indeed. What has this to do with me?"

The man smiled. His scar reddened and seemed to smile, too. "Are we to play games?"

"Why should I play games with the anti-pope's men?"

"Anti-pope?" The man straightened and toyed with the long chain that hung over the breast of his elaborately patterned cotehardie. The coat gleamed blood red in the firelight. The tippet sleeves dragged along the floor almost meeting his long-toed slippers.

The man's dark hair framed his face in its coifed perfection; fringe perfectly straight, ends of his brown locks curled inward. His men, however, were dressed like monks in long, dark robes that hid—Crispin was certain—their armor. "He is the rightful successor of Peter duly elected by the cardinals. You would call his holiness Clement VII the 'anti-pope'? You should be flogged for such insolence. And yet…." He chuckled again. "You already have been."

"Yes," said Crispin. "I have been. So what now? You know I do not have the grail so why trouble me?"

"The grail?" The man pretended to examine his manicured fingernails and flicked them once before returning his attention to Crispin. "So you *do* know."

"Come, sir. I tire of this. Begin the torture, if you will. My patience for talking has expired."

"I told you. We have not come to torture." He approached the fire and warmed his hands in its amber glow. "My name is Guillaume de Marcherne. I know you have never heard of me. I, on the other hand, have heard a great deal about you since our last encounter."

"Oh? Am I expected to be flattered?"

De Marcherne smiled. The scar lifted it higher. "You are a brave one. One wonders how you withstood the shame of your dishonor; how you continue to live despite the humiliation that must be repeated in a thousand different ways each day."

The men in the shadowy perimeter laughed in low growls.

Crispin smiled. "And yet, I am not the one working for the anti-Christ."

De Marcherne frowned for the first time. He walked to the coffer by the door and sat, facing Crispin. "Let me tell you a tale, then you may decide if I am in the employ of the 'anti-Christ' or not."

"Everyone wants to tell me a tale," Crispin grumbled. He shrugged. "Well, why not?"

De Marcherne settled on the chest and leaned forward, resting his fists on his thighs. "When our lord Pope Gregory died in 1378—*requiescat in pace*—" he becrossed himself—"the cardinals assembled in conclave in the papal palace in Rome. Immediately there was an uproar in the city. Bells in every tower rang out and the people clambered up the palace steps and overtook the guards. Some entered the precincts and, with a force of hundreds, demanded the cardinals elect a Roman or Italian pope. What could they do, poor clerics that they were? They feared for their lives. Forthwith, they elected Edwin, Bishop of Bari. They believed, under the circumstances, that he would reject the vote, telling the mob that popes are not elected by the threats of criminals and villains. But much to their chagrin, he did not decline their hasty election. He allowed Man's frail ambition to sway him to the detriment of his soul. He all but seized the crown and the seat of Peter. Can you blame the cardinals for retiring to a safe haven outside Rome to set things aright? Even after Robert of Geneva was hailed the new pope, Bishop Edwin would not step down. It is he who is responsible for the divisions we now see in Christendom, not Clement VII."

Crispin frowned. "I know all that. I do not pretend to be a

theologian. Far from it. But there has never been precedent for putting aside a pope, whether that election was under pressure of malice or not. Perhaps it is the Holy Ghost who moved the mob to make the very decision the cardinals deride. Who can say?"

"Men with more knowledge of Church matters, Master Guest. Not dispossessed knights."

"And just who are you, my Lord de Marcherne? A tool of the anti-pope, or of the King of France? Or both?"

De Marcherne waved his hand and leaned his arm against the bedpost. "Does it matter? I am here to make a proposal."

"Indeed. I do not care for your kind of proposals, my lord." Even though the flesh began to heal, Crispin still felt the raw soreness inflicted only two days ago.

"This is a proposal you may have difficulty refusing." De Marcherne moved away from the bed and sauntered toward Crispin, squaring with him. "We wish to hire you."

Crispin did not even try to stop the spitting guffaw that left his lips. "Hire me? You jest!"

"Indeed, no. I fail to understand your reaction. By the looks of things—" De Marcherne glanced about the mean room—"you could use the money."

"Go to Hell," said Crispin.

De Marcherne slowly turned. His scar seemed to redden. He tapped the pommel of his sword and stared down his considerable nose at Crispin. "You do not even know why I wish to hire you."

"I would never work for the anti-pope. Despite your eloquence, I do not believe Robert of Geneva's right to the seat of Peter."

"Whoever said you would be working for the anti-pope?"

"Are you not his tool?"

"There is much you do not know about me." He made a gesture to one of his men who fetched the wine jug. Before Crispin could say it was empty, he watched the man pour red wine into the two wooden bowls he owned. The man handed one first to de Marcherne and the second to Crispin.

Crispin took it but did not drink.

"Go ahead, Master Crispin. It is good wine."

Crispin looked into the wine cup. The berry aromas wafted up his sharp nose. He smiled a crooked smile. "There was recently a man poisoned from wine. Perhaps you know of him. Gaston D'Arcy."

"D'Arcy was a fool and very sloppy. He deserved to die. Do you think we intend to poison you?"

Crispin's smile did not fade. "Did you kill him?"

"You already have a man in gaol for this heinous crime. Do you doubt your own work now?"

"No. I merely wondered. He could have had an accomplice."

De Marcherne laughed and gestured with the cup again. "Drink."

Crispin's smile widened. "You first."

De Marcherne grinned, saluted with the cup, and drank heartily. Wine dribbled down the side of his mouth where it met the bowl. With a flourish he swept the bowl away from his lips and made a satisfied exhale. "Excellent. French, of course."

With a shrug, Crispin put the bowl to his lips and downed the cup. He barely tasted it, but the residual flavor on his tongue spoke of the wine's good character. Better than he had tasted in a long while. "You are correct. It is good wine. For French stock."

De Marcherne laughed. "You are an amiable man, Master Crispin. I regret my earlier treatment of you. Shall we be more civilized now?" He walked toward the bed and sat on it. He held the bowl out for his man to refill.

Crispin did likewise and this time took a smaller sip.

"No, you would not be working for His Holiness, Master Crispin, but for me. I am...how would you say...a free agent. I work for myself and for whoever is the highest bidder."

"Then why do you need me?"

"You are an accomplished investigator. They call you the Tracker." He smiled, amused by the title. "And this item is most definitely in need of tracking."

The bowl stopped short of Crispin's lips. "What item?"

"The Holy Grail, of course."

Crispin hesitated, then brought the cup to his lips and drank the entire contents again. He wiped his mouth with the back of his hand and set the wooden bowl aside. "This is a very popular occupation for me of late."

"Oh? Who else? Ah. I see. D'Arcy's compatriots have gotten to you."

Crispin said nothing. He kicked back, balancing his chair on its hind legs.

"These fine and noble Templar knights," de Marcherne purred. "Would you like to know something about them?"

"From you?"

"I have not deceived you as to my nature, Master Guest. I am all you see. Deceitful, hungry, pugnacious, greedy. Qualities found in most knights in most courts, wouldn't you say? I am not like the precious Templars. Their deceit is couched in the odor of sanctity, wrapped in the mantle of piety, and sanctioned by well-wishers everywhere. The Templars want nothing more than to rule and dominate and they use goodhearted dupes such as you to accomplish their goals. But do not take my word for it. Discover for yourself the character of Gaston D'Arcy. Why don't you ask Lady Stancliff?"

Crispin's face remained neutral. The chair settled on all four legs again. "Lady Stancliff?"

"You know the lady in question. My operatives tell me that you know her...very well indeed."

"I warn you. Do not delve into my privacy."

"Privacy? For such a public lady? A lady whose indiscretions span the court? Ask her what she had to do with the pious Gaston D'Arcy. Ask her. Then ask her about Stephen St Albans. There are more paramours, but we do not have that much time." He chuckled but there was little mirth behind it. "Perhaps the lady knows the grail's whereabouts."

Crispin's strained fingers clutched his knees. Her vulnerability did seem a little too studied, a little too convenient. He suddenly

163

felt the fool.

"*Mon Dieu!*" De Marcherne laughed. "I did not burst any bubbles, did I? You are not in love with her, are you?"

"I am under no delusions as concerns Lady Stancliff."

"Good. Then I suggest you ask her about the grail. Or would you rather *I* ask her?"

A chill ran down Crispin's spine. Wily she may be, but he did not relish the thought of Vivienne enduring de Marcherne's kind of query.

"What say you, Crispin? Make a pact with me to find the grail? I will make it worth your while."

"I am already being paid to find it."

"But when you find it for them," he said, leaning closer, "you must surrender it. Find it for me and there will be no reason to. Think Crispin. There are forces here far greater than we. If you covet the return of your knighthood, if you believe that without it you are only half a man, you will do this. The grail can recover everything for you."

Crispin tried to shut it out. It was true, then, that the Devil knew your greatest weakness and could use it to tempt you.

He wondered how much he owed to the Templars. Wynchecombe did not care if the grail was recovered or not because he did not believe in its existence. Legend, myth. Who could truly say what the grail was or who it belonged to?

"It is not treason when one works for the greater good," continued de Marcherne. "How foolish are the English. They do not perceive your value. Come to the French court and your knighthood and all that goes with it will be restored."

"If I find the grail and give it to you?"

"Yes. Simple."

Crispin rubbed his chest. "You could have asked before. Why didn't you?"

De Marcherne sipped his wine. "When one is accustomed to certain methods it is hard to change. As I said, I do regret my earlier treatment of you."

"I work for a fee of one shilling a day, plus expenses."

"You work for sixpence a day. But I will pay you twelve." He motioned to one of the men who handed him a pouch. "Here is a sennight's worth in advance."

Crispin looked at the pouch but did not take it. "What if I don't find it? What if it falls to another?"

De Marcherne smiled, took Crispin's hand, and placed the pouch within it. "Don't disappoint me."

CHAPTER TWENTY-ONE

Crispin looked up from his wax slate when Jack returned early the next morning,

"Ah. Jack. What have you to tell me?"

Jack stood before Crispin, pulling on the hem of his tunic. "Well, Master. I followed Lady Stancliff like you told me."

"And?"

Jack moved to the fire and warmed his hands. He turned and aimed his backside at the hearth and rubbed that, too. "She went to the Spur just like you said she would. She went to the room at the top of the gallery but it was locked. Then she went and fetched the tavern keeper. When she entered that room upstairs, I could no longer see her, but it did not take her long to come out."

"Did she have anything in her hands?"

"No, master. Naught that I could see."

He nodded and resumed drawing. "Continue."

"After that, I followed her to another inn: the Bell on Ropery. That is where she is lodged. But then, before I left…she had a visitor."

"Oh? Who was it?"

The boy hesitated. "I… I did not know him. But he was a gentleman. He was tall and dark and he had a scar going up from his mouth to his eye."

Crispin froze. "Did you hear him speak?"

166

"Aye. He was a Frenchman."

"What happened?"

"She was surprised to see him. Unpleasantly so, but it was clear she knew him. But she welcomed him in."

"And then?"

"Naught. For about half past. And then he left. Alone." Jack hesitated and ran his hand up the back of his neck. He sensed the boy wished to say more, but though he waited, Jack remained silent.

Crispin did not press the matter. "If you ever see that man again, Jack, fetch me. And stay clear of him. He is very dangerous." He eased back into the chair. "You have done very well. Now bring us both some wine."

Jack scrambled to the larder and pulled down the jug. He brought the bowls to Crispin's table and offered him a cup.

Casually, Crispin said, "I had a visit yesterday from the anti-pope's men."

Jack froze. "Jesus mercy! What did you do?"

"Not much but listen. Their leader, one Guillaume de Marcherne, hired me to find the grail."

"After they'd gone and flogged you? Madness!"

"Yes. Of a sort. But it did give me pause."

"You aren't going to work for no anti-pope, are you, Master?"

He shook his head. "By the way, de Marcherne has a very distinctive feature: a scar running up from his mouth to his eye."

Jack seemed less than surprised but kept his lips shut up tight.

Crispin said no more and hid his thoughts in his wine bowl. Jack pondered quietly and finally sidled up to him and glanced sideways at the drawings on the wax slate. He took a swallow from his own cup and said, "I've been thinking about all this," said Jack quietly.

"'All this'?" asked Crispin, jotting down more notes.

"Aye. This tracking you do. That I done for you. I took a nice long time to think about it. About all them people mixed up in this murder. And I think I've come to some ideas, beggin' your pardon."

Crispin set down his quill and did his best to repress a smile. "Have you, now. I'd like to hear."

"Well…" Jack straightened his disreputable tunic and, much like a minstrel launching into a song, he postured and began. "The way I see it, it's all mixed up, isn't it? All them people coming and going. They can't all be involved. So I carved it down to bits and pieces. Seems easier to think of it all in that way."

Crispin sharpened his gaze. "How very enterprising."

"First, you got this Vivienne woman—"

"*Lady* Stancliff."

"As you will. *Lady* Stancliff—wanting you to find some fellow who has some fine thing she'd like to get a hold of. Then there's Stephen St Albans, a knave if there ever was one. Then this vile, devil of a man—what did you call him? G-Guillaume de Marcherne." He shuddered. "He abducts you and treats you right foully. He wants the sarding Holy Grail, of all things… Who am I forgetting?"

"You've done very well," said Crispin, surprised. "I was unaware of your talent for juggling information."

"Oh aye," said Jack, ignoring Crispin's compliment. "Them Templars. I don't trust them. Why you hold such store by them I do not know. Perhaps it is the unwariness of noblemen." Crispin frowned at that. "And so. I've come to some conclusions, as I said."

"I am all ears."

"First of all, I'm not so certain there is a grail."

Flicking extra wax from the nib of the quill, Crispin stopped to look at Jack. "Why would you say that?"

"I'm just saying. All these men certain it exists yet who has actually seen it?"

Crispin raised a brow of amusement. "Then let us say, for the sake of argument that the grail exists."

"Well then. This is the list of people that seek it," Jack said, ticking them off on his fingers. "The Templars, of course.

Guillaume de Marcherne of the anti-pope's camp—the foul devil— and Lady Stancliff... And you." Jack offered the last timidly.

"Yes. I am hired to return it to one of these." He scratched a word onto the slate. "But Sir Stephen says he knows nothing of the grail. He admitted that he did not even know D'Arcy was a Knight Templar. He could be lying, of course...."

"Ah! Then I would remove his name from the hunt for the grail. So *that* means he didn't kill no one for no grail."

Crispin nodded.

"So if Sir Stephen didn't want the grail," Jack continued, "then why did he kill him?"

"That has yet to be seen, for he will not say." He tapped the slate with the quill nib. "By Lady Stancliff's actions, it appears she well knew of D'Arcy's Templar history but believes, for some reason, that the grail belongs to her, and may stop at nothing to get it. She is a woman of questionable character."

Nodding, Jack fingered the edge of the slate. "That sounds like you might be blaming her for the murder."

"I very well might be."

"But Master! What of Sir Stephen?"

"It does not remove the possibility that they worked together."

"But you said Sir Stephen knew naught of the grail."

"Lady Stancliff can be very persuasive."

Jack whistled. "Aye. You have not yet mentioned about Lady Rothwell. You were hired to find her brother and find him you did."

"Yes. She was seen arguing with Sir Stephen during the time she said he was missing. Obviously, he was missing for far less time than she admitted. She must have feared something in that brief disappearance. Yet she, too, was seen talking to D'Arcy."

"How does she know him?"

He shook his head. "She will not say. She says it is a private matter."

"The grail?"

"I know not."

"There's something I left out. What of the dead apothecary, Rupert of Kent? I think he was killed to silence him."

"Very good, Jack." Crispin drew another line on the slate. "Rupert was indeed killed for that reason so that the identity of the person to whom he sold the poison would remain a secret."

"How about the dagger that killed him?"

"It was of very ordinary origin. It was even possibly owned by Rupert himself. No clue there."

Jack studied the slate and cocked his head, sipping his wine. "So what's this you're at, sir?"

Crispin chuckled at the boy's audacity. "It is a diagram of what transpired so far and those involved. It's everything you just talked about."

"God blind me!" Jack stared at the slate with renewed interest, though Crispin knew he could not read the names.

"You said you came to a conclusion, Tucker. Do you now name a different murderer?"

"Well, sir, you say it is Stephen St Albans but I think it is the anti-pope's men. They are the ones that wanted the grail so badly. For the murderer must know something of the grail as it seems of great import. Whether it exists or not. And as you said, Stephen don't seem to know ought of the grail."

"I see." He eyed Jack with admiration. Not only was Jack greatly skilled with nimble fingers, but his mind seemed equally so. Crispin supposed it would have to be for Jack to have survived on his own in London at so young an age.

Crispin looked at the slate and pushed his hair back from his forehead, flattening the dark locks with his hand. "I thought this list would help. There is still something missing. Something I am forgetting."

Slurping his wine, Jack returned to the fire. "I say that you do not worry further over it. You have captured your murderer and will get your revenge. Either Stephen is lying about the grail or there is no grail. Either way it don't affect you. Forget the grail. Take the money you have and go in hiding for a time until this blows over. You will be in good stead with the sheriff and you will have made some coin from it all. And you will remain alive."

"But what of Rosamunde?"

Caught in mid breath, Jack deflated. "Ah now. The lady. I did not consider…"

"It doesn't matter," he said tossing the slate on the table. "She no longer loves me and will not have me. She said so."

"And Lady Stancliff?"

"Lady Stancliff," he said, though it came out a growl. "I must go to see Lady Stancliff. I need some answers. I'm off to the Bell. Stay by the fire and warm yourself, if you like. You have earned it."

Crispin headed down the lane toward the Bell, never considering what he was going to say. Instead, his emotions took over and bubbled in his chest like a kettle's dancing lid. The feeling of being a cuckold remained strong, though the lady had a husband and only Lord Stancliff had the right to any feelings on the matter. But still. If de Marcherne paid her a call… Crispin thought of that night at the inn when Vivienne met a mysterious man. He was now fairly certain it was de Marcherne.

Crispin talked briefly with the innkeeper and found her chamber door. When he knocked, he heard her voice calling out, expecting a servant.

Crispin entered, closed the door behind him, and leaned against it. "Vivienne."

She whirled. "Crispin!"

He noticed chests and baskets packed and stationed by the door. "Yes, Madam. It's me." He strolled forward and, with a smile, curled his arm around her waist and yanked her hip against him.

She tried to extricate herself. "Crispin. What an unexpected surprise. How did you find me?"

"I am the Tracker. Is a lost lady so difficult?" He nuzzled her neck, sniffing first the aroma of lavender, then perspiration. "Vivienne." He raised his face and kissed her, though he noticed the return of that kiss seemed distracted and less ardent than before. "Since last we met," he whispered and nipped her lips, "I have not been able to get you out of my mind."

She stood stiffly against him with his arms wound tightly around her. "Truly? That is very flattering, though I regret we should have become so entangled. I *am* a married woman."

Crispin drew back to look at her askance. "Surely this should have occurred to you before. It is rumored that I am not the first."

"Well. Rumors…."

"Are you leaving, Madam? I see your baggage is prepared."

She laughed nervously and touched her throat. "I must return to my estates. I have been too long away."

"But the object of great value? Did you find it?"

"Alas, no. I must leave it for now and return at a later time."

His hand inched toward her wrist, grabbed it, and shoved her arm up her back. She cried out but he yanked her hard against him. "What troubles you, sweeting?" he said, teeth clenched. "It did not tax you to be so close to me the last time."

"You are hurting my arm!"

"Am I? It is only to impress upon you the seriousness in which I take my work. Though I was diverted before, I will keep my attention focused this time."

She struggled but could not free herself. In any other circumstance, Crispin might have found such physical contact delightful, but he knew he had to keep his anger in check. He did not wish to inflict any real damage. Not yet.

"So tell me," he said, tightening his grip on her wrist. "Did you find what you were looking for?"

"No. I told you…"

"I hope you do not intend to lie to me further. I have no more patience for it. Tell me again. Do you have the grail?"

"The what?"

"The Holy Grail. Where is it?"

She smiled even in her agitation. "*Holy Grail?* You can't be serious."

"I am extremely serious."

"You thought I sought the Holy Grail? Blessed Virgin!"

Crispin still held her tightly, but now he began to doubt his reasons for doing so. He released her and stepped back. Vivienne lowered her arm and rubbed her wrist.

"What, then? What had you to do with Gaston D'Arcy?"

She raised her shoulders but only to heave a great sigh. She turned from him. "Is it so important?"

"If your neck is at all important to you, for I shall surely break it if you do not say!"

Her lips evened to a tight line. "Gaston D'Arcy was my lover. Is that what you wanted to hear?"

Expected, but it still hurt. "Did you know he was a Templar?"

"No! I knew he was a secret knight, for he kept his armor hidden and I saw the cross upon his surcote, but it was a game to me. Never could I have dreamed..."

"Then what went awry? Did he tire of your promiscuity?"

She delivered a hearty slap to his face. Crispin did not react except to feel the cold sting of her hand and the hot aftermath that radiated outward from his cheek.

"As a matter of fact," she said, resting her fist in her hip, "I tired of *his*."

Her expression appeared defiant, but with an underlying streak of pain, the kind on a child wrongfully punished. Something about it stabbed his heart with empathy. He knew he should say something. He wanted to ask about de Marcherne, but somehow, to utter his name now when she looked so vulnerable, seemed unnaturally cruel. Instead, he said nothing.

He approached slowly. She did not react at first, but allowed his arms to encompass her. Stubbornly, she would not raise her face to his, so he captured her chin between his thumb and forefinger and lifted it. Silver tears glistened on her cheek, darkening her long lashes. Her eyes were her history, written in the pain of almost as many hurts and humiliations as he had suffered.

Her red lips parted. To curse him? He would never know.

Leaning forward, his mouth took possession of hers with unexpected fervor. It did not take long for her arms to encircle his neck, and once they did, *his* arms tightened about her and mashed her breasts against his chest.

He remembered unlacing her gown, and she pushing his shirt out of the way, and very little else but the sweetness of passionate oblivion.

When Crispin awoke, he forgot where he was. He raised his head and noted the darkness of the room. No candle burned and the fire had dispersed to warm ashes.

Wrapped in the sheet and nothing else, Crispin lay for a while. Once the cloud of pleasure dissipated from his head, his memory returned.

A sinking feeling suddenly thumped his gut. "Vivienne?" he called weakly.

But even a cursory look about the room confirmed that she, along with her baggage, had vanished.

Another perusal made Crispin's lips part with dismay. "God's blood!"

All of his clothes were gone as well.

CHAPTER TWENTY-TWO

"It's not like me to say 'I told you so,'" Jack rattled, "but breaking one of the Almighty's commandments never bodes well."

"For God' sake, be still, Jack!" Crispin's angry voice muffled under the shirt he pulled over his head.

"Master Kemp was kind enough to give you them clothes and shoes. A proper payment should be made to him to set things aright."

"Why don't you just 'come by' more of his coins and balance the books!"

"I would, Master, but you told me not... Oh, I see. You are angry with me. Well, don't kill the messenger."

Crispin wrestled with the shirt's laces. "No. I am not angry with you, but with myself." He sat heavily on the end of the bed and pulled on each stocking, tying them to the braies' waistband. "I let myself be duped by a woman!"

"She could not have gotten far."

"The tavern keeper said she left before nightfall."

"Then she would have to stay at an inn or a monastery along the way to her estate, eh, Master Crispin? You said they were near Chelmsford."

"Yes." He yanked on the oversized coat and pulled mercilessly on the buttons. "But I will never be able to catch up to her without a horse and that takes money."

Jack absently brushed the dust from Crispin's shoulder. "There's the money from de Marcherne." Crispin's glare told him that topic was prohibited. "Or...er... you could talk to the sheriff. He might see his way to lending you an animal if it was on the king's business."

Crispin sighed heavily and sat back. His body sagged, crumpling the coat. "That is good advice, Jack. And I must pursue her."

"Aye, Master. This makes me reluctant to tell you that Lady Rothwell has sent a messenger saying she wants to see you."

Crispin dragged his hand over his head and down to the back of his neck. His muscles stiffened and ached. "I am compelled to see her first." What would the boy do now? Stay at Crispin's side? He certainly proved his worth by bringing him some clothes.

"You may...do what you will, I suppose. Er...return to my lodgings, if you wish."

The lad's grateful expression smoothed his own sour temperament.

"Or perhaps go to the sheriff and tell him..."

Jack frowned. "I'd rather not, Master. The sheriff gets me skittery."

"Yes. He gets me equally 'skittery.' But if you will, go ahead of me and wait outside Newgate. I will hurry back as quickly as I can from the White Hart."

Pinched and drawn, Rosamunde's face looked like a mummer's mask. "Crispin. I thank you for coming."

"My lady." He bowed and waited. She wrung her hands and paced. He could hear Jenkyn and her maidservant behind the anteroom's curtain. When Crispin served as a page many years ago, he had ears only for the needs of his master. Any other conversation was sacrosanct, though he could not vouch for the integrity of servants of a lower class. He flicked his gaze toward the still curtains and frowned.

"Yesterday I went to see Stephen," she said.

He thought he could, but when the moment arrived, he could

not look her in the eye. He listened to his own breathing, and felt the strangeness of his feet in borrowed shoes and his body in Martin Kemp's long shirt and coat.

"Oh, Crispin," she whispered. "How could you have done it?"

"The evidence—"

"Damn the evidence. He is my brother. He has done nothing. I know it."

"He knew the dead man, he argued with him, and he was the last to see him alive. There is little left to infer."

"He did not do it. He could not have done," she pleaded, wringing her hands. "Poison, Crispin? You know Stephen well. Would a man of honor use poison?"

"A jury must decide."

"He told me you captured him."

At first it had felt good to apprehend Stephen and escort him to prison; to see him in that cell, a cell similar to the one Crispin resided in all those years ago. It did feel good, but only briefly. Now he stood before Rosamunde like a schoolboy awaiting the rod. He entwined his fingers. "That is so."

"I hate your vengeance. I hate your anger. Is your revenge for me, too? To make me suffer so?"

"A crime was committed."

"And yet you would hang an innocent man."

"He has not proven that!" Crispin jerked away from her scrutiny and stood by the window. The open shutters threw a wash of pale light across the floor before him. "He says nothing. He is as stubborn as you are."

She moved to him and raised her delicate hands. "Once, you loved me. You were even Stephen's bosom friend. We were to be family. All of us. But your selfish, stupid act ruined it all. We barely recovered from it."

"Bless me." He exhaled into the cold air of the open shutter. "What a pity. *You* barely survived. Well. I must say a rosary or two in repentance for that."

"Do not jest…"

"No, indeed. I do not jest. What a pity that your honor barely survived." He turned to her then. "Do you know what living hell I endured for the last seven years? I *starved*, Rosamunde. I took scraps from almoners before I could find some kind of work to feed myself. I slept in church doorways and nearly froze to death. And the very first employment I got—and I was damned lucky to get it—was mucking out latrines for one penny a day. And do you know what I discovered, Rosamunde? Shit is shit no matter who expels it, king or beggar." He tore away from her and walked stiffly across the room.

"After three months of that I became a henchman for a rich burgess. It was my duty to protect him and, on occasion and for extra pay, I beat nearly to death his debtors." He rubbed his knuckles absently, remembering.

"The next year was better. I was a scribe and worked for merchants. They were kind to me, for the most part. I received more generosity from their little gestures than can be found in all of court." He heaved a breath. "I can assure you, my dear lady, that you, too, would muck out a privy if it meant one more day alive. So do not weep over your poor little life. Because I know what it is to hang from the lowest rung."

She shook her head slowly. "I felt so sorry for you once. How bitter you have become."

"Bitter?" He grabbed his hair in frustration and bellowed out a guffaw. "You have a great gift for understatement!"

She pressed her hands together prayerfully and touched her fingertips to her lips. "I asked you here to plead for my brother's life."

He straightened and brushed off his coat. "Why come to me? You would have greater luck petitioning the sheriff."

"I know you. At least, I used to."

"Yes, yes. While your honor suffered so."

"Crispin, please. You know he could not have done it. Surely there are other suspects."

His gaze was steady. "How do you know Gaston D'Arcy?"

"I met him at court."

"And how do you know Lady Stancliff?"

"I told you before. Also from court. We do not know one another well."

"What is it you spoke to D'Arcy about?"

Her hands were still linked in prayer. The skin was white and veined in blue. Her wedding band encircled her left ring finger. "I cannot say."

"Damn you, Rosamunde! I cannot help you unless you speak!"

"There are just some things, Crispin, that cannot be said aloud."

"Yet you said it to him?"

"Try to understand."

"Never, Rosamunde. Never!" Only now he recalled their devilish arguments. Why did he fail to remember that until this moment?

He grabbed his beard-stubbled chin and rubbed it raw. He simply could not stomach deceit. She never hid anything from him before. What was so terrible that she could not say? He wanted it to be the key to the case, but he feared it was only his frustration at being cast aside.

"Then there is nothing more to say. I must go." He reached the doorway and even stepped through it before he made himself stop. Over his shoulder he said, "You are tying the noose about his neck yourself by refusing to say."

"But *you* could stop it, Crispin."

"I will testify at his trial and nothing will stop me then. If he is innocent, then I am certain the jury will find him so. But trouble me no more about it. I have too much work to do."

He stalked forward out of the room, but Jenkyn pushed out from the anteroom curtains and stood in his way. A frown darkened the servant's features and he would not move. His smooth face free of lines belonged to a younger man. He wore his years well. Crispin wanted to say something to the man, wanted to warn him of her unreliable devotion, but in the end he could say nothing out loud. There were no more words for him at the moment; nothing articulate except to growl his sentiments.

Angrily Crispin shoved Jenkyn aside without a word. Outside, he rumbled along the lane. He must get to Newgate. That thought and only that thought drummed in his ears. He hated to ask the sheriff for a mount. What if he refused? Would he be forced to tell him the whole degrading tale? His dagger, purse, and shabby cloak were all Vivienne left him and he pulled that mantle over his chest with a grunt.

"I have to get to Newgate," he grumbled, and felt uncertain relief when it came into view.

A shadowy figure stomped before the walls to keep warm and it suddenly cheered Crispin to see it. He slapped Jack on the back in greeting and told him to wait by the stables. Jack trotted away gratefully, but when Crispin entered Wynchecombe's chamber, the sheriff did not look pleased to see him.

"This writ is done, Crispin," he said over a mound of parchments.

Crispin shook his head reluctantly. "No, my lord. I fear it is not."

"Damn you, Guest! What is it you want? More money? I will not pay."

"My lord, I believe Stephen has an accomplice. I must pursue her, but I need a horse."

"What? Now you want a horse? From my stable?"

Crispin studied his borrowed shoes. They were slightly larger than his own shoes and less worn. He decided he would stuff them with straw the next time he donned them. "As you know, my lord, I no longer own a horse, nor can I afford to hire one."

"How do I know you will bring it back?"

Crispin raised his face.

"Never mind," said Wynchecombe. "I suppose you will berate me until I relent?"

"You are generous, my lord," he said flatly.

"I have not yet said I would agree to this." He furrowed his brow and bristled his mustache in his most sincere expression of displeasure. Hastily he scribbled his name on a writ and thrust it forward. "Here! Get you to the stable and bring back your prisoner, or I swear my oath to the Almighty that I shall lock you in a cell and throw away the key!"

Crispin waved the writ at the stable's guard, relieved the sheriff's man did not choose to argue. He met Jack and the boy watched as he quickly saddled a mare, the only horse the sheriff was willing to give him. "I will take Aldgate. There is a small convent she may be staying in outside of London. She will not expect me to follow."

"And what of me, sir?"

What *of* him? How many days ago now was it that he caught the cutpurse stealing his last bit of money? And now Jack was becoming a permanent feature in his life. It was with a certain amount of irony that he reached into his purse. He gestured to the surprised boy and dropped the coins into Jack's open hand. "Take them. You may need them if I am gone longer than a day. Keep all well in my lodgings."

Jack was momentarily silenced before he was able to rasp a hasty, "Thank you, Master." He held tightly to the bridle. "God keep you, sir. Come back safe and sound." From his tunic he pulled a small loaf of bread and a wedge of cheese. "For your journey, sir."

Crispin took them solemnly and stuffed them into the scrip at his belt. He dared not ask where Tucker got them, for he did not remember such from his own pantry.

He swung up onto the saddle and settled like he used to do on the smooth leather. He grasped the reins and wrapped them about his hand. "I will, Jack." He pulled up on the reins and spun the horse about. He squeezed with his thighs and felt the horse surge ahead over the stony courtyard until he was free of Newgate's confines and headed down Newgate Market to the other end of town toward Aldgate, where he could take a road into the countryside.

London's streets were crowded as they always were, and he maneuvered the beast down narrow lanes clogged with donkey carts and pedestrians. It took less time than he reckoned to reach the gatehouse at Aldgate, he tipped a bow to the guards there, who didn't give him more than a glance.

Once out on the open road, he let the scenery pass him by without much note, and though his mission was a mixed bag of embarrassment and anger, he allowed his thoughts to turn to the pleasant sensation of sitting aloft a horse.

The feel of the horse's gait beneath him, the leather in his hand, and the pungent scent of the animal, was all a salve to his aching heart. Such simple joys. He missed them the most. He almost missed them more than the jousts and the finery and the huge feasts that lasted for hours. And the dancing. An accomplished dancer, Crispin had taken his turn with the women of court and they'd compete for their place with him. He remembered the halls filled with candles. How the smoky galleries above the dance floor would crowd with intimate couples seeking a quiet and discreet place, and how he would find himself there many a time with a willing lady. He missed that, too. He missed the artful games of courting, their subtleties and rules. He missed the masculine camaraderie of knights discussing the lists or a battle.

But the simplest of pleasures like riding his own horse with his own tack tailored to him, were particularly missed.

Perhaps it took his meeting again with Rosamunde to finally believe he would never have those things again. They were gone. As ephemeral as mist.

He stroked the horse's mane and patted the neck while it bobbed with the rhythm of her gait. London fell behind him and gave way to green rolling hills and farmland. Windmills on distant hillocks moved their sweeps sluggishly, like squires flagging down a knight on the lists. The occasional grange house spilled into the view, their rambling stone gates along the road marking their territories. He saw little else but sheep and cows grazing over the hillsides.

By midday, he took a small portion of Jack's bread and cheese from his scrip and nibbled as he rode, letting the horse take his own pace.

He reached the small convent by early evening. The porter at the gatehouse stared uncomprehendingly at the writ Crispin held out for him to see. "If it's the sheriff's business," he said, "then I'll oblige. What is it you want?"

"I am looking for a lady who may or may not be using her true name. She is Lady Stancliff, Vivienne by name."

"Oh, aye. She is here. She is traveling to Chelmsford." He leaned forward bearing a burning cage of coals. Bits of burning embers spit and fell from his cresset. "Are you going to arrest her?"

"I might. Has she an entourage with her?"

"Only two maids and one manservant. But he is older than I. He won't put up much of a fight."

Crispin tightened his hold of the reins. "Then where may I find the lady?"

"Through the arch and to the right. There's a small cottage there near the stewponds. Will you be needing help?" The porter grasped a large staff propped in a corner. "I used to be a fair fighter with the staff in my day."

"I do not think that will be necessary, but I thank you."

Crispin dismounted and tied the horse near the gatehouse arch. On foot he approached the cottage and stealthily made his way to the window. The shutters were barred but he made out the lay of the room through a crack. The hearth light glowed enough for him to see two maids working on the seated Vivienne. Her hair lay unbound from their braids and each maid brushed out a long strand of it like a horse's tail. The light shimmered along her black tresses and fell in feathery layers to her uncovered shoulders, for she wore only her shift.

He smiled. Leaving the window he went to the door and knocked gently.

A maid's muffled voice asked, "Who is there?"

In his best imitation of the porter, Crispin said, "There is a message for your lady."

"Very well," she sighed. "One moment."

He knew they would cover Vivienne with her gown before they would unlatch the door. He pulled the dagger free from its sheath and stood ready.

The bolt lifted and the door opened a crack. Crispin shoved hard and the maid fell over with a squeal. The other screamed and ran to a far corner. Vivienne jumped to her feet and grabbed the nearest object of any weight, an iron poker.

Crispin sheathed the dagger and rushed her. He grabbed the wrist holding the poker and twisted. With a cry she dropped the makeshift weapon to the floor. The maids rushed out screaming into the night and when they did, he lunged for the door and bolted it after them.

With a snort he stood back to gaze at Vivienne. Her gown fell open exposing the light shift beneath. He fondly recalled touching all the curves and valleys revealed by the shift's transparency, until he also remembered in what manner she left him.

"Surprised?" He sat in her chair.

She inhaled deeply and strolled to the hearth, all the while rubbing her wrenched wrist. "Indeed. I did not think you had a horse."

His smile was not meant to comfort, and by her pale expression he could tell it did not offer it. "We have unfinished business."

"Do we? I said all I intended to say."

"I believe you have something of mine."

A ghost of a smile raised one corner of her mouth. "Yes. I do." She moved to the chest and opened it. Neatly folded, she took out Crispin's clothes.

He took them without ceremony and tucked them beside him in the chair. "I am obliged to you for not taking my belt with its dagger and money pouch."

"I am not a monster, after all."

His lips curled but not to smile. "No indeed. Let us begin, then, where we left off. What is it you sought from Gaston D'Arcy?

What is this 'object of great price'?"

"Well it certainly is not the Holy Grail." She relaxed and leaned against the wall. She did not try to close the gap of her gown.

At first, Crispin did his best not to look, but then decided that courtly manners had no place with her. "For the sake of argument, I will believe you on this point…for now. If not the grail, what then?"

"It is something of mine. Rather, of my husband's. Something he gave me and wishes to see me wear again. A valuable piece of jewelry."

"D'Arcy stole it?"

She rolled her eyes and ran her hand up her other arm. "No. I gave it to him. A love token."

Crispin laughed. "You gave your husband's love token to your lover?"

"Do not laugh at me!" The relaxed stance dissolved. "You do not know what I endured at the disgusting hands of my husband! Do you know how old he is? How fat and how diseased? How would you like to be sold like livestock to the highest bidder?"

"Forgive me for stating the obvious," he said, "but you agreed to the marriage."

"And my alternative? Some other old wealthy creature? Or worse, a nunnery. Could you imagine me in such a place?"

"No, my lady. I admit I cannot."

"You think your choices were few without your knighthood. Imagine it as a woman."

He sighed and stared at his boots. "Very well. I concede it. And what does this have to do with Stephen St Albans?"

"Gaston sold it to him."

"Ah!"

"And he would not sell it back to me."

"So you became St Alban's lover as well."

"It was not for lack of trying, but he would do neither. The last time I confronted him he claimed he did not have it."

"May I ask?"

"You are a stubborn man!" She whirled again and paced erratically, casting her arms about and rippling the gown that tried vainly to follow her unpredictable moves. "It is a ring! A ring. Now I must return to my husband empty-handed. He will surely suspect the worst and I shall be put in a nunnery after all. How would I look, I wonder, in habit and veil? I do not favor black, Crispin."

Crispin burst into laughter, so much so that he leaned forward to slap his thigh.

Amazed, she planted her fists in her hips and glared.

He tried to stop but just as it subsided it flared up again. Finally, he reached into his purse and pulled out D'Arcy's pouch. He opened it and pulled out what he took for a man's pinky ring. "Is this your ring?"

She fell on it with a cry and landed at Crispin's feet. "Where did you find it?"

"Forgive me, Madam, but I had it all along. And this you did not manage to steal. Had you but said earlier…"

"Oh, Crispin, I could kiss you!"

His laughter rumbled down to a low chuckle. "Can you?"

Looking up at him, she rested her hands on his knees. "Yes," she whispered. "And more, if you wish."

He sat back and gazed at her languidly. "You already paid me. Remember?"

"Was it enough?"

Vivienne was a most pleasant sight kneeling between his thighs, her fingers resting lightly on his knees. He could think of any number of ways she could repay him. By the flush of her cheek and the dewy moisture of her lips, she must have thought of them, too. He took a breath. "Yes," he said reluctantly. "It was enough." He rose and her hands fell away from him. He stood beside the shuttered window and inhaled the fresh, cold air creeping in from a chink in the wall. "I always thought that a Knight Templar is bound by a vow of celibacy."

She rose. "He never told me he was a Knight Templar."

"Do you know a Guillaume de Marcherne?" He turned to

watch her face.

She said nothing for a long time. Too long. "No. Should I?"

Crispin scowled. "Vivienne."

She gathered her gown about her with trembling fingers. "Perhaps…I have heard of him."

"In what sense?"

"He…is from court, no?"

"A guest of the court. How do you know him?"

She squared her gaze on him. "Perhaps I simply met him there." She said nothing more.

He debated with himself whether to confront her with his knowledge that she knew him far better than that, but the truth seemed more painful to bear. "Didn't he ask you to get the grail? From me, perhaps?"

Her gaze wavered toward Crispin but mostly stayed fixed on the fire. "Why should he do that?"

He grabbed her shoulders and spun her to face him. "Don't lie to me. I will take almost anything but a lie. I'll only ask you once more."

"Yes! *Yes!* So he did. You may recall, I never did ask you for such."

"Not directly. But instead you sent me on a futile errand to find D'Arcy when you knew—"

"I did not know he was dead. Not then. Not when I first came to you." Her eyes searched Crispin's. Once more he was uncertain if that look was calculated or sincere. "But once I did know he was dead," she went on, "I thought Guillaume did it."

Guillaume? He growled and pushed her back. "Did he?"

"I thought so at first. But now…" She shrugged. "I don't know. So many people despised Gaston. It matters not," she said, dismissing him with a wave of her hand. Her hair fell away from her cheek.

Walking away from her, he ruminated on her words and the unnaturally harsh manner she said them. So if it was true that de Marcherne tried to force her to find the grail, her own purpose was stronger. But did this mean she had nothing to do with D'Arcy's death? He wasn't so certain. "Do you know Lady Rothwell, Sir Stephen's sister?"

"You asked me this before and I told you that we are only acquainted by sight." She lifted her chin to throw back her tossled hair. "Don't you believe me, Crispin?"

"There should be no reason in your lying now that you have your 'object of great price'."

She clutched it in her fist and held that fist to her heart. "You have saved my life. I thank you."

He bowed. "You are welcome." When he lifted his head his mouth hardened. "Did you kill Gaston D'Arcy?"

The fist lowered to her side. She opened her hand and stared down at the ring for a long time before she took it from her palm and placed it on her finger. "Why do you ask me such a question?"

"I have asked so many today. Surely one more will not break you."

She paused. "I certainly had good reason to."

He had wanted so badly for Stephen to have worked alone that he did not wish to entertain the possibility that the crime might also include her.

"You are displeased," she said. "Is it because I left you as I did?" She smiled and waved her hand in dismissal. "No, that is not the reason. Very well. I will give you cause to celebrate. I did not kill him. But I cannot say I am aggrieved to see him dead."

"Vivienne, for the love of Christ, if you are lying to me I will find you out."

"I know." Her bravado faded. "And so I do not lie to you now. I killed no one. And I should not hang for a crime I did not commit."

"Did Stephen act alone?"

"I know nothing of it. I should think the sheriff would know more than I."

"If Stephen did it, then why?"

She shrugged. "For the grail?"

"He knew nothing of it either."

"Then for another reason. As I said, Gaston had many lovers. Maybe Stephen's woman was one of them." She lifted her hand to examine her ring. "Do you believe me, Crispin? Or will you arrest me? I know that is why you came."

He crossed his arms over his chest. "I thought you had ties to Stephen."

"No. Not beyond this ring. It was all I sought. It was all I ever sought. De Marcherne be hanged. I only wanted my ring. He can look for his grail on his own." She looked at him with squared shoulders. "Do I seem like the kind of woman who needs to resort to murder?"

Vivienne was resourceful, to be sure, and competent. But he agreed that her wilier nature was capable of much more intricate means to serve her ends.

"I confess I used you ill," she went on. "I am sorry for that. But I am only sorry for lying *to* you…not *with* you."

He paused before he approached her.

"Will the sheriff arrest me?"

He sighed. "Guillaume de Marcherne is a dangerous man. But I suppose you already know that. If he threatened you in some way…"

She sighed, a world-weary expulsion of breath and soul. Moving toward the fire she stood before it, head bowed, gown gathered tightly about her. "And if he did?"

"Vivienne. You must tell me."

"Why? Why must I? Is not our business now over? I'm leaving as much for your sake as mine."

"He *did* threaten you. Extortion? Worse?"

"Do what he says, Crispin," she whispered. "I fear for you."

"For me? Do not worry over me. I can take care of myself."

Her brightened eyes roamed over his borrowed coat and stockings. "Of course," she said.

He took her shoulders and turned her to him, gently this time. Her head hung listlessly. "He forced you to try to get the grail from me?"

"He only wanted to know if you already possessed it. But he frightens me. And extortion or no, I fled London. I am not brave like you, Crispin. I thought I could fool my husband for a time should de Marcherne make good on his threats."

"But now you have your ring. His threats are groundless."

She smiled. "Thanks to you."

"If I were you, I would stay on your estates for a good long time. With your husband."

Her smile sagged.

"And I will deal with de Marcherne in my own way."

He turned to go but she stopped him by touching his arm. "If someday...I should find myself a widow...and in London..."

He did not face her. He gathered his things in silence and left.

CHAPTER TWENTY-THREE

After leaving Vivienne, he decided to accept the convent's humble hospitality. Once the morning light brightened his small room, he donned his own garments and stuffed those donated by Martin Kemp into the saddle bag. He could now happily return the clothes to his landlord and owe nothing.

But as he stretched into the damp morning and pulled himself into the saddle again, he could think of nothing better than Gilbert's wine and the comfort of the Boar's Tusk. Of course he would have to first return the horse to the sheriff and explain why he did not have a prisoner.

His hips rolled along with the mare's gait. "I do not have to tell him the whole truth," he muttered, and put up his hood.

He rode silently, reviewing his diagram in his head and rearranging the names to piece together the new information. *The least initial deviation from the truth is multiplied later a thousand fold.* How many lies were there now? How many more were there to find?

He arrived in London after sext and slowed his mount to a dull plod before dipping down toward Newgate.

He left the horse in the stable courtyard with a groom, and took his time reaching Wynchecombe's hall, but when he neared it, he heard him arguing with someone.

Rosamunde.

Flattening against the wall, Crispin considered. He certainly did not wish to challenge Rosamunde again, and the sheriff would not be pleased that he returned empty-handed. The Boar's Tusk was looking better and better. He felt a bit of a coward when he turned on his heel, but he consoled himself that another confrontation with Rosamunde was bad for his disposition and a bowl of wine was the only cure.

Crispin pushed his way through the throng blocking the entrance to the Boar's Tusk. After finally freeing himself, he staggered into the room and scowled at the crowd still pushing their way in.

All he wanted was some peace and quiet. What the hell was all this?

He spotted Gilbert near the back doorway and tried to make his way toward him, but the crush of people overwhelmed. No way through. He jumped up onto a long table instead and walked across the planks to the next table until he reached him.

Gilbert looked up just as Crispin leapt to the ground.

"Sweet *Jesu*, Gilbert. What goes on here?"

"I do not know," he shouted back over the noise. "There is a rumor about the wine. Now everyone wants it, but I am nearly out. I fear a riot."

"The wine? Surely not yours."

He shook his head. "I know not. People have come saying they were healed of infirmities, and they think it is my wine."

Crispin scoffed. "All because of rumor?"

"Aye. But the casks are nearly empty. What can I do?"

"You may have to call in the sheriffs."

Gilbert cast his gaze across the heads and faces angrily shouting for drink. "What will they do to my place?"

"I don't know. I only came for the peace and quiet. And of course your excellent wine."

Gilbert looked at him and suddenly laughed. "Come with me," he gestured, and Crispin followed him through the back courtyard and down a staircase to the lower mews.

"At least it is quieter here," he said, leading Crispin to a table and stools. Oil lamps lit the store room and shadowed the large casks that lined the walls. "If it is wine you want, wine you shall have." He took a jug from a shelf and filled it from a spigot. He raised the jug triumphantly and brought it and two clay cups to the table.

"So now your wine has miracle properties, eh? I always thought it was the water."

"There now! You know I do not water my wine."

They both drank. Gilbert's face concentrated on the flavors. Crispin found himself doing the same and trying to discern anything new.

"This is madness," Crispin said at last, putting the cup down. "There is nothing to this wine. It is a miracle if it tastes good."

Gilbert feigned shock. "Indeed! And yet you return day after day."

With a nod Crispin drank again. "Hope over experience."

"Well, if no miracle, then perhaps a special cask, but I cannot seem to taste a difference from one to the other."

Footsteps rushed down the stairs and they both turned to spy Gilbert's servant clinging to the stair rail.

"What it is, boy?"

"Master, forgive me, but I've taken the liberty of telling them people that we sent all our wine to the Monk Tavern, and they've begun to clear out."

"Ned, my boy!" Gilbert rushed up, grabbed Ned by his ears, and turned his head downward to kiss his crown. "That's good thinking. Now it's the Monk's problem." Ned shook his head and rushed back up the stairs.

Gilbert returned to the table and sat with a sigh of relief. "I tell you, Crispin, strange things seem to be happening of late. I owe it to that murder. You don't suppose that dead knight haunts us, do you?"

"I do not believe in ghosts, Gilbert. But this murder definitely haunts."

Gilbert licked the wine from his lips and leaned forward. "How goes your investigation?"

Crispin settled his elbows on the table and curled his fingers around the cup. "That is madness, too, Gilbert."

"Rumor has it you have your man. Stephen St Albans. And may the Devil take him, if he will have him." He raised the bowl and drank to it.

"Yes, I apprehended Stephen."

Gilbert settled his cup on his thigh and studied Crispin's expression. "For God's sake, Crispin! Does nothing make you merry? Why so glum? This must be good news."

Crispin sat silently, looking into his cup.

Gilbert knocked his knuckles on the table. "Oi, Crispin? What ails you? You are miles away."

Lifting the cup Crispin slurped its contents. The wine burned its way down his throat. No, this was certainly no miracle wine, but Gilbert's open expression did much to ease his troubled soul, and he leaned forward, the cup imprisoned within his fingers.

"It seems to be a hollow victory, Gilbert. Rosamunde has changed. She does not love me and I fear she never will again. Certainly hanging her brother will not endear me." He sat back still clutching the cup, his nails tapping against the chipped ceramic. "I fear I might have let an accomplice go because of sentiment. Do I grow soft, Gilbert? Have I lost all sense of perspective?" He dropped his face into his wide palm and left it there, breathing through his open fingers. "I could be completely wrong about all of it. I don't know what's the matter with me. I have never been so personally involved in these matters. Always, I solved whatever puzzle and walked away. But this time…"

"Well, it seems to me you have put your finger on it," said Gilbert, wiping his lips and brown beard with his hand. "Everywhere you turn you are personally involved, whether by these Templar fellows or those dangerous men who abducted you, or by ghosts from your past." He drank another dose and set the cup down. "This accomplice you have let go. It isn't a woman by any chance?"

Crispin nodded.

"I see. Crispin, this convinces me of something I have considered for a long time: you need a woman."

"God's blood." Crispin sank his head to the table and wrapped his arms around his head, hoping to muffle Gilbert's words. He heard them anyway.

"Not the sort you crave for a time and cast away, mind you. But a woman to straighten you out. A woman to marry."

Crispin rolled his head within his arms. All the protestations in the world would not make Gilbert stop, and where he left off Eleanor was certain to take it up again. "Gilbert, for the love of Christ, please!"

"I'm only saying…"

"My life is complicated enough without a woman mixed in it."

"And yet you do entangle yourself."

Crispin stopped moaning and cracked a weak smile. He raised his head. "I do indeed. Would you deprive me of that?"

Gilbert shot a quick glance up the stairs. "Well now. I am not a man to stifle a man's appetites. What sort of tavern keeper would I be then, eh?"

Crispin's smile grew broader and he took up his wine again. "In truth, Gilbert, this is a vexing case."

"With the murderer caught and imprisoned, you should be in better stead with the sheriffs. *That* is a good thing, at least."

"Yes. It is."

"But?"

"But I can't help but feel that the wrong man awaits the gallows."

Gilbert smacked the table with his hand, sloshing Crispin's wine onto the stained wood. "For God's sake! It is the man who ruined you. What better scoundrel could there be?"

"And I truly wish I could see it that way. Indeed, I did at first. But now…there is no sense to it. Stephen is an intensely honorable man. Both of them were knights. If he wanted him dead or needed to avenge himself, he would have challenged him on the field. They would have fought it out like true knights, not in deception with poison. I tell you truly, I cannot picture Stephen doing such a thing."

Gilbert set down his bowl and nudged his stool closer to the table. The oil light behind him glowed the stray strands of his brown hair with a golden edge. "Then you have a problem. You need to discover his motive in killing him in this secret fashion, or…"

"Or, I need to find who did do it."

"What about this woman you let slip through your fingers?"

"I believe she is capable, but…"

"Did you swyve her?"

Crispin drew up sharply and peered down his nose at Gilbert. "That is hardly your business."

"No. It isn't *my* business. It's the king's. If you let yourself be influenced by every quim that comes your way, then justice cannot be served."

Crispin launched to his feet and paced across the dusty floor. "I made a decision and I stand by it."

"Well then. It looks like you made up your own mind at last. Perhaps you best question Sir Stephen and find a motive you can live with."

Crispin stopped pacing and swiveled his head in Gilbert's direction. "Yes. There is a lot of sense to what you say."

Gilbert laid his hand on his heart. "I am a man of many gifts."

Crispin set down the cup and headed for the steps. "God keep you, Gilbert. And your good wife," he said over his shoulder and raced up the stairs.

He turned up Gutter Lane, heading toward the Shambles, concentrating on what he would say to Stephen as well as what he would be forced to admit to the sheriff. He hoped that Rosamunde had left Newgate by now so he could be alone with the sheriff and the prisoner.

The Shambles was crowded with a man moving pigs down the avenue and Crispin slipped up an alley to skirt around them. Until three figures blocked his way.

It didn't matter, he decided. His spirits were high and a fight would do him good.

CHAPTER TWENTY-FOUR

He stood his ground and let the men approach. He knew these alleys. By coming to Crispin, they cut off their own escape. He tensed with fists clenched, wondering if he would need his dagger.

They breached the boundary of shadows, and light flooded their faces.

"Forgive us," said Parsifal holding out his empty hand.

"We did not startle you, did we?" Edwin gestured to another knight Crispin did not know.

Crispin relaxed his guard but not completely. "I did not expect to see you. What is it you want?"

"We are only asking about your progress in finding the object we seek."

Crispin's instinct included glancing behind him, which he did. The alley lay empty. "I have not yet found it."

Parsifal lowered his head and shook it slowly. His tonsured scalp caught the vague sunlight and gleamed. "We are sorry to hear that. We hoped to be gone from this place by now."

"My apologies. But these things take time. In the interim, why don't you tell me something of Gaston D'Arcy."

Edwin kept his steady gaze on Crispin. Parsifal and the other knight exchanged furtive glances. "And so you know his name," said Edwin.

"Yes. A piece of information you did not deign to share with me. Tell me of his character."

Edwin smiled. "It matters little now. He is dead."

"Yes. He is. And no end of trouble has come from it. Tell me about his character."

"We do not see the point. It is past; over and done with."

"A man sits in gaol for his murder. Do you care nothing for that?"

"It is no longer our affair."

Crispin guffawed and slowly paced around the three disguised knights. "No longer your affair? A pretty picture, this. Funny you should mention affairs. It seems Gaston D'Arcy was involved in many 'affairs.' Your celibate knight had many paramours, I hear tell."

Edwin snorted. "Rumor and innuendo."

"On the contrary. I have reliable testimony. Did you know your Cup Bearer was so engaged?"

The unnamed knight drew forward, his hand on his sword hilt. He began to withdraw it. "You are insulting, sir, to the honorable order of Templars!"

"Hold, Anselm" said Edwin, stepping in front of the knight. "Crispin is our ally."

"He does not sound like an ally," grunted Anselm.

Crispin postured. "Do you draw your blade on me?"

"Yes. To any man who makes such accusations."

"Then hear this," said Crispin. "Lately I have heard much about Templars; how they deceive in order to conquer; how their only aim is to dominate. Perhaps the grail is how you wish to achieve it. Perhaps you never had it to begin with." He glared at each solemn knight. "Maybe to silence the rumor and innuendo, you killed your own comrade."

Anselm drew his sword and shoved Edwin aside. Crispin backed away from him, desperately searching for something that could serve for a shield.

"Crispin!"

He saw Parsifal offer his sword. The knight tossed it and Crispin caught its hilt. He curled his fingers around the leather and wood-covered grip and felt the heft and perfect balance of the weapon. How good it was to feel a sword in his hand again! But with almost the same breath he glanced up at the oncoming knight and realized that it had been seven years since he had last used one.

Anselm slashed. Crispin swung his own sword to block it. The metal clanged. Anselm swung again. Crispin ducked in time to save his head. While low, he jammed the heavy pommel into Anselm's boot. The knight yowled and staggered back. Anger flushed his face and he increased his volley of blows upon Crispin. Crispin backed away. The shock of Anselm's blade against his sword weakened his arm. His unused muscles screamed at the new activity demanded of them. Anselm backed him against the wall but Crispin blocked his blade with a heavy downward stroke and kept it there with a trembling hand.

Anselm bared his teeth. Close enough to feel his angry breath upon him, Crispin cocked back his left fist and punched.

He heard a satisfying crunch, and blood rushed from Anselm's nostrils. The knight's eyes rolled upward, he dropped his blade, and fell backward into the mud.

Crispin stood over him and panted for a moment before he handed Parsifal his sword. "Much thanks," he said once he caught his breath.

Edwin sighed and looked down at the supine Anselm. "I am sorry for my brother's hot-headedness. Believe me. He is a good knight. Far better than…than our dearly departed."

"And so," said Crispin, straightening his coat. "You admit it."

"Yes," he said stiffly. "He was unable to keep his vows. His time with the grail was almost up and once it was, I was to take him to the Master and have him removed from the order."

"Why did you wait?"

"It was hoped the grail would change him," offered Parsifal. He lowered to one knee to minister to Anselm. "It changes many who guard it."

"Then you still maintain there is such an object."

"Of course!" cried Parsifal. "We have all seen it. Touched it."

"Then who is Guillaume de Marcherne?"

The three knights froze. Edwin was the first to move and he seized Crispin's arm. "Do not have congress with that man. He is the Devil incarnate."

"That much I gathered. But who is he? I believe he is allied with the anti-pope."

"That and more," said Edwin.

Anselm rose to his feet, a torn piece of his shirt was stuffed into his bloody nose. "You fought right well," he said good-naturedly and offered Crispin his hand.

"As did you," Crispin answered somewhat perplexed. He took Anselm's hand and gripped it once before letting it go. "You are no longer angry with me?"

Anselm shook his head. "I was never angry with you. It was a test."

"A test? What nonsense is this?"

Edwin eased Crispin aside with a gentle tug on his arm. "Crispin. Your king may have seen fit to degrade and dispossess you, but we recognize a noble nature that cannot be suppressed. We offer you your knighthood as a brother in Christ."

"What?" It came out as a puff of air.

"Yes, Crispin," he went on. "We ask you to join us as a Knight of the Temple. Don your sword again and be a soldier of Christ. Once you find the grail you shall be one of us."

Crispin took a step back and studied their solemn faces. "Me? A Templar? You must...It is a jest."

"No. Our brethren are chosen carefully. D'Arcy was once a young idealist but he strayed and allowed the face of woman to lead him away from the straight path. He was weak."

"Gentlemen," said Crispin. He opened and closed his fists. "'The face of woman' is oft foremost on my mind. I am afraid I am not made for chastity."

"A man can learn," said Parsifal. Crispin looked at him for

seemingly the first time. So young. The same age as Crispin was when he was knighted. At that age, he, too, might have pledged his chastity. He had been just as fervent to do his job well and to find his honor in it.

"What you offer…" Crispin shook his head and paced around the men. "It's extraordinary." De Marcherne offered the same, but it wore the stench of dishonor about it. And how could Crispin ever raise his head and serve in the French court?

But here, in the Templars, there was great honor and just enough mystique for added enticement. The feel of a sword again; a horse; armor. All the accouterments he yearned for, the trappings that defined him. Even the vow of chastity did not seem as repellent as it first appeared. What had women done for him except to cause him pain and disappointment? There could be great nobility in this notion of sacrifice.

"I do not know what to say," he offered feebly.

"Then say nothing for now," said Edwin. "When you find the grail, you will find your way. It is God's manner to work in us in this fashion."

The two knights bid their farewells and each took one of Anselm's arms to help him.

Crispin watched them, these noble knights. Then the thought occurred to him. How well they distracted him with the one thing he most wanted. Like the Devil, they found the weakness in his armor. "One thing more," called Crispin before they disappeared around the corner. He strained to keep the anger from his voice. "Do any of you know of a man named Stephen St Albans?"

Subtly, almost too subtle to detect in the half shadows of the alleyway, Crispin saw a look pass between Edwin and Parsifal. He could not describe it with any accuracy, and any other man might have missed it. But Crispin's instincts always served him well and he carefully noted the fleeting moment like a scribe scratches a quick, black mark with the tip of his quill.

"No," said Edwin. "We do not."

They nodded their farewells again and left Crispin alone in the alley.

CHAPTER TWENTY-FIVE

Crispin waited in the dark passageway to be announced to the sheriff. He rocked on his heels. Newgate's darkness seemed blacker than ordinary night, more oppressive than cellars and storerooms. Perhaps the density of its gloom was fed by the many souls who had passed through its portals. Even an oil lamp could not seem to pierce the murkiness that hovered in each corner, keeping its mysteries tightly concealed.

The bailiff startled him from his musings and motioned for him to go into the sheriffs' hall.

Crispin yanked at his coat and tried to smooth out its permanent wrinkles. He took a deep breath and walked in with head held high.

"Well?" bellowed Sheriff Wynchecombe before Crispin took two steps. "Where is this prisoner you were so keen to bring in?"

John More hovered beside Wynchecombe, silent and studied. As always, he seemed pleased enough just to let Wynchecombe take charge.

"My lords," said Crispin with a deep bow.

Wynchecombe sneered. "None of that. That only means you are about to lie to me. But I warn you," he said, pointing a bejeweled finger at him, "if you perjure yourself, I will not keep that spare cell idle."

More huffed and turned away, looking out the window toward the rising mist.

Crispin sighed. "I fully intended to return with a prisoner. But after my interview, I did not believe she had much to do with this crime."

"*You* don't believe? Since when have you designated yourself my keeper of the peace? You have no authority to decide such things. I should send you out again on a donkey to retrieve her."

"Why must we content ourselves with Master Guest?" sighed More. "Send him away, Simon."

Crispin persisted. "You must trust my judgment in this, my lord."

Wynchecombe ignored More's bored sighing. "Why? Give me one good reason to do so. Why is your judgment better than my own? It does not seem to be touched with gold. Nothing about you, in fact, is touched with gold."

With tensed hands pressed behind his back, Crispin cleared his throat. "I have no better explanation than my instincts, my lord. Such instincts have kept me alive."

Wynchecombe laughed, sharing it with More's back. "Bollocks to your instincts."

"If my instincts prove wrong, I still know where to find her. She is going nowhere."

Wynchecombe cracked a smile. "A contingency strategy? Well, you are no fool, at least. A stubborn whoreson, but not a fool." Wynchecombe rose and picked up the silver flagon. "Wine?" he asked, gesturing with the ornate jug.

Crispin's mouth felt dry but he forced himself to shake his head. "I did not come simply to present myself to you, Lord Sheriff."

Wynchecombe poured his wine and made as if to offer some to More, but with the man's back still to him he huffed his displeasure and held his full cup. "Oh? Why, then?"

"I wish to speak with Sir Stephen again."

The sheriff frowned and shook his head. "No. Enough. He is

not your personal whipping boy. He is a knight of the court, even if he is guilty of murder. You have no further jurisdiction in this."

"My lord—"

"I told you," said More. "Send the whoreson away. By my lady, Master Guest, you are a vexation."

"I said enough!" cried Wynchecombe. Crispin wasn't certain if he was talking to him or to John More, until Wynchecombe swiveled toward him. "You think because I allow you certain liberties that we are equals in this. You are not my equal."

Crispin knew he should drop his gaze and appease the sheriff's temper, but he could not quite make himself do it. Instead, he looked straight at him and nodded. "Yes, my lord. It is only that I am a man of justice. And I would see it served to its fullest."

In the same quietly malevolent tone, Wynchecombe asked, "And do you think that justice is not being served?"

"Not yet to its fullest, my lord. And it is my fault."

"Ha!" Wynchecombe's guffaw broke the tension. He jabbed the air with his finger and swept up the goblet with the other hand. "That is the first sensible thing you have said."

"Then will you allow me to further question Sir Stephen?"

"Oh, for the love of Christ, Simon, let him do it." More turned, disgust twisting his face. "Then we'll be rid of him. Rid of them both."

Wynchecombe threw More a glare. "Guest," he growled, still pinning his gaze to More, who had already turned his back again. "Perhaps. First, you must prove yourself to me."

Everything is a test. He sighed. "In what way?"

"I have a visitor arriving. Some foreign dignitary. I have no patience for such like. He wishes to speak to Sir Stephen as well."

"My lord?"

"That's simple enough, isn't it?" Wynchecombe sat again and leaned back in the chair. "You take care of it. And I will see my way to being generous to you."

"Would not the gaoler be better suited—"

"No. I want you to do it." He glanced at More. "Does that suit you as well, my lord?"

More shrugged, still gazing out the window.

Wynchecombe scowled and fixed his gaze on Crispin.

Crispin raised his chin. "What is it I am to do, Lord Sheriff?"

"Just show him through. That's all. When the page comes, meet him at the gate." He smiled. "When you meet him, give him my apologies. Tell him that I am too concerned with the king's business to welcome him personally, but convey my sincerest greetings. Tell him you are my lackey and that you will serve him as well as if you were the 'sheriff himself'. Did you get all that?"

For a moment, the most fleeting of intervals, Crispin thought of overturning Wynchecombe's table and spilling the wine and his papers across his floor. He thought of his hand already clenched in a tight fist, and of his knuckles meeting Wynchecombe's white teeth, causing some of them to loosen with a rush of bright red blood.

He thought of it, and then let it go. He must talk to Stephen, and if it meant gulping more than his fair share of pride, then so be it.

Crispin bowed to both sheriffs and straightened his spine. Almost at the same time, a breathless page entered and said that the foreign dignitary waited at the gate.

He followed the page down the dim stairs to the gatehouse. Newgate's guards were there hovering near a fire in an iron cage. They glanced with disinterest toward Crispin, but nudged each other to attention when other men approached from the courtyard.

Crispin went out to meet them. The tall dignitary wore his hood over his head. Five men accompanied him. When he threw back his hood, his familiar face smiled wide. A scar pulled up his lip.

Crispin narrowed his eyes.

"My good friend Crispin!" said the man, his accent purring off his tongue. "You come in the sheriff's place? How fitting."

"My Lord de Marcherne," said Crispin with a curt bow.

"Though," said de Marcherne feigning concern and speaking in a stage whisper, "we are not supposed to know each other." He tossed his cloak over his shoulders and opened his arms, encompassing the presence of his companions who walked at a considerable distance behind him. "I am a dignitary from the French court and I humbly asked permission from King Richard to interview one of his prisoners." De Marcherne chuckled and walked with Crispin across the courtyard back toward the gatehouse. "I did not expect to find *you* here, however."

They passed under the arch into the building, but de Marcherne stopped and motioned for his men to return to the outer courtyard leaving Crispin and himself alone. Once the men left, he turned to Crispin. "Lead me."

"Where? Which prisoner?"

De Marcherne smiled with an airless chuckle. "You know which one."

It was Crispin's turn to smile. His lips drew up crookedly. "I do not think he is accessible."

"I was given to understand I was to be denied nothing."

"What a shame you were misled."

De Marcherne stepped away from Crispin to glance across the gatehouse. The stone ceiling arched over them. A long wooden staircase clambered up the walls in a meandering pattern. One way led to the sheriff's chamber. The other way to the prisoners in the tower. "I could go to the sheriffs myself and tell them how you were dismissive of me and insulted the French court."

"Should I go against custom?"

"Insults to the face of a dignitary, and from a lackey? What would your master say to that?"

Crispin did not need to consider. He tried not to frown but was unsuccessful. "I will only allow it if I am present."

De Marcherne was about to protest but at the last moment seemed to think better of it. "Very well," he said, and gestured Crispin forward.

Crispin took his time and toured de Marcherne throughout the narrow passages and distasteful corners of the prison, hoping to try his patience.

De Marcherne did not indicate by look or gesture that his patience had reached its limit, except that his face looked stiff and drawn. He made almost no comment the entire length of the wearying tour. On the rooftop, Crispin gazed down through the embrasure at London on one side, and its fields and marshes on the other.

"This looks nothing like a cell," said de Marcherne.

Crispin breathed the air and after standing in the wind for a time, he gestured for de Marcherne to precede him down the stairs again through another dark passageway.

"I understand," said de Marcherne suddenly, "that you were visited again by your Templar friends."

Crispin said nothing.

"Did you ask about me?"

"Yes. I believe they called you the 'Devil incarnate'."

When they approached Stephen's cell at last Crispin slowed.

"The Devil incarnate. How refreshing. Did they say nothing else?"

Crispin turned to him quizzically. "What else needed to be said?"

They stopped before the cell door and de Marcherne stared steadily at Crispin. "They did not say, for instance, that I used to be a Templar? The Grand Master, in fact?"

Crispin's lips parted while de Marcherne smiled and looked at the door. "Is this the place?"

CHAPTER TWENTY-SIX

Crispin stepped back against the wall and absorbed de Marcherne's words. The Templars had been so persuasive. He had even considered their offer with some amount of soul-searching. Was this just another deception on de Marcherne's part? Or the Templars'?

De Marcherne grabbed the grate of the door's spy hole. "My lord," he called within. "I would speak with you."

Crispin looked over de Marcherne's shoulder and watched Stephen approach the door. He wore a five-day-old beard and his hair fell dirty and mussed about his cheeks. "Who the hell are you?"

"I could be a friend."

"I know that voice," Stephen hissed. "You bastard!"

"Alas," said de Marcherne. "Such a recognizable voice. Unfortunately, my companions haven't the subtly to question a prisoner properly and I am forced to do it myself. I must look into instructing them."

"I have nothing to say to you that I haven't said before."

"Yes. Such colorful metaphors they were. So many intriguing ways to blaspheme myself."

"And I meant every one of them!"

"Yes, I know. I only have the one question left."

Stephen sneered at Crispin. "What's he got to do with it?"

209

De Marcherne sent only a perfunctory glance back. "Him? He has nothing to do with it. He is merely the sheriff's lap dog and insists on accompanying me. Do not bother with him."

"I will not bother with either of you. Have you not heard? I am under a sentence of death even before my trial. Do you think I care what you have to say to me?" He turned his back, and leaned against the grate.

"Even if it will free you?"

He did not move except to adjust his shoulder. "Lies," he spat.

"I can have you freed with one word to the king. But I require something from you in return."

He whirled and grabbed the grate, though it failed to startle de Marcherne. "The damned grail, is that it?"

De Marcherne turned to Crispin. "You told him?"

"Yes," said Crispin dispassionately. "I wondered if he had it. He doesn't."

"No? Are you certain?" Crispin nodded and de Marcherne ticked his head. "You do not have the grail?" he asked Stephen.

"I never saw it. As I *said.*"

"Alas. It means you have nothing to bargain with. Pity." He lowered his face for a moment before bringing up a sardonic smile. "Good luck with your trial."

De Marcherne turned and appraised Crispin. "I thank you for your most interesting tour. I hope we shall meet again." He leaned closer and said in quieter tones, "My offer to you still stands. Think on it." He cast a dismissing glance to Stephen before he waved to a gaoler standing some distance down the passage. "Do not bother to escort me, Master Crispin. This fine gaoler will lead me out. *Au revoir.*"

His footsteps stopped echoing long before his stately figure disappeared into the shrouding shadows.

"Why did you bring that bastard here?" Stephen grimaced. "Never mind. I know. To further torment me. Satisfied?"

"In fact, no. Yet I have some questions of my own."

"Do you? Well you know what you can do with your

questions."

Crispin toed the dirt at the foot of the door and then peered into the dim cell. A dismal fire sputtered in the hearth. A stool, a table, and a pallet with a straw mattress were the only furniture in the room. He remembered it well from his own incarceration seven years ago.

"I am trying to discover what possible motive my future brother-in-law would have for murder in this deceitful manner."

Stephen rushed the window again but instead of flinging insults he pealed his lips back and bared his teeth in a smile. "You are bluffing. Rosamunde would never marry you. She's already betrothed."

"Liar," he growled. "She never said—"

"Why should she discuss such a matter with you? I tell you she is betrothed. It is only a matter of months before she is wed again."

As if struck by an arrow, Crispin staggered back and took a moment to catch his breath. When he looked up again Stephen calmly appraised him.

Crispin shook his head. How tired he was of games. Everyone, it seemed, lied to him. Rosamunde, the Templars, Vivienne, Stephen. He straightened, rolled his shoulders. "Why would Rosamunde tell me you were missing longer than was true?"

Stephen sniffed. "Gone one day? Would you have bothered to search?"

"Why was she suspicious?"

"Because I went to speak with D'Arcy and she did not trust him."

"Why?"

Stephen pressed his lips together.

"Lady Stancliff was his lover. Did she want the grail?"

"I know nothing of that. I never knew he was a Templar."

"And what of your affair with Lady Stancliff?"

"Mine? Never."

"You lie. She said you were together. She remarked how cruel you were to her."

"She made accusations. And that kind of woman does not get away with insults to me."

"You never had an affair with her?"

"No. She is a liar if she claims so."

"At first I believed the object she sought was the grail, but she has since told me it was something as innocuous as a ring. A ring I happened to have in my possession all this time."

Stephen's face changed, growing pale. "So? Did you give it to her?"

"Yes. It belonged to her, after all. Did it not?"

Stephen scowled and ran his hand over his chin. With that simple gesture, he seemed to release something, and his eyes surrendered into an expression of bleak indifference. "So she said."

"What troubles you? That she was not your mistress?"

Stephen laughed bitterly. "That harridan? As if I would have her."

"She warned me you would speak ill of her."

Stephen measured Crispin and cracked a wry smile, a smile devoid of joy. "You slept with her. Well and why not! The both of you are whores. She with her cadre of men and you selling your time to the highest bidder."

Crispin's hands curled into fists but he checked his anger. After all, Stephen sat in a cell marked for death, not him.

"You are right. She did not, in fact, claim you were her lover."

"And so."

"But there was another lover. She said so. D'Arcy had many, in fact."

Stephen turned away from the door and crossed his arms over his chest.

"Lady Stancliff," Crispin continued, "told me of his many conquests. If he became the lover of another man's woman...say, yours, perhaps..."

"I have no one in my life now."

"There must have been another lover involved." Jealousy. He could easily see jealousy as a motive, and jealousy worked well with poison. Crispin struggled with his thoughts, trying to think if he missed something or someone who could possibly be D'Arcy's lover. And then the sudden insight came to him and struck like a pike piercing his heart. "*Jesu*! Why did I not see that before?"

At the same moment Crispin pronounced, "Rosamunde!" Stephen challenged him with a stout, "No!"

"Rosamunde. It was Rosamunde, wasn't it?" Stephen's expression was a muddled mix of anger and fear. Fear? Crispin drew closer, examined his face, and frowned. "That was not the name you expected me to say, was it?"

Stephen glowered into the fire. "I do not know your meaning."

"You were prepared with a denial. Whom did you think I meant to say?"

"No one. If you suspect Rosamunde then I dare you to accuse her yourself!"

"Who else, Stephen? You know something, damn you! Are you prepared to die for it? Answer me! Who else?"

"Go to the Devil, Crispin!"

Crispin postured and leaned with both hands on the door. "If you had no lady for D'Arcy to woo, then why do you act like a jilted lover? It's as if…" He stared at Stephen's bewildered face; saw grief suddenly on his features and something else. Terror. Not the same fear Stephen wore when he spoke of de Marcherne's men torturing him. This look in his eyes was deeper, older. He studied Stephen, from the rich leather of his boots up to his broad shoulders.

Like a cascade of icy water, his mind snapped to.

"Christ's blood," Crispin muttered. "Christ's merciful blood!" He planted his feet before the door and crossed his arms over his chest. "You. Dammit, it was you."

Stephen never moved from his haven by the fire but he turned to Crispin. One side of his face bronzed from the flames while the other fell into shadow. "You…you have no proof."

"Your expression is proof enough! And you do not deny it! You killed him to keep your secret."

Stephen hurled himself at the cell door. "I did not kill him!"

"You were lovers. Answer me!"

Stephen trembled, but not from fear. "Damn you."

"Well, well, well!" Crispin drew back and strutted before the cell door. "Not only will you be hanged for his murder, but you will be exposed for the disgrace you are!"

"Crispin."

Crispin spun on him. "Do you plead with me? *You?*"

Stephen took a deep breath. "Hang me if you must. But I implore you. Say nothing for Rosamunde's sake."

"Then you admit to murder?"

"If it will spare her, yes."

Crispin frowned. This man he had known, who had been his friend. Crispin never suspected this secret side of him. But why then did he murder D'Arcy in such a cowardly way? Why did he lie about the grail, for surely he must have known D'Arcy had it, knew where it was? What was the point in keeping it secret now?

The more Crispin thought about the murder, the harder it was to imagine it. A crime of passion required the spilling of blood. From experience, Crispin knew that it felt far more satisfactory to let the offender see the blade coming, for him to feel it slice into him, and for him to know that his life's blood would ebb away.

He looked up at Stephen's woeful expression and gritted his teeth. He could walk away now, satisfied of his revenge. He could. Instead, he took a tentative step closer and peered through the grate almost nose to nose with him. "You did not kill him, did you?"

Stephen shrugged and pulled his cloak over his chest. "I might as well have done. Perhaps I should have. And so," he said with a shuddering sigh. "You can still have your revenge. Just let me hang."

Crispin's lips peeled back in snarl. "Not if you're innocent!" He pushed away from the door and furiously paced.

"You have a strange sense of honor."

"Why shouldn't I have my revenge?"

"That is the core of it, isn't it?" Stephen shook his head. "This isn't about justice. It's about you. You blame everyone else but yourself. God's bones! You committed treason, Crispin! You acted against the rightful heir! You acted against England itself. Why can't you see that?"

"I did what I thought was just."

"*You* thought! What about the law? Oh how well you now uphold the law, but what about then? If we have not our laws and the rule of succession, we are nothing. We might as well go back to wearing skins and painting our faces blue."

"But Lancaster—"

"Never had rights! God, Crispin! Lancaster was not in line! It was Richard. Richard was the rightful heir. No matter that he was a child at the time. It would not matter if he was a babe. He *was* king, not your Lancaster. Mother of God! It's been seven years and you still don't see how wrong you were. Revenge? Everyone else is to blame but you." He shook his head and wiped the spittle from his lips with the back of a trembling hand. Stephen's anger fell away. His shoulders slumped and he turned from the door. "But as for me," he whispered, placing his hand on his chest. "This has been champing at my heels all my life. Don't you think I would change if I could? Try to understand…"

Crispin shook his head. "Understand? You must be mad!"

"Yes. I thought as much. The great Crispin Guest. Protégé to Lancaster." He gestured to Crispin's clothes, his lack of a sword. "See where your pride has taken you."

"At least I am not behind a prison door."

"No visible door."

"No." His eyes narrowed again with vicious fury. "And I have you to thank."

"Seven years ago," Stephen said solemnly, "I discovered a plot and I was honor bound to reveal it. I did not know that it involved you. Not at first. But by then it was far too late. Don't you realize? You were not the only one destroyed. It destroyed Rosamunde. It destroyed our family. You and I. We were friends. That, too, was lost."

Crispin shook his head and swallowed a hard lump in his throat.

"I did not kill him," Stephen said softly. "Not for me and not for Rosamunde, for I know she and he…" He sighed. "It was one of the reasons I broke it off with Gaston. For God's sake, she was my sister! And he knew it, the bastard. Another reason was…oh, there were many reasons." He threw his head back to gaze up at the arched ceiling. His lashes were moist. "He said many things, made many promises."

Crispin grimaced. "Spare me."

"He gave that ring to *me*! I thought it was mine. When I discovered it was not I threw it back at him."

Crispin wiped his face with a clammy hand. "So you are saying Rosamunde… She *was* his…his…" Crispin could not bring himself to say it. It was worse than D'Arcy and Stephen. Almost.

"Yes," Stephen finally answered, covering his face with one hand before dropping that hand away. "But she does not know about me."

Crispin suddenly wished he never came to Newgate, never met Templars and dead men and courtly ladies. He wished to go back to the Boar's Tusk and drown his senses in bad wine and smoky hearths.

Wearily, he heard himself ask, "What of her betrothed?"

"I know not. The last I heard, he was still in France."

Crispin froze. "France? Your French business?"

"Yes," nodded Stephen. "We have been negotiating for months."

Crispin fell silent. The neat package tied up in a tight string was now unraveling and so much else with it. He pulled distractedly at his coat. Suddenly he felt weary. "For what it is worth," he said, voice hoarse. "I believe you. And whatever you believe about me, I am a man of honor, however misplaced. I will do my best to see you freed, though the sheriff will not like it." He strained on the next part, wondering even at the last moment what he was going to say. "I will say nothing to Rosamunde about the…the other matter."

Stephen lowered his head and heaved a long sigh. "Thank you."

"You..." He stopped and started again. "It's..." No use. What could he say? Crispin compressed his lips and shook his head. "I do not understand any of this."

"I'm..."

"No." Crispin held up his hand and grimaced. Now more than ever he longed to strike Stephen, but the man was safe, for now, behind a barred door.

Crispin turned, but the ragged thoughts would not leave him. "For God's sake, Stephen! You frequented a brothel!"

Stephen shrugged. "To keep up appearances."

"What in hell did you do there?"

He smiled sheepishly. "I played cards."

Crispin kicked at the straw-littered floor.

Stephen stood at the door, fingers resting on the iron bars. His pensive expression flickered in the torch light. "Will you truly ask the sheriff to release me?"

"Yes. I said I would. I will not be responsible for hanging an innocent man. But he will ask me what I shall ask you now." He turned to face him. "If you did not kill D'Arcy, who did?"

Stephen shook his head. "I don't know."

"Wynchecombe will not like that answer and will require convincing."

"If anyone can do it," he said, eyes locked on Crispin's, "it will be you."

CHAPTER TWENTY-SEVEN

Crispin sat at home and stared into his untouched bowl of wine. After he left Newgate and returned to his lodgings, he realized he was back to the beginning, with no murderer.

De Marcherne and his henchmen. Crispin had all but ignored him in favor of convicting Stephen.

"Stephen," he muttered. He did not want to envisage it, but now his mind could not erase the image of Stephen St Albans and Gaston D'Arcy. Crispin met Stephen a year before encountering Rosamunde. He fought beside him in battle. He never suspected the man capable of what his mind conjured. It wasn't as if he had not known sodomites. Some were even his friends, but Stephen…

He shook his head and quaffed the wine. Rubbing his face, he listened to the silence of his room. Below, he could hear Martin Kemp's wife Alice berating him for some husbandly error among the clatter of pots and pans. Not long after, a door slammed and the quantity of smoke from the outdoor furnace suddenly billowed, cascading across Crispin's open window and tumbling into his room. Crispin took two strides to close the shutters, but not before watching Martin Kemp jam wood into the inferno, no doubt thinking of something other than wood burning in the fierce blaze and going up in smoke.

Crispin sighed and leaned his hand against the lintel. "I must return to the problem," he reminded himself. "Who is the murderer?"

He started when Jack Tucker opened the door and walked in as if he'd lived there all his life. He smiled upon seeing Crispin. "Master. What's the news?"

Crispin stared, unused to the ease with which Tucker had insinuated himself. He still wasn't quite sure what to make of the lad and his motives, but he shook his head and walked away from the window. Standing in front of the fire, he mechanically raised his fingers to the flames. It did little to warm him.

"The news, Jack, is far from good."

"Oh?" Jack settled on the floor beside the fire. He took out a wedge of cheese from his pouch and began eating it. With a wad bulging his cheek, he stopped and offered the hunk in his hand to Crispin. Crispin glanced disinterestedly at the food and shook his head.

"Stephen St Albans is not guilty of murder."

"No! It's that wretched sheriff to blame."

"No, no. It is not the sheriff. It's me. I have talked with Stephen and mulled over the evidence and I do not believe him guilty."

Jack eyed him and continued chewing. "The woman, then," he offered slowly. "That Lady Stancliff."

Crispin shook his head. "Nor her."

"Blind me, Master. Who's left?"

"Exactly." Crispin sat on the hard wood of the chair.

"Maybe it's them anti-pope men like I said."

"Yes. I do consider them. But I also consider D'Arcy's Templar companions."

"Eh? Why would they murder him? They were his friends, weren't they?"

Crispin tapped the wooden bowl with his fingers. "Not entirely. I cannot tell you all, Jack, but it might have been simpler for them to merely eliminate him. Remember, they did steal the body."

"Oh, aye." He chewed and thought. "It's complicated, isn't it?"

"That it is."

Crispin rose again to retrieve the wine jug and poured more into the bowl. He stood for a moment with the jug still in his hand and stared into nothing.

"Master," said Jack at his elbow. "Why don't you ask them Templars. Get it straight from them."

"Because I cannot find them. They find me."

"Then what of de Marcherne?"

"At least I do know where *he* is." He put the jug down and ran his hand over his day-old beard.

"Where, Master?"

He sighed, but it came from a weariness far beyond the rigors of the day. "Court," he answered.

Jack whistled. "Have you been lately to court, Master Crispin? Since...well, since..."

"No. I have not. But I have made many a deal with the Devil today. One more won't hurt."

Two strides took him to his wash basin, and he proceeded to shave without a word.

Jack insisted upon escorting him to Westminster Palace, and in the back of his mind, Crispin felt glad the boy came. He tried to look his best. Crispin had shaved, clipped his hair, and groomed his poor clothes as best he could, and though Jack's attire obviously belonged in no court, it was better to have some kind of retainer than none at all.

But the closer Crispin got to the gates, the harder it was to breathe. "I wish to God I had a horse," he muttered.

Jack nodded. "It would be more seemly, but a man has to make do." He glanced up at the walls and the finery of the guards ahead and moved closer to Crispin. "How long ago did you say you were last here?"

"Seven years. Yet it seems like only yesterday."

They reached the gatehouse and the porters looked them over. Each guard wore a mail hood that covered their chins and rested under their lower lip. Their conical helms fit snugly to their heads. One man-at-arms stood back under the shadows while the other approached. "And what would *you* want?" he asked.

Crispin resisted the urge to straighten his coat. No amount of tugging would hide its repairs. "I am here to see the dignitary from the French court; Guillaume de Marcherne."

The guard squinted at him before glancing back to his companion. Although Crispin looked like a common tradesman his manner of speech gave them pause.

"And what would the likes of his worthy want to see you for?" asked the man-at-arms.

"I have business with him. I would send my man here to give him a message."

The man glanced at Jack and sneered. "What? Him?"

"There now!" cried Jack. He gestured with a jerk of his thumb. "This here is Sir Crispin Guest, and you best show the proper respect for him. He has business at court."

The man made no effort to move except to lick his lips. "So?"

Crispin tried on his haughtiest expression. "I am sending my man with a message. Now."

But the guard dropped his hand on his sword pommel. "Take the tradesman's entrance. Back there." He gestured half-heartedly and turned his back.

Crispin felt his muscles tense and the urge to grab for his own sword was strong, even though no sword hung at his side.

Tight-lipped, he gestured for Jack to follow him and they walked around the palace by another arch. Men unloaded sacks from a cart and carried them in under the distracted eye of a man-at-arms. Crispin nodded for Jack to follow his lead and they each picked up a sack, hoisted it over their shoulders, and carried it inside. Once they were out of sight of the knights in the courtyard, they dropped their loads and entered a long corridor. Crispin found a wooden staircase and grabbed the railing. "Come along, Jack. Keep close."

"Aye, Master," he murmured, grasping Crispin's cloak.

They reached the top of the landing and entered a wide hall. The space was as large as any nave in London's bigger churches, spanned by huge trusses and ornate beams, all held aloft by two rows of pillars. The floor, painted in a large checkerboard of blue and white, stretched forward. Long banners hung from the far walls while the closer walls near a raised dais glittered with a colorful scene of men on horseback hunting a boar, and ladies plucking flowers. Crispin glanced at the shimmering banners and the many pallets still set up for sleeping servants, and headed across the expanse of floor. But Jack's tugging at his cloak slowed him to a stop.

"Jack! What are you doing?"

"Sweet Jesus." His voice seemed smaller amidst the hall's echoes. "What is this place?"

Crispin wanted to hurry through. He did not want to be forced to look about the hall, to remember where he had sat many a time, recalling the great feasts and the fine food. He did not wish to bring to mind with whom he talked and the women with whom he danced. But Jack's fear forced him to take stock and he made himself survey the place that had been home to him since before the time he was Jack's age.

"It is the great hall. This is where the evening meals are served."

Jack clutched Crispin's cloak tight and peered around him. "Does the king eat here?" he asked, still whispering.

"Yes." Crispin sighed and turned toward the dais. He pointed to the largest and most ornate chair situated in the center of the long plank table. "There, next to his ministers and now his wife."

"Blind me! Did you ever sit up there?"

"Sometimes. That was in Edward III's court. Before Richard was ever heir."

Jack raised his eyes to the high ceiling and its ornate beams painted in stripes and diamonds. Gold leaf gleamed from carved leaves, and below them hung huge, round coronas filled with candles, none of which were now lit. The hall's light came from large clerestory windows and flaming cressets.

The tapestries lining the walls rustled from a draft from the open passage doors. Above them hung the banners of knights and houses nearly as old as England itself. Crispin's banner once hung there. The family name of Guest had thrown in their fortunes with Henry II, and for two hundred years counted themselves among the elite of court society.

The banner was gone. Every memory of it wiped clean from English recollection. Others stood in its place, proudly jutting upward toward the arched ceiling, like angels' wings stretched protectively over the throne.

Jack turned a melancholy face to Crispin. His eyes were wide and moist. "By the saints. *This* is what you lost?"

Crispin turned away. He tried to swallow the ache in his throat. "Come along."

Quickly they passed through the great hall to an outer chamber framed by clerestory windows. Here, oil lamps lit their way along more painted floors. Murals and tapestries enlivened the plaster walls.

A cluster of maids bustled ahead and Crispin drew back to allow them distance. Except that the maids had a familiar look about them. And one in particular.

He rushed forward, Jack trying vainly to catch up.

"Vivienne!"

She stopped and turned. Her maids stood before her protectively, especially the ones who recognized Crispin.

A small smile formed on her lips and she shook her head. "Crispin Guest. You do turn up at the most unexpected places."

"As do you, Madam." He bowed. Nudging Jack, the boy followed suit.

She glanced at her maids but seemed to decide she needed a shield. She did not dismiss them or move to stand before them. "I found it necessary to return to court. I made a, perhaps, too hasty departure."

"Indeed. What brings you back so swiftly?"

"Unfinished business."

"And yet I thought your business *was* finished."

The smile on her lips now appeared painted there. "This is

other business."

Crispin glanced at the maids and then at a perplexed and defensive Jack. There was only so much he could say in front of an audience. "Then…I hope you will come to me if there is anything more I can do for you."

She bowed her head and curtseyed. "You will be the first to know." She turned on those words, and without looking back, proceeded up the corridor.

Crispin watched her leave with a wave of anxiety. He took a step forward, but stopped. He longed to ask her about Guillaume de Marcherne, but too many eyes and ears made that impossible. And he had been as good as dismissed. He knew in his current standing he had no authority to delay her.

"But she left London…" Jack whispered.

"Yes. She had." He pressed a fist to his hip. "And now she is back. And I wonder now if I was right in not apprehending her. The sheriff will have my hide if I change my mind on it."

"Then don't change your mind," Jack muttered under his breath.

Ahead, he heard voices and hoped it came from the pages he sought. He moved quickly and turned the corner much too fast and ran into a lordly man surrounded by a cadre of equally attired knights and squires.

Crispin blanched and stepped back. Belatedly, he bowed in apology and tried to skirt them by walking backwards, trying to escape before they recognized him, but the lordly man shot out a hand and grabbed his arm.

Crispin gasped and looked up. The man was older. The beard running along the underside of his jaw and his neatly trimmed mustache were black but graying, yet there was no mistaking that stern nose and those aggressive eyes.

He glared at Crispin for a long moment. His pale lips parted to speak, but in the end, he said nothing. He released Crispin's arm and turned from him abruptly, striding quickly down the corridor with his entourage of knights. He never looked back, but his entourage did, with scowls and accusing expressions.

Crispin froze. *Careless. Incredibly careless.*

Jack waited for the men to disappear through an arched doorway before he tugged on Crispin's cloak. "Who was that, Master?"

Crispin breathed again, unaware he had held his breath. "That was John of Gaunt, duke of Lancaster."

"Jesus mercy," whispered Jack and becrossed himself.

Crispin did not move except to shake his head. "It was a mistake to come here."

"But you have to question de Marcherne, do you not?"

"To what end? I cannot arrest him. He could easily escape to France before the sheriff ever decides to make his writ. Wynchecombe already has his murderer, remember?"

"Then what are you going to do?"

His body felt numb, his limbs limp. "I do not know." Curse his impetuosity! It had been a proud choice to return to court. He believed that if he summoned the courage to do this, then nothing, not even the cold reality of Rosamunde's broken chastity, could crack him. But he was wrong. This was too insurmountable.

The Tracker. He snorted. He could not even find his own dignity. He thought he did find a portion of it through feats with the lower classes, but all of it was mummery.

The palace walls closed in on him, trapping him in the illusion of the freedom he mistakenly thought he possessed.

"Crispin Guest?"

Crispin spun and stared at a young page. His fears gathered about him again. "Yes?"

"His grace the duke wishes to speak with you."

Crispin felt his skin go cold. "With me?"

"Yes. Follow me."

Crispin looked once at Jack before he lifted his deadened feet to trail the page. Jack followed a little further behind.

They entered a small door to an anteroom where Lancaster sat on a sumptuous chair.

"Your servant can wait outside," said Lancaster.

Jack seemed only too happy to oblige and he bowed to the duke very low and once more to Crispin before exiting.

Warm. Familiar. Crispin recalled gazing at this room's rich tapestries many a time, losing himself in the adventures depicted on their clever panels. He and his fellow squires and knights used to warm themselves by that same fire, sharing cups of wine and speaking of deep things that only men who had shared the experience of war could discuss.

Being Lancaster's protégé, Crispin had been allowed in the next chamber, Lancaster's bedroom. Pleased to serve as Lancaster's personal varlet, Crispin's training began with these menial tasks for his lord. He had cut his meat at dinner and he had served him cups of wine. They never seemed like lowly chores then, for he loved the man who raised him, knighted him, trained him, and took him on his campaigns.

Yet now, Crispin stood before him like the menial he had become. He kept silent knowing he no longer had the right to speak freely.

Lancaster studied him. "It has been a long time, Crispin," he said at last.

Crispin tried to smile but could not recall how. "Yes, your grace. A very long time."

"I did not know of your return to court."

Crispin tapped his scabbard with nervous fingers. "I have not exactly been brought back, your grace."

"Oh?" Lancaster's gaze began its slow travel over Crispin's shoddy clothes, lighting last on his left hip, the place where his sword should have been. "Well," he said, seeming not to know just what to reply. "You look well, at any rate. A bit thin, perhaps. What do you do with yourself?"

Never had Crispin felt so aware of his lack of a sword, as if he were standing naked before Lancaster. "I solve puzzles, your grace," he managed to say. "I recover stolen goods, bring criminals to justice, right wrongs."

"Right wrongs, eh?" Lancaster's lips curved into an ironic smile. "If not for yourself than for others, is that it?"

"Perhaps it is a penance, your grace."

Lancaster ticked his head. "I have missed you, Crispin. But I have also been extremely angry with you. And disappointed."

Crispin shut his eyes. "I know, your grace. I say again, I apologize. And I do thank you for speaking for me, for asking the king to spare my life. I was never able to convey that. I was ushered away so quickly, and then…"

Lancaster nodded and stared at the floor. "Yes. Well. I am surprised you are in London. I would have thought…"

Crispin raised his head. "There was truly nowhere else to go."

Lancaster nodded. "Just so."

Crispin wondered if he should say more. Lancaster looked old suddenly, and very tired. When Richard took the throne at the tender age of ten, a council had been appointed to rule until he came of age, and Lancaster ruled that council. For all intents and purposes, he *was* the power of the throne. In the end, Crispin's traitorous efforts toward that resolution had been premature.

Being outside the sphere of court, Crispin had been unable to determine if Lancaster had any further influence on his nephew and charge. But now, at sixteen, King Richard showed himself to be the petulant autocrat Crispin feared he would become, even though he was not at full majority. Like his doomed great grandfather Edward II, Richard kept close too many favorites who were given too many privileges and too much access. Crispin believed if this continued into Richard's majority, the king's fate might follow that of his unfortunate ancestor.

"What is your business here, Crispin?"

"Strange business, your grace. I am investigating a murder."

Lancaster raised a brow in a familiar way. It eased Crispin somewhat to think that Lancaster might find something in him to be proud of again.

"You work with the sheriff, then? I had not heard this."

"Not exactly, your grace. I am a free agent but the sheriff does call upon me from time to time."

Lancaster mulled this while examining Crispin's shabby clothes. "You have a retainer. That boy."

Crispin smiled. "Yes. He won't seem to take 'no' for an answer."

"Who is he? An apprentice investigator?"

Crispin's smile fell. "No. A cutpurse."

"What?"

"Reformed."

"I see. This is the manner of men you traffic with?"

"It is now."

Lancaster acceded with a nod. "I take it there is someone here you wish to interview about this murder."

"Yes, your grace. It is somewhat thorny."

"It isn't the king, is it?" His voice carried a familiar sardonic lilt.

"No." Crispin smiled. "It is only the French dignitary, Guillaume de Marcherne."

"'Only', eh? Crispin, can I trust you in this?"

"With my life, your grace. I owe it to you at any rate. I need only talk with him. But, in truth, it would help a great deal if I could examine his rooms without his presence."

"Crispin, Crispin." Lancaster rose and walked across the Saracen rug before the hearth. He stood just as Crispin remembered: strong, straight, tall. His posture reminded him of those days on the battlefield and especially after, when Lancaster walked amongst his men and toasted them with a shared cup of ale.

The hearth flames were kind to his aging features, and Crispin could almost transport himself back to those lost days when he grew to maturity under this man's shadow. Strange, he thought, that a man only ten years his senior could seem so much older and wiser.

"What are you thinking, Crispin?" he said in his mentor's voice. "Are you trying to get yourself hanged?"

"No, my lord. Far from it. But I must know more of this man. There are some facts I know already, but I must be certain if they are true. He is a master of lies."

"What is your plan?"

With an awkward smile, Crispin shrugged. "I have no plan."

Lancaster shook his head with disdain. "After all these years, still hot-headed as ever. Do you recall nothing of my lessons? I told you to curb these impulses or you will get yourself killed."

"As you see," he said, opening his arms, "I am still alive."

"Yes. God must love you greatly. Or does not wish eternity yet with you."

Crispin waited. Was he to be escorted from court? Surely Lancaster would not turn him in. He wondered just why Lancaster asked to see him at all. He hoped it was because of their mutual affection. But times had changed. Crispin was no longer the asset he had been. If he were found in Lancaster's quarters, even now after seven years...

Lancaster turned back to the fire. The years fell away and it was again him and Crispin plotting and planning. He remembered quiet evenings in these chambers while Lancaster's first wife Blanche played a psaltery. They would sit together, a family, listening to the quiet strains of music before a roaring fire. Occasionally, Lancaster's son Henry would join them. Henry, the same age as Richard, seemed a world apart in temperament from his monarch cousin. Not often at court, Henry likely stayed busy with his own knight's training. After Blanche died, Lancaster married Costanza of Castile. She was not the motherly matron that Blanche had been to him, but he missed her, too, and her kind attention.

Crispin suddenly frowned. It didn't do to fall into the trap of sentimentality. There would be no more quiet evenings by Lancaster's fire, no more private moments with the man. He looked up at the duke and saw all the same thoughts pass over Lancaster's features. Lancaster scowled and he suddenly seemed much older.

"Listen carefully," Lancaster said at last. "I will have de Marcherne brought to me now and you will have no more than a quarter hour to see to your business in his rooms. After that, I am no longer responsible. I did not see you and I did not speak with you. Do you understand?"

"Yes, your grace."

"Go now. If I recall, he is in the west corridor."

Crispin longed to clasp Lancaster's hand, but that intimacy had long past. Crispin bowed low instead before he hastily departed.

Jack hovered in the shadows trying to disappear when he noticed Crispin. "Master!" Jack scurried alongside him. "What happened?"

"He's helping us, but we must hurry."

Crispin trotted and Jack followed. They skirted pages and servants and finally made it to the west corridor. Crispin moved Jack and himself into a small window alcove and pulled the drapery around them. "We must wait here," he whispered. He grabbed the two curtains with his fists and peered through a small crevice.

A page strode down the passageway and entered the door to a suite of apartments. Not long after, he came out again followed by de Marcherne and two of his men. Like a military unit, they marched down the passage and soon disappeared into the distant shadows.

Crispin opened the curtains and without bothering to motion to Jack, went up to the door and pulled on the door ring.

Locked.

He knelt. Using the long metal aiglet from one lace of his shirt and his dagger's point, he inserted both into the lock. He fished and jiggled until the pins set and the lock released.

Jack whistled. "Blind me. Where'd you learn that?"

"You'd be surprised at the things I've learned." He pushed open the door and peered inside. At first he feared the other men would be lying in wait for him, but a cursory examination of the chamber told him otherwise.

Crispin moved to one of the chests and opened it. He rummaged through the many layers of rich clothing until his fingers encountered something hard. He removed a box, tripped the lock in the same way as he had the door, and opened it. Brooches, rings, other fine jewels. Nothing of any consequence. He handed the box to Jack to return to the chest and immediately grabbed the boy's hand. "Jack, there are no spoils from this venture. Put it back."

"But Master! Surely you don't think—"

"Jack, I am not a fool. I saw you take the ring. Now return it."

Grumbling, Jack cupped his palm and spit the ring into it. He stuffed the wet object back in the box which he placed with care under the clothes in the first chest.

Crispin checked the other chests and found nothing. He stood looking at them before he knelt to the first chest again. Opening the lid, he examined the inside, running his fingers along its edges. A soft click, and a panel opened. He reached in and removed an empty pouch. Embroidered on it was the Templar's cross.

"Jesus mercy," whispered Jack.

"Indeed."

Crispin rummaged inside the trunk's secret hiding places but found nothing more. He likewise searched the other chests and found similar hiding places, but those contained only silver and gold coins.

Crispin returned all to its proper order when they heard footsteps approach from the passageway. "Quick, Jack. Go to the window and hide behind the curtains."

"What about you?"

"Don't worry about me."

Jack complied and Crispin moved to a large chair and relaxed into its velvet cushion just as the door opened.

De Marcherne's men noticed Crispin first. Both drew their swords and advanced on him. De Marcherne turned and his surprised expression changed to one of admiration.

"Hold!" he told his men. Crispin did not move and glanced from one sword tip to the other. "Well, Crispin," said de Marcherne. "What a welcomed surprise." He assessed the room. Satisfied, he addressed his henchmen. "Put away your weapons. I would speak with this man alone."

The henchmen did as told but moved hesitantly toward the

door. "Go on," de Marcherne insisted, encouraging them with a sweep of his hand.

Once alone he sat in the chair opposite Crispin. "Have you come to accept my offer?"

"To be a knight in the French court?" Crispin chuckled mirthlessly. "I would not ask a dog to do that."

De Marcherne frowned. "Well then. Why are you here?"

"I have some questions for you. I would rather ask them in the manner you asked me." He smiled unpleasantly. "Unfortunately, I am in no position to do any such thing."

De Marcherne's face relaxed. "No, of course not. I do wonder at the gall of your being here at all. I will not even ask how you got in here."

Crispin shook his head. "*I* am asking the questions."

"I could easily call the palace guards. It would not go well for you."

"It hasn't gone well for me for some years. However. My questions. Tell me about being Grand Master."

De Marcherne laughed, a long, rolling laugh, one that included his clapping in amusement. A laugh that only made Crispin's apprehension tighten and his anger sizzle.

"I am amused that you are so intrigued by this." He shook his head. "Yes, I was Grand Master of the Order of the Knights of the Temple. For many years. I knew their secrets, I knew their membership, and where each resided. I knew who was loyal and who was not. I meted out punishment and my word was law. It was a sacred task of unimaginable power. 'So', you must be thinking, 'why did he leave? Was he ousted? Threatened?' The answer, my dear Crispin, is that *I* left it all behind."

"Forgive me," he said dispassionately. "But I think you are lying."

"Indeed? No. *I* left it. I foreswore my brothers and I sold their secrets, and I nearly got away with the grail. Why?" His smile widened and his even teeth gleamed in the firelight. He lifted an index finger and ticked it from side to side.

"You won't tell me."

"Patience, Crispin. I must keep you interested and involved. I do not think of you as my quarry, as I think of so many men. I think of you as an equal."

"Merciful God."

"Oh, it is a compliment, though you may not recognize it now. You see," he said leaning forward, "I believe you will convert to my way of thinking once you know all. You will become my ally."

"I doubt that."

"Do not dismiss me so quickly. You have no idea how far this thing extends. Or how far back."

Crispin blinked, hiding his bewilderment behind his lids. "This 'thing'?"

"This coven of the grail, Crispin. Indeed, the grail goes back nearly fourteen hundred years. And for fourteen hundred years men have sought it. Do you ever ask yourself why?"

Crispin snorted. "It is the Last Supper cup. It held the Savior's blood."

"So pedestrian." He sighed. "Of course it did. But do you think most men are sentimental fools? Do you think they want it simply to cherish such a thing?"

"Yes, I do."

"Crispin, Crispin. I did not take *you* for a maudlin man. To cherish it! Bah! There are relics aplenty for reverence. No. The reason men want the grail is for power. Unimaginable power."

"Power?"

"Yes. Of course there is the power of healing, but there are more secrets to the grail. Power over others in ways that can never be resisted by trebuchet or arrow."

Crispin's neck hairs stood up and he drew forward. "What are you talking about?"

"I am talking about the power of God."

Crispin shot out of the chair and stood over de Marcherne. "You and these Templars! I am supposed to believe that God's power is there in the grail for the taking?"

"Yes. That and more. Do you not listen to your priest's sermons? Do you not know that God's ways are not our ways?"

Crispin stared at de Marcherne's unruffled demeanor and felt a chill run down his spine. "You do not speak of God at all," he said in a low voice. "You *are* the Devil incarnate."

"You don't believe me. I expected as much."

"I believe many things about you, to be sure. And I wonder if you killed Gaston D'Arcy to get the grail. You and I both know you will get away with it. I cannot apprehend you. The sheriff cannot touch you. But I have the need to know."

"Is that why you came? To investigate an unimportant murder? How commonplace."

"Did you?"

"He was not in the plan for the grail. Ask your Templar friends. They know."

"Dammit! *Did you?*"

De Marcherne stood and glared nose to nose with Crispin. "Why is this so important? I tell you, there are far greater things at stake than catching a murderer."

Crispin grabbed de Marcherne's coat and fisted the cloth in his hands. He brought his face within inches of de Marcherne's. "Tell me now, or I swear I will kill you!"

The curtains rustled. Suddenly they crumpled upon themselves with a great, thunderous crash of rod and plaster that startled Crispin and de Marcherne from their confrontation.

Jack stood alone in the little alcove, the thick curtains encircling his feet, his face white. "For the love of Christ, Master, let us leave this hellish place!"

Livid, Crispin released de Marcherne and glared at Jack.

The Frenchman straightened his houppelande and brushed it off. "Perhaps your little friend is right. Perhaps it is time for you to leave before I call the palace guards. Or mine."

Crispin swept the room with a furious glance. He grasped Jack by the collar and hoisted him inches above the floor while dragging him forward, but de Marcherne's parting words slowed him.

"And Crispin. Since we no longer have an agreement, I must warn you. If you find the grail first, it will be the last thing you ever do."

CHAPTER TWENTY-EIGHT

They reached the foot of Crispin's lodgings and he finally spun on Jack. "All I needed was one more moment, one more word from him, you senseless, sorry thief!"

Jack pouted. "Now, Master. That isn't no way to speak to me. I'm a good lad, I am. I'm loyal to you. But when that man talked about God! I started gripping the curtains and...well it wasn't my fault they fell! I got all queer inside. Like he didn't have the right to speak the name of the Lord with his poisonous breath."

Crispin mashed his lips together and stared at Jack a long time. He ran his hand over his face and nodded solemnly. "You may be right."

"'Course I am. And you don't truly believe he done it, do you?"

"Why not? He is evil enough."

"Aye. That's my point. If he did it he wouldn't fear telling you. He'd be proud of it. I think he's toying with you because he only wished he done it!"

Crispin said nothing. He climbed the stairs, unlocked the door, and dropped into his chair.

Jack went to the hearth to coax fire from the ashes.

Crispin watched the renewing flames. The boy busied himself tidying up the room and swept stray ashes back into the hearth.

"Very well," Crispin said, answering Jack's question at last. "No.

236

I suppose I don't believe he did it, and for the reason you cite. But God's blood, I want him to be guilty!"

He sat with his face in his hands a long while, feeling the room grow warmer from the fire. But he also felt weary and strangely out of place. Returning to court drained his senses. His limbs even felt heavy as if he had been running in full armor.

"Again, we are placed in the unfortunate circumstance of not knowing who the murderer is."

Jack handed Crispin a bowl of wine. "Aye. But you've solved difficult puzzles before, have you not?"

Crispin drank thirstily. His throat felt like parchment. "Yes. But not quite like this."

Jack went to the larder and poured himself a bowl of wine and stood over Crispin, contemplating his pinched expression. "I wish I could help you, Master. I truly do. I haven't a head for puzzles, I'm afraid. That is what you do."

"So they tell me," he said with a sigh. Jack hurried to refill Crispin's cup.

"Jack, what am I forgetting? What small clue have I missed?"

The boy settled on the floor by the fire and hugged his legs, his bowl beside him. "I know not, Master. It seems so long ago now, though it was less than a sennight. I was only at the Boar's Tusk very briefly."

"That's right. I was asleep and I felt you cut my purse—"

"Sloppy, that. You never should have felt it," he said with a brush of hurt in his voice.

Crispin's mind summoned the scene from one of many wine-soaked memories. "Let me think. I was asleep and…who else was there?"

"Master Gilbert, but was asleep, too."

"Yes. And then there was you, and John the piper, and the dead man, and some assorted fellows I've seen a thousand times before."

"And the servant."

"And the servant." Crispin squinted, trying to see the tavern in the dim corners of his memory. "The servant. He was sitting next to D'Arcy." He thumped his elbow on the table and rested his chin in his hand. "I only saw him…" He tilted his head to the side trying to recollect. "I only saw him through the haze of hearth smoke. And it was shadowy. But I knew he was a servant because he wore livery. Whose? Jack, do you recall his colors?"

"Ah me no, sir. I know they was dark."

"Dark. Green or blue. I can't remember. But he sat beside Gaston D'Arcy. How long?"

"He was there when I entered."

"And how long were you there before you began to thieve from me?"

Jack blushed and lowered his face. "I had to get the sense of the room, Master. And though I knew the rest were in their cups— begging your pardon—I had to wait until no one was mindful of me."

"And how long was that?"

"'Bout quarter past the hour. Once no one paid me any heed…well, that's when I made me move."

"So he sat beside D'Arcy all that time? Doing what?"

"Naught. Not even drinking."

Crispin sat up. "But I saw him. He was drunk when he got up. He even fell against you."

"Ah no, good Master. That is *my* way, you see. 'Twas I that stumbled against him."

Crispin saw the room in his mind's eye. The smoky interior flickered in the firelight. The windows were shuttered against the rain and mist. Candles on the tables offered some light but only sparsely. Crispin's wine bowl sat before him but there were many discarded on the table, just as there had been in front of the dead man. "There were many bowls on that table. Do you tell me the servant drank from none of them?"

"I only know what I saw, Master, and as you know, I had naught to drink. Until I drank that cursed poison."

Crispin looked at his wine but did not drink. "Jack, when you bumped into him, did you take his purse as well?"

"Ah, no, Master. He moved too swiftly for me."

"Damn!"

"Oh, but I did get his broach."

Crispin slowly raised his face. "Tell me, Jack," he said, trying to calm the excitement in his voice. "You do not, by any chance, still have that broach, do you?"

"Oh, aye."

Crispin shot from his chair and grabbed Jack by the shoulders. Jack squealed in surprise and pushed away from him. "Here now!"

"That broach, Jack. Get it!"

"Very well," he said cautiously once Crispin let him go. He went to the door and grasped the jamb. He guiltily looked back once at Crispin before he pulled and loosened the board and reached with his stick-thin arm into the opening.

Crispin marveled that such a secret place hid under his very nose, but he admired Jack all the more for his ingenuity.

At last, Jack pulled out a parcel wrapped in a rag and tied with string. He laid it on the table and ran his hand under his nose. "Now then," Jack said, the same hand resting on the parcel. "When I open this, you may be surprised by what's inside. But there's no sense in your insisting I return these items to their owners for I have long since forgotten who owned them. I am at your mercy, sir."

Crispin returned a solemn countenance to Jack's grave one. "I swear on my honor, Jack, that I will say nothing."

"Right then." Jack took his knife and cut the parcel's string and opened the rag. Crispin's eyes widened when he beheld the many folded documents, wax seals and leather ribbons in tact. But there were also rings, brooches, pins, and loose gems.

"Jack!" he gasped. "God's blood!"

"It's me treasure," he said sheepishly. "For my retirement. A man can't be a thief all his life."

Crispin laughed and touched the boy good-naturedly on the shoulder. "No indeed. My hope is that no new items of late have been added to this cache."

Jack lowered his face and muttered, "'Of late'? Well, that depends on what you mean by that."

"Never mind for now. How is it I missed these things when I caught you that night?"

·Jack smiled. "It's a clever thief with more than one place to hide his spoils."

Crispin eagerly scanned the cache again. "Which one belonged to the servant?"

"Now let me think." Jack picked through his bounty and finally weighed something in his hand, nodding. "This one. I think it is this one. With the bird."

Crispin took the broach and stared at ivory and silver. A bird, a crane. His mind put it together and he shook his head. "Oh, Jack. What a pity."

"Eh? Someone you know, then?"

"Yes. Someone I know."

He took his cloak but left his hood behind and said over his shoulder, "Jack, you'd best come with me."

Crispin struggled to remember. He put himself back in the setting of the Boar's Tusk almost a week ago; watched the servant in dark livery—certain now it was blue. The man would be familiar, but Crispin's position across the room and his drunken state contributed to his not recognizing him.

When they reached the White Hart, Crispin told Jack to stand guard at the door until called. Crispin entered and stood in the doorway to get his bearings and to allow his eyes to become accustomed to the dimness. He scanned the room and strode across the tavern until he reached a table near the stairwell. A man sat alone, staring into his bowl of wine. His dark blue coat had a high collar and buttoned up the throat. The skirt, split in the middle, made it easier for him to run and better serve his masters. A black leather belt cinched his waist. A lengthy strap of leather, it wrapped around him almost a second time and folded and tucked over the buckle. It sported a scabbard with a dagger and a leather scrip at his hip near his back. An embroidered crane eyed Crispin from the left breast, the signet of Rothwell.

"Jenkyn," said Crispin.

He jerked up his head and stared. Crispin made his way to the table and sat opposite him. "What do *you* want?"

"Now, Jenkyn. Is that any way to talk to an old friend?"

Jenkyn stared up at Crispin with cool gray eyes. Not steel gray like Crispin's, but light with just the barest blue tint to them. His bushy brows hung over his lids. His nose, straight and aristocratic, belonged more to his betters than his long lineage of servants serving the St Albans household as far back as anyone could remember. His hair, slightly wilder than fashion called for, shined darkly, but gray streaks tangled through it and the hairline shot high up his lengthened forehead. "I was not your friend," he said. "I was my master's servant. And now I am the servant of my mistress."

"Just so. We were never friends, but I feel I know you."

"No, you don't. You were just another lord like all the rest, and now you're not even that. Begone. I have no use for you."

Crispin curled his fingers into fists. He would have struck the man, but Jenkyn was in the right. Crispin was no longer a lord. He could talk to Crispin any way he liked.

"So that is how you truly feel? Interesting. If only our masters could hear what is in our heads, eh? We'd all be released from service."

"Then it's a good thing none are mind readers." He took up the bowl but still did not drink.

Crispin watched him. "You do not drink."

"I am not thirsty."

"Yet you ordered wine."

Jenkyn looked at the bowl in his hand as if recognizing it for the first time. Hastily he put it down. "Habit."

"Perhaps you have no more taste for drinking wine in taverns. To see a man die from such imbibing…"

Jenkyn rose but Crispin drew his blade and motioned for him to sit again. "I do not believe I am done talking with you," he said and slowly sat again, echoing Jenkyn's cautious movements. He kept the knife in plain view. Jenkyn stared at it. His forehead beaded with sweat and his breath became hard and rasping.

"Why don't you tell me about that night," Crispin urged.

Jenkyn wrung his hands. "Jesus mercy," he muttered. "I don't want to hang."

"That is the punishment for murder, is it not?"

"Have I not been a loyal servant? Have I not served the house of St Albans for most of my life?"

"There is no denying it." Crispin's stomach turned. He had no belly for what was to come; for the pleading and the crying. A man should take his punishment. He knew he should be angrier at Jenkyn for all the flurry he'd caused, for Crispin's sometimes disastrous meetings with Lady Vivienne and for his trouble with Stephen. And even for Crispin's encounters with Templars and de Marcherne. Jenkyn had given him a merry chase and now was time to finish it. "Tell me what happened."

"Oh my poor Lady Rothwell. He was a devil. He...he..."

Jenkyn succumbed to weeping and laid his head on his arms. Crispin sat back and sheathed his knife. He glanced at the others who turned to look. "Pull yourself together. You were surely defending your mistress' honor."

"Yes, yes. That is so!" He raised his wet face. His trembling hands opened and closed until he finally grasped them together and dropped them into his lap. "She has been good to me. So good. When I discovered what that knave intended..."

"There's no need to speak of that," Crispin interrupted. He looked behind at the curious faces and suddenly thought better of a public encounter. "Come now. We will discuss this with the sheriff."

Jenkyn's face drained of its ruddiness and became flat and white like a plaster wall. "The sheriff? Gaol? Oh, Sir Crispin! You don't mean to turn me in, do you? Was I not equally loyal to you, good sir?"

So swiftly Crispin changed from a troublesome nobody to "Sir

Crispin" again. He had no time to enjoy the irony. "Though that is true, there has been a crime, Jenkyn. As a knight…well, even though a knight no more, I still have sworn to uphold the king's laws, and I must."

The servant's speed caught Crispin off guard. Jenkyn sprinted from the table and zigzagged through the benches and chairs. Crispin snapped from his seat to pursue, but the man was always an arm's length out of reach. Just as Crispin almost caught up, he got tangled in a crowd of men playing dice, and tried vainly to shove them aside.

Jenkyn slipped out the door, knocking down Jack Tucker. Crispin called out, "Get him, Jack!" but Jenkyn disappeared far from sight by then, having ducked down a nearby alley.

When Crispin reached the door he scowled at Jack. "Did I not tell you to be on your guard?"

Jack picked himself up and wiped the mud from his sagging stockings. "I'm sorry, Master. Forgive me."

Crispin glared down the bleak avenue, with its few passersby, and thrust his fists in his hips. "No, Jack, I was at fault. I am the one who was not on guard. But there is nowhere for him to run. We will wrest him yet."

"Is he the murderer?"

"Yes, Jack. Right under our very noses all along."

"Why'd he do it? Did he know the gentleman?"

"He knew him. He did it for his mistress' honor," he said, looking up at the threatening sky. He remembered he left his chaperon hood back at his room. "But he will tell all when we apprehend him. We must go to Newgate and inform the sheriff."

"He won't like this. Will he believe you, I wonder? Enough to release Sir Stephen?"

"I don't know. Pray he does. Then this whole matter will be over with."

"Except for one thing." Jack glanced behind him as if expecting doom to descend upon him with his utterance. "The Holy Grail."

CHAPTER TWENTY-NINE

"Let me sum this up," said Wynchecombe. He left his houppelande unbuttoned down to the waist revealing the white shirt beneath. His wide sleeves were rolled up past a hairy length of wrist. He wore no hat and his black hair lay in mussed waves. "You want me to release our prisoner because you do not believe him guilty. Instead, you wish to implicate a servant who escaped from your easy grasp. Is that the gist of it?"

Crispin gritted his teeth. His hand rested on his dagger hilt. "Close enough."

"You must be mad!"

"Only slightly."

"I don't understand you, Crispin." Wynchecombe rose to walk around the table. He planted himself firmly beside Crispin and cast a shadow, blocking the oil lamp's flame. "Your chance at revenge. Fame for such a coup. You would give it up—"

"For the truth, my lord."

"But as Pilate said, 'What is truth?' Anything can be made to be the truth."

"Not anything. Sir Stephen is not guilty, and though nothing would please me more than to see him die, I would not have it so through a lie. In truth…" He shook his head. "I do not even know if I feel the same about my vengeance any longer."

"Crispin! God's teeth! A change of heart? Truly a miracle has

244

come to pass."

Crispin thought he knew Stephen, thought he understood his own misery, but none of it seemed to matter of late. "I know not. All I know is that I believe him when he protests his innocence. And this servant was there sitting beside Gaston D'Arcy with the means and the motive to kill him."

"Oh? What motive was that?"

He wondered how much to divulge. Perhaps Wynchecombe could keep his tongue. "He was defending the honor of his mistress."

"Lady Rothwell? How so?"

"My lord, discretion is tantamount. The lady is betrothed."

"Indeed? You show an unusual amount of restraint for a man who was once betrothed to her yourself."

Scowling, Crispin turned away. Not given permission to sit, Crispin stood at the window and gazed into Newgate's courtyard. The rain began again, and the courtyard was bathed in gray light and misty lines of drizzle. Stagnant puddles came alive with jumping dots of raindrops, and the few wooly horses tethered there stomped impatiently for dryer paddocks. "That was a long time ago, my Lord Sheriff. I have put the matter aside."

"Then what is this secret that must be so hushed?"

"The lady," Crispin began in a subdued tone, "was having a love affair with D'Arcy."

Wynchecombe's laugh infuriated but Crispin did not turn from the window. He clutched the shutter, grasping so tightly he felt the wood crack.

Wynchecombe composed himself and merrily poured more wine in his silver cup. "Such a motive could be equally applied to Sir Stephen. Or you, for that matter."

"Not with poison. Stephen would have slit the man's throat. I know I would have."

Wynchecombe chuckled and nodded. "And so would I."

"My witness claims Jenkyn did not drink, and sat beside D'Arcy for at least a quarter of an hour."

"Your witness? Who?"

"Jack Tucker."

"Who is Jack Tucker?"

Crispin licked his lips. "The cutpurse."

The cup flew across the room nearly hitting Crispin in the head. Red wine splattered on Crispin's coat and face. He wiped his cheek.

"You whoreson! What are you playing at? Do you toy with me?" Wynchecombe pulled his dagger and advanced on Crispin. Not knowing what else to do, Crispin allowed the sheriff to back him against the shutter and hold the blade to his throat.

"How about I slit *your* throat, eh?" The sheriff's wine breath puffed on Crispin's cheek. "Wouldn't that be the end of all my troubles? Including yours?"

"Don't you want the truth, my Lord Sheriff? Or are half-lies better than disagreeable facts?"

Crispin felt the cold steel press to the flesh under his jaw. The sharp edge sliced him by his mere breathing. He waited interminably for the sheriff to pull away, and when he did not, Crispin wondered if he ever would.

Then be done with it! Let me leave this world while I have tried to do justice in it. Then maybe God, if not my fellow man, will forgive me.

Wynchecombe breathed raggedly and began to loosen his grip. With reluctance in his eyes, he lowered the dagger.

Crispin reached up to his throat and wiped away the blood.

"You are a damnable man!" the sheriff bellowed. He threw his knife into the table where it stuck. "What am I supposed to do now? I trusted your judgment. I arrested Sir Stephen on your word. I will have the king down on my head because of you." Wynchecombe faced him. "You've betrayed me!"

"Not so, my lord. I have done good work for you in the past. Our history together must surely—"

"History means nothing!"

Crispin surprised himself with the vehemence of his reaction. It bubbled up out of nowhere, yet always it lay just below the crust of emotions. "Nothing?" he cried. "History is everything!"

Wynchecombe drew back, startled, but Crispin didn't bother with civility any longer.

"How you can stand there and tell me…" Crispin held out his arms showing himself in all the rags and shabby finery of days past. "Look at me, Wynchecombe. I am nothing *but* history!" He laughed, slightly hysterically, and dropped his arms to his sides. Advancing toward the table he smiled when Wynchecombe subtly retreated. "You are not a brilliant man, Wynchecombe. But surely even you must recognize that history plays the most important part in a man's life. Mine especially. If it were not so, I should have taken a sword to you years ago."

Wynchecombe said nothing. He hovered over the table, eyeing his knife. His sword and baldric lay out of reach. "You'd take a sword to me, eh?" asked Wynchecombe warily. "Why? Because I give you the insolence you deserve?"

Crispin nodded. His face felt hot. Anger reddened it and forced his mouth into a grimace. "The insolence I deserve," he echoed, thinking about the words. "Who knows what I deserve? Perhaps I taunt you so that you will thrust that knife into my gut. You want to, don't you? Why don't you take it up? I won't stop you."

Wynchecombe grasped the dagger hilt and pulled it free of the wood. He held the blade but not to strike. Crispin could imagine the heft of it. He knew it was well made with soft leather strips carefully wound about the wooden grip. A red gem crowned the pommel.

The dagger hanging from Crispin's belt was the same he owned for three decades. They did not see fit to take it from him when they stripped him of everything else. It was as fine a thing as Wynchecombe's blade.

But Crispin made no move to retrieve it. He was as anxious as Wynchecombe to discover what would transpire next.

"Enough of your arrogance," the sheriff said at last. "Yes, you have a history. You are not a great lord anymore. You are not a knight. You are…what? What are you now, Crispin? A day ago you were my lackey. Is that what you are?"

All the vitality and anger released from him, rushing out with a long, ragged sigh. "Yes," Crispin said gravely. "That is what I am. That is all I will ever be."

The sheriff toyed with his knife. He touched the blade's tip with his finger and turned the hilt, catching the light in flashes on its polished brass. All at once he laughed.

Crispin drew himself up and stared at the sheriff's ruddy countenance: eyes squinted, teeth bared, mustache lifted up at the corners.

Has he gone mad, too?

"Crispin, you sorrowful bastard!" He slammed the knife into its scabbard and stood back, looking at him.

Crispin knew he had done a terribly stupid thing. Not only had he been uncivil and rude to a better, but he showed his hand, revealed his vulnerability. In a fight, he never would have done so. But in a true fight, he would have been better armed.

The sheriff swung and caught Crispin's jaw with his fist.

Flashes of light, motes of black. Crispin looked up at the sheriff from the floor.

"That's for your ill manners," Wynchecombe said and walked around the table, but not to help Crispin up. Instead, he kicked him hard in the side. Crispin rolled away with a gasp and curled inward to protect the damage.

"And that is for using me."

He grabbed Crispin by his collar and lifted his shoulders off the floor long enough to snap his fist at Crispin's face a second time. He let him fall back down. His head hit the wood floor with a bang.

"And that is because I felt like it."

Crispin lay on his back and groaned. He tasted blood and probed his teeth with his tongue, searching for loose molars. His jaw swelled. The room spun and his bruised side caused nausea to tighten his belly.

"Now," said the sheriff standing over him. To Crispin's blurry vision, he looked like a dark, shaggy bear. "Tell me again why I must release Stephen St Albans."

Slowly, Crispin moved his hand to feel the floor, making certain he knew exactly where it was before trying to push himself into a sitting position. Once he sat up he gave himself a moment to quell his uneasy belly. "My lord," he began, and gingerly touched his jaw. He glanced admiringly at the sheriff. "Stephen may have had a motive and the means, but he never would have dishonored himself by using poison. He covets his honor almost as much as I do." He tried to smile but his jaw hurt and he winced instead.

Wynchecombe jerked his head in a satisfied nod and offered his hand to Crispin. When Crispin hesitated the sheriff thrust it forward. "Come now. Take it."

Crispin slapped his hand into the sheriff's and allowed Wynchecombe to haul him to his feet. He stood unsteadily, surprised when a wine cup was thrust into his hand.

"You have made a proper mess of this, Crispin."

Crispin slurped the wine and nodded, wiping his face with the back of his hand. "I admit as much. I was fortunate that the servant Jenkyn all but confessed. He knew he was caught."

"That is all very well for you but what of me? Sir Stephen has no love for me for throwing him in prison. If he goes to the king…"

"I might be persuaded to influence Stephen to press no countercharges."

Wynchecombe studied Crispin. "I see." He nodded and released a sound not quite a chuckle. "How much will this cost me?"

Crispin dabbed his sleeve on his bloody lip. "I require no payment."

"Not in coin, eh?"

Crispin said nothing. He blinked and touched his fingertips gently to his swollen jaw.

Wynchecombe scowled. "What about this Jenkyn, then? Are you certain this time?"

"As certain as I can be. Jenkyn knows too much to be

completely innocent. We will have to thoroughly question him."

"Then I will send my men with a description of him. He will be apprehended anon." He cleared his throat and postured beside his chair. "I will release the prisoner. But I tell you truly, I shall not arrest him again if you are wrong."

The Boar's Tusk was crowded full of men drinking and making merry. Crispin edged his bruised body through the throng and found a quiet place in the back. He eased down onto a bench and cradled his face in his hand, hoping he could dull the throb in his jaw with Gilbert's wine.

"Crispin, dear." He looked up at Eleanor through his fingers and he saw her tick her head at him while planting one hand on her ample hip. "Tsk! You look awful. What happened?"

"The sheriff and I have come to a mutual understanding, is all."

She waited for more explanation, but since Crispin offered none she asked, "Will you have wine?"

"Ah, such sweet words," he sighed. "I will have wine. And plenty of it."

She left for only a moment. When she returned she set a wooden bowl before him and poured wine into it. She did not leave the jug as expected. Instead, she cradled it in a ragged cloth and stared at him worriedly until he gestured for her to put the jug down.

"I don't know, Crispin. Mayhap you should just go home."

"I am home. And since I am home I am master here. Put down the jug."

"Now Crispin—"

"Down!" He slapped the table with the flat of his hand.

She hesitated a moment more before slowly setting the jug beside the cup. "I should bring you something to eat. You look like the ragged end of a battle."

"I don't want food."

"But Crispin—"

"Madam, please!"

She swiped once at the table with her apron as if to punctuate her hurt feelings and thumped away with hard steps.

"Bless you," he said, barely realizing her absence, and then filled the half empty bowl to the rim. He lifted it to his lips and drank gratefully, rolling his upturned throat in long swallows before he set the empty bowl down. He refilled it and settled more comfortably on the bench.

After a few minutes his jaw did not feel so sore and he relaxed and closed his eyes. Alone in his dark corner, he felt the companionable solace from so many men sharing the same experience. The low murmur of their voices and laughter resonated in his chest. A bagpipe merrily played and further eased his mood.

The wine did its work, and the ache of his body and the anxiety of his mind relaxed into the distant haze of alcohol. He sat with eyes closed for some time, simply enjoying the peace of the place he called home until a tingle of discomfort and the sense that someone stood over him ruined that peace.

Rosamunde. A corona of candles flickered behind her, and with her position above him and alcohol warming his senses, it looked like a halo glowing behind her head. He lifted his bowl to her and smiled his crooked grin. "Hail, saintly Rosamunde! How fare you?"

But her saintly demeanor soon changed. Her face grew almost as scarlet as her gown. She sat hastily beside him. Her white fingers clutched the table. "I fare not well at all! How could you? It was not bad enough that you arrested my brother, but you have to abuse my servants and arrest them too?"

"Jenkyn is not arrested. Yet. He escaped, but not for long." His tongue cleaved to his mouth and did not seem to want to cooperate with his words. They slurred on the pleasant flavors of the dark wine. "And what do you care? He is merely a servant. He is nothing to you. Why should you care that he has done you a service out of loyalty?"

"Done me a service?"

He slammed his free hand on the table. "Do not play games with me." He eased back and chuckled unpleasantly. "I happen to know that saintly Rosamunde spent her free time swyving Gaston D'Arcy."

This time she slapped his face. He expected it, relished its sharp thwack and the sting. He smiled broader and slurped the wine. "Such coy games you used to play with me. Only letting honorable Crispin go so far, touch only so much. What was the matter? Was I not comely enough for you?" He slid closer and looked her over like a man scrutinizing a tavern wench. His hand snaked forward to capture her waist and he pulled her snuggly against him. "How about now?" He tightened his grip and kissed her noisily and sloppily, prizing open her cold mouth and stabbing in with his tongue. When she would not react, he let her go and sagged back. He smiled again. "No. I didn't think so."

He drank his wine and poured more into the bowl. "Will you drink with me, Rosamunde? Like old times?"

"You're drunk."

"Maybe. Maybe. But not quite as drunk as I intend to be. Not yet."

"And this," she gestured distastefully to him, "is what stands in the way of freeing my brother and my servant? You. Look at you. Bruised and beaten from some tavern brawl, no doubt. You, of all people, are a witness to their character and their actions."

He nodded and chuckled. "Yes. Amusing, is it not? I am the witness, who has witnessed so much in this life already." He raised his head unsteadily to look at her. Her eyes were dark like coal smudges on her pale face, and even the candlelight could not warm it with its generous yellow tones. "You have a look on your face, my dear. Do I disgust you?"

"Yes, you do."

He laughed. "Then why did you not wipe my kiss from your mouth?"

Her expression hardened but her pouting lips remained moist. "Crispin, I came to reason with you."

"I am beyond reason, my lady. Well beyond. And if you will excuse me, I must go to the latrine and piss away the rest of my reason." He rose but grabbed his wine bowl and drank it down. Setting it back on the table he kissed her cheek wetly. "I shall be back. Don't go away."

He staggered to the door and found a privy in the rear courtyard. He hummed to himself and made water down the privy's pit, thinking about his early days of disgrace when he spaded out such muck and dumped it into his wheelbarrow. In the earliest hours of the morning, he would roll that wheelbarrow throughout London, his frown deep behind his scarf. "How the mighty have fallen," he had muttered to himself, never thinking he deserved any of it. He'd go back to the hovel he lived in, reeking from the morning's activity.

He brushed the memories aside. Tying his braies and adjusting his coat, he smiled to himself. At least those days were behind him. He found respect amongst his fellows at the Tusk and even begrudgingly with the sheriff. Perhaps time could erase the past and make a new life, remake him anew. If not with Rosamunde then some other willing woman.

He sauntered back inside, not shoving his way this time, but patting the men on the shoulders whom he moved past, smiling in wine-soaked congeniality at grins and hoisted cups.

He returned to his table in the dark shadows of the back of the room and was surprised to find Rosamunde still there. She refilled his wine bowl and set it before him with a grim expression.

He took it up and drank. "Much thanks, Rosamunde," he said and took another swallow, downing almost all of the bowl's contents.

Steadily she watched him drink, every motion he made—tilting back the cup, drinking deeply, licking his lips—until he put the cup down and smiled at her. "Perhaps you are having second thoughts about me," he said, leaning on an elbow. "It's not too late, you know. You don't have to marry that Frenchman."

She was surprised but it quickly faded. "You know about that too."

He patted her hand. It was cold. "Dearling, I know much about you."

"Yes. I was afraid you did."

Her hand clenched something which he tried to decipher in the dim light. "What's that?"

"This?" She raised it so he could see the small ceramic vial with a cork stopper. "It is an empty vial."

He chuckled, his sodden mind believing the most mundane things to be funny. "Why do you carry an empty vial, my dear?"

"It was not empty a moment ago."

"Oh? Where did it go?" Yet even as he asked, he felt an unnatural sensation creep through his limbs. Not ordinary drunkenness. That was familiar. This was different. It dragged his extremities into thick heaviness like weights were attached to points of his body and he was falling down an abyss. And then his vision blurred and his heart quickened. His throat unaccountably tightened, like fingers pressing harder and harder.

He glared at Rosamunde, but her bland expression revealed nothing.

"Rosamunde," he rasped. "What have you done?"

"I have killed you," she said calmly.

She spoke so plainly as if to a servant asking for something as simple as a bowl of wine. Her deed meant no more to her than that. "Rosamunde…" He couldn't say more. His lungs screamed. He clutched the table in order to breathe. His heart hammered so hard he thought it would burst.

"You were getting much too close," she said in the same becalmed manner. She looked at the vial in her hand and turned it in the dim light. "But without you, there will be no reason to condemn Stephen or Jenkyn. Stephen knew nothing of this. I told you that. Jenkyn wanted to help but he was too afraid. In the end, I was the one to buy the poison, and I was only too happy to administer it. You were right about Gaston and me. I do not know how you discovered it, but you are a clever man." She sighed deeply and stared at the table. "It was lovely at first. Such a change from the dried lips and cankerous hands of my husband." She smiled, the dimpled corners of her mouth rising. "Oh, you needn't worry over him. He died a natural death. Though had I known how easy it was, I should have killed him years ago."

Crispin's chest ached and burned, partly from the poison's effects, but mostly because he could not believe her words. He did not want to listen, but he couldn't move.

"But Gaston…such a passionate man. I imagined you might have been the same. For many years, you see, when lying in my husband's bed, I did think of you, Crispin. When he touched me, I closed my eyes and told myself it was you. And when he put his foul-breathed mouth on me, my thoughts were only of you and your sweet lips. But as the years past, I could no longer conjure your face. You abandoned me, abandoned us. When Gaston came along, it was as if new life was breathed into me. I had been a corpse for seven years and suddenly for seven weeks I was reborn. But he became demanding, coarse. When Stephen secured my betrothal I told Gaston it was over, but he would have none of it. Gaston threatened to tell my betrothed, to extort me for his silence. That was when Jenkyn suggested I kill him. But he was too weak to do it himself. So I did it." She glanced over Crispin in his effort to breathe. "I know what you are thinking. Why did I not go to Stephen? But how could I confess my disgrace? It was not possible to ask him to do it. So I came here to Gaston one last time, not too far from where we are now sitting, and I poured him a bowl of wine—just as I did for you—and I added the poison. It did not take him long to die, but I did not wait to see his final breaths. Later, Jenkyn told me he came here to do the deed himself, but again, his courage failed him. Of course Gaston was already dead, but poor Jenkyn did not know that."

Crispin sank toward the table. Only the weakening strength of his forearms upheld him. Every muscle in his body cramped and his heart hammered relentlessly. He gasped, casting blindly about the room for someone to notice, someone to come to his aid. He saw neither Gilbert nor Eleanor.

"The apothecary was more difficult," she went on. "When I

255

discovered you were investigating the murder and that you were seeking the man who sold the poison, I could not risk his discovery. By chance, I was there the same moment you arrived. I was in the back room listening, and when I saw my opportunity I stabbed him with his own dagger." She looked at her hand, flexed the fingers. "Such a strange sensation, stabbing someone. I had no idea how hard the body is. Of course, with a sharp knife, it is easier." She raised her chin. Her small nostrils flared with the scents of smoke, sweat, and spoiled ale. "I have no regrets for killing him. He was a vile man. I have no regrets about killing Gaston, for he, too, was a cruel and vile man." Her gaze returned from far away and rested on Crispin. She cocked her head. Her moist lips pressed together, pouting. "But I do have regrets over killing you, Crispin, for you were dear to me once. You do not know how many times in my marriage bed you saved my sanity." She rose and looked at him curiously.

Crispin struggled for consciousness. She wavered in his blurry vision. A tear left his eye to run down his sallow cheek.

She leaned forward and touched her lips to his gasping mouth, ignoring his struggle to breathe. "Farewell, my love. I do you a favor. It hurt me deeply to see you so degraded, living this horrid life in that decrepit little hovel." She leaned forward, and with her lips brushing his, she whispered, "Surely your reward will be greater in Heaven."

She closed her fingers over the vial and stepped back. She looked at him once more with a pitying expression, and walked from the Boar's Tusk.

CHAPTER THIRTY

Crispin's eyes followed her until she disappeared out the door into the gray sunshine.

Rosamunde! He longed to scream it aloud, but no breath came; only a rushing sound in his ears and the approach of blessed death. Slowly—it seemed so slowly—he laid his face on the table. He made no more choking noises. He simply felt his cheek hit the surface and closed his eyes.

Oh God! Oh blessed Jesu! How could she? How could she kill me after all we were to one another?

There seemed little left to think about but this last betrayal. He wondered why it hurt so much. Why was it taking so long to die?

Through his closed eyelids, a bright light pierced the darkness, and he stared through the vibrant red. A moment passed before he realized the color was his own blood through his lids, but he wondered at the light, and with difficulty, pried open his eyes. The light shone starkly white and filled his view. Strangely, though he expected it to, the light did not hurt or make him squint. He simply looked into it and it seemed to go on a long way, a tunnel of pure light. He speculated about this strange apparition for some time. Shadowy figures moved past him but he did not fear them. He knew, without knowing why he knew, that they were friendly, even loving. He felt it a comforting place and he longed to move forward and join the figures that came into sharper focus. He felt glad to be away from whatever disturbed him, and he vaguely wondered why his memory of those events seemed so foggy.

A figure approached out of the bright light, coming closer. Crispin spoke to him, though he was slightly surprised that he did not need to open his mouth.

What is this place?

The figure looked at him. Crispin could not see his face clearly, but he felt the expression was one of paternal amusement. *Don't you know?*

Crispin didn't answer. The situation had all the earmarks of a dream. Yet it also felt distinctly unlike any dream he had ever had. *No. Where am I?*

Not yet, Crispin Guest. Not yet. There is more for you to do. Much more.

Before he could question the figure again, before he had time to contemplate the sensations rippling about him, the vision receded. Something wrenched him away from the light and the warm sensation of love.

He awoke and snapped upright with a long gasp. His body spasmed and ached, but even that subsided and he slowly warmed from the nearby hearth. He put his hand to his throat. The passageway opened and he felt only a vague sense of grogginess.

He froze with an awful realization. Was he a ghost? Doomed to haunt this place?

He turned to the man behind him and poked him in the shoulder. His finger did not pass through and the man turned to him with a stern but quizzical look. "What the hell do you want?" he growled at Crispin. But upon receiving no reply, he cursed, and turned back to his ale.

I am not a ghost. He ran his hand over his corporeal chest, trying to believe it. She poisoned him, didn't she? Where was the death he expected?

He lifted his head and darted his glance about the room. No one seemed to take notice of him. He was just another patron in the Boar's Tusk, one of many men who spent their evenings forgetting their troubles in the bottom of a wine bowl.

Wine bowl.

Crispin looked down. It sat where he left it, almost directly before him. Only dregs remained of the red wine now, and, he assumed, the deadly poison. A simple wooden bowl, much like the two he owned at home. But as he looked around the room, he saw only clay bowls and horn cups. None but this one was made of wood.

He gingerly grasped its edges with his fingertips and turned it. It was worn, with the faintest of etched designs running along its outer rim, a simple design of static waves, lines zigzagging around the circumference creating a border one inch wide. The bowl seemed more worn than the others. Quite old. Wood, smooth to the touch and well-crafted, made by a very skilled carpenter.

Hands now trembling, Crispin lifted it up and looked closely at it, turning it tenderly in the dim light. Such a simple thing. No one would take note of it. And no one had. Countless men drank from it, this humble cup, this wooden bowl.

"The Holy Grail," he whispered, unable to fathom the immensity. "It's impossible." He dumped the last of the poisoned wine on the table and ran his hand reverently over its outer surface.

Still, his analytical mind reasoned. How did it get here?

He recreated the incident in his mind. He saw Gaston D'Arcy sitting here in the tavern hatching his plots, and with a pang of an unnamed emotion, he saw Rosamunde enter and argue with D'Arcy. Somehow, without his seeing, she administered the deadly potion. He drank it, and she left him to choke to death just like she did to Crispin.

Crispin wiped the sweat from his brow. Unimaginable that she murdered two men and tried to add him to her list. Him!

His knuckle removed the last tear he would shed for Rosamunde, and he resettled his mind again to the puzzle. D'Arcy struggled to breathe just as Crispin had, and no doubt D'Arcy suspected poison. What then did he do?

He had the grail. The scrip. It held the grail. After all, he was the 'Cup Bearer'. He did the only thing he could do to try to save his life; he tried to get the cup. And he succeeded. He brought it forth, but he was perhaps too ill to pour the wine into it and drink. He believed that it would heal him, but he could not manage to do it. It was on the table. There were several cups there, but it was the only one of wood and it was the only one empty. *My God. It's been here all along and no one knew it.*

He stared at the cup and felt its solidity.

But what of me? Did the grail heal me?

He glanced toward an open shutter and noticed the darkness. He had lain unconscious a long time, for hours, allowing the poison to work itself out of his system. Isn't that what the apothecary said? If he had only consumed a small portion of it, a grain or two, it would have caused a great deal of unpleasantness but he would survive. How much did Rosamunde have left in the vial? Not enough to kill, that much was certain. He couldn't quite make himself believe that this cup healed him. But others believed it and believed in the other powers they said it possessed. So many men wanted it so badly.

Even if it were just the true cup of Christ, wouldn't it be worth fighting for?

He examined the cup one last time before he slipped it under his cloak. Rising from the bench, he glanced anxiously about the room, fearing someone saw him and knew what he had. Hastily he left the Boar's Tusk and hurried down the lane. He made it several yards before he slowed and suddenly stopped. Where should he go? To the sheriff? To his lodgings? He wiped his face with a clammy hand.

A horseman galloped down the lane and forced Crispin against a wall, spattering him with clods of mud. Crispin took no notice and simply leaned there, thinking, his hand pressed to the object beneath his cloak.

"I need guidance," he whispered. And before he truly knew the direction he traveled, he made for the little chapel of Father Timothy.

The chapel lay in darkness but the altar glowed in a wash of candlelight. The cross's gold beckoned, and Crispin threw himself forward, clutching the cup at his side. When he knelt, he felt a sense of gratitude and relief. Even if the grail had not healed him, Divine intervention had still saved his life. He had not forgotten the strange vision of the figure.

Behind him he heard steps approach, and he jumped to his feet. Father Timothy strode down the short nave and smiled upon recognizing Crispin. "Welcome again, my friend. It is good to see you."

"Oh, Father, you do not know how good it is to see you. Can we talk in your rectory?"

"Of course." The young priest led the way and soon Crispin sat on a stool by the humble hearth. He forced himself to drop his hand away from his cloak, but he satisfied himself with the feel of the cup against his thigh. Silently he gazed into the fire.

"There must be something I can do for you, friend," urged Timothy, sitting on a stool across from him. "Else why would you be here? Has it to do with what we discussed before?"

"Father." Crispin leaned forward, closed fists resting on his thighs. "When we die, what exactly happens to us? What do we see?"

"Our hope is to see the face of God."

"Yes. But before that, what else?"

"I know not. When a man dies, he cannot return to tell the tale."

Crispin shook his head and sat back. "I am not so certain. At least…" He managed a chuckle. "Perhaps a man *can* rise from the dead."

Timothy's gaze was steady.

Crispin scowled. "I was vilely betrayed by a woman I once loved. She poisoned me and I…I nearly died."

"By the blood of Christ, tell me! What happened?"

Crispin lifted his hand and touched the rounded belly of the cup under the cloak, testing its substantiality with his fingertips. "There was not enough poison to kill me. But in so doing I might have discovered the whereabouts of the Holy Grail."

The priest becrossed himself and rested his trembling fingers on his lips. "Blessed be God," he whispered through his fingers. "Where is the grail now?"

Crispin hesitated. How could he be sure of anyone? He looked at the priest's strong-boned hands and his ring. "Safe," he replied curtly. "If this is the grail, then I see no end of trouble with it. Too many are affected by it."

"You never truly believed."

"I do not know whether I believe in it now. But some men do. And those men are dangerous."

"What are your plans?"

Crispin rose and paced the length of the little room. "I know not. Perhaps I should drop the thing down the nearest well. Or leave it on the highest mountaintop, or throw it into the ocean. Miraculous or no, nowhere is safe enough or far enough from the greed of mankind. I wish God would simply take it back!"

The priest tapped his fingers on his lips for some time. "I can well see your reasoning," he said at last. "But it can also do great good in the world."

"But has it?"

"'I have come not to bring peace'. So spake Jesus. Sometimes spilt blood is necessary. 'We make war that we may live in peace.'"

Crispin measured him. "You quote Aristotle well for a parish priest." He smiled. "Our kings would have us believe such about war. Its necessity. Yet kings can betray—"

"Or be betrayed."

Crispin looked up suddenly at the steely expression in the priest's eyes, not as young as they once looked. "Yes, I know who you are," admitted Timothy. "And your history. You are a man of sorrows but capable of so much valor. You must weigh very carefully what you do for the next few hours. What you possess is miraculous."

"There is no proof of that."

"How do you know?"

"It did not heal me. My body healed itself."

The priest smiled, a little sadly. "But you will never know for certain."

Crispin frowned at his own uncertainty and at Timothy's smug conviction. "I came to ask your guidance in this."

"I have no more guidance to give you now than I did before. God chose you to be the bearer of this burden. *You* must decide."

"And if I make the wrong choice?"

Timothy smiled faintly and then let it go. "I pray...you do not."

Crispin returned to his lodgings and sat in the chair. He looked about the shabby room, the rickety shelves and nicked table; the shutters that would not quite close; the chipped jug of water and the empty one of wine. He once believed this was the sum total of what he had become, but the last few days told a different story. There may yet be more to him than he ever imagined, for why else should he be chosen to suffer this burden of the grail when all the world seemed filled with more learned and more deserving men than he?

He sat and stared a long time at his few possessions before he slowly inched his hand within his coat. He took out the cup and stared at it. His fingers ran over the carvings along the rim and he wondered just where Jesus had laid his lips. Was it here? He ran a finger on the spot. Or here? His fingers trailed. He couldn't even be certain that this was the actual Holy Grail. Oh, he was certain that this was the cup that caused so many to lose their lives, but was it the cup of Christ?

De Marcherne hinted that it wielded power. Maybe it healed Crispin. Maybe it didn't. Maybe he'd never know, like Father Timothy said.

There was only one way to know.

If he asked it, asked the grail, what would it do? What did he want the most?

He picked it up and stood. He thrust his arms forward and lifted it up, as if offering it as a sacrifice.

Was it his imagination? Did his arms tingle from the grail's power, or was it the stiffness in which he held them? Suddenly, he felt the crawling sensation of fear. Not of death, for he'd faced that too many times to count. Not of dishonor, for he'd lost it all already. But of something else, something he was loath to identify.

Power. He feared the power, the terrible and awesome power that did not come from taking a castle with an army or standing above a defeated opponent. This was different. Was this the power of God?

A lump in his gut sat heavily like a stone within him. If he dared ask the grail, might his fondest desire be granted?

He opened his fingers and the cup hit the table with a pop, and spun, finally landing on its rim. Crispin stared at the grail for a long time. He listened to his breath fill and escape his lungs; he listened to the wooden ceiling beams creak and to a puff of a draft whine past his shutter. "Superstition," he whispered. He touched the cup with his fingertips and laughed nervously. No tingle. No strange visions. Only a cup. Perhaps an old one, but only a cup nonetheless.

He scooped it up, dropped it through the buttons of his coat, and reached for a cup from his shelf. He sat with it in his lap and drew his dagger.

Jack entered with a cursory knock and moved directly to where Crispin sat. "The sheriff is still searching for Jenkyn."

"He'd best give it up," Crispin said distractedly, working diligently. "He's not the killer."

Jack sat hard on the chest. "'Slud, Master! If he isn't the killer then who the hell is?"

"A woman."

"Ah ha! It's that Lady Vivienne! I knew it. She's—"

"No," he said looking up from his work. "I almost wish it were. And yet, for that lady I have much sympathy."

"Then who?"

He put his knife aside and sighed. To say it aloud meant it was real, that it happened, but this he could not deny. Could he swallow his feelings and fulfill the king's justice?

Quietly he said, "Rosamunde. Lady Rothwell."

Jack peered carefully at Crispin's lowered face. "Eh? What's that you say? I thought for a moment you said it was Lady Rothwell what killed him."

"Yes, Jack. That is what I said. She confessed to me…before she attempted to poison me."

"No!" Jack slid to Crispin's feet and gazed up at him. He laid his hands on Crispin's knees. "Master, is it true?"

Crispin smiled fondly. "Yes, Jack. There never was a more pitiful end to a sadder tale."

"Aye, that's the truth. Save the brother only to hang the sister." But as soon as he said it he slapped his hand over his mouth. "Oh, Master! Forgive me."

"Well and why not?" Crispin snapped to his feet and strode to the window. "The bitch tried to kill me with no more consideration given it than a mud stain on her gown. She killed two men—the apothecary, remember?—and would have happily killed me. She thought she did."

Jack sat back on his feet. He let his hands drop to his thighs. "What happened, Master? Will you tell me?"

Crispin pushed open the shutter and leaned against the window frame. Martin Kemp's furnace had quieted for the evening and no smoke marred the air he inhaled. The rooftops of slate, tile, and lead marched away from his view, undulating like an angry sea, their hearth smoke like charred masts standing straight and stiff. "She poisoned me, Jack. The same she used on Gaston D'Arcy. And it would have killed me, too, if…if I had not drunk it from the Holy Grail."

"Christ!" He becrossed himself. "You don't mean it?"

"I don't know. Maybe there was not enough poison to kill. Maybe it was a dream. See for yourself, Jack." He went to the table and took up the bowl, showing Jack its simple design and etchings.

Jack drew back, shaking his head. "I'm not worthy to come nigh it, sir. I'm only a thief."

Crispin gazed at it fondly and put it up on the shelf. "And yet a thief joined our Lord in Heaven the day he died on the cross." He glanced at Jack, but the boy's fear was clear on his face. Crispin sighed. "The thing is, Jack, I don't know what to do with it."

"May I make a suggestion?"

Both Jack and Crispin wheeled toward the voice coming from the open window. Crispin frowned and drew his dagger upon recognizing Guillaume de Marcherne climbing in. But de Marcherne ticked his finger. Three men entered behind him.

"He's like a spider, he is," sneered Jack, "climbing up the side of a building like that."

"A ladder is a most convenient tool, *n'est pas*? Now, my dear Crispin." He centered himself and straightened his brilliantly scarlet houppelande. "I am ready to take possession of the grail. That is, to take it off your hands."

The door suddenly flung open and Edwin, Parsifal, and Anselm burst through, their swords drawn. Jack dived under the table and Crispin wished he'd thought of it first.

"Go back to Hell, de Marcherne!" cried Parsifal.

De Marcherne drew his sword and squared on the Templar. "Your purpose is forfeit. I claim the grail."

"It cannot be 'claimed' by anyone, Guillaume," said Edwin, his sword bobbing between de Marcherne and the men at the window. "In all this time, you failed to learn that."

"Oh, I have learned much more since the time I left your noble order. Much more than you could imagine."

"I am certain it is nothing a Christian should know."

"Dear me. The same self-righteous Edwin. I thought you would have grown by now. Instead, you stagnated with the same pathetic platitudes. Tell me again how I am a disgrace to the name of Templar."

Edwin bared his teeth and raised his blade.

"Gentlemen!" Crispin cried. They all turned to him. "Can you take this elsewhere? I would rather not bloody my floor."

Parsifal gestured with his blade toward de Marcherne's men but

Crispin felt the underlying threat to himself. "Surrender the grail, Master Crispin. You have been a good caretaker, but now the duty falls to us."

De Marcherne laughed. "Do not be a fool, Crispin. I shall give you all I promised…and more. Give it to me and regain your manhood."

"I have no reason to believe I am not a man now, de Marcherne. In fact, only a man of character would refuse you."

De Marcherne stared. His severe expression gave way to an admiring guffaw. His scar reddened. He sheathed his sword brusquely but the Templars kept theirs at the ready. Their sword tips followed his approach toward Crispin. "You asked why I left the Templars. Shall I now tell you?" He glanced at the knights. Their blades bobbed uneasily. He chuckled. "Because they refused to use this power that was given to them. They betrayed and deceived to keep the grail safe when they could have done so much more. I do not talk of wealth or power. I am talking of the good they could have done."

"Do not listen to him, Crispin," cried Edwin.

Crispin glanced quizzically at the Templars.

"It is true," said de Marcherne. "They would only play the one game. A foolish game. I do not even think they believed in it anymore. It was all by rote, like some poor school boy under the rod. There are worse kinds of corruption than that of greed, my dear Crispin. Complacency is a great sin. See your catechism. It is there."

Crispin glanced again at the Templars and their unreadable expressions. Why didn't they deny de Marcherne's words? Maybe they didn't think they needed to. Maybe he spoke lies. Or maybe the truth cut deeper than they cared to admit.

Crispin stared at the floor. He wanted to ask them, he wanted to say something, but before he could think of a reply, de Marcherne suddenly grabbed him and pulled him back against his chest, holding a blade to his throat.

The Templars advanced but de Marcherne pressed the blade

deeper, reopening the scab the sheriff made earlier. Crispin felt hot blood trickle down his neck.

De Marcherne's breath puffed harshly in Crispin's ear. "It is time to stop playing the hero. I want the grail. Where is it?"

"This is a very poor show, de Marcherne," rasped Crispin. "Where is that famous French courtesy?"

"Gone, as is my patience. Though I would regret it, you know I do not have an aversion to killing you."

"That seems to be a popular theme this evening," Crispin muttered. "What makes you think I care?"

He released a reptilian chuckle. "I have learned, through years of experience, that even when a man is tortured, he always holds dear his life. Though it were easier and less painful for him to lose it, he cradles it as precious. And so you will excuse me if I take your scorn with little enthusiasm."

"Do not tell him, Master Crispin!" Anselm lurched forward. De Marcherne's men crept closer in a countermove. "'He that loveth his life shall lose it; and he that hateth his life in this world shall keep it unto life eternal.'"

Crispin glared at the Templars. The blade felt cold against his hot neck. *All very well for you!*

"Must I resort to counting to three?" asked de Marcherne in a bored voice. "Very well, then. One…two…"

"Wait!" Jack leapt from his hiding place and stood between de Marcherne and the Templars. "Release my master and I will tell you!"

"Jack! For the love of Christ, be still!"

To quiet Crispin, de Marcherne dug the edge of the blade deeper into his flesh. Crispin felt the cold steel slice. More sticky blood trickled, soaking the collar of his shirt. He stiffened against de Marcherne.

"You are a good servant, Jack," placated de Marcherne. "I am certain you want your master unharmed. Now then, tell me where it is."

"If I get it for you, you'll release Master Crispin?"

"Of course. On my word as a knight."

"Don't believe him, boy," said Parsifal. "His words are Satan's!"

De Marcherne grinned and raised his elbow, slicing another thin line of red across Crispin's neck. Crispin gurgled stiffly. "Time is passing, boy," said de Marcherne. "I'm waiting."

Jack licked his pale lips and swept his glance over the helpless Templars. He wiped his hands down his dirty shirt and nodded. "Right, sir. I'll get it." He went to the shelf and took down the wooden bowl, carefully cradling it in his hands. "May Jesus forgive me."

"Ah!" De Marcherne's face brightened. He motioned for Jack to set it on the table. "Hiding in plain sight. You are a clever man, friend Crispin. I regret that we shall not serve together as knights."

"You said you'd let him go!" Jack's eyes filled with frustrated tears.

De Marcherne looked down at Crispin before he shrugged and shoved him into Jack's arms. Jack and Crispin tumbled to the floor.

De Marcherne snatched the cup and sprinted toward the window flanked by his men, but the Templars pursued, until a shout behind them stopped them. In the doorway, more of de Marcherne's men stood with swords drawn.

The Templars spun on their heels and engaged the two knights at the door, while Edwin continued his pursuit of de Marcherne.

The Frenchman crouched in the window. The men who entered with him guarded his escape and postured in front of Edwin.

De Marcherne grinned and threw a kiss to the Templars. "*Au revoir*, Edwin! Farewell, Crispin. I do not think we shall meet again. At least, it would be unhealthy for you to do so."

He dropped out the window, the cup in his hand. His men fought in earnest. Edwin slashed one man across the chest and he dropped with a groan. Without thinking, Crispin snatched up the discarded blade and stood beside the old Templar. With a feral smile, Crispin raised the blade with remembered skill. The sharp sound of steel on steel rang out in the little room. An abrupt appetite for blood swelled in Crispin and he gathered all his aggression.

He chopped unmercifully and countered each blow before he backed his opponent against the window. Just when Crispin raised the sword for the final strike, the man slipped backwards over the sill, sliding along the broken roof tiles in a whirlwind of crashing slate.

The other two engaged by the Templars turned tail and fled down the stairs, leaving their wounded comrade behind.

Edwin stopped only to wipe his forehead and to grab Crispin's arm with his sword hand. "You fought well, Crispin. I am only sorry your servant did not have your strength of courage."

Crispin stopped to catch his breath and only then did he raise his hand to his bloody neck. "He followed his conscience and his loyalty. I cannot fault the boy for protecting me."

"Yes. But what is lost today! We must follow him." Edwin nodded to Crispin and directed his fellows out the door. They darted down the stairs in pursuit.

Crispin stood panting, sword still in hand. He looked at the empty window, then the doorway, and finally toward Jack cowering in a corner.

"You won't beat me, will you, Master? I only did what I thought best. I don't know naught about no grail but I do know you've been right good to me. I didn't want that harm should befall you."

Crispin lowered the sword and tossed it aside. He pressed his bloodied hand on Jack's shoulder. "Peace, Jack. I am not angry with me. I am gratified that you feel such affection for me, as indeed...I feel for you." He patted Jack a moment before he felt his legs give out and he fell into the chair. "This has not been an easy day," he admitted. He glanced at the injured man groaning on the floor. "I will keep him at bay while you fetch the sheriff, eh, Jack?"

CHAPTER THIRTY-ONE

It took a long time to explain fully, especially since the sheriff wanted Crispin to repeat several parts of the tale again. They took away the injured man to Newgate, and the sheriff's men dispersed. Wynchecombe sat on the chair leaving Crispin to sit on the edge of the bed.

"Crispin. You promised to make no more mistakes."

Crispin studied his hands. Grimy creases. Palms smudged with dried blood and dirty sweat. "Jenkyn knew what happened. How could I have guessed? How could I have made the leap?"

Wynchecombe, in a rare show of parity, shook his head. "I know. Such a betrayal." He raised his face to Crispin. His gaze steadied. "She will hang, you know."

Crispin felt a cold hand clutch his heart. "I know. The law is the law. And she deserves the punishment."

"Leave her arrest to me."

"No. I will do it."

"Crispin—"

"Simon. Give me this. It's owed me."

Wynchecombe breathed a long sigh through his nostrils. Crispin knew the sheriff's thoughts: that Crispin would find an opportunity to let her go and escape the king's justice. He couldn't be certain he did not entertain such thoughts. But in the end, Crispin knew he would bring her in. He knew her. She would not stop with his attempted murder. When she tired of her new husband, what would stop her from eliminating him?

"'It is not always the same thing to be a good man and a good citizen,'" quoted Crispin wearily.

The sheriff huffed. "That damned Aristotle again." But Crispin nodded and rose. He looked about the shattered room in the ragged first light of morning; at the blood spattered on the wall and the broken end of the chair. A shelf hung aslant from one hook. Crispin's razor and soap cake lay on the floor. "It wasn't much to look at, but your fee may repair what is here."

"Yes," Crispin answered mechanically. He did not look up when the sheriff left, nor did he stir when Jack cautiously returned to the room and straightened what he could.

"Would you have me fetch wine, sir? I can run to the Boar's Tusk with the jug."

"Yes, Jack. Do that."

Jack hoisted the jug—miraculously untouched in the melee—and hugged it to his chest. "I'll go now, shall I?"

Crispin nodded but Jack made no move to leave.

"Master," said the boy, "it is a sore thing to lose your lady. But in truth, you lost her long ago and not in the way you think. The moment she thought you were less than her, that is when you lost her. A true love would not have felt so. A true love would have moved Heaven and Earth to stay with you."

Crispin turned a tender smile on Jack. "When did you become such a philosopher?"

Jack blushed. "Well, I'm no such, but I heard a thing or two in me day." He made for the door and stopped on the threshold. "Don't be hard on yourself, Master. You solved the murder. You did the best you could for the grail. It was I what lost it."

"Don't fret, Jack. I am well. At least I will be." Stoically, he rose and went to his basin to sponge away the blood from his neck.

Jack made a half-hearted smile. "There's....there's always that Lady Vivienne, Master. You said you were fond of her. And she is back at court."

Crispin nodded. Yes. And he wondered why, though of late he

seemed to have no time to wonder. He unbuttoned his coat and yanked off the dirty shirt blotched with dried blood, and replaced it with a cleaner one. He pulled on his coat again, buttoned it, and brushed it with a rag.

"Sometimes," Jack went on, "my wanderings take me to Westminster." He ducked his head and blushed. "Er...I'm a man of habits, Master. Best not to ask what I was about."

Crispin closed his eyes briefly. "Go on."

"Well, I saw Lady Vivienne—Lady Stancliff—at Westminster Palace."

"And so I saw her myself. What of it?"

"That is true, Master, but she was with that vile Guillaume de Marcherne. I suppose...we *could* let it lie."

Crispin rubbed his fingers into his eyes. "What I wouldn't give to let it lie."

Jack perked up. "Will we go? We don't want that villain coming back to haunt us."

It took only a moment to decide. "Yes, we'll go." Anger propelled Crispin. He'd had quite enough of all of it. To deal first with this was to put off having to see Rosamunde, and that was something his sick belly could delay for a long time. Was there no one to be trusted? No one he could be certain of? Well, he was certain of one thing: he wanted to stop Guillaume de Marcherne. One way or another.

Crispin and Jack made the journey to Westminster, avoiding the front gate altogether. Throughout the long walk, Crispin tried to decide what it was that was going on between Vivienne and de Marcherne. She lied, that was plain enough. Her "other business," no doubt. But what hold did de Marcherne have over her if she had her ring? Was there something more?

They entered the palace by the tradesmen's entrance, skirting as many wide eyes as they could. "What I need to discover," said Crispin, "is where Lady Stancliff is lodged. And I am uncertain exactly how to do that."

"Oh, that's easy!"

Surprised at Jack's flippant observance, he allowed the boy to do his will. Jack moved toward a gaggle of serving maids gathering cots and hay-stuffed mattresses from the alcoves in which they were hidden. Crispin watched him talk to them, a swagger in the young boy's bearing. The maids—girls, really—responded with giggles and coy expressions, swaying their ragged skirts and fanning their fingers before missing teeth. Jack bowed to them and they curtseyed back, and then he trotted to rejoin Crispin.

"South wing," said Jack and led the way.

Crispin grabbed hold of Jack's shoulder. When the boy looked up, Crispin's words dried up on his tongue. He shook his head instead and let the boy lead him, vowing to keep a sharp eye on Young Jack Tucker.

They came to the south corridor and Jack counted the doors. "I was told this one, Master." Crispin recognized the place where minor nobility were housed. Certainly Lady Stancliff qualified. Crispin strode up to the door and lifted his fist to knock when Jack jumped up and grabbed his hand.

"What you think you're doing? *He* could be in there!"

Crispin made an altogether unpleasant grin. "I'm counting on it."

He rapped on the door and a servant answered, one who had encountered Crispin before and who also tried—unsuccessfully— to block Crispin's entrance. Crispin shook his head at him while stiff-arming the door. "I wouldn't," he said.

He pushed the door open and strode in, Jack behind him. Vivienne stood in the middle of the room, her expression neutral, except for sparkling eyes.

"Again, Crispin. A most unexpected visit."

"Is it? Somehow, sweet Vivienne, I do not think so. I think you enjoy this game. You said so yourself: you prefer the company of men. You fancy playing it innocent, as if you were the victim. First of your husband, then of D'Arcy, and then of St Albans. And finally, of course, of de Marcherne. It amuses me to wonder to

274

whom you will play the victim from me."

Her eyes didn't sparkle as much, and her lip curled in a sneer. "So you think you know me, do you? Men have such pride. And it is so futile. What good is your pride, Crispin? Did it win you back your knighthood? Are your coin purses filled with gold?"

"My honor is my pride and I wear it freely under the sun. I need not hide it in secret rooms…or behind the curtains."

Jack startled when the hangings were pushed aside by a sword blade and then de Marcherne stepped through. The boy moved in front of Crispin protectively, but Crispin gently pulled him back and stashed him behind him.

De Marcherne's blade was aimed toward the floor as he stepped closer to Crispin. "My dear Vivienne," he said, looking at Crispin instead of Lady Stancliff. "I do not think you are an adequate judge of a man's pride or his honor. Best to keep to what you do know." His eyes flicked toward her. "And that you do so well."

Crispin backed toward the hearth. "What is your business with Lady Stancliff, de Marcherne? Aren't you done in London?"

"A funny thing about my business, Crispin. That grail you gave me. A fake. One has to wonder where such fakery originated. With D'Arcy? No, he was much too stupid for such a trick. Edwin?" He slid his foot closer, inching his way forward. The sword slowly rose toward Crispin's chest. "Again, no. He is not deceitful in this manner. He only wished he was. That, of course, leaves either you," he said gesturing with the sword toward Vivienne, "or you." The sword tip again aimed toward Crispin. "Now my dear Vivienne might conjure such an idea to stay in the game, for you are correct in your assessment of her. She is obsessed with danger. Aren't you, love?"

She spat at de Marcherne. He only smiled in reply. "Did she treat you thus? Or is it only me who elicits such behavior?" He ticked his head. "I fear it may be me."

Crispin stumbled over the hearth. The flames licked at his back.

"She left me once," said de Marcherne. "But then she returned. She sought revenge of me. I knew the object she sought but I

275

wanted her help in finding the one I was looking for. Now that she has her ring, she thinks she can be rid of me. But I am not easily cast aside. You just missed a very amusing scene in which she tried to stab me to death. I simply disarmed her. Imagine. Returning all this way to Westminster only to commit murder. Would you have arrested her then, Crispin? Or is the death of a Frenchmen not worth the Tracker's time."

"For *your* murder? I would have found the time."

"Enough of this. I have been saddled with a fake grail and I wish to have the original. Which I think you still have, no?"

"Do you plan to cut me in two, de Marcherne? You'll never find it that way."

"*Au contraire.* You see, I perceive it in the outline of your coat. You should at least have given it to your servant to carry."

Slight miscalculation. Crispin smiled weakly at Jack who stared at him and then ran that gaze down the bulge in Crispin's cotehardie. De Marcherne's eyes narrowed. With a sense of danger tingling his neck, Crispin looked around the room, picking out defensive strategy, weapons, shields.

Just as de Marcherne raised his sword, Crispin dove for the poker by the hearth and brought it up to block the blade. Steel clanged against iron. De Marcherne stepped back, momentarily stunned, but he soon recovered, frowned, and chopped down with the blade again. Crispin swung the poker upward and parried the blow, trying to knock the sword out of the man's hand, but he would not yield it.

Crispin maneuvered his opponent away from the fire, holding the poker two-handed.

He heard a muffled scream and at the corner of his eye, he caught Jack struggling with Vivienne. She grabbed a large candlestick and Jack clutched her hands. Vaguely, Crispin wondered which one of them she intended to threaten with it. They wrestled, the taller Vivienne glaring wild-eyed at the boy. Jack hung desperately on to Vivienne's wrists, trying to use his weight to pull it from her. When that failed to work, he swung his leg back

and kicked her shin. Hard. The candlestick fell from her grasp and
Jack stumbled back with a whoosh of air and hit the floor on his
backside. Vivienne shrieked and fell on him with her bare hands.
Jack let out a yell and scrabbled on the floor in an attempt to gain
his feet but Vivienne grabbed an ankle and yanked him back. He
kicked to free himself, and Vivienne, now sobbing in frustration
released him. He stood unsteadily and pulled his small dagger.
"You'll have to behave yourself, m'lady. I don't want to use this
but I will."

"You're a foolish boy," she sneered. She was inelegant regaining
her feet, but once upright her comportment returned. "Can't you
see that evil man is going to hurt your master? I was only trying to
stop him!"

"If that were so," he panted, "then why were you aiming for
Master Crispin?"

"Because *I* want to be the one who kills the bastard!"

De Marcherne laughed. He waved his sword at Vivienne. "You
see, Crispin. No love lost. Worry not, Fair Vivienne. As soon as I
have dispatched Master Guest, I will see that you suffer no more."
His smiled faded even as the blush drained from Vivienne's face.

De Marcherne wasted no more time and swung at Crispin's
head. He ducked, slid to the right, and brought up the iron at an
awkward angle, but it was still enough to block. Barely.

Not even winded, de Marcherne lowered his sword and
grinned. His scar darkened. "One wonders what damage you could
have done with a sword, Crispin. I regret I will never get the
opportunity to see."

"This bit of iron can do enough damage, I assure you."

"Ah, but will you get the chance?"

De Marcherne's casual poise masked his wariness. Without
warning, he swung again. Crispin dodged it, but this time the tip of
the blade nicked Crispin's ear. He felt the sting but didn't react
except to search the floor. No ear. A good sign.

He swung the poker at de Marcherne's feet and the nimble man
leapt straight up out of harm's way, but this time he was winded

and he stepped back from Crispin a few feet to catch his breath.

Crispin wasn't about to allow that.

He charged, a battle cry exploding from his lips. But de Marcherne was as seasoned as Crispin and he knew each battle trick as well. Perhaps even a few more. He parried the blow with a cry of his own and Crispin's momentum sent him toward the floor, the one place he knew he did not want to be. Crispin tried to roll and recover, but Vivienne and Jack were in the way. Like kayles pins, they all tumbled against the wall together.

De Marcherne panted and stood over them with the blade levered forward. He smiled. "I could have killed you all with one long stroke. But where is the merriment in that?"

Crispin recovered his feet first and slid against the wall. Another place he did not want to be. He raised the poker again. He was beginning to have his doubts about winning.

De Marcherne never lost his smile. He was able to assess the situation, too. He seemed to sense—as Crispin used to do—the moment a duel was about to end. Crispin adjusted his sweaty hands on the poker. He knew it wasn't going to end well.

De Marcherne raised his weapon and Crispin cringed, but instead of the slash of steel across his midsection that he expected, de Marcherne threw back his head and howled in pain.

Crispin looked down. Jack's knife slammed deep into the man's foot through his boot and pinned him to the floor.

Crispin didn't hesitate. He swung. The poker shattered de Marcherne's knee. The man dropped as far as he could with his foot pinned to the floor. Finishing the swing, Crispin heaved the poker upward and connected with de Marcherne's jaw. A sickening crack, and his head snapped back. His body arched for only a moment before awkwardly slamming to the floor, and lay still.

Crispin tossed the poker aside. Jack pulled his dagger free of the boot and stood up with it, eyes transfixed on the bloody blade. With trembling hands he hastily wiped the knife on his tunic. "Well done, Jack," Crispin panted. He turned his eyes on the suddenly terrified Lady Stancliff. "Call in the sheriff. Or the palace guards. I care not which. Whatever de Marcherne's game, it is now over. As is yours. I don't care why you returned. If it was to kill him he is as good as dead now. If it was for some other pursuit…well." His lip curled in a sneer. "I'm not interested. I suggest you leave for Chelmsford and stay there. I think King Richard's court has tired of you. Stay with your husband, Lady Vivienne. If he will still have you. Pray that he does."

He straightened his coat and flicked his hand for Jack to follow. One more to confront.

It took a quarter hour to reach the White Hart. Stopping before the door of the inn, he turned to Jack. "Go back to our lodgings, Jack. The sheriff may come to call and I would have you explain to him about de Marcherne."

Jack eyed the inn, eyes scanning the windows. He measured Crispin and stood his ground. "Wouldn't you rather have me here, sir? With you?"

Crispin felt his muscles tense. "No. Please, Jack."

Jack bowed, as well as any page at court.

Crispin did not watch him depart, but pushed opened the inn's doors and climbed the stairs to the gallery. He strode purposely across the plank passageway and stopped before Rosamunde's apartments, lifted his closed fist, and pounded on the door.

To his surprise, Stephen opened the door and grinned upon seeing him. "Crispin! My God! I am actually glad to see you. Come in. Come in."

Taking a breath, Crispin entered and glanced about. The door to the inner chamber was closed and no one stood in the parlor but Stephen and small leather bound chests and valises. They were preparing to leave.

"We return to my estates," said Stephen in reply to Crispin's appraisal of the room. "There is no more reason to stay now that all is well. I will fetch Rosamunde. She will be surprised to see you."

Crispin smiled dryly. "Won't she."

He waited while Stephen disappeared behind the closed door. At the sound of a shriek, he spun and encountered a wide-eyed Rosamunde. He smiled unpleasantly at her look of horror.

"Beloved," he said between clenched teeth.

She put her hand to her throat.

"No words?" he said, circling her. "You were so full of words before at the Boar's Tusk. You had much to say. Surely there is more."

Stephen frowned and stepped forward. "What is this, Crispin? What transpires between you? Rosamunde? Why do you look so pale? What does he say to you?"

"Yes, Rosamunde. Why don't you tell your brother your story? Why don't you tell him how you were willing to let him hang? Why won't you say how you were willing to let poor Jenkyn take the noose in your stead?"

Stephen grabbed Crispin's shoulder and squeezed painfully. "What lies are these? I thought you had become our friend again."

Crispin shook him loose and strode toward Rosamunde. She recoiled. "Tell him, Rosamunde. Tell him how you killed Gaston D'Arcy. Tell him how you slew that despicable apothecary. Tell him how you poisoned me."

Breathing hard, Stephen stared at Crispin. "Why do you say this?"

Crispin twisted towards Stephen. "Because it is true. This precious creature tried to kill me to save you, but she would have easily let you die for her crime. You or Jenkyn. She cared not which."

"No!"

Crispin turned. Jenkyn emerged from the inner room.

"No. That cannot be true," he said, imploring his mistress. "She tried to prove my innocence."

"And if she failed," said Crispin matter-of-factly, "she would have let you hang. Or poisoned you before you could implicate her."

"No." But this time his avowal was not nearly as robust.

Stephen went to his sister and took her shoulders. "Rosamunde. Tell him what a liar he is."

Rosamunde closed her eyes and breathed. She wore her green gown again, the one he favored. And the jewels she so hastily gave to Crispin graced her neck. Now he wished he hadn't returned them. His gut churned. He realized those jewels would be the last thing she would wear around her neck. Almost the last thing.

Slowly she opened her eyes. Calm descended within them and her look of horror fled. "How did you do it, Crispin? That is twice you cheated certain death."

"Rosamunde!" Stephen shook her, but she only gazed up at him with a curious smile.

"You do not know what I have endured," she said. "Gaston promised so much. And yet he took so much."

Her words were muffled when Stephen gathered her hard against his chest. "Rosamunde," he whimpered, lips trembling. "For God's sake, say no more."

"It's too late for that," said Crispin.

"So now your revenge extends to my sister," he cried over his shoulder. "I thought you were done with this."

"So did I. But a man has a change of heart when his former love tries to murder him. How many more would have died, Rosamunde, to satisfy you? Rupert of Kent was another, but you did not poison him. No. For him, you used a blade and stabbed him in cold blood. How many more? Stephen? Jenkyn? Your betrothed when he ceased to entertain you? How many?"

Crispin's words changed the expression on Stephen's face. He glanced at Jenkyn's puzzlement before turning to Crispin. "Rupert of Kent?" he asked softly.

"The apothecary who sold her the poison. I was there when he was killed. I saw the back of the killer's hooded head and no more. I did not even know it was a woman, but there was still something familiar about it that struck me, though I never would have connected it had she not confessed it to me while I lay dying at the Boar's Tusk."

Stephen released Rosamunde and stepped back to stare at her. "Tell him he lies. Why will you not tell him he lies?"

She shook her head and Stephen turned a desperate face to Crispin. "We will go away then," he said. "Will that satisfy you? Does our history together mean nothing?"

"History," Crispin sneered. "It is a matter of responsibility. You were willing to die for love of her," he said to Stephen, "as I might have done at one time. But she was not willing to do the same for you."

"A woman hasn't the courage of a man."

"It has less to do with courage and more with self-interest."

Stephen stared at Crispin. At last, the knight turned to Rosamunde. His face paled with bewilderment. "You would have let *me* hang for a murder *you* committed?"

Rosamunde seemed to awaken and she moved imploringly toward him. He recoiled. She stopped halfway and pressed her hands together prayerfully. "I tried to prove you innocent."

He frowned, his dark lips now gray. "And if you failed?"

"With Crispin out of the way no one would have implicated you."

"And do you think this is justice?"

"What do you fear?" Her chin rose arrogantly. "You are a knight. You have faced worse."

"No. I have never faced worse than this. You do not know...you cannot begin to know..."

She shrugged. "It does not matter. Crispin is alive and Gaston is dead with good reason. Leave it at that."

"I am very much afraid," said Crispin, "that we cannot."

She laughed. "Do not be a fool. What are your plans? To arrest me? Who will believe you? Look at you. A rusted knight; a shabby banner of days past. You are no one. You are less than no one. You told me you were once a gong farmer. What is lower than that? No one will ever believe you."

Stephen slumped his shoulders. "I do."

Rosamunde's gaze snap toward him. "Stephen!"

"I once thought the world of you. How innocent you were. Now look at you. I was silent when you became Gaston's lover. If I were a better brother…" He shivered. "Instead, I said nothing and fled to France to secure your marriage, hoping you would come to your senses and end it. But this. This is no game of courtly love. This is *murder*. For the love of Christ, Rosamunde! You killed two men!"

Crispin grasped her arm. She looked down at his chapped fingers curled tight over her sleeve.

No anger, no pity. Nothing lay in the hollow of his chest. He knew it would not last but he savored the numbness so he could do his duty. "It is time to pay, my dear. Perhaps there will be mercy. Perhaps the law will judge you kindly. But do not doubt that I will convey you myself to Newgate."

Her eyes were quizzical and subtly changed the longer she appraised him. She turned toward him and placed her free hand on his chest. "Crispin. You cannot mean what you say. Consider it. Consider *us*."

He leaned forward and kissed her gravely on the lips. She raised her hand to cup his face, and they held that pose for several moments before he drew away.

"I do have my regrets over killing you, my dear," said Crispin. "For you were dear to me once. Surely your reward will be greater in Heaven."

Her face paled in the recognition of her own words and she suddenly struck out at him, beating him on the chest with her clenched hands.

He drew back his fist and punched her jaw. Her head snapped back and she slumped. He caught her before she hit the floor.

"I am taking her to Newgate. Do you interfere with me?" he asked Stephen.

Stephen's gaze met Crispin's. "She is my blood." He slowly withdrew his sword.

Crispin laid her on the bed. "I expected no less." He looked at Stephen's blade and scowled. "I do not have a sword."

Stephen nodded and sheathed his weapon. He pulled his dagger instead and Crispin did likewise.

The room fell silent except for their labored breathing. Neither wanted to lift his blade first until a pall of resignation bleached Stephen's features. With a roar through grit teeth, he fell toward Crispin. Crispin raised his arm in defense.

Stephen made no half-hearted feints. He stabbed toward Crispin, and Crispin deftly dodged each attempt. They both fought in earnest, maneuvering their way around the room, casting furniture aside.

Stephen's blade struck upward and the tip caught Crispin on the cheek. He felt the sharp sting only momentarily, but it was enough to spur him on. He tossed the blade into his left hand and landed several blows with his fist into Stephen face with his right. Stephen wobbled and Crispin maneuvered him into a corner. He pinned Stephen's dagger arm to the wall and pressed his own blade to Stephen's throat.

Stephen looked up miserably at Crispin. "Do it," he rasped. "Take me out of this world. Oh *Jesu*! I should have let you hang me!"

Crispin clamped his lips together and breathed furiously through his nose. All at once, he lowered the blade. "For Jesus' sake, let us make an end to this."

"How can I let you arrest her? She cannot bear it."

"Two men have died. Are they to suffer no retribution?" He looked past Stephen at Jenkyn's stark face. The servant had pressed himself against the wall trying to avoid the fighting. "What say you, Jenkyn? She almost made a murderer of you and then would have let you hang. You have a say."

"I was loyal all my life to this house. Why would she do that to me?"

Crispin gestured with the knife. "She is a selfish creature, Jenkyn. Best concern yourself—"

Jenkyn's eyes widened. "Look out, Master Crispin!"

Instinct moved his hand before he turned. His dagger sunk

deep with that familiar sensation of slicing flesh and oozing blood. When his head swiveled enough to spy the edge of her disarrayed hair he let go of the blade with a horrified gasp. With a silent rend of his own heart he knew it was too late.

Rosamunde pulled the dagger from her belly at once but it only served to blot her gown in a growing irregular stain. The dagger clattered to the floor.

Rosamunde looked up at Crispin and smiled. Blood tinged her lips. She let her own jeweled dagger fall from her hand. "Justice?" she whispered before crumpling to his feet.

CHAPTER THIRTY-TWO

Crispin sat in the dark. He barred the door even from Jack, who gave up trying to enter hours ago. Gilbert and Eleanor tried to coax him free of his lodgings. Even Martin Kemp made an effort, but none could budge him.

Today, especially today, he would not leave the haven of his shabby room. Though the day ended, he could not bring himself to light a candle. He did not feel deserving of even that singular illumination while they buried her.

The knock on the door surprised him. He hoped they had all given up by now.

At first he didn't answer. But the gentle voice on the other side of the oak roused him to his feet. He stood at the door and stared at the bolt. Finally, he threw it back and returned to his chair and sat.

The door slowly creaked open and Father Timothy peered in. He blinked into the darkness. "Do you invite me in, Crispin?"

Crispin did not reply. He only sighed, but Timothy acknowledged it and entered, closing the door behind him. "Surely we can light a candle?"

"It is dark where she is." His voice cracked. He realized he had not actually spoken in some days.

"We do not know that," Timothy said and sat on the chest.

"It is dark in the grave."

"Stephen St Albans sent word after the burial. She is safe at her ancestral estates."

Crispin absorbed this and nodded. He didn't know whether the news pleased him or not.

"May we light a candle, then?"

Crispin said nothing. Timothy proceeded to the hearth and lit a straw. Cupping the glowing sprig in his hand, he brought it to the table and lit the tallow candle in its dish on the table.

The priest's young face immediately sprang into view. He smiled. "There now. A little flame does no harm."

"What have I done?"

Timothy eyed Crispin with sympathy. "It was an accident. The justices declared it so. It spared her an arrest and a trial, after all. And the punishment. It is justice, when all is said and done."

"Yes, but whose?"

"She was a murderer, one who killed more than once for vain reasons. It was a mercy this way."

"Then why is it *I* feel like a murderer?"

"Not so. In the end, she forgave you."

He raised his face to the priest, gazing into his sympathetic eyes. They glittered in the candlelight. "Were you there?"

"Yes. I gave her absolution. She lasted two days, as I'm certain you know. And as a faithful Christian, she forgave you for all of it. Without reservation."

Crispin stared at the candle a long time and finally raised his hand to his face. He wiped his dry features before dropping his hand away. "I am glad."

"Now then. There is other business I came to you about. It is time for you to arise from this tomb you have made. You have much to do."

"And what is that?"

"Your life!" Timothy rose and threw open the shutters. The sunset spilled streaks of red and gold across the floor. A fresh breeze washed the stuffy room and puffed a breath across the hearth's embers, awakening their dormant glow to flames. The room came alive with golden light and even Crispin's gray features warmed.

Crispin sat back against the chair. "Why?"

"Because many people care about you and would help you."

"Yes. I suppose."

"And there is much good you do. It still needs to be done."

Crispin would have shrugged if he could summon the energy. He chose not to.

"A terrible thing has happened," Timothy continued. "But you proved your worth in this. In fact, you have nullified your shame of years ago."

"Oh? Who says so?"

"I do. And others who know and respect you."

Crispin grunted. These were empty sentiments now. "It does not make all this go away."

"No. Not today. But someday."

Crispin took in Timothy's kind but stern expression and allowed himself a reluctant smile. "Your optimism astounds me."

"And me at times," Timothy chuckled.

"But that is not the only reason you came."

Timothy's gentle laughter petered out and his dark eyes settled on Crispin's. His smile changed to a wry one. "No. No, indeed."

"How did you know?"

"I have my sources."

"Of that, I have no doubt."

Timothy smiled and leaned on the table. "Well? Have you decided?"

"Yes. I decided some time ago." Crispin reached into his coat and carefully removed the object. He laid it reverently on the table but kept his hands upon it, his thumbs rubbing the etchings along the rim. "I toyed with the idea of trying to use it on Rosamunde. I dismissed it just as quickly."

"Yes. You understand, then."

"If indeed it is miraculous, it must not be used in that way."

"But others would."

Crispin nodded. "Like Guillaume de Marcherne. I recognized his character."

"His mistake was in not recognizing yours. But as I understand it, he will be making no more bargains. I believe I heard that he is dead."

"Good."

"I know he promised you much."

"I never took those promises seriously."

"But Edwin also made promises to you."

"And I do not hold you to them."

"On the contrary." Timothy watched Crispin stroke the cup but did not reach for it. "I make the same offer."

Crispin smiled and shook his head. "And I make the same answer. The 'face of woman' is too much on my mind. Especially today."

Timothy sighed. "Very well." Timothy rose and held out his hand. It wasn't to bid Crispin farewell.

Crispin, too, rose. Now he noticed the sword hanging from Timothy's belt hidden beneath the cleric's mantle. It didn't surprise him in the least. He picked up the cup and placed it into the priest's open palm. Timothy held it for a moment. He turned it to examine the markings and to run his finger over them. He smiled at Crispin before he consigned it to his scrip.

Wordlessly, he turned toward the door.

"I will not see you again, will I?" said Crispin.

Without turning back, Timothy said, "No. I should think not."

"That is as it should be. You *are* the new Grand Master, are you not?"

Timothy smiled and nodded. He turned. His bearing was completely different from before. No longer the contemplative priest. He stood like a knight. "How did you guess?"

"Your ring. The light was dim in your rectory, but that is no priestly ring."

The young cleric raised his hand and ran his fingers over the gold band with its shield of a cross potent. "In all these years, you are the only one to have noticed."

Crispin shrugged. "My mind may have been on Templars and Templar badges."

"It is a pity you will not join us."

"You have your cross to bear, and so do I. But I would know something before you go." He stared at the scrip disappearing into the shadows of the priest's gown. "I wonder. Is it...*does* it perform miracles?"

Timothy's cheeks creased with a smile. "*You* would know that better than I." He offered a final nod, pulled open the door, and was swallowed by the shadows of the landing.

Crispin sat again and stared at the empty table, empty but for the candle, its flame flickering from a draft.

The door opened again. Crispin didn't move. The candle wavered, sputtered, but remained stubbornly lit. He was not surprised to see the small shadow of a boy stretch across the floor.

He turned and took in the sight of Jack Tucker. A pathetic child of the streets. A wretched thief. His tunic was nearly as threadbare as Crispin's coat. His shoes had holes and his cloak's hem hung with loose threads. Probably from the way the boy always worried at it. He was secrets and stolen trinkets and noise when Crispin desired only peace. Trouble was written all over him. "What to do with you, Young Master Tucker," he sighed after a thoughtful pause.

The shadow lengthened and soon the boy came into the light. His face was wet from tears, making tracks through the dirt, and he wiped his nose absently with his sleeve. "It's cold outside."

"Yes," Crispin agreed. The warmth from the fire was meager but it was warmth, of a sort.

"Master Crispin...I was wondering. I mean...I know you said you never wanted..." He twisted his cloak in his fingers again. "Blessed Saint Anthony," he muttered. He looked down at his feet, huffed a breath, and started again. Amber eyes soft, his gaze settled on Crispin. "I promise...I won't be no trouble. I swear to you, sir. I...I can cook. And clean. And do for you, sir. Fetch fuel and water."

Crispin turned away from the boy to stare at the hearth. "A proper servant keeps his face and hands clean."

A shuffle close behind him. "They do?"

"And never use their sleeves for snotty noses."

Jack was now at his elbow. "A proper servant?"

Crispin sighed deeply and even smiled a little. It *was* cold outside. And getting late. "I'm thirsty, Jack." He closed his eyes and leaned back in his chair, feeling the warmth from the hearth on his face. "Go fetch me a bowl of wine. There's a lad."

AUTHOR'S AFTERWORD

Let's talk Templars. Let me set the record straight. Templars had *nothing* to do with the grail's legend *until* the twelfth century when German poet Wolfram von Eschenbach wrote his epic poem *Parzival*. Here is where it is believed the tenuous thread between the grail legend and Templars originated. In the poem, Templars are mentioned guarding the "grail castle." Arthurian legends furthered the tale and incorporated the grail into the expanding saga, integrating Parsifal and Galahad on a grail quest. The grail story begins to get very convoluted with different traditions melding and trading off. Wolfram's grail, for instance, is a stone fallen from heaven. The grail from Celtic lore is a dish, or a flagon, one of many sacred vessels. Christian tradition has it as Christ's cup from the Last Supper. It's that last one that seems to stick.

Templars connected to the Holy Grail are fiction, fiction, fiction. Twelfth century fiction, but fiction nonetheless. But then again, we're talking about the grail. Did that even exist? Who can know?

And let's not forget real history. Vatican documents unearthed in March of 2002, shed new light on the Templars and their relationship to Pope Clement V. History claimed he denounced them in 1308. These documents were known but thought destroyed by Napoleon when his men looted the Vatican during their invasion of Italy. According to the document known as the

"Chinon Parchment," the pope sent emissaries to conduct what was essentially a secret trial and exonerated the Templars for allegations of sodomy and blasphemy. But, as was explained in the book, such a decree of exoneration would not be popular, and many of the crowned heads of Europe did what they liked first before informing the pope of their activities. And Clement V was said to be easily manipulated. So good-bye Templars.

The information regarding the anti-pope is also true, though it is my own fabrication concerning his network of international spies and operatives.

Or *is* it?

But I digress. The Catholic Church has always been stuck with anti-popes throughout its history. It wasn't quite the "universal" ideal it touted. At one time, there were three popes: the "official" one in Rome, one in Avignon, and one in Pisa. It wasn't until 1449 that the final anti-pope had his last gasp.

Crispin's tale is far from over. My intent is to get back to the series and tell his story till the end. So, if you are just beginning the series, go on next to *Veil of Lies*. If you are continuing the series, then look for *The Silence of Stones* next. As always, if you want to find me, go to my website at JeriWesterson.com or on Facebook. Feel free to ask questions or just chat. By the way, you might wish to get yourself on my e-newsletter where there is always more medievally goodness and news. Crispin also has a blog on my website, so there's a lot more about our favorite ex-knight there.

Thank you all for reading!

GLOSSARY

There are a few words in the novel that may defy context. Some are simply archaic words, used only at the time with no contemporary equivalent. Only historians and scholars are likely to understand them. Since it is not my intention to confuse but to enlighten, I have included some words here. I hope this will help clarify.

CHAPERON A combination hood and shoulder cape, with the cape edged in fancy shapes. Since most cloaks did not yet have attached hoods, these supplied much needed protection from the elements and cold interiors. Often worn without the cloak.

CHAUSSES Stockings, in this case made of mail as flexible armor for the legs.

CHEMISE Shirt for both male and female, usually white linen. All-purpose, used also as a nightshirt.

COTEHARDIE (coat) Any variety of upper body outer wear popular from the early middle ages to the Renaissance. A coat reaching to the thighs or below the knee, with buttons all the way down the front and sometimes at the sleeves. Worn over a chemise. Early part of the fourteenth century, the belt was worn at the hips. The belt moved up to the waist as the century progressed, and stayed there. Some women's gowns were also called cotehardies.

DIVINE OFFICE They were first used for monastics, denoting the specific hours of the day for certain prayers. Also called the canonical hours, these soon became how the laity could divide the day, since the monks and nuns rang bells to call their community to prayer. It was a precursor to clocks, and Crispin and the other occupants of village and city alike, knew what specific time of the day it was by the ringing of the bells. They were divided roughly like this:

Matins (during the night, usually midnight, sometimes called Vigils)

Lauds (at dawn or 3:00 a.m.)

Prime (first hour, 6:00 a.m.)

Terce (third hour, 9:00 a.m.)

Sext (sixth hour, noon)

None (ninth hour, 3:00 p.m.)

Vespers (6:00 p.m.)

Compline (9:00 p.m.)

HOUPPELANDE Fourteenth century upper body outer wear with fashionably long sleeves that touched the ground. As fashion changed, so did the collar, growing in height, the sleeves in length, with pleats on the bodice front and back.

KAYLES A game of medieval ninepins.

SCRIP A small bag, wallet, or satchel.

SHERIFF The word is derived from the *shire reeve*, a man appointed to settle disputes and keep the peace in a region made up of several villages and towns known as a shire. The duties of the sheriffs changed with the times. The sheriffs of London were appointed for one year and served their term with little compensation except that which they could obtain by benefit of their office, that is, what bribes they could collect from those brought to justice. They appointed the juries, after all, and decided what situations would go to trial. They also served as judges.

VARLET Valet. A menial or groom. A fourteenth century term.

ABOUT THE AUTHOR

Los Angeles native and award-winning author **Jeri Westerson** writes the critically acclaimed Crispin Guest Medieval Noir mysteries. Her books have garnered nominations for the Shamus, the Macavity, the Agatha, Romantic Times Reviewer's Choice, and the Bruce Alexander Historical Mystery Award. When not writing, Jeri dabbles in beekeeping, gourmet cooking, fine wines, cheap chocolate, and swoons over anything British.
JeriWesterson.com

Craig Westerson ©

Made in the USA
San Bernardino, CA
01 July 2014